C000021529

Lino Omoboni

The
Quest
for
Glorious

novum pocket

All rights of distribution, including via film, radio, and television, photomechanical reproduction, audio storage media, electronic data storage media, and the reprinting of portions of text, are reserved.

Printed in the European Union on environmentally friendly, chlorine- and acid-free paper.

© 2019 novum publishing

ISBN 978-3-99010-871-0
Cover photos: Dmitrijs Bindemanis, Godfer, Mirafilm | Dreamstime.com
Cover design, layout & typesetting: novum publishing

www.novum-publishing.co.uk

In the ancient Kingdom of Onuvar ruled by a Queen, life was pleasant and the economy was thriving.

The weather was semi tropical and so warm most of the time.

The dowager Queen Amanda was the last monarch descended from the ancient hero Bonamor. She had one son, Prince Neno, now in his early twenties.

The kingdom's population was mixed between white, black and oriental people that had great respect and love for their Queen.

Queen Amanda had dark brown hair with a light Mediterranean complexion, as did most of the people of her kingdom.

In ancient times, King Bonamor abolished slavery and there was freedom in the land.

*

There has been peace for two hundred years, since the great warrior King Bonamor defeated a terrible invader that had conquered and subjugated all the land.

That ancient King was the son of a farmer prince and after an illness that killed many people and most of the royals, he was the only survivor left to rule the kingdom. Something he did very wisely until that dreadful invasion.

The kingdom had guards to deal with the city walls and the gates but no army.

That invasion was terrible. The people were terrified and didn't know what to do.

He was hiding with his Queen and children inside the forest using it as a refuge until he decided to do something and became their freedom fighter.

On his own at first and then with an army made up of everyone who rallied to his flag – a white background with a blue shield and golden crown in the centre and a shining sun on top with its rays pointing in all directions.

*

In the final battle, he killed his enemy but arrows mortally wounded him.

He died surrounded by his close friends and after the battle; they put his body in a tomb at the site of the battlegrounds.

Years passed and a rumour started that they buried him with his flag and the sword known as "Glorious".

According to the legend, all his strength came from that sword given to him by an old and wise woman who lived in a cave deep inside the hills at the foot of the mountains south of the forest.

Legend has it that the good magic of the earth created the sword and the fairies polished it.

Since that famous battle, many Kings and Queens had been in the throne.

*

The palace was a tall building in the east of the city with several towers and balconies all around with embellished corridors showing many vases with fresh flowers on console tables attached to the walls.

The throne hall was at ground level with the royal quarters above and there was an avenue flanked by tall trees between the palace gates and the city square.

The walled capital city was big with towers and catapults at certain distance of each other all around though nowadays gathering dust.

*

A walled canal under several bridges runs through the city with its waters filtering into many wells providing drinking water. It comes into the city from under the west wall running on the west side of the city square.

Some small boats bringing goods from the countryside used the canal that starts well inside the forest fed by a river. It comes out under the wall on the east side of the main gates on the north wall and under a wooden bridge wide as the road that comes from the east. It is flanked by many bushes and after, it finishes close to the seaside where the overflow finishes in a small cove.

*

The east of the country is a desert and after it is the territory of another kingdom. There is a forest in the west that stretches all the way to the sea in the north and close to the mountains in the south with many hills, gorges and ravines carved by a couple of small rivers and streams. The prairie is on higher ground with mountains overlooking it.

*

In a small village, a short walking distance from the city and facing a bay, there were many young people including a young man and a young woman who used to do many things together since they were young children.

In fact, it was mostly him playing games while she enjoyed herself by helping him. Since she was little, she followed him like she would an older brother.

His name was Eloy and her name was Pearl. They both had light brown hair with a lovely suntan, which was the result from living by the seaside.

He was in his early twenties and she was eighteen.

Like most of the women in the kingdom, she was wearing a light-yellow dress just under her knees though very colourful with plenty of embroidery showing mainly flowers.

Eloy's clothes were very simple like the majority of men in the kingdom. He just wore brown trousers and a brown sleeveless jacket on top of a thick multi-coloured shirt made of cotton. He wore leather sandals the same as his father and most of the people in the kingdom though some people wore shoes obviously make by cobblers in the forest villages.

His father was a prosperous farmer and Eloy used to help him in the fields where they had a couple of oxen to pull a plough.

Hedges with many bushes and trees marked the boundaries surrounding all the farms' fields.

Her father was a fisherman, but his main income came from fishing for pearls in the bay where the water was not too deep for him and his daughter to dive and well protected by a natural rocky wall with a narrow entrance for the boats.

He always said his most precious pearl was his daughter and that's why he gave her that name.

*

In the kingdom, the only religion they had was the worshiping of the Holy Spirit and though they never had a temple or priests, for hundreds of years they had one priestess and now Pearl's mother was the one. At the same time, she was a herbalist dealing with people's health – helped by many other women in the city. One of her main jobs was to perform weddings during weekends.

*

It was common for everybody in the village to get up early.

After helping her mother to prepare breakfast, Pearl's hobby was to practice every morning in an area outside the walls on the right side of the main city gates with the bow as a sort of exercise and after she help her father pushing the boat to the water.

For Eloy, the beginning of the day was similar because of some ancient custom young men had to practice with the sword just outside of the gates under the instructions of an expert swordsman for one hour before going to the fields to help his father. It was the same for many farmers' boys.

The practice area was on the left side of the gates and just before the wooden bridge on the canal.

*

At the end of the day they used to get together, and as good friends walk on the beach enjoying the fresh breeze coming from the sea.

Chapter One

One day, Eloy was in the fields helping his father by guiding the oxen pulling the heavy plough. Their land was between the village and the main road coming to the city from the east. At that time of the day, it was busy with caravans mainly formed by wagons.

*

It was heavy work for both of them because the field was big. Eloy was not doing his job as enthusiastically as he used to and his father noticed. "What is with you?"

"Oh, I don't know. I feel bored."

"But why? Every month we have a big party in the city square for all the young people to come together and enjoy life. There is always the chance for you to find a young woman and who knows maybe get married and have a family to make me a grandfather." He said the last words holding his laughter.

"I know father, but the point is that there is nothing exciting happening. It is like a routine."

His father thought about it for a moment. "Maybe what you need is to go to another country and see how other people live and I'm sure you will return happy to be here and not there."

Eloy didn't answer and instead he carried on ploughing.

*

Suddenly Eloy stopped ploughing and his father noticed. "What is it Eloy?"

"Look over there, Dad. It's another emissary from that General Dictator probably bringing a valuable present for our Queen."

They knew it was an Emissary because of his rich clothes and followed by two servants on horse with a mule carrying a small coffer.

"I think you are right son and as usual she will reject it."

They looked at each other and laughed loudly.

*

At the end of that day, Eloy and Pearl got together and as usual, they went to sit on the rocks by the seaside.

He was very quiet and Pearl noticed. "You are too quiet what is it with you today. Did you work hard helping your father?"

"Yes, I did but that's not a problem and there's nothing wrong with me but I feel bored."

Pearl was confused for a moment. "You feel bored with me? With my presence?"

Eloy looked at her and opened his eyes wide. "Oh no, I'm not bored with you at the contrary the only time I'm not bored is when you are close to me. After all you are my best friend," and with his strong arm he pulled her closer and kissed her forehead making her giggle.

Pearl thought about it and shrugged her shoulders. "I guess you are right. I see you as my best friend too because I talk to you about subjects I never mention to my girlfriends or my parents."

"Still I feel that I'm wasting my life here. Everything is beginning to look like the same every day, you know, doing the same things. There's no action."

"I don't understand you. Every day we have plenty to do. I have my practice with the bow and after I work with my father. At the end of the day I practice my writing and reading with my mother, and sometimes I go to the library."

"I know Pearl and I do more or less the same."

"And don't you forget about the dancing and music we have every month in the city square by royal command where the palace chefs cook several barbeques and there is always the opportunity for young people to make friends.

"Yes, I do enjoy those parties."

"I've got an idea, why don't you come with me on a boat and maybe you will be lucky and find some pearls. It will be a change in your routine and I'm sure your father won't mind."

Eloy looked at her with open eyes. "Of course, he won't mind but me dive for pearls? I don't think so my swimming is not that good."

She started giggling. "Eloy to search for pearls you do it underwater and all you need is to hold your breath; it isn't like swimming on the water."

Eloy thought about it. "I will take your word for it but I won't try."

Pearl just giggled. "Wouldn't you try to learn?"

Eloy looked at her smiling. "Let me put it in a different way. Fish swim and it is caught by people and eaten."

Pearl started to laugh. "Eloy if you dive nobody will fish you out and eat you."

"Oh, I don't know about that but maybe a sea creature will try," he said while putting his arms up with his hands like claws and showing his teeth.

They look at each other and burst with laughter.

*

At that moment in one of the palace balconies, the Queen was listening to the Prime Minister.

She was wearing a beautiful long green and yellow dress and the minister was richly clothed though mainly with a black robe with plenty of golden and silvery embroidery and a colourful round hat.

"Lately, we are having some problems with the extra population in the city. There are not enough houses for them."

"Tell me prime minister. What are the possibilities of building more houses outside the city; after all there is quite a lot of empty land."

"Yes, Your Majesty but in an emergency, they will be unprotected outside the city walls."

"True Prime Minister but we have been at peace for at least two centuries."

"Yes, Your Majesty it has been considered and right now I have given instructions to prepare the land outside the city on the east side though it will take some time before anything happens. The idea is to build houses with some land around to create gardens."

"Brilliant idea Prime Minister and do carry on with it, after all we are not short of clay to make bricks and there's no shortness of stones in the rocky desert but make sure you do it away from the cemetery."

"As you wish Your Majesty but in the last couple of weeks there is another problem with people coming close to the city though strangely they don't bring anything to do business with. So far they bring their own food and camp in big groups."

"They bring their own food?"

"Yes, Your Majesty though some of them buy what they need from the city market."

"Well, we cannot build houses for them as well."

"No, Your Majesty," he said gleefully and bowing he left leaving the Queen looking upon the city.

Prince Neno came to the balcony. He was not dressed as was expected of a prince with his brown trousers and colourful cotton waistcoat paired with his green silk shirt.

"It's a peaceful city mother."

"Yes, my son but for how long? You know about that foreign dictator trying to wow me."

"Yes, mother but what he really wants is our kingdom."

"I know son and I don't like him. He's a very rude man and I've heard about how he treats his people."

"Yes, mother and not to mention the size of his army. We don't have an army and our city guards are not enough to stop any invasion."

"Yes, that's true and we must consider organising an army but first we must make sure we can afford it."

At that moment, a palace guard approached. "Excuse me Your Majesty an emissary has arrived."

"Very well, show him to the throne hall."

The soldier bowed and left.

"It could be an emissary from that General we were talking about mother."

"Yes, I know but we must always be polite with visitors and careful not to provoke or insult. Diplomacy is very important."

*

Moments later the Queen entered the throne hall that was very spacious, in the company of her son. There were two thrones with armed guards standing at either side and she sat on the left with Prince Neno sitting on the other.

She signals for other guards to open the doors.

*

The emissary approached and bowed. He clapped his hands and the two servants approached with a small coffer they put at the Queen's feet and opened it.

"This is a small token from my master and he hopes you will accept it and be his bride."

Prince Neno looked at the coffer with wide-open eyes. "Mother, it's a treasure."

"Yes, I know," then she stood up, "emissary, take the coffer back to your master and tell him though his present is very impressive, I am not looking for a husband and I cannot take his present under false pretences."

For a moment, the emissary stood there perplexed but then he clapped his hands and signalled for the servants to take the coffer away and bowing to the Queen he left.

"So much for diplomacy Mother. Don't you think that was a bit too harsh? The General might take offence and you said not to provoke an insult."

"Yes, I know son but to accept his present would have been like saying yes."

"Yes, mother you have a very good point there."

*

Pearl finished helping her father a bit earlier than usual and went to meet Eloy who by that time of the day should have finished ploughing.

They met on the road from the city to the village.

"How was your day?"

"The same as every day and this time of the year is all ploughing."

*

Before reaching the village, Eloy and Pearl saw the emissary leaving with his servants all on horseback and the mule carrying the coffer.

"Another emissary leaving with his present," said a giggling Eloy.

"Eloy, everybody knows about those amorous approaches from that dictator and everybody knows it is his way to get our country. If our Queen marries him, it will be the easiest way to conquer us."

"Yes, Pearl that is very possible but as you can see the emissary is leaving."

Pearl was quiet for a moment.

"Have you noticed lately all those people coming to our country from the east? A few are merchants but most of them are men and they carry everything on their back or on horseback."

"Yes, I have and it worries me too. If it wasn't that we are at peace with our neighbours, I could say we are being invaded."

*

Moments later, they both came close to their homes.
"I'll leave you now Eloy and I'll see you tomorrow."
"Yes, Pearl, I'll see you tomorrow."

*

Their homes were not far apart facing each other from across the road connecting the farmland with the sea through the centre of the village, with tall trees at both sides. The stone-built houses were painted with whitewash.

A small white wall surrounded the properties. Some houses had big fig trees and a garden with many lemons and fruit trees all around. Most of the village houses had not only trees but also a small vegetable garden.

The village was on higher grounds protected from any big wave coming from a stormy sea.

*

Pearl entered her home and went straight to a metal basin pouring some water from a jag in it to wash her hands and face. Her mother was there setting the table for the evening meal. "You are spending too much time with Eloy. It will get you nowhere. Instead, you should pay more attention to some young and strong men; get married and have a family. Some of your friends are already married and with children."

Pearl shook her head dismayed while drying her hands and face with a towel. "Mum, I'm too young to get married and on the other hand I might join the female guards in the palace. You know I practice with the bow every morning."

"Yes, I know it used to be a man's job but since the Queen decided to have women guards the male guards are quite happy with females close to them even if they are wearing a uniform." Then she had a thought. "Hey, maybe you could find a steady relation with one of the guards."

"Oh, Mum can we change the subject?"

*

Eloy entered his home and mother was putting some bowls with boiled potatoes on the table. His father was already sitting, eating a piece of bread.

"How is Pearl?"

"She's all right Dad," and he went to wash his hands and face with the water in a metal basin close to a window.

"She will make a good wife for you," said mother while adding a bowl with salad on the table.

Eloy finished drying his hands and face. Looked at his mother shaking his head and holding back his laughter, while sitting close to his father. "I'm sure she can be a good wife but we are just good friends."

*

Carrying a net on his shoulders Pearl's father approached his home and stopped just outside the door putting the net on some pieces of wood sticking out of the wall. Then he stopped outside the house door looking towards the city. "I have never seen so many people coming to our country. A few are entering the city but most of them are making camp outside. Something very strange is going on."

Pearl's mother came to the door. "Come inside and refresh yourself before your meal."

He entered and after washing his hands and face sat at the table and started eating a piece of bread looking at his daughter. "Well? Has Eloy proposed to you or not."

"Oh, father not you too, we are very good friends and we enjoy our company."

Father gave a loud laugh. "All right, I'm only joking."

Mother put some food in front of them. "Darling, you are the only daughter we have and the only one to make us grandparents."

"Oh, I see, that's the reason for you to see me married."

"No, darling," said father, "it will be your decision."

"We only want you to be happy," added mother.

Pearl was getting impatient. "I am happy and right now all I want is to have my meal and then go to bed early. Tomorrow morning, I want to be the first in the archery field."

"What about your studies?" asked father.

"Can I take a book to read in bed instead?"

Mother looked at her fondly. "Of course, you can, darling."

Pearl went to some shelves with scrolls and choosing one, she went back to the table.

They all sat together enjoying their meal of fried fish and salad while Pearl was browsing through the scroll by unrolling it.

"No, darling," said mother, "reading while you are eating is bad manners.

"Sorry," and she carried on eating.

Chapter Two

Early in the morning, Pearl left home when it was still dark going to the archery field with a bow across her shoulders and a quiver full of arrows.

Eloy left his home carrying a sword in a sheath hanging from his belt and runs to join her outside the village.

"Good morning Eloy feeling energetic today?"

"Good morning Pearl and yes, I feel great."

*

After a short walk, they reached the outskirts of the city and separated. "See you later."

"See you later Pearl."

She was happy to see she was the first but soon all the other archers arrived and the practice started by taking turns with the use of the targets. It was a mixed group of young men and women.

Not far from the city gates, she saw many strange men sitting outside their tents and watching their practice.

*

In the meantime, Eloy was practicing with his sword together with many other young men on the other side of the gates.

After an hour or so, he was send back home and soon joined by Pearl they had reached their homes.

"Here we go again Pearl. Another working day."

"Yes, another of those days and I'll see you later."

*

Moments later Pearl was leaving home walking to the beach with her father and Eloy was leaving home with his father going to the fields and carrying some tools.

"Don't work too hard!"

Eloy just waived his hand.

*

Moments later Pearl and her father reached the sandy beach where their boat was and could see in the distance many more men on the road approaching the city on foot.

"This is very strange," said her father while walking toward the boat. "They are not entering the city instead they are going to places where most of the foreigners are camping and strangely they are not here to do any trading. They have no goods to sell."

At one side of the boat and lying on the cross sits there was a small mast with a folded sail.

They put a couple of baskets inside the boat with Pearl putting her satchel inside as well and started pushing and pulling it towards the water.

Soon they were rowing away inside the bay from where they could see the waves clashing against the rocks that protect them from rough sea.

It was a big bay and other boats were also fishing.

They dropped their anchor that was not more than a rock at the end of a rope and father was the first to dive followed by Pearl. They both had a small bag made of fine fishing netting attached to their belt and a sharp knife in their hands.

The underwater world was beautiful with so many varieties of fish coming to look at them; after all fish is supposed to be curious creatures but Pearl and her father were only interested in shellfish that was in abundance, mainly oysters. After all, they used to do their fishing in the afternoon.

A moment later, they were back on the boat emptying their bag on the floor. Pearl had many muscles and a couple of oysters while her father had only oysters.

"That's a very good catch Pearl. Very soon we'll have enough muscles for the fish market and hopefully more pearls to take to the pearl dealer."

They dived twice more bringing more muscles and oysters up.

*

Later on, they had enough and father started to open the oysters searching for pearls.

Then they heard some horns in the distance. "It seems the guards are practicing with their horns," her father mused.

Pearl carried on cleaning the muscles shells from barnacles before putting them in the basket. They were very busy and father was quite happy to have five pearls, which he put in a small pouch hanging of his belt.

"Look," said father showing a black pearl. "This will get a good price."

After, he started putting the oysters in small bamboo skewers for the sun to dry. Pearl was doing the same with some of the muscles.

*

Suddenly they heard somebody calling and a boat with a couple of very excited fishermen approached. Pearl noticed they had their families with them.

"Forget about the fishing! We are not going to the city market today!"

"What are you talking about?" asked father.

The boat came closer to them. "Something is going on and many people are running away from the city," said one of the fishermen.

"We could hear the sound of horns used by the city guards," said another.

Pearl wanted to know more. "Do you know why?"

"No, nobody is sure but we better be safe than sorry."

At that moment, they saw mother waiving her hands from the beach.

Pearl's father took the initiative. "First we go for your mother and maybe she has some more news for us."

"Do you know that cavern further west?" asked one of the fishermen.

"Yes, I know."

"We are going there right now. We'll warn other fishing boats out at sea."

*

Pearl and her father rowed as fast as they could towards the beach.

"Hurry up!" cried mother.

They hit the beach ploughing into the sand and Pearl's father put a ladder made of manila ropes and short pieces of wood overboard.

Mother came on board carrying a big bundle. "It's terrible. When we heard the news everybody in the village grabbed whatever they could and ran away to the west towards the forest. I had to come and get you and I managed to put some fruit, bread, salamis and cheese in this bundle." Then she shows him a small bag made of thick cotton fabric. "And here are the rest of the pearls."

Pearl's father embraced his wife and gave her a kiss. "Sanila you are my real treasure and thank you for saving the family wealth. I intended to take them to the city dealers, tomorrow morning."

Pearl jumped out of the boat to push it back to the water and soon they were rowing away while mother carried on talking. "Some of the neighbours came back telling the city was under attack and there was plenty of fighting in the streets. The attack is mainly done by those people that were camping outside the walls."

"What happens with the rest of the villagers," Pearl wanted to know.

"The fishermen's families went to the forest. They could not wait for the boats to come for them."

"Somehow, I knew those foreigners were after no good," said father.

Rowing as fast as they could they leave the bay hitting the open sea waves. They could see in the distance other boats that managed to put their small mast with a sail up.

Father stopped rowing. "This is it daughter and now we can put our sail up."

They didn't take long to put it up and soon joined the small flotilla of fishing boats sailing west.

In this part of the sea, the wind was from the west and they had no choice but to navigate in zigzag for the sails to catch the wind in diagonal.

"Do you think we'll be safe in the cavern father?"

"Yes, I think so, that cavern has not been used for a long time.

Ancient fishermen used to live there before the city and the village was built."

Pearl looked towards the coast made up of tall rocks and cliffs. She was deep in thought. "I wander what happened to Eloy and his family."

"Don't you worry about them now; I'm sure if they join the people going west they will be all right," said father.

"But why to go west father."

"Because it makes sense, they can take refuge inside the forest. You know how big that forest is and in there they will be safe because of so many hills, gorges and ravines big enough to hide a whole army. It can take up a whole day to cross it and, in the east, there's only a rocky desert and the invaders came from there."

*

As soon as the troubles started Eloy and his father had managed to go back to the village and with mother, they left carrying everything they could but mainly food in rucksacks and something in a satchel with a blanket for each one of them.

In the company of many other people, they reached the top of a small hill in the north of the forest and from there they could see a terrible spectacle. Dark smoke was rising straight to the sky because of the lack of wind. Part of the city was on fire.

Eloy could not hide his anger. "Now we know what all those strange people were here for. They are an enemy army that sneaked into our country right under our noses."

"I know son and our brave guards are no match for them."

"What can we do?" asked a woman.

"We don't have an army and there is no hero to lead us," said an old man.

"You worry too much old man. A hero will come," said Eloy's father and started to walk going deep inside the forest. The rest of the people did the same though using different paths.

Eloy became curious. "Why are we going west father?"

"I'm not quite sure son but according to what I know, in the west and on higher grounds after the forest there are high hills after a big prairie and there is no better place to hide."

Eloy was deep in thought. "Or to organise some defence." Then his expression changed and he opened his eyes wide. "How stupid of me. I forgot my sword in the house."

Mother didn't like what she heard. "Don't you worry about your sword now, son. These will be dangerous times and you better stay close to your father."

"I can fight mother; I can use a sword."

Tenderly his mother embraced him. "Please don't say that, I know you can use a sword but I don't want you to get hurt. You are the only son we have and I don't want to lose you."

Eloy lowered his head. "Yes, mother."

His mother followed her husband deeper into the forest following a narrow path but Eloy stayed behind for a moment just looking at the horrible spectacle.

"Hurry up son!"

"It's all right mother. I'll be with you in a moment!"

"It's all right Mavina he'll follow us," said father already behind some trees.

Soon they were walking on the north side of a stream with many banana trees.

They didn't waste any time and gorged themselves with ripe bananas.

*

As soon as the news reached the farms, small villages and hamlets inside the forest, there was chaos and all the people were leaving trying to reach the heart of it well away from danger.

Somehow all the forest population was on the move.

*

The small fleet of fishing boats carried on sailing for most of the morning until they reached rough coastland with many tall cliffs but above all, there were many little uninhabited rocky islands.

Suddenly the sails didn't help them because the wind had stopped. They had a very calm sea so they all put their sails and masts down and carried on rowing. Contrary of the wind flow from the west, the current always flow west and that help them very much with less rowing efforts.

"That cavern should be close by and I'm happy to say we have calm seas otherwise we wouldn't be able to enter," said Pearl. "I understand the entrance is supposed to be narrow."

Father stood up and scouted the coast ahead. "I don't know about that because we fishermen know how to manoeuvre our boats with rough seas and narrow places as well."

Somebody shouted. "There! Over there!"

They look and could see a kind of a strange shaped dark hole in the rocky cliff not far from where they were, though apparently wide enough for boats to get in.

It looked to Pearl like a tall crack in the cliff.

*

One by one, they entered what it was a deep and very spacious cavern with a wide sandy beach all around a lagoon big enough for all the boats.

Though it looked like a cavern, it was not a real one because it was between two very tall cliffs with the tops nearly touching leaving some daylight come in.

Pearl with her parents pulled their boat bow on dry sand and she grabbed her satchel putting it on her shoulders.

They found a place to sit down on dry soil well above the sea level at high tide marked by a line of dead seaweed.

Pearl looked at all those people and, in a way, she felt optimistic. "At least we have plenty of food and I'm sure most of the boats have a good catch of fish."

Mother was happy. "Yes, my love and I can see some dry seaweed we can use for fuel," and off she went collecting some while Pearl's father started using more bamboo skewers filling them up with the oysters and muscles.

*

Pearl started to explore the cavern and went well inside and up a slope where the top of the cliffs where almost touching. The light was dim but soon her eyes become used to it and further she went.

Fallen rocks strewed the path making it a little bit difficult for her to walk. Nevertheless, she carried on.

Moments later, she reached a narrow exit and outside she found herself surrounded by tall rocks though she managed very well to go through and finally she could see her surroundings.

She was at the top of a hill and she could see the edge of the forest not far below. On the east and at the other side of the forest, she could see the glare of the city fires putting some colour to some white passing clouds. She stood there just looking at a terrifying spectacle and suddenly she closed her eyes and put her arms up.

"Holy Spirit, please hear my prayer. Please put good thoughts in the mind of the people of our country in this our hour of need. Don't let them loose their hopes for freedom."

She put her arms down and opened her eyes.

While turning back the smell of cooked fish hit her nostrils and some smoke was coming out of the narrow cavern entrance in the opening at the top.

Immediately her expression changed and she looked worried.

*

She entered the narrow entrance and reaching the people in the cavern, she saw several small fires and people cooking their meals.

Standing on a rock, she called for their attention. "Listen to me my friends! Right now, the back and top of this cavern is working as a chimney and the smoke of your fires is going out through it for anybody to see from far away.

"We need to cook our food!" cried a man.

"Of course, you do but the smoke will alert the invaders and if they come they could kill as all! What you should use is charcoal to do your cooking; it produces less smoke."

"But we don't have any charcoal!" said a man.

"True but there are charcoal makers in the forest and maybe later on somebody could go and get some!" There was a lot of murmuring amongst the people though they carried on cooking.

As soon as the cooking ended, all the fires were put out. So far, they had managed to cook oysters, muscles, crabs and some fish.

*

The day was almost over, Eloy with his parents were walking through the forest on a path at the side of a small stream between hills and they were beginning to feel very tired.

"We should stop and rest for the night father."

"I know son but I want to do it well away from other people. We will have better chances to defend ourselves as a small group because it could be easier for us to disappear inside the forest and by moving closer to the north edge of it we'll be closer to the rocks and cliffs close to the sea."

"As you wish father." Then he had a thought, "father, I guess that to run away is the only possible action because without any weapons we cannot defend ourselves."

"In that case my son we have no choice but to make our own using some dead wood. We could make some maces and with some bamboo make some spears."

His father's opinion put some sparkle in Eloy. "Yes, you are right father."

*

In the city, the initial chaos when the invasion started was over and the last groups of fighting guards surrendered and were kept sitting on the roads and surrounded by enemy soldiers; most of them in the square. They were mostly men though at least one third of them were women.

The city dwellers were confused and didn't know what to do so they stayed indoors.

The enemy General patrolled the streets with his second in command right at his side and surrounded by his personal bodyguards looking at the defeated guards with arrogance. Then he addressed his soldiers. "Well done men! The city is ours!" All the soldiers around started yelling while waiving their swords and spears. "This country is ours!" and the yelling was louder.

Then he looked up the avenue to the palace at the end of it.

"Any news from the palace?"

"Yes, General the palace is surrounded," said his second in command.

"Very well, come with me."

He started to walk up to the palace with many soldiers following him.

When he reached the palace gates, they all stopped and he could see some guards at the top of the walls.

"Open the gates! The war is over and there is no more fighting in the city. Your Queen will be respected!"

*

The garrison commander entered the throne hall where the Queen was. "Your Majesty the enemy General is outside the gates demanding entrance."

For a moment, the Queen was silent and then with an adamant attitude and her eyes welling, gave the orders. "Stop any resistance and open the gates for the enemy to enter."

The commander saluted in military fashion and left.

*

The gates of the palace were open and the General entered walking straight to the throne hall where he found the Queen facing him surrounded only by her attendants, the garrison commander and some guards.

For a moment, he stood in front of her and then spoke calmly. "The city and obviously the whole of your country are under my control but do not fear. All the fighting has stopped and no harm will come to you."

Then she came down some steps to face him. "What do you want General?"

He smiled arrogantly. "But Your Majesty you know what I want. I have sent emissaries with valuable presents for you and you have refused my advances. All I want is for you to be my wife and both countries will be one."

"General, you know perfectly well that I don't want a husband."

"Just think Your Majesty how powerful our two countries will be when united. We can build an empire."

Still adamant the Queen responded. "With the power you have, you don't need me to build an empire and obviously you don't need me as your wife. I'm sure your concubines can please you."

The General grinned at her. "That's true and you don't have to answer today. Think about it and I will visit you again."

Then he turned to his second in command. "All our troops will leave the palace and the Queen guards will take over again and send our soldiers to put the fires out."

"What are we doing with the city guards?"

"They are not guards anymore. Let them go home but make sure they don't have any weapons with them and above all, let them wear their uniforms so we will always know where they are."

He left the throne hall at the head of his soldiers.

*

Those had been nervous moments and the Queen went to sit on the throne drying her eyes with a handkerchief.

Moments later the palace guard's commander entered the hall and bowed to her. "The palace is in our hands once again and the enemy has left Your Majesty."

"Very good commander, do your job but do not provoke the enemy soldiers outside the walls though you will leave the palace gates open as a sign of good will."

"As you wish Your Majesty."

The Queen's attendants closed the throne hall gates.

"What can we do now?" asked one of the attendants with an Asian complexion.

"From now on I need to be informed every day about the conditions in the city. These will be very tough times for all of them. I hope the people outside the city will do something to help."

"But we don't have an army and we don't have a General or a leader to organise any resistance," said the same young woman.

"Yes, you are right Amina but one will come forward and I'm sure the people will rebel." then she had a thought. "Where is my son?"

Amina look at the other attendants and they shrugged their shoulders to her.

*

The day was coming to an end and by nightfall, Eloy's family found a small clearing between the trees where some forest people had been making charcoal.

They could see several earth mounds with some smoke coming out little holes. There was a small hut were the charcoal makers are supposed to live but there was nobody.

"Mavina we'll stay here for the night and don't make a fire," said father. "This place is warm enough with those smoky mounds."

"It's all right my husband and I need some rest."

"We are not too far from the sea father. I can smell it."

His father breathed in deeply and nodded while smiling. "Very invigorating."

They lay down but Eloy felt restless and after a few moments, he started to perambulate between the trees making his mother nervous.

"Don't go too far son!"

"No, mother don't you worry I'll be all right. The invaders have not invaded the forest yet!"

*

Eloy walked up a hill until he came to the edge of the forest and saw at the top of the hill some tall rocks. "Maybe from there I can have a better view," he thought and by then night had fallen.

He took a flat clay bottle of the satchel and drunk some water before continuing.

*

Pearl was feeling restless and decided to try the exit at the top of the cavern once again.

"Where are you going?" asked mother.

"Don't you worry Mum I need to stretch my legs."

Slowly she followed the path and moments later, she came out of it though this time it was dark. Nevertheless, she managed to climb on top of one of the tall rocks and sat on it.

Though it was dark, she could see the city fires were still burning and producing quite a lot of smoke rising straight to the sky because of the luck of wind. Above, she had a small quarter moon giving some little light to the land and she was admiring the forest at night with some stars in the sky. There were no sounds and she started dowsing with a warm breeze touching her face.

Suddenly she heard the sound of a broken twig and leaned forwards trying to see if something was moving. Nothing happened for a moment and then she saw a shadow coming closer to where she was. Slowly she slipped down to the ground and grabbing a stone, she lay in waiting.

The shadow came closer and jumping on it, she hit it in the head knocking it down. She leaned over ready to strike again but somehow, she could see the face and dropped the stone. "Eloy!"

Immediately she tried to help him to sit. Eloy had both hands holding his head and full of surprise spoke with a very weak voice. "Pearl? From where do you come from and why did you hit me?"

Pearl was feeling very apologetic. "I'm sorry Eloy but I didn't know it was you. I thought it was an enemy prowler."

He managed to stand up but still with his hands on his head. "That hurts you know?"

"I can guess that and I'm sorry."

"What are you doing on top of this hill?"

"It's a long story but I'll try. When we knew what was happening we just went to sea joining other fishing boats going west and finally we all reached a huge cavern giving us good shelter."

"All right, I can understand that but still my question is the same. What are you doing here on top of this hill? I have been so worried about you and your family."

"Well, that's an easy one. There's an entrance to the cavern right behind these rocks. Come, I'll show you."

Soon they entered the gap between rocks and though they were in semidarkness, they could see their way because some of the moonlight was coming through but started coughing because some smoke was coming out of the cavern.

He followed her though still rubbing his head. He looked at his fingers and saw some blood. "My head is bleeding."

She came closer to him and looked at his head. "Yes, you have a very tiny cut and I'm sorry Eloy. I'm sure that my mother will help you because as you know she's a very good nurse."

*

Moments later, they reached the lagoon with the flotilla of fishing boats and lit by many torches. "Wow, this is big."

"I knew you'd like it, come to see my parents."

*

Her parents were very surprised with Eloy's presence.

"Come," said father. "Have something to eat."

"Where did you find him?" asked mother.

Pearl's father gave him a skewer with cooked oysters.

"Thank you, sir actually we met in a very peculiar way," he said while rubbing his head.

"I didn't know it was him and I hit him with a stone and now he's bleeding. Can you take care of his wound, Mum?"

"Of course, dear, let me take a look young man," and separating his hair examined his head.

Father was surprised. "Pearl, you didn't."

"It's all right, sir, I'll be all right though it still hurts."

"There's only a little cut but the bleeding has stopped and you'll be all right, here," said Sanila taking some salt out of a small pouch and rubbing it in the wound."

Eloy reaction was loud. "Ouch! That hurts."

"Of course, it hurts but the salt will disinfect and very soon you'll be all right."

A woman approached them with two mugs of coffee.

"Tell me," asked her father, "where is your family. Are they all right?"

"Yes, they are and they are not far from here. We managed to run away with many other people and now all of them are hiding in the forest."

"I think you better go and bring them here," said mother.

"Yes, that's a good idea," said an enthusiastic Pearl pulling Eloy by a hand and he felt he had no choice but to go with her.

"By the way," said Eloy, "where my family is, there are people making charcoal you might buy from them."

"Now that's a very god idea," said her father standing up, "we'll do that. It will be much better than to burn wood or seaweed considering charcoal produce very little amount of smoke."

*

They came out of the rocks and had to wait for a moment for their eyes to get used to the dim light of the night and for Eloy was a surprise to see the light of the city fires reflecting on some passing clouds.

For a brief moment, they stayed there mesmerised by the impressive spectacle.

"Hey, this time you are the one guiding me," said a smiling Pearl.

"If I can remember the way," he said looking down to the edge of the forest.

Pearl had a funny thought and asked giggling. "Are you still bored?"

"No, Pearl," he said as well giggling, "I'm not bored anymore."

*

They moved slowly and very cautiously reaching the first trees and always trying to listen for any sort of noises but fortunately for them, there were none.

Suddenly they heard something and they heard his father's voice. "Eloy? Is that you?"

"Yes, father and I have a surprise for you."

They came out of the trees facing his parents and father was holding a piece of branch that looks like a staff, as a weapon with a couple of charcoal makers doing the same.

"Pearl?" said mother, "but how come?"

"It's a long story mother but she is the one that found me," and looked at Pearl while touching his head.

She spoke holding her laughter. "That's true and now you must come with me to join my family. They are all in a very safe place close to the sea."

"All right, what are we waiting for," said a happy father.

"Hold on," said mother, "let's buy some charcoal."

They did so and after paying the charcoal makers with some coins, they left each carrying a small sack with it.

*

Soon, they reached the rocks at the top of the hill and Pearl shows them the entrance.

Inside father was curious. "I don't understand, when you mention the safe place close to the sea I expected to be by a sandy beach but not inside a cavern."

"I know, sir but though this is a cavern, it is very big and the lagoon is enough for many boats."

His father and mother were very impressed with the size of it.

Soon her happy parents welcome them.

"Happy to see you my friend," said Eloy's father, "we were all very worried about your fate."

"Thank you, my friend but we managed very well."

"And we brought some charcoal for you," added Eloy's mother and Sanila took some while other women approached and took the rest of it.

*

They were sitting in a circle having some fish and bread.

"I know we are so far safe from the invaders but what we don't have are weapons and I don't think we can use the fishing gear to defend ourselves," was Eloy's opinion.

For a moment, they remained in silence thinking about the subject.

Father spoke first. "I know son but we are not soldiers nor warriors and I have never had the chance to use a sword or a bow."

"That's true father but I have."

"And I have been trained in the use of the bow," added Pearl.

"Her mother didn't like that sort of talking. "I don't want for young people to risk their lives."

"That's fine," said father, "I don't like that either but now we have no choice and the point is from where can we get any weapons?"

Eloy had an idea. "I think I could go and try to find people that might have some spare weapons but the point is that we don't have any money to buy them and I don't think those people will be willing to give them up. Mother only has a few coins in her pouch."

Her father took the pouch with the pearls of his belt and grabbed a handful out of it giving them to Eloy. "Here son, you can use this for money."

"Thank you, sir," and he put them in a small purse he had in his pockets.

Pearl was curious. "What are you trying to do father?"

"These pearls are valuable and I guess Eloy can use them to by at least a sword and probably a bow."

There was a moment of hesitation in Eloy but Pearl was prompt to react.

"Come on Eloy we can try; there must be some merchants in the forest or somewhere else and I'm sure they must have taken most of their merchandise with them."

"Pearl, I don't think the merchants in the city could have done so."

"True but there have always been some traveling merchants in other towns and villages and I'm sure some of them must have some weapons for sale."

"True," said Eloy, "but in the meantime some fishermen can go to the forest and look for some straight dead wood they can turn into spears by sharpening the tip with their sharp knives and there are some bamboos they can use for that purpose."

"Very good idea," said Pearl's father, "I'll organise some of the boys to do that early in the morning."

His father was getting impatient. "I think you two better go."

"Come on," said Pearl taking the lead.

Eloy felt he had no choice but to follow her and off they went.

*

They came out of the tall rocks and straight into the night.

"Eloy, I think we better try to get some sleep before we carry on."

"Yes, you are right and I'm happy to say the night isn't cold. I don't have a blanket."

"You are right; it is very warm."

They accommodated themselves against a reclined rock and soon they were asleep.

Chapter Three

Night was over and a bright sun shining from the east forced them to wake up.

Eloy stretched his arms as much as possible and Pearl did the same.

"Oh, my back," complained Eloy, "I'm not used to sleeping rough."

"Neither am I but if you do some of the exercises I do, you'll feel much better."

She started with some contortions and Eloy tried to follow by imitating her though his body was a bit stiff.

"Sorry Pearl but my body is not so flexible like yours."

She stopped and looked at him shaking her head. "Men, they can do many things but when it comes to do some little exercise."

"Come on Pearl don't try to tell me off, you know perfectly well that women are more flexible than men," and he just walked away from her who was looking at him fondly.

They looked in the direction of the city and noticed the fires were out. There was no more smoke.

Eloy had a thought. "I think we better go east."

For a brief moment, Pearl was astonished. "Eloy if we do so we'll be coming closer to the city and to possible enemy patrols."

"Yes, I know but if we keep close to the sea we'll eventually come close to our village and there we might find some weapons too. Hopefully I can get my sword."

Pearl frowned deep in thought and then she smiled. "I guess you are right and I might get my own bow and arrows."

"There you are, now let's go without wasting more time."

They entered the forest and for a moment, they didn't know which way to go.

"I think it will be better to carry on outside the forest and the closer to the sea will be better and safer There are some narrow paths going east and west," was Pearl's opinion.

"Of course, and I think I know them all."

*

Though they had left the forest behind, the terrain was very rough but there was some fertile soil in some places with some bushes and banana trees at either side of the path meandering around tall rocks but been young people it was not a serious obstacle.

In some places, the footpath took them higher above the cliffs and in others they came very close to the water. So close that several times the drizzle coming from where the waves were clashing against the rocks makes them wet.

*

For several hours, they didn't see a soul, which made them relax.

"This is very strange. We haven't seen anybody."

Eloy looked around. "Maybe because apparently there is no rebellion against the enemy; people are still very afraid and who ever run away from the invasion is hiding in the forest."

"I hope you are right."

"Why?"

For a moment, Pearl felt angry. "Because I don't like to see people getting hurt and I don't want to see any enemies either."

"Neither do I but I'm sure people will get hurt when we organise ourselves and eventually the enemy will send patrols into the forest."

Some voices from behind some rocks interrupted them. They looked and were shocked to see an enemy patrol passing by forcing them to freeze where they were.

They stayed there for a few moments until the soldiers had passed.

"Hey," said Pearl in a whisper, "that was scary."

"This means they are sending patrols towards the north of the forest and I hope the people there will be clever enough to carry on further west," said Eloy also in a whisper.

"Or maybe attack them and take their weapons."

"Yes, that will always be a possibility."

She could not see the enemy anymore. "I wish I had my bow and arrows. I could have hit some of them."

"I'm sure you could have done it and after we would have had no choice but to run away very fast been chased by the survivors."

She looked at him and thought about it. "I see what you mean."

*

The peril had passed and they continued their walk, but this time keeping an eye on any possible danger.

Several hours had passed and they had to stop to have some rest. By then the sun was well above them and the air was warm and pleasant.

"I never thought we were so far away from our homes," said Pearl sinking her teeth into a piece of smoked fish, "you know the smell of smoked fish can go a long way and people can smell it far away."

Eloy thought about it and smiled. "If that's the case then we better finished it quickly don't you think so?"

"Eh? Oh yes," she said eating as fast as she could and soon she had a long drink of water and was ready to continue. She looked at the sky. "We've taken the whole morning to reach here."

*

They carried on without any dangers until Eloy stopped looking around. "Do you recognise this place?"

Pearl looked and smiled. "We are close to our village."

"Yes, we are and that means to be more careful."

They carried on but this time though close to the seaside and well protected by some tall rocks still they could not see anybody.

Soon they saw the village and after making sure there was nobody inside, they approached cautiously coming from the beach using the road in the middle of it but there was not even a dog.

"I have the feeling that the invaders have taken everything and most probably found my bow and arrows."

"Yeah, that's a thought and probably they found my sword too."

Before they entered, they noticed all the trees had been stripped of fruit.

Pearl went to her house and Eloy did the same to his.

He entered his home to face a spectacle of devastation. The kitchen and bedrooms looked like they'd been turned upside down. Then he went to the place where he kept his sword on a beam on top of the main entrance and there it was. The looters missed it because the sword was inside an indent carved into the beam so nobody could possibly see it.

He put it on the table and cleans it with a piece of rack lying on the floor then he put the sheath in his belt but when he exits the house the shock for terrible.

Right outside there were two enemy soldiers looking at him very surprised.

He swiftly drew his sword but immediately those soldiers saw the sword in his hand and drew theirs.

There were a couple of seconds with no reaction and then they jumped forward with their swords high.

His reaction was fast avoiding the stroke of one sword and he blocked the second trying to defend himself but though he had good training he had never been in a real fight. Nevertheless, he had no choice but to defend himself walking back and blocking the enemy strokes in the best possible way. Unfortunately, they were too fast for him and he didn't have a chance to do any attack.

At that moment, an arrow hit one of the soldiers and the other stopped fighting and stepped back completely surprised.

Pearl was approaching them with her bow ready and the surviving soldier decided to run away.

For a moment, Pearl didn't say a word. She was shocked. Then she spoke slowly. "This is the first time I have killed a man and somehow I don't feel so good."

It took a moment for Eloy to recover from the shock. "I have never killed anybody but I think I can understand your feelings." Then he saw the bow in her hands and his mood changed, "well, I'm happy to see they didn't take your bow either."

Pearl had quickly recovered from the sad emotions. "No, they didn't and look," she said turning around for him to see her cloak, "I found it on my bed where they left it."

"I can well understand that because that's a woman's garment. I must say that's a beautiful cloak."

"True but we haven't got extra time and we better leave now."

Eloy approached the soldier's body and stripped him of his sword, shield, dagger and his pouch with money. "Now we've got more money to buy maybe another sword or just a bow."

Pearl nodded. "Or maybe some food?"

Eloy sighed. "Yes, that's more likely."

"Swords are very expensive and we have no choice but to eat," she said while nervously approaching the dead soldier pulling her arrow out of the body and cleaning the blood on it with some dry grass. "Come on Eloy stop dreaming and let's go." Then she looked at him with a smile. "Maybe what you need is the famous Bonamor's sword."

"Oh yeah? Very funny. All I need is more practice with real fighting. This was the first time ever for me to fight for real and somehow I was not sure if I could really do it."

"I understand what you mean because this was the first time for me too and I feel a bit scared. From now on, we must be more careful. There could be some patrols in the forest."

"Yes, Pearl you are right and the soldier who ran away must be right now reporting and they are bound to find the dead one and I'm sure they will send a patrol to find us."

"A big patrol because they don't know how many we are," said a worried Pearl and her voice sounded like if she was trembling and forced a smile. "It makes me feel like if I am an army."

"Okay," said a giggling Eloy, "come with me one-woman army."

Before leaving the village, they went to the side facing the farms and no matter how much Eloy looked, he could not see the oxen they had left in the fields. There was no sign of them.

"What are you looking for?"

"Our oxen but I can only guess they have been eaten by now. Sad because I grow up very attached to them. They were good animals."

*

They left the village but not before looking around a bit nostalgic.

"I've got the feeling that everything will be all right Pearl and one day we will be back."

"This time and as soon as possible we better try to go back to the cavern."

"Yes, Pearl let's do it." He looked at the farm once again and sighed.

*

The forest started not far from the village, nevertheless, instead of going back the same way they used to come in, they decided to enter and before long, they were under the protection of the trees. They could not see any people and soon they were following a path around a hill with a small stream running at the side of it and flanked by small hills at the other side. It was the same path used by Eloy and parents the day before.

"Hey, look," said Pearl approaching the trees, "ripe bananas."

Eloy didn't say a word and went straight to some yellow bananas.

*

Things in the city were terrifying for the city dwellers and the invaders had put many guards in all the gates to prevent anybody trying to open them.

There were no more fires but still some smoke was coming out of some of the burned buildings. Although the library was not burnt.

Many families had all the belongings they could safe, on the streets close to their burned homes and taking shelter under makeup tents. Some of them were chopping some of the half-burnt wood to use it to cook whatever there was to eat though by then there was almost no food available.

Other people had made up some shacks with some wood rescue from the ruins.

Some merchants were brave enough to open their stalls but there was panic shopping and soon they had to close down because they had nothing more to sell. All what's left was some squashed fruit on the streets for some birds to feed.

The same was happening with the chicken people had in their back gardens that they could sell to the neighbours.

*

Very few city dwellers were venturing onto the streets to look for anything they could find to feed their families and were walking around like ghosts with sadness in their faces, overwhelmed by a great number of enemy soldiers. By then the city guards had completely disappeared.

*

In the palace, things were calm though very worried for the Queen who could not leave.

In the meantime, her son Prince Neno was in a dungeon inside one of the wall towers facing west.

It was a dreadful place. There was just a little hole close to the ceiling to give him some light but too high for him to look outside and he was in shackles.

*

The dictator General Agaram came back to the palace and entered the Queen's chambers without any ceremony.

"I always knew you had no manners General."

"But Your Majesty I have conquered your city and feel free to go anywhere I want."

"Hopefully not for long and considering you have entered my chambers, you should have shown some respect for my person."

"But I do respect you and you shouldn't say things like that considering your people are doing nothing and I'm sure all those who ran away to the hills and forest will soon come to their senses and return. After all there is no fighting anywhere."

"General, a long time ago in the times of my forefathers another invader conquered our land but there was the hero warrior King Bonamor who rallied the fighting people and defeated the invader by killing him in battle."

The General paced in front of the Queen deep in thought and then smiled arrogantly. "Oh yes, those times. I understand the invader was no other than one of my ancestors but he didn't have the army I have. As you already know, there's no fighting and everything will go back to normal as soon as you accept to marry me. Think about it; when you are married to me the people will see I am their legitimate ruler."

For a moment, the Queen felt very angry but soon controlled herself though feeling very adamant. "You have conquered my country and brought plenty of pain to my people but I will not marry you. Not even if you put me in chains down in a deep dungeon with no food or water."

First, the General had a serious face but immediately it changed to a broad smile. "Ah yes, that was my first thought but then I have decided that I could not possibly treat my future wife with such bad manners and so instead I have decided for something completely different."

He went to the Queen Chambers balcony. "Come here Your Majesty I want to show you something."

Reluctantly the Queen approached him.

"Now, look upon the city."

The Queen did so.

"There is no fighting but unfortunately your people are not allowed to leave and very soon they will have no choice but to eat the horses, donkeys, mules and who knows, maybe their dogs too and as you know in all cities there are mice and rats. There is a very strong possibility for the people to start catching them for the same purpose. Food will be almost nothing in a few days and all your people will have is water from the many wells they have and the canal that runs across the city. After all, I don't want them to die from thirst. I don't want the people to think I am a cruel man." Saying that he burst into a loud laughter.

The Queen had tears running down her cheeks. "You are a very cruel man but still I have hope and I'm sure my people have it as well. After all evil cannot endure."

"As you wish Your Majesty but do not forget about your son. I hope the shackles in his wrists and ankles won't be too painful. Now I will leave you with your thoughts."

The Queen turned to face him with desperation in her face. "My son in shackles?"

Without bowing, General Agaram turned arrogantly and left.

Immediately the attendants approached running to console her.

*

The General was walking in a corridor inside the palace and a captain approached him saluting in military fashion.

"Yes, what is it?"

"One of our soldiers has been killed in the village close to the seaside."

"What? How did it happen? How many villagers attack them?"

"I'm not sure General but the other soldier with him managed to run away and reported they had an encounter with a man and a woman."

"Only two? There must have been more hiding behind the houses. Very well, take fifty well-armed men and a wagon, go to that village by the seaside to bring all those people to the city and make sure the fishermen go out to do some fishing and at the same time make sure to bring all the food they have. Our soldiers must be fed."

The captain once again saluted in military fashion.

Moments later, he left through the north city gates followed by his soldiers all on horseback and a wagon pulled by four horses.

*

Inside the forest, Eloy and Pearl were following the path meandering through the trees passing close to another hill.

"Eloy, we've been walking for quite a while and still haven't found any merchants or people as a matter of fact."

"Yes, I know but knowing merchants I'm sure they have gone further west as far as possible from any danger and we must take into consideration, most of the villages are further south."

"All right, let's hope you are right but tell me, why they won't approach the invaders to sell what they have."

"Eloy thought about it for a brief moment. "I can only give you an educating guess. If they do that the enemy will not buy anything from them but simply take it without paying."

At that moment, some deer running not far from them distracted their attention.

*

In the meantime, the enemy captain has reached the fishermen's village and some of his soldiers dismount and search it thoroughly.

They did it with their bows ready and went to all the houses and after checking there was nobody, they returned to report.

"Well? What is it?"

"There is nobody in captain."

"And there is no food either," said another.

"Very well we'll go east and see if we can get anything from another village."

*

Eloy with Pearl carried on ambling without any hurry and surrounded by beautiful wild flowers and a gentle warm breeze was making them feel relaxed.

"I like the forest scents. It makes me feel very close to nature."

"I know Pearl and I feel the same."

Pearl felts sad. "I hope the refugees won't start killing the wild animals. That would be terrible."

"Yes, Pearl I hope so too but we must not forget that at this time of the year there are many wild fruits in the forest and many edible roots as well."

Pearl frowned and then smiled. "Yes, you are right and especially if they try to eat horse-radish."

They look at each other and burst into laughter.

They heard some noises from some excited birds.

"What you know, chickens," said Eloy.

"Yes, there are supposed to be plenty of those in the wild and at least some people will feed on fresh eggs."

"Yes, Pearl and some chickens as well. After all they reproduce so fast they are not in danger of extinction."

After a couple of hours, they had arrived where the charcoal makers were and though they didn't see anybody, they could see the smoking mounds in the clearance. By then the sun has started to go down though there was still plenty of daylight left.

*

Eloy and Pearl reached a group of people camping in another clearing and joined them.

"You are the first people we see with weapons," said a woman.

"Hopefully not the last," said Eloy.

A man approached them with a jar and the woman gave them a couple of mugs. "Have some sweet coffee and tell us if there are more people in this forest."

Eloy and Pearl were a bit confused.

"I'm beginning to believe that you have just arrived," said Eloy, "otherwise you wouldn't ask that question."

"We arrived yesterday," said a woman.

"Very well and yes, there are more people in the forest but what can you tell us about what's going on in the city."

For a moment, those people remained in silence and then a man spoke. "When it started it was very confusing because first we saw many men entering through the gates and suddenly they took their cloaks off showing a uniform and producing their swords and bows. They attacked the city guards in such a way, there was no time to organise any defence. The guard's commander was very brave but with some of his men they were slaughtered and in the confusion many people managed to leave using the gates, mainly in the south wall."

Pearl wanted to know more. "What about the Queen and Prince Neno."

"Not much to tell," said the woman, "we know the Queen is still in the palace but we heard Prince Neno was taken away to one of the dungeons in one of the west wall towers."

Eloy with Pearl were for a moment speechless and the man continued. "The main problem for the city dwellers will be food because the enemy has closed both gates and nobody is allowed to leave."

"Tell me," said Eloy, "anybody knows who is behind the invasion?"

"Yes, the leader of that army is no other than General Agaram."

"Now I'm beginning to understand," said Eloy, "because he could not attract the Queen's love he simply decided to invade to force her to marry him. If she accepts him the two countries will be united and obviously he will be the ruler and who knows how many more dreams of grandeur, he has in his little brain."

They all remained in silence once again.

Pearl had some more coffee. "This coffee is delicious. Tell me how did you managed to leave the city. Did you do it with other people using some of the gates?"

"No, friend it was too late for us," said the woman, "we used the sewers that run out of the west wall instead and I can assure you it wasn't easy because the smell is horrible and we had to carry all of our belongings in a bag over our heads."

"Happy to say," said the man laughing, "we managed to have a bath in a small stream and after we had to wash our clothes thoroughly."

"Yes," said the woman, "lucky for us we had brought many soap bars with us."

Eloy scratched his head. "The sewers you say, well now that's a thought to keep in mind but why the sewers when there are other ways like the channels for the rain water which are mostly covered by stone slabs and the canal running through."

"I know," said the woman, "I kept telling them but no, they had to follow him into the sewers."

"Yes, I know," said the man with the entire group laughing, "but by using the sewers we make sure the soldiers wouldn't dare to follow us."

"Never mind that," said Pearl, "further west you'll find many more people."

"Is there any resistance?" asked the man.

"That I don't know," said Eloy, "but eventually I'm sure somebody will do something about it."

Pearl was eager to carry on. "We must go now and if you carry on further west you'll be all right."

"I think so," said the man, "and good luck to you both."

*

They left and Pearl was curious. "Why didn't you tell them about the cavern?"

"Very simple, they don't have to go to the cavern because the weather is holding very well and they will be more comfortable inside the forest."

*

Once again, they carried on west and Pearl noticed Eloy's look. "You are thinking about something, aren't you?"

"Yes, I do. It is what they said about leaving the city using the sewers."

"Yes?"

"Well, if they managed to leave the city using that system it means we can enter it using the same way."

Pearl thought about it for a brief moment and looked at Eloy frowning. "Who will be so stupid to try and get inside the city which is occupied by foreign soldiers? And not to mention the sewers; can you imagine for us walking anywhere inside the city and smelling of body waist?"

Eloy thought about it. "Oh, I don't know who will, I won't for sure."

Pearl shook her head holding her laughter and they carried on in silence for a few moments.

"Eloy."

"Yes."

"Further west and way after the forest there is the sacred place where Bonamor tomb is supposed to be."

"What are you trying to say?"

"To me it will be the right place where people willing to fight for the freedom of our country should gather."

"Gather for what?"

"To organise an army."

"I don't think that will be the place to do it, considering it is supposed to be in a prairie with no rocks or trees to use for protection."

"People can build some defences."

Eloy looked at her sympathetically. "So far it is just you and me with weapons and you are talking about an army?"

"Eloy, I'm sure there are more armed people and I'm sure there will be somebody willing to lead them."

"How do you come to that?"

"Because it is the obvious."

Eloy smiled at her. "Come fighting woman."

"I don't know about you but I'm good with the bow."

"Yes, of course you are. I've seen it."

*

Eloy and Pearl carried on towards the west following some paths usually at the side of a stream between hills and by then the sun has started to go down.

*

A few hours Later on in the east, the enemy captain found another fishermen's village though strangely there were no women or children.

"Where are your families?"

The leading fisherman spokes. "When we heard about the invasion we send them to the hills but with the intention to bring them back as soon as the fighting stops."

"I understand that and I can assure you the fighting has stopped; the city garrison has surrendered and, in the meantime, we need plenty of fish and shellfish so you will carry on as usual.

"As you wish, sir but we'll need the women and children to help us."

"Very well so be it but we'll be back tomorrow for the fish!" he cried.

They left the village and moved west towards the city.

*

It took Eloy and Pearl some time but finally after following the path at the side of a stream, they reached the western edge of the forest without meeting more people and in front of them was the emptiness of the prairie and well into the west, they could see some tall hills.

"Eloy."

"Yes."

"This is very strange but we should have met quite a lot of people by now."

"I know Pearl but I'm sure there is a good reason for it. After all this is a big forest with some villages mainly in the south of it and I wouldn't be surprised if many of the refugees are in those villages."

"Eloy."

"What."

The top of those hills looks strange to me."

"How strange?"

"Somehow the top looks like if there is a wall."

"Well, we are too far to find out."

"Why don't we go back to the cavern? At least there we can have something to eat even if it is just fish or shellfish," and taking the water bottle out of her satchel, had a good drink.

Eloy touched his belly. "Yes, my friend, now that is a very good idea but first we rest. We've been walking most of the day and you can see the sun is going down."

"I know and right now I can hear some rumbling coming out of my belly."

*

The enemy commander had reached the city and passed Eloy and Pearl's village.

"We'll go and find other villages this time in the forest but we must harry up because it's getting dark."

They moved at a gallop but soon they realised they were facing a kind of green wall and though they saw the beginning of some paths, there was no road for the wagon and had no choice but to enter without it.

They didn't know the forest and after searching for a while, they could not find any village and it was getting darker. Because they didn't have any experience with a forest, the vegetation was a serious obstacle and had no choice but to get out.

Their commander signals for them to follow him though they had to do it outside the forest. "This time we'll go south where we might find some villages!" Lucky for them there was clear land outside the city wall with a gap of about hundred metres between the walls and the first trees so they could bring the wagon with them.

By now, night was upon them.

Suddenly he stopped. "Stop!" he cried and then he looks around and up realising it was getting too dark. "This is a waste of time and night is already upon us. Let's go back to the city."

"There must be some other villages further west," said one of the soldiers.

"What? You want me to take the risk of been ambushed? No, I will not and now we'll go back to the city."

*

After a good rest, Eloy and Pearl turned back and followed a very narrow footpath meandering between the trees, which made Pearl happy. "At least who ever made this path didn't cut any trees."

There were no more birds singing. Night was upon them and they felt at peace. There was a crescent moon giving some dim light to their surroundings.

*

They were coming close to the rocks with the entrance to the cavern when they heard some people talking and slowly came out of the trees.

What they saw was a surprise because they never thought to see people queuing to get in.

They approached and talk to those people.

"What's going on?" asked Pearl.

"We are getting into the refuge," said a man and they saw they had no choice but to put themselves in the queue.

Inside the tunnel entrance, it was a bit wider and they managed to pass many of those people.

*

Finally, they reached the sandy beach and found their parents close to a boat.

"What's going on father," asked Eloy.

"After you left we decided to go out and search for more people in need of refuge and this is the result. We found many people from our village. At the same time, we managed to meet the people making charcoal and bought some. Now you can see our fires are not producing so much smoke."

Pearl was happy. "No wonder because we found only a small group and after we went all the way to the other side of the forest seeing only some animals and birds."

"Maybe some of the people we found are those you encountered."

"I understand what you've done father but by doing that now the cavern is overcrowded and that will create a problem with food and above all with some hygiene and we cannot have latrines close to the sea water."

"You are right son but what else can we do to help."

"Come," said Pearl's mother, "first have something to eat. It will help you to think."

Eloy gave the extra sword and the dagger to his father. "Here, now you've got a sword and a dagger but I don't have the time to teach you how to use it."

"Thank you, son and don't you worry about teaching me, I'm sure eventually somebody will. But tell me how much did you pay for it?"

"Nothing father. In fact, it was easy because we went to our village to get our weapons and in there I was attacked by two enemies."

Both mothers were shocked.

"And by then I had my bow and arrows and when I saw him fighting, I killed one of the soldiers and the other ran away," she said with her chin up.

Her mother was astonished. "Pearl, you killed a man?"

"Well, I'm not proud of it but I had to protect Eloy. They could have killed him."

Her father was happy. "Now that's the way to deal with the invaders. You've done well daughter."

They remained silent for a moment and Eloy with Pearl sat on the sandy beach to eat some fish brought to them by a couple of women but Eloy was thinking on how to solve the situation and noticed he s deep in thought.

"You are very quiet."

"Yes, Pearl I am. I'm thinking about what you said earlier on about concentrating the people where Bonamor's tomb is and I remember seen the tall hills further west where there must be rocks, trees and bushes that can be a good refuge and there must be some small streams to provide the drinking water."

"I have never been that far but maybe what I saw is a real wall and that means there could be a place for us to stay."

"That could be possible because the land is different than where we live. In those hills, there are many passes that can protect a whole army."

"How do you know that?"

"I remember people talking about it and there is something else."

Pearl look at him. "Come on, tell me."

"I've heard that in some streams there is gold that can be washed out and some people can get it and we can use it to buy whatever we need."

They all remained silent for a moment just looking at him and Pearl became inpatient. "Go on tell us, do you have an idea?"

"Well, most of these people can be guided to those hills where they will be well protected. The hills on the north side go as far as the seaside and people can do some fishing. I don't think the invaders have enough soldiers to send patrols that far away from the city."

Pearl stood up checking if the bow was all right on her shoulders. "What are we waiting for?"

Eloy's father went to some rocks away from the sand and stood on one of them clapping his hands vigorously calling for attention. "Hear me good people!"

Everybody stopped talking and listened to him.

"According to my son Eloy, there is a place further west where there are tall hills that will give a better protection to all of us and above all you will be outside instead of been in a claustrophobic place like this."

There was plenty of murmuring amongst the people but soon they were all nodding approving the idea.

"Very well then, prepare to leave!" were Eloy's orders, "and when outside wait there!"

*

There was a great deal of movement amongst the people gathering their belongings. Eloy's and Pearl's mothers in the company of other women were giving them some food and moments later those people started to move going up to the narrow entrance but not the fishermen. They stayed with their boats.

Eloy's father took the lead and off they went up and out of the cavern.

The moonlight was not enough but at least they could see something.

Her father and mother went with them following the people and Eloy with Pearl took positions well in front as scouts.

This time his father was wearing the sword and Eloy noticed that her father had the dagger.

*

First, the column of refugees followed the narrow path Eloy and Pearl had used earlier.

The prairie was not too far away from the cavern, nevertheless, they took a few hours to come out of the forest facing a strange landscape with undulating terrain showing a strange colour because of the dim moonlight covering the grass and a few scattered bushes in the depressions though no trees between the forest and the mountains.

In that part, the prairie between the forest and the hills was narrower. The wider part of the prairie was further south.

Eloy and Pearl went to some higher grounds and look back. What they saw was impressive. They never thought they were leading so many people with so many torches. Then they noticed another column coming out of the forest further south and moving closer to them. In that column, they could see two wagons pulled by mules and above all, they had a small herd of cows. Most of those people had torches and some of them were black people and others were oriental.

Other people in that column had sheep, pigs and goats.

"From where are these people coming from. We only saw a small group when we went through the forest," said Pearl.

"Well, they are here now and I can only guess they are from the villages in the south of the forest. There are some villages close to the hills in that area."

"They are so many Eloy. I can say they are in their hundreds."

Yes, they are and we'll have the task to organise them but above all, to organise all of those people willing to form the resistance army."

"I can notice that some of them have bows and arrows with a few holding spears but apart of the mules there are no horses."

"I wouldn't worry about horses now. I'm sure we'll find some, after all villagers use horses."

Their parents joined them looking at that immense number of people moving steadily across the prairie.

"We are following your idea son but do you know how long it will take to reach that safe place?"

"Yes, father if it was just us we can do it in a couple of hours but considering the slow movement of animals and children, we should be there by daybreak."

*

The refugees walked as far as they could, reaching close to the foot of the hills. It was the right place to make camp and Eloy asked his father to tell them so and the people lay down for the night.

"I'll have to organise some women to deal with the feeding of those people," said his mother.

"And I'll give you a hand with it Mavina," said Pearl's mother.

"What you need is a wagon where you can put most of the supplies," was his father's opinion. "Now we have stopped for the night, the people can make some fires. I don't think the enemy had sent patrols so far away from the city"

"That's true father but you must calm the people by telling them the truth."

Night had covered all of the land and the two columns amalgamated into one and Eloy's mother Mavina in the company of Sanila was already talking to some of those people with the wagons led by a few village leaders, mainly older people.

*

The crescent moon was climbing up the firmament though still not big enough to give them enough light.

Eloy and Pearl joined by their parents gathered on higher grounds from where they could keep an eye on the people in case the enemy attacks them.

Pearl observed something. "Look, some of them are standing with their weapons as guards all around."

"That's very good, it means they are showing initiative and above all it means there are more armed people," said Eloy, "and that means by tomorrow we can start choosing some of them as commanders to organise the others."

Pearl shook her head. "Why wait till tomorrow, we can do a round later on and see who's who and by tomorrow we'll have those commanders in place."

Eloy grinned at her. "Very well young warrior, we'll do it now."

"Now?"

"What's wrong with now? It is your idea."

"Very well, now it is," she said shrugging her shoulders and off they went.

*

In the meantime, back in the palace things were not so peaceful.

General Agaram entered the Queen's chambers, lit with many candles, with two bodyguards and as usual without announcing himself.

She was not completely dressed and immediately her attendants rush to put a robe over her shoulders and she faced him in strong character.

"Well General once again you have showed us your good manners."

"Manners? Oh that. It's all right Your Majesty I can go anywhere I want. Your country is mine and once we are married it won't be important anymore."

"Not quite General."

The General looked surprised for a brief moment. "Ah yes, the possibility of some resistance, nevertheless, I'm sure that you will eventually accept me as your husband. Down in the streets the people are getting hungry and already many animals have disappeared but don't you worry about your son, we keep him well fed for the time being of course."

"Oh, you are a very cruel man."

The General became angry and exploded with rage. "Cruel! Me? What about leaving your people to starve just to protect yourself! You don't even care for your son." There was silence for a moment and the General started pacing in front of the Queen. Then he spoke calmly. "You can stop all that by saying yes and marry me." Saying that he stared at her with a cheeky look.

She looked at him with her chin up while her servants were sobbing. "No, General I'm not cruel because I have not done anything to harm my people and all of their suffering has so far been caused by you."

Once again, the General exploded with a rage. "You will marry me!"

"No! I will not!"

"I have the power to put you in shackles!"

"Do it and you'll see how strong I am," she said with a very defiant attitude.

For a moment, the General just looked at the Queen and then left the chambers mumbling something in a rage. "This woman is impossible, but all will be different when she marries me."

*

Moments later, the returning captain had entered the city through the south gates.

Some supplicants approached the General who was inspecting his soldiers in the square.

"Please, sir, allow us to go out of the city to search for food. Our children are hungry."

"Move aside you filthy beggars!" he shouted and his soldiers pushed them away.

*

Coming closer to the General, the captain signalled for his men to stop and dismount. By then they were all exhausted.

"Well, any news?"

"Yes, General in the village way east we found only fishermen because their families had run to the hills."

The General thought for a moment. "Tell me, when you went to that fishermen's village with only men in it did you see any boats doing some fishing?"

"Yes, we saw many boats but they were not going out to do any fishing but I told them to do it and I'll send some of my soldiers tomorrow to get it."

"Very well but what about the other villages?"

"The fishermen's village closer to the city is empty and the villagers have taken everything with them. There's no food left. All the signs are that all of them went west. There must be some villages deeper inside the forest."

The General thought about it and then look at the captain frowning. "It's too late now but tomorrow morning with the first lights and after you send some of your men to get the fish, you will take two hundred well-armed men and you will search for those people deeper inside the forest until you find them, if they offer any resistance kill them. I don't want them to get any ideas about any kind of organising, understood?"

"Yes, General."

*

Eloy and Pearl started their rounds and met several people of all ages selecting four. One of them was a woman.

The three men had a sword and the woman bow and arrows.

One man was Oriental, another was white and the third was black; the woman had a Mediterranean look.

"My name is Eloy her name is Pearl and from now on you will be commanders of people who will eventually become warriors."

"As you command Eloy," said one of the men.

"As soon as you can, start selecting the people you think are the best," were Pearl instructions and the four new commanders touched their chest with their right fist and left.

"Come let's join with our parents," said Eloy.

Pearl looked at him with a wide grin. "So, you are our leader now."

For Eloy, it was like a punch and reacted by looking at her very surprised. "Me a leader?"

"Of course, you saw how they reacted to your instructions."

"Oh, I don't know about that. They followed your instructions too."

"Yes, true but I have no intention of being a leader and if you don't do it, I don't know who will."

He thought about it. "Mmm, let's wait and see."

Chapter Four

Early in the morning, some soldiers left the city through the north gates.

One column of two hundred soldiers turns left going west and right behind them a small detachment with a wagon left going right towards the fishing village in the east.

*

In the prairie, the people started to wake up and many of them started with exercising their limps while others were eating something cold and many children had a piece of bread in their hands.

Pearl looked at the top of the hills and saw something strange. "Eloy look."

He looked and what he saw was something that looked like a ruined wall.

"Not to worry Pearl because very soon we'll find out."

*

Eloy and Pearl mothers had managed to organise two wagons to keep their supplies in.

Eloy's mother approached her son. "Another wagon arrived during the night and it belongs to a merchant."

"Eloy gave her a sympathetic smile. "And what are they selling mother, clothes, pots, makeup or maybe shoes?"

His mother was surprised. "Don't you dare to laugh at your mother."

Immediately Eloy embraced and kissed her on the forehead. "No mother I'm not laughing at you but tell me what is in that wagon."

Mother laughed. "Well, he has some shoes and clothes with some cooking pots and makeup but above all he has some swords, shields, steel helmets and some bows and arrows as well."

"Now this is the kind of news we need from now on," was Pearl's opinion.

"Very well," said Eloy, "we'll deal with that later in the hills."

*

The smoke of the cooking was spraying the smell of fried eggs.

"I'm happy to see that they have something to eat," said Pearl.

Once again, Eloy with Pearl and their fathers took the lead and Eloy was beginning to get used to be at the head of people.

Close to them were the four commanders.

It didn't take long for them to reach the foot of the hills after all, they had camped close to it and Pearl was curious. "I'm glad to see we have some hills first though the mountains behind look impressive."

"Yes, they are but if you could see the mountains in the south of the prairie, they are very much bigger though far away and hopefully we won't have to reach them."

"I wonder what's behind those mountains."

Eloy shrugged his shoulders. "All I know there are other countries in the west and south though they don't trade with us because they are too far away; although sometimes some traders come to us once a year."

His father interrupted. "From now on we must find a way to go to the top of the hills to find the protection we need, and we must leave the people here for us to go further and find the way."

Eloy agreed with him. "All right, you commanders come with us."

"And all of you be prepared to move," said Pearl addressing the people.

*

By following an animal trail, they soon found themselves walking in between taller hills and many trees and bushes at either side of a road and Eloy signalled for them to stop.

"Why are you stopping son."

"Very simple father, I feel tired."

"So am I," corroborated Pearl.

That gave them the chance to look all around familiarising themselves with the surroundings.

Pearl looked at the road meandering at the side of a hill. "It seems to me somebody has gone to the top of these hills before making this road that is wide enough for wagons."

His father talked to the four new commanders. "I think you better go back and stay with the people until we return. Do your best to organise them."

The commanders hit their chest with their right hand and returned to the people.

*

The road was going up and they could see that on the left side were many rocks big enough for anybody to hide and on the right, there was a sharp fall.

*

About half an hour later, they had reached a plateau about two hundred metres in all directions and surrounded by walls partially collapsed.

It was a mysterious place with many walls showing something like the houses in a village showing damaged roofs and walls.

Right in the centre there was what it looks like a palace with a badly damaged roof and the stained glass in many windows was partially gone.

They entered the building cautiously.

"Somebody lived here a long time ago and by the look of it, it might have been a beautiful building," said Pearl, "though now a bit draughty."

"I'm sure of it but I have never heard of this place," said his father.

"I'm sure there won't be any problems for some of the people to rebuild this building and the houses, after all the stones are still here. Maybe some villagers can provide some glass for the windows later on."

"Yes, Pearl and I think this village is big enough for all the people coming with us and a few more. Outside on the north side we can have some corrals."

"Come with me Pearl," he said going outside the building and with her they carried on to the west side of the ruins where outside the wall they found some flat grounds with a path going down to a place with many rocks and a small stream at the bottom. "Here, this will be a good place to make up the latrines for all those people."

"Yes, you are right, and it will be a very good exercise going down and after coming up here.

"Something else to think about is to make sure the waist doesn't filter down to the stream between these hills just in case it feeds other streams we might use for other purposes, like to wash vegetables and for us and the animals to drink."

"That's true but I can guess that when this village was alive with people, they must have had some latrines in different places. Don't you worry Pearl, I'm sure my mother will check on that and it will be better for somebody to dig a long trench that will be covered by wooden planks with holes to use as toilets."

"Yes, you are right and some people could build a wall to make it more private."

"Yes, that's right Pearl and as you can see there is a foot path going down to the right following the cliff contours and hopefully there are more of those paths for warriors to walk all around this village."

"All right," said Pearl, "I've seen enough and now one of us will go back to the prairie and guide the people up here."

"I'll do it," said Eloy's father and without waiting for Eloy to say anything, he left running.

"I must say your father has a lot of energy."

"Yes, he has always been a strong man."

Eloy and Pearl started to ambulate through the ruins and in a way, Eloy was very optimistic with it.

"Some of the buildings are not bad at all and can be restored. We don't know for how long we'll stay here but we must do our best to make our stay as comfortable as possible."

Pearl agreed with him. "All this is the size of a big village. In a way, it looks bigger than the villages in the forest and looking like if in ancient times it was a village fortress."

"That's right Pearl it gives me the same impression."

"Hey, maybe this was Bonamor's headquarters."

*

Eloy's father reached the people that were ready to move already organised in four big groups and spoke to the four commanders. "We've seen a wonderful place at the top with a kind of village in ruins that can be rebuilt. Now it is for you to guide the people up there," and the four commanders moved swiftly to be at the head of each group and in a few moments, they were all moving forward followed by the animals.

*

Back in the village fortress Pearl looked at Eloy grinning and he noticed. "What? Why are you looking at me?"

"Well, it seems to me that you will be the leader from now on."

"Pearl, please don't say it."

Pearl opened her eyes wide. "Oh no, you won't get out of your leadership just like that."

"But Pearl, I'm not the leader."

"Oh yes, you are and stop trying to avoid it," she said and moved away leaving him without a chance to say a word. He just looked at her and shrugged his shoulders.

*

Without wasting any time, his father with the four commanders led the people up to the top of the hill.

Sanila with Mavina with their husbands were the first to reach the top.

"This is big," said Sanila.

"Come on Sanila," said his mother, "we must find a place for the communal kitchen," and off they went searching.

Eloy started to look around. "What we need now it to find a place for us to use as headquarters, a place big enough for both families and for us to spend the nights in it. You and I must stay close at all times."

"And I know the right place for it. The building that looks like a palace will be big enough though it needs to be repaired."

"Okay, let's have a look."

They went back to the palace ruins and looking around Pearl saw at the other end of the big hall stone stairs in very good condition.

They went upstairs and saw several rooms though the roof was just wooden beams with wooden tiles showing a few holes. Stone debris and many wooden tiles covered the floor.

*

By then more people were arriving and immediately they started to disperse just looking for a house.

*

Eloy and Pearl carried on and they found two rooms in better condition than the rest of the building. "All right, this room will do for me and my family," said Eloy, "and you can use the other for your family."

Pearl was surprised. "Why are you separating our families?"

"Very simple my friend because you must stay with your parents. Think about it woman, you cannot stay with us sleeping in the same room. It wouldn't be proper. People could start murmuring and your family need some privacy."

"Oh yes, of course," she said realisation dawning. Then she had a thought. "If the people wanted to murmur they could have done it by now, because we've been together for most of the time on our own since the beginning of the invasion and so far, they have not," saying that she started looking inside the other room.

"This one is big enough for my family!" she cried and Eloy joined her. "There, now our families will be together under the same roof and in a palace; now we have solved that problem let's carry on exploring the rest of the ruins."

Pearl looked at the building and sighed. "Not much of a palace right now. It's more like a palatial ruin."

"Yes, it is and from now on it will be our headquarters. The hall is big enough for having meetings with the people in command."

They look at their surroundings and saw just damaged walls with no furniture and a roof.

"The walls can be repaired and we can put a few more wooden tiles on the roof," said Pearl, "there must be some carpenters amongst the people."

Immediately Eloy collected some small rocks and started to repair the wall in his room. His father entered the room and started to collect some of the stones from the ground. "Leave it to me son, I'll carry on and you can go about your business as a leader."

"Oh, father, please."

"Please nothing, you are the leader and that's final."

Her mother came in and saw the room selected for them. "This will be a wonderful bedroom Pearl, but we must make our beds on the floor."

Immediately her father started to do some repairs in their room.

In the other room, Mavina was very happy with their lodgings. "This is all right to keep us from any strong wind."

*

Eloy left the building followed by Pearl and soon they were mingling with the people and feeling happy to see so many children already playing and running.

They walked through a gap out of the east wall and found a ledge just outside of it from where they could have a panoramic view of the prairie.

By then the animals were arriving.

*

In the meantime, Pearl's father had left the headquarters with the two mothers calling for volunteers to restore the walls of a place that in ancient times must have been a sort of communal kitchen with a big cooker made of stones and several ovens big enough not just to make bread but to roast as well.

*

A column of mainly women was leaving the place with jars on their shoulder to try to find a stream to bring water for the people.

Though it took them a couple of hours to reach the plateau, finally the last of the refugees reached the ruins.

*

Some people started to build on the north slopes outside the village fortress four corrals made of stones. One for the cows and the other three for the goats, pigs and sheep. Everybody was doing something.

One thing is for sure," said Eloy, "we won't be short of food."

"And there will be enough wool for people to spin and knit pullovers," added Pearl, "at this height, the air is a bit colder and they'll need some wormer clothes."

"And not to mention the manure we'll have, that can be used for the vegetables some people will start growing on the north slopes."

Pearl thought about it. "Can we really have vegetables growing in here?"

"Of course, but it will have to be done further down the hills and away from the prairie. You know, closer to the streams and where they will catch the first sun every morning."

Pearl was feeling more at home. "This will be a wonderful place to live."

*

Three men and a young woman approached them. They were the four warriors chosen by Eloy and Pearl the night before, to be the commanders. They were all in their early twenties.

"You've done very well," said Pearl.

"Yes," said Eloy, "but now we need to know you better."

The black man spoke first. "I'm Marum."

"I'm Bo," said the oriental man.

"I'm Barum," said the white man.

"And I am Lera," said the young woman and Eloy noticed she was about his age with a light brown complexion and sporting some short light brown long hair she kept like a pony tail and he felt some attraction towards her.

Barum was an impressive tall and muscular man with dark short brown hair and a moustache connected with his sideburns.

The contrast was Bo of an average height, with a white complexion. and long brown hair resting on his shoulders.

Marum had a light black look with short curly black hair with a moustache and beard.

"I'm happy to know you all," said Pearl, "come with me to the headquarters," and led them into the spacious hall in the heart of the palace. Some men were there already repairing the walls while others were repairing the roof. In fact, the whole population of this revived village fortress was on the move with all of them doing something and showing plenty of enthusiasm.

"Very well," said Eloy, "from now on you will be selecting more people into your groups and you will pass your knowledge in the use of your weapons turning them into warriors."

Commander Barum looked surprised. "Warriors?"

"We don't have any warriors," said Lera.

Eloy nodded. "That's true but from now on you will select the people who are willing to form our new army and later on, I will with Pearl help you to train them."

"With what weapons? We don't have any apart of our own," was Marum's opinion.

"Not to worry because one of the wagons belongs to a merchant selling weapon and we won't have any problem to buy them. You must remember that in the near future we might get some from the enemy. What you must do now is to put some sentinels all around mainly on the east wall to keep an eye on the prairie in case the enemy sends patrols to find us."

"Now you know what to do, go to the people and carry on making your selection," were Pearl's instructions and the new commanders left.

"What do you think?"

"What I think Pearl is that we have a difficult task ahead and there is nothing we can do to avoid it."

"We won't have any problems with you in the lead," she said once again showing a wide grin.

"Oh, stop that," he said shaking his head.

"And I will be always at your side."
He breathed in, looked at her and smiled.
"I know that."

*

The plateau was big enough for all the people but some of them had gone outside of the north wall to build some stone rooms for their families leaving a road in between for everybody to walk freely. However, they did it away from the corrals.

Inside the village fortress, many family groups started using blankets as a roof while they carried on rebuilding their homes.

The citadel with its surroundings started to look more like as it was in ancient times.

*

Later on, while walking and mingling with the people Eloy and Pearl noticed, some guards have appeared on top of tall rocks and part of the rebuilt wall. With some of them simply holding staves.

"What we need now are some skilful people like carpenters and blacksmiths with some people in the knowledge on how to make walls, like bricklayers." said Eloy.

"You are right." and she called commander Lera. "Go and mingle with the people and find out if there are any carpenters, blacksmiths and some stone masons or bricklayers."

Lera left immediately.

"Good," said Eloy. "Now we wait."

*

Moments later, three men approached them with Lera and they all had a rucksack and holding a bag with some tools.

"I am a carpenter," said one of them.

"And I am a blacksmith," said the other," "and this is my assistant."

"Very well then but I hope you have the tools of your trade," said Pearl.

They showed the tools they had in their bags.

"Very well," said Eloy, "choose a place where you can build up your workshops blacksmith, you need to try to find a well-ventilated place. I don't want you to smoke the people out, eh?"

Then he instructed the carpenter. "Try to instruct some young people in your skill making bows and arrows and don't you forget to put somebody to split pieces of tree trunks to make tiles for the roofs."

Cheerfully they bowed to him and left.

At that moment, several people approached. "We are stonemasons and bricklayers," said one of them.

"I'm happy you are here because as you have already seen, there is quite a lot of work to be done to bring this village to habitable conditions. The people will need not just a roof on their heads but walls as well. Don't forget to train some young people in your skills and to supervise the people already doing some repairs."

They bowed to Eloy and Pearl, leaving talking enthusiastically.

*

Eloy and Pearl approached their fathers. "What we need now is for you to organise some people to go down to the prairie and see if they can go to the forest to collect some wood for the carpenters to start making bows and arrows and hopefully some deadwood for our fires but you must make sure not to damage the forest. Some trees can be cut in such a way that they will carry on living and producing new branches and saplings."

Remember to choose straight branches for the carpenter to make bows and dry dead wood for the making of arrows," said Pearl.

"All right, we'll do that," said his father, "but don't forget that some people had managed to bring some charcoal."

"Yes, I know but the charcoal will be better use by the blacksmith and in here it doesn't matter to have open fires. We are well away from the enemy."

*

Some selected people that were just sitting and doing nothing with commander Marum in the lead, left helped by commander Bo and some of his men.

"Don't forget to collect the dry animal's droppings!" cried Eloy.

Her mother interrupted him. "That's the job for women and we'll start right now," she said calling Eloy's mother.

The two mothers call other women instructing them to bring sacks and to follow the men down the hill.

*

Eloy and Pearl were happy to see how people were organising themselves.

"I hope some of them will go down to the stream and bring back some mud to use as mortar to repair the walls and to make some new stone homes."

Pearl agreed with him. "This place is big enough to shelter many people," then she had a thought. "With so many people, we must deal with hygiene and for that purpose what we need is a communal bath for men and another for women."

Eloy looked around and agreed. "I think you are right and we have all the people we need for the building of that bathroom." Then he looked at their surroundings, "and when the wall is completed this will be what it was a long time ago; a fortified citadel or we can carry on calling it the village fortress."

Pearl felt enthusiastic. "I must say you are thinking big but I agree with you because right now I need a bath. I have not had a chance to clean myself since we left our homes."

Eloy looked at her and covered his nose with a hand. "Yes, Pearl you are so right."

She was shocked for a moment and then gave him a push. "And you smell too!"

Eloy was holding his laughter back. "Yes, my friend and I need a bath too."

They carried on mingling and no matter where they went, people approached them asking all sorts of questions.

*

About an hour later, they went to stand on the ledge they found earlier from where they could see the prairie and Eloy father joined them.

"We have a good view of the prairie."

"Yes, father."

They could clearly see the two commanders walking on the prairie followed by many people.

"I hope you agree to have those sentinels I've put on the walls."

Eloy felt surprised. "Yes, father that was a very good idea, thank you."

*

In the meantime, the enemy captain at the head of two hundred soldiers was meandering in between the forest hills, this time all of them on foot.

He ordered a few of them with their bows ready to carry on ahead as scouts.

There was enough room on the path between the hills for them to move until they reached the foot of another hill, where he led them following a path inside of a small gorge carved by a stream.

*

Though the north of the prairie had a narrow distance between the hills and the forest than the rest of it, commanders Marum and Bo with their helping hands took two hours to reach the forest. Immediately they started work by collecting the dead wood and choosing the right trees they could cut properly.

In no time, they had chopped some trees and branches to the right size and with some ropes; they started to pull them towards the prairie.

Commander Marum was keeping an eye on everything and he sends a few of his men as lookouts further inside the forest walking at the side of a narrow stream running in from the prairie.

They cut several more trees and commander Marum told those people to stop and start back to the hills though he stayed behind waiting for his men to return. Commander Bo did the same.

*

The enemy Captain had passed the gorge and was advancing very cautiously still going west without seen any refugees.

The scouts were walking on a path at the side of the same stream that had carved the gorge but surprised there were no people in the forest though they found the remnants of some old fires.

*

After some time, the scouts send by commander Marum heard people walking not far from where they were.

One of them carried on very slowly until he saw one of the enemy scouts and immediately run back to report.

He joined the other scouts and together they run to the end of the forest to report.

*

Though exhausted, the scouts reached commander Marum. "Enemies commander and they will soon be here!"

"All right, let's go back to the hills and help those people pulling the tree trunks."

They run as fast as they could with some of them helping the others. It wasn't easy because some of the tree trunks were heavy, but they did their best. The rest of the men carrying dead wood could do it faster.

Mavina and Sanila saw what was going on and immediately they call the other women to leave with whatever they had collected.

*

Up in the hills the guards from their lookout positions saw what was going on and gave the alarm.

"People in the prairie are in trouble!" cried one.

"What kind of trouble?" asked Eloy.

"I don't know, sir but some of them are running."

Once again, Eloy and Pearl came to the ledge.

Pearl agreed. "Yes, they are returning with some of them running. Commander Barum! Some of you go down there and help those people. Something is not right!"

Immediately, commander Barum ran down to help followed by several men of his new group of would-be warriors.

Eloy's father joined them. "Shall I send some of my warriors?"

"No, father this time Barum's warriors are enough."

It was some distance between the forest and the hills and Commanders Marum and Bo had crossed most of the prairie getting very tired when the reinforcements arrived.

Though the enemy had not come out of the forest yet, with their combine efforts soon they were leaving the prairie.

*

Eloy, Pearl and Eloy's father were nervously watching upon the prairie.

*

It didn't take long for the enemy Captain to come out of the trees and from there he could see in the distance the last of Marum and Bo's men using the road and ordered his men to stop.

"I don't think we should go there. If we do it we'll be ambushed."

"I don't see many trees for them to hide behind," said one of his soldiers.

"True, not enough trees but there are many rocks for them to hide behind."

"Come on Captain let me go with some volunteers."

The captain thought about it for a moment and then he nodded. "All right do it."

The soldier called some of his friends and off they went.

*

Eloy and Pearl noticed some movement on the prairie.

"They are sending a patrol to investigate," said Eloy and Pearl look at him waiting for instructions.

He called Lera. "We'll go to that place where the road has the sharp side and lay in waiting behind the rocks for the enemy to arrive. We will ambush them.

*

It didn't take long for them to encounter the commanders Marum and Bo who immediately stop and organised their warriors to hide behind the rocks letting the rest of their men to carry on with the wood and the women carrying sacks with the animal droppings.

"This time we can use our swords for the first time," said commander Barum.

Eloy had a thought. "It's true you can use them but you Lera can reach them first with your arrows and the rest of you can bombard them with plenty of stones before engaging them."

"All right, we are ready," said commander Bo.

"Same here," said Marum.

"And here too," said Barum.

"I'm ready too," said Lera.

"Be careful Lera, this time you'll stay behind the fighters," was Eloy instruction. "You can reach them with your arrows."

Somehow, Lera felt disappointed with Pearl feeling sympathetic. "Don't you worry Lera, Eloy don't want for you to get injured."

*

Moments later Eloy, Pearl, Barum, Marum, Lera and Bo were in position waiting in silence.

The commanders had about ten warriors each.

Time was passing with no signs of the enemy and the new warriors were getting impatient.

Then they heard something and got ready.

The first soldiers approached with their bows ready but Eloy and Pearl didn't give the signal.

More soldiers came behind the first and they too had their weapons ready. They were twenty and soon they were all at the mercy of the resistance warriors and Eloy cried the order. "Now!"

Pearl with Lera shoots their arrow hitting several soldiers while the warriors, after throwing some stones, just jumped forwards with their swords high.

The enemy was completely surprised though they managed to shoot some arrows lightly hurting some of the warriors.

Soon the fight was man-to-man and very fast; Pearl and Lera stayed where they were shooting their arrows and a few moments later, all the enemies were dead.

"All right! Let's collect their weapons and help me to take care of our wounded!" instructed Pearl while leaning at the side of one of the warriors with an arrow in his left leg. She broke the arrow and other warriors helped him to walk. All the wounded could walk.

"Some of them fall down the hill," said commander Bo.

"That's right," said Eloy, "and somebody will have to go down there and get their purses and weapons."

For their amusement, some of the men went down though reluctantly and mumbling all the way.

"That will be the best place to bury them," were Pearl's instructions, "some of you push the other bodies down after stripping them from their money and weapons.

Moments later, some warriors were covering the bodies with stones. After all, they didn't have any shovels.

*

The enemy Commander was getting worried when his men didn't return.

"That's it, they are not coming back, any more volunteers?" He looked at his men but they all look inconspicuously in different directions.

"All right, let's go back to the city." His orders make his men happy and relieved.

*

In the meantime, Eloy with Pearl and their warriors returned to the top of the hill in triumph and the people celebrated with singing and dancing.

Several would-be warriors grabbed the bows and the swords Eloy's group had brought for them while trying the steel helmets.

Pearl's mother Sanila with the help of other women started taking care of the wounded that were clearly in pain.

Pearl noticed Eloy once again in deep thought. "What is it this time?"

"This time I'm thinking about the people in the city and the Queen with Prince Neno."

"Ah, Prince Neno. I saw him once and I think he's cute."

Eloy looked at her sympathetically. "Of course, you would."

She frowned at him. "What do you mean by that?"

"Very simple, by been a young woman you would find a young man cute."

She thought about it for a moment. "I don't find you cute."

"Of course, not because we are friends. It's different."

Pearl was shocked for a moment but then she smiled and shrugged her shoulders.

They remained in silence for a moment and Eloy had an idea. "I think we should do something to rescue the Queen or at least Prince Neno. If the people know they are safe, it will encourage the city dwellers to resist the invaders."

Pearl thought about it. "How can they resist without weapons? All they have is water." Then she smiled. "Maybe they can attack them by throwing water by the bucket?"

"Come on Pearl be serious," he said holding his laughter, "we must do something to help the people inside the city."

Her expression became radiant. "Now that is a good idea but how can we do it?"

Commander Lera was nearby and Eloy called her. "Commander will you please call the other commanders for a meeting."

Lera bowed and left.

Pearl's curiosity was aroused. "How can we do that? To go through the forest can be very dangerous. Some warriors can have accidents like to break a leg and we already know the enemy is in there. If we have an encounter with them it is possible for some of our warriors to be killed and that will reduce our power to carry on."

"Pearl, I don't now but I'm sure there is a way to do it. Come let's wait for them in the headquarters."

*

Lera returned a moment later with the others. They still didn't have chairs or a table in the hall so they all sat on the ground in a semicircle facing Eloy and Pearl.

"I have an idea but I need your opinion. It could be very good for the moral of the people in the city if we rescue the Queen or the prince. It will increase their will to resist."

"We could go in small groups and enter the city," was Barum's opinion.

"Yes," said Pearl, "but the point is on how to do it because we cannot use the gates."

"That's true but first the point is on how to get there because, as Pearl mentioned to me earlier on, we cannot go through the forest without having a possible encounter with the enemy that could finish with several warriors, dead," said Eloy.

There was an uneasy moment for all of them thinking but then Marum had an idea. "Why don't we go by sea?"

They all look at him first and then at Eloy and Pearl.

Eloy was happy with the idea. "Yes, that's another way. Stay here and wait for us, I will have a talk with Pearl's father, come Pearl." and they both left.

*

They found Harmon with his wife. "We need to have a talk father."

"I'm listening."

"Do you think your friends the fishermen could come further west and closer to us?" asked Eloy.

"Yes, I don't see why not. All I need is for me to go to the cavern and organise them but I need to know why because they will ask me."

"I intend to organise a raid on the city to try and rescue the Queen or Prince Neno."

Harmon frowned. "Very good idea in principle but very dangerous."

"Yes, the point is can the fishermen, do it? What I mean is for them to take us closer to the city."

"Oh yes, in the sea we are the masters and my boat is the fastest. The enemy cannot challenge us; they have no boats," he said with pride, "the problem is with the sea current and in these parts of the coast it runs west, which means it will be easy for the boats to come to get you but going east we'll have no choice but to use the sails and that means we can be seen from the distance."

"Very well then, we'll think about that problem later and now you go and prepare your boats and we will prepare the warriors for our daring action, which will be the first for our newly form army. How many people can your boats carry?

Pearl's father scratched his chin. "Unfortunately, only six or maybe seven at the most."

"Now that will be a problem because I will need at least twenty-five warriors to come with us."

"In that case we'll need at least five boats but don't you worry, I'll pick the best and I don't have to go east to ask other villages. That I can do another day."

"All right, you go and we'll prepare."

His wife gave him some food in a satchel and he left.

"Be careful father."

"Don't you worry Pearl, I'll be all right. I intend to follow the sea shores; it will be a bit longer but safe."

They returned to the other commanders.

"Part of the plan is already on the move and we'll have boats for the transport but now you must choose the best warriors you can find and form a group of twenty-five armed mostly with swords and at least five will be archers."

"How much time we have to get our force together?" asked Lera.

"You'll have until tomorrow because hopefully by then the boats will be close to us by the seaside."

"That will be quite a walk because the seaside is not so close," was Marum's worried opinion.

"True my friend but it will be a good exercise for everybody and it will be safe because the invaders have not come so far west."

Lera was ready to start. "Eloy is right and I think we'd better spend our time putting the warriors together and leave him to do the worrying."

Eloy felt a strange emotion towards her. "Thank you Lera."

She just looked at him and smiled. "It's all right, any time."

"All right," said Barum standing up with the others. "Let's do it and leave the leader to deal with all the worries."

Eloy was beginning to realise that he has become the leader and didn't feel happy. "Yeah, right."

Then he called for his father to come forward. "I have a task for you father. After we have left, you will organise the rest of the people into an improvised army and then go down to the forest and advance until you are close to any enemy and instead of attacking, you will form a line of defence to prevent them moving west. Though you will do your best to tease them and make them believe it is a serious attack."

"Thank you, son, I was beginning to feel left aside like an old man but I won't have enough people to do that."

"Of course not, but the enemy won't know and then you will retreat back to the hills; all that will be to deceit them and don't waste any opportunity to take some of their weapons."

"Yes, my son it will be done but what about if they follow us until here?"

"In that case father, you'll have no choice but to face them and do your best to stop them but if that happens out in the prairie our sentinels will see whatever happens and reinforce you."

"Yes, son as you wish."

*

The sea was not that far from the village fortress and after a few hours walk following the path towards the sea flanked by trees, Pearl's father had come to the seashores, and after resting for a while, started to follow the beach going east.

Sometimes later, he had passed a cove he thought it was ideal to use later with the boats, it was a place surrounded by tall rocks and well protected from any strong wind.

After resting for a while to have something to eat and drink some water from his flat bottle he followed the coast that was in many places covered with sandy beaches and some dunes. On his right side, he could see lower hills that in a way stopped the dunes advancing on the prairie.

The sea was calm with many noisy sea birds and the breeze was refreshing.

He manages very well to go to that part of the seaside where the cavern was though it was impossible for him to approach the main entrance; it was high tide and the sea was a bit too rough.

Nevertheless, he changed direction going up the hill to reach the cavern entrance used by the refugees.

*

It took him some time but finally he reached the place that by now had several guards with spears and soon he was inside rallying all the fishermen to listen to him.

"Eloy, our leader, needs some boats to take some of the warriors of our new army for a very special mission. My boat will be one but he'll need five."

The news of having an army put a sparkle of enthusiasm in all those people.

The fishermen started to deliberate and finally four more boats were selected to go but they had to wait until night to leave the safety of their refuge, to prevent any possibility for the enemy that might have come close to the seaside, to see them.

*

After an exhausting force-march crossing of the forest the enemy captain arrived at the city and immediately went searching for the General who had taken residence in the palace.

"Well?" he said arrogantly, "did you find them?"

"I saw them and now I know where they are."

The General became impatient. "Come on speak, where are they?"

"They are in the hills further west of the prairie and I lost twenty soldiers that were ambushed by them on the road to the hills."

The General thought about it for a moment. "You will go back to the forest but you'll stay outside and form a sort of a barrier to prevent anybody coming out of it to attack us. Now go."

The captain saluted in military fashion and left.

*

In the hills, the commanders had selected their warriors and soon they were on the march with Eloy and Pearl in the lead. All the mail warriors had swords and five female warriors were archers under Lera's command.

"Our warriors are well armed but so far, we don't have them in abundance and they don't have enough experience." was Pearl's opinion.

"Don't you worry I'm sure that eventually the rest of the army will increase in numbers. Have some faith in the people."

"I do have faith in the people and above all in our cause, but I don't think that weapons will just come to us."

"Eventually they will; if my father is successful in the forest he will get some from the enemy."

Pearl expression changed. "The problem will be that for every sword taken from the enemy he might lose a warrior."

"Yes, Pearl that is always possible."

*

The enemy captain at the head of a bigger infantry force arrived close to the first line of trees and ordered his men to make camp in several places but in a straight line, like a barrier though he didn't have enough soldiers to cover all the edge of the forest. Nevertheless, he managed to cover the area facing the main gates until a bit further south. In fact, he didn't have enough soldiers to cover the entire west wall.

*

The day had come to an end and in the city the Queen tried to leave the palace with two of her attendants and a couple of her personal guards holding torches but she was stopped by some enemy soldiers guarding the main entrance.

"Your Majesty I'm sorry but we have orders not to let you leave the palace."

She was adamant. "I am still the Queen and I intend to see my son Prince Neno."

For a moment, the soldiers weren't sure about what to do. They were facing a woman with a strong personality. "Stay here and I will consult with the General," said the commander and left leaving the Queen and attendants surrounded by his soldiers.

He entered the General's room where he was feasting with a bowl full of fruit. "What is it?"

"The Queen is trying to leave the palace to see her son."

The General frowned. "Very well let her pass but with our escort and don't let anyone come too close to her, understood? She must not communicate with other people."

The commander saluted in military fashion and returned to the Queen. "It's all right but you will be escorted by some of my men," and he gave the order. "You will show Her Majesty the way and will make sure she returns to the palace. Above all don't let anybody coming too close to her."

The soldiers saluted in military fashion and led her with her attendants holding the torches leaving the two guards behind.

The night was not very dark because the crescent moon was already up and they crossed the streets with no city dwellers, only soldiers.

It was very strange for the Queen to cross a city looking like a military garrison and after going over one of the bridges, they reached the tower in the wall and had to go down using a spiral staircase.

Deep below a dungeon's guard opened the cell and the Queen was very impressed with the smells and filth.

Her son was lying on some straw. When he saw his mother, he stood up with some difficulty making sounds with the chains attached to his ankles and wrists.

With tears in her eyes, the Queen approached and embraced him. "Don't you worry son there's always hope and I will try to get you free."

"Don't bow to his demands mother. If they haven't killed me, they must have a good reason for it."

"Are they feeding you?"

"I wouldn't call it food mother. It's just some watery gruel with absolutely no taste."

The attendants provided the prince with some fruit they have hidden in their clothes and the prince didn't waste any time devouring them.

"Now go mother and do not take this risk anymore. I'm sure the people will do something."

The Queen gave him a kiss and left with tears running down her cheeks.

*

With the cover of darkness, the fishermen were ready to leave the cavern. After loading some food, the boats left and did it using the currents, which meant it was easy for the two fishermen on board to row. The currents help by taking the boats west.

"I hope that somebody will help with the rowing later on," said one of the fishermen.

"I'm sure some of the warriors will consider doing some rowing that will be a good exercise for their muscles."

*

Eloy and Pearl moved through a land that they had never seen though the terrain was not difficult. Wisely, they followed the paths made up by many animals and sometimes they noticed some gazelles not far from them.

By then the crescent moon was giving more light to the land and there were no clouds.

*

Using the moonlight, Lera with her female warriors managed very well to hunt for rabbits and proved to be very good archers and sometime later, they joined the warring party with their catch.

"You and your archers did very well," said Eloy, "and tonight when we camp by the seaside we'll have roasted rabbits."

"My girls are very good with their weapons and hunting rabbits was a very good exercise. With the moonlight we have, they had to find their targets in semi-darkness.

*

They had reached the seashores and moved east walking on the wet beach that was very much easier than to walk on dry sand.

They reached the place with a cove surrounded by tall rocks and made camp. Nearby there was a small stream running into it.

Commander Marum had an idea. "I think the tide is low and that means only one thing."

"Shellfish," said commander Bo and without saying another word all the warriors left their weapons on the ground and taking their trousers and sandals off, they went to the nearby rocks with some of them lighting their surroundings with torches.

The female warriors only folded their skirts up.

Though the moonlight was dim, they managed to see their surroundings. A warm breeze kept them warm though their feet in the water were very cold.

"Well," said Pearl, "I think we'll have shellfish and rabbits."

They put the torches all around their camp and immediately some of the warriors started to make up some stony structures using the mud from the nearby stream as a mortar, finishing with stony cookers.

*

They collected dry seaweed for the fires and moments later the first rabbits started to roast at the side of the fires held by thick wooden twigs.

"It is all right for us to have some fires because we are well away from the enemy and I can't wait to try some of those rabbits," said Eloy gleefully, "and some of you can get some salt from the rocks." Immediately some of the warriors went to collect some.

Moments later, there were several small fires all around. By then the sea breeze was turning a bid too fresh.

It didn't take long for them to get enough muscles and a few crabs. They put the muscles in some long thin wooden skewers to roast on the fire and throw the crabs at the side of the fires to cook. It was like a little feast or a seaside banquet though all of them were using their fingers.

*

Later, most of them were asleep and Eloy, Pearl and the commanders were sitting together not far from the rest of the group.

"Do you have any idea how we'll enter the city?" asked Lera.

"No, not really" said Eloy, "I know that some of the city dwellers left the city by using the sewers but I have no intention of doing the same. It would be very embarrassing to mingle with the city dwellers smelling of sewer."

"Argh," exclaimed Pearl, "certainly, I wouldn't."

"What we'll do when we reach the city is to look for another way to get in."

*

Later, commander Barum pointed to the sea. "There, the boats are coming in!"

All the boats had some lanterns and were all guided by the fires in the warrior's camp.

The five boats approached the shore that was not made of sand but shingle instead, awaking some of the sleeping warriors.

Very carefully and with their help, they pulled the boats bow out of the water.

"First have something to eat and then try to get some sleep. You'll need all the rest you can get because tomorrow will be a hectic day." Were Eloy's instructions and as it was expected the fishermen used their boats to sleep inside.

Eloy with Pearl and the commanders choose a place away from the seaside sheltered from the cold breeze coming from the sea by some tall rocks and wrapped themselves with their blankets.

They could see a handful of the male warriors sitting together with female archers close to a fire in a very friendly way.

"See that?" said Pearl looking at them with a very happy expression.

Eloy sat closer to her. "Yes, even in the middle of a tragedy friendship between men and women is always there."

Then he noticed that Lera was sitting at his side and shivering, though she had a blanket over her shoulders. "Let me help you," and used his blanket on both of them.

For a moment, she was confused but then she smiled and leaned her head on his shoulder.

They lay down looking at the sky and admiring the firmament. A couple of shooting stars crossed the sky and moments later, they were asleep.

Chapter Five

A young sun shining from the horizon woke all of them up.

There was no time to do any fishing or to build up a fire and all they had for breakfast was bread and some fruit from their satchels. There was no rabbit or seafood left and moments later, they were ready to go.

Eloy called the entire group for a meeting and with a long piece of wood; he made a kind of a map on dry sand away from the shingle.

He made a line to show were the coastline was and a mark where they were. Then he made a cross to show where the cavern was.

"Because it is day you will take your boats as far as the cavern and from there out at sea navigating east but as far as possible from the coast until you cannot see it and later on well pass our fishing village you will approach the coast. We'll use a small cove facing a cliff and surrounded by tall rocks and sandy beaches."

Pearl's father spoke. "I know the place you are talking about and you must know too Pearl; we stopped in that cove a couple of times to wait for the sea to calm down."

"Yes," said Pearl happily, "I remember."

"But why go so far away from the coast?" asked another fisherman.

"Because as I have mentioned this before, going east you must use the sails to navigate against the current and we must avoid for any enemy patrolling the seaside to see them."

The fishermen nodded and all the warriors were ready.

"All right," said Pearl, "let's go."

First, they pushed the boats back to the water and then by getting their feet wet, climbed on board.

Commander Barum climbed on a boat and started to laugh.

"What's funny?" asked Pearl.

"We haven't had a shower or bath for some days but this time at least our feet are washed even if it is with sea water."

It was easy for them to do so because thy all wore sandals.

In another boat was Lera and Pearl. "Yes," said Lera, "but the water is very cold." Taking her sandals off she started to massage her feet. Suddenly she started laughing.

"Why are you laughing," asked a curious Pearl.

"Very simple because last night all I had was muscles and crab using my hands, now my feet will smell the same."

The warriors and sailors in the boat couldn't stop laughing.

*

First, the fishermen row to leave the cove and then they put the mast and sail up.

From then on, it was just navigating going east and the warriors could relax. Because of the currents, they moved forward slowly but steadily.

*

Eloy's father had followed his son's instructions and early in the morning and just before the sun show itself in the east, with all the men and women who could hold a weapon marched out of the village fortress and down to the prairie.

They were all a happy bunch of about two hundred would be warriors.

Many people had only a long piece of wood to use as a staff and some of them using their knives were making one end of it very sharp.

By the time they reached the forest, the sun was getting higher and they entered walking at the side of a stream without encountering anybody though the improvised army was getting very apprehensive. They all stopped fooling about and there was no more laughter.

*

Some rain clouds covered the sun and it started raining which make them very unhappy though they had no choice but to get wet.

Fortunately for them, it was only a couple of clouds and soon the sun was warming the air.

"What can we do commander if the enemy attack us?" was one of the warrior's nervous questions.

"My instructions are to face them and then retreat back to the hills, that's all." Then he looked at the sky. "I don't think we'll find them inside the forest because so far only one group has tried by sending a patrol that was defeated." Then he smiled. "They don't know how many we are and most probably they are getting very nervous."

*

Eloy's father was right because the enemy captain in command of the soldiers just outside the forest was getting very nervous and was pacing right and left holding his sword.

*

It didn't take long for Eloy to see the cavern entrance though they could not see the people inside. From then on and according to their instructions, the fishermen sailed their boats going north and negotiating the islands very well.

The small flotilla was lucky to have a calm sea and the west wind was very helpful pushing the boats forward at a steady speed. In some places, the wind was channelled between the rocky islands making it faster and soon they were in open sea.

They have been very lucky to have calm seas but nevertheless, they could see the sun moving over them and it was well passed midday. That was the time for Pearl's father who was ahead to turn his boat heading towards the coast and it was exciting for the warriors to see once again the coastline though they could not see the cove they were supposed to reach.

The navigating skills of the fishermen were commendable and soon they could all see the opening between some tall rocks. They used all their skills going through the narrow entrance and there they were inside a very well sheltered cove with very calm waters and protected from any wind though there was a small waterfall falling from over a rocky cliff with its waters cutting through the beach finishing in the cove's waters.

"That's a beautiful waterfall but where is that water coming from," asked Lera.

"That is supposed to be the water that overflows from the canal that runs through the city," said Eloy, "isn't it beautiful?"

For a moment, Lera was ecstatic. "Oh yes."

Without slowing down and just before hitting the beach, they put the sails and masts down.

With certain speed, they hit the sand and immediately the fishermen jumped out and started to pull the boats bow out of the water.

The warriors jumped on the sand without getting their feet wet.

"Make sure to secure the boats properly considering the tide is coming in," were Pearl father instructions.

Following his instructions, the fishermen pushed a piece of steel in the sand and tied the boats with a rope to it.

Her father decided to stay with the boats and the rest of the group followed Eloy.

"We have taken most of the day to come here," said Eloy, "and by the time we reach the city it will be getting darker."

"Have you thought about a way to get inside the city?" asked Lera.

"No, I have not and so far, probably the only place we can try is to go over the east wall." Then he had a thought. "But of course," he said slapping his forehead, "that's the best way to get in; the canal that runs through the city."

Pearl reacted with great enthusiasm. "Yes, you are right but it must be done under the cover of darkness, to prevent the soldiers in the battlement to see us."

"That's true but first we must come closer to it," was Eloy's opinion.

He took the lead and started to look for a way to climb out of the beach and soon he found a narrow footpath on the left side of the cove taking them to the top.

*

They could see the city walls in the distance to their right though still far away.

What they saw in front of them was not flat land and there was some kind of protection because of the undulating terrain with many small trees and bushes close to the canal. There were many trees marking the edge of the farming fields giving them extra cover from the soldiers on the battlements. That was in fact the end of the arable land. From there it was the beginning of the desert to their left.

They advanced towards the city but didn't encounter any enemies though they did it very carefully and Eloy ordered them to stop and rest.

*

What was left of the day passed calmly and by then the sun was almost all gone behind the mountains.

"All right," said Pearl, "when we start moving you must make sure not to be seen from the battlements. The bushes and small trees at either side of the canal will give some protection."

*

Suddenly Pearl saw something. "Look some soldiers are coming from the east with a wagon."

They all observed and Eloy had an idea. "It could be a wagon with food from their country."

"Or fish from the other fishing village in the east. Thinking of it, I think that Harmon could try to get some boats from that village for later on." was Eloy's opinion.

*

The General was on the battlements observing those soldiers approaching with the wagon. "Good, now we'll have some good food."

*

The improvised army led by Eloy's father carried on through the forest without any difficulties. Nevertheless, they did it very carefully. They tried to come out at the other side not far from his village and there the enemy spotted them.

The enemy Captain gave the orders to shoot their arrows but the warriors used the trees as shields and nobody was hurt.

Immediately after, he sent a messenger to the city. "Tell the General we have been attacked from the forest but we are holding our positions."

The messenger was confused for a moment looking at the forest with no rebels on site. "Attack?" Then he shrugged his shoulders and saluting in military fashion he left.

*

Eloy's father ordered his warriors to stay where they were and to shoot some arrows at the enemy and a small skirmish started with arrows flying from both sides but without any close encounter.

*

Most of the day has gone and night has fallen and he decided to make camp and order to retreat for about hundred metres and put several sentinels to keep an eye on the enemy in case they decided to attack.

Most of his warriors make themselves comfortable as much as possible in between the trees.

*

The enemy commander ordered his soldiers to start building up some fires to give him enough light to see anything that could move at the edge of the forest.

*

The Queen was in her chambers attended by several of her female attendants.

"Is it possible for any one of you to get out of the palace?"

Her attendant Amina nodded. "I can, I've done it a couple of times to visit my parents. My tactic is to leave with a jar to get some water from the well in the square to take to my family and so far, the soldiers like to see me and let me pass."

"That's very dangerous Amina but have you heard anything about any rebellion?"

"No, Your Majesty nothing at all but perhaps one of these days I will."

"Don't take unnecessary risks."

"No, Your Majesty I won't."

"When will you go out again?"

"I will like to go in a few moments."

"Very well and do keep me informed about the people."

"Yes, Your Majesty I will."

*

Night was upon them and Eloy gave the signal to move forward though cautiously and soon they were closer to the canal and the city walls, though very well camouflage behind trees and bushes. By then the crescent moon was a bit bigger shining on them making the situation a bit dangerous because they could be seen from the battlements.

They remained in that place while Eloy and Pearl looked at the soldiers pacing behind the battlement.

"Over there," pointed out Pearl, "there is the opening under the wall with the canal running out of the city."

Then they noticed some soldiers behind the battlements lit with many torches.

"With those soldiers on the wall we cannot do it. What we need is a distraction for them to move away."

"I have an idea," said commander Bo, "with five archers I can go towards the right and attack the wall closer to the city gates with a few arrows and hopefully that will attract those soldier's attention."

"Very well," said Eloy, "you do that and as soon as the soldiers move we'll enter the canal."

Commander Bo moved back with the five female archers until he was sure nobody from the walls could see them. There he crossed where the overflow stream was and moved towards the village carefully while Eloy signal for the rest of the warriors to follow him crawling very slowly.

*

From the village, Bo moved towards the city. It wasn't difficult for him to move because they used the trees and bushes in the hedges planted by the farmers to mark their land.

He saw in the distance the line of defence from the enemy soldiers, closer to the forest and move coming closer to the city. As soon as he was close enough, he gave the order to start shooting arrows at the soldiers in the battlements. Many soldiers sounded their horns giving the alarm. The soldiers in the streets close to the main gates immediately run up to the battlements.

The action worked very well and after shooting a few more arrows Bo started running right and left with his warriors systematically shooting arrows while coming close to the gates.

*

Eloy heard the sound of the horns and the soldiers on the wall he was facing, left running taking the torches with them. That was the signal for him to run towards the canal followed by his warriors with Pearl and Lera close behind him and Marum not far behind.

They moved towards the road bridge and passed a couple of wooden portals used by the farmers.

"I'm happy the canal isn't too deep," whispered Eloy, "though it seems to me to be a bit brown in colour."

"That's the usual colour for this water because of the silt and you should know about it because you farmers use this water for irrigation." Then she had a thought. "And I'm happy it isn't the sewers." She managed to move closer to him. "Somehow I've got the feeling that you lied to me and you really can swim."

"Of course, I can. What I don't like is to dive."

*

Moments later, they went under the wooden bridge and soon after under the wall entering the city with only their heads above the water carrying their satchels with food and their weapons on top of their heads.

*

Bo noticed some of the soldiers close to the forest moving towards him and that was the moment for him to decide it was time to leave. "All right! Let's get out of here!" Without a word, they all left running through the farmland towards the coast.

The enemy commander ordered his men to stop and go back to the line of defence. "Let them be, they are a small insignificant group!"

*

The soldier's commander above the main gates looked at the land outside the city for a few moments. "Argh, just a few rebels trying to impress us, stop wasting arrows and go back to your post!"

*

Once inside the city Eloy and Pearl used some stone steps attached to the wall to climb out of the water. They were lucky there were no soldiers in those streets.

They also had the protection of many boxes and baskets piled on the wall at the side of the canal. Some people came out of the houses to look at the commotion and Eloy with his little fighting force mingled with them. Soon those people, living in the houses close to the city walls, realised who they were and immediately help them to take refuge inside their homes. Other city dwellers did the same with the rest of the group.

By the time, the soldiers returned to that part of the battlements, they were all in a safe house.

*

In the meantime, commander Bo had done very well getting away with his female archers and had disappeared from the enemy sight.

They could see the fires of the enemy close to the trees but they managed very well to make the enemy believe they were going to the seaside when in fact they just moved closer to the stream.

*

Immediately the news that something had happened passed through to some scattered people in the streets moving between houses holding torches. It didn't take long for all the city dwellers to know, giving them some hope.

*

Inside a house, a few metres from the wall and a small bridge over the canal, Eloy, Pearl, Lera, Marum and Barum with some of their warriors were sitting close to a hearth.

Now you'll have something to eat," said the man, "but all we have is dehydrated fruit and some bread with plenty of water, tea or coffee."

"No, my friend let us share the food we have," said Eloy and with the others he gave the man and his family some fresh fruit and smoked fish which they happily eat. Soon the kettle was boiling and the pots with tea and coffee were percolating.

"Tell us what we can do," said the man of the house.

"Thank you for your help good man. What we need is to hide the weapons and for us to mingle with the people in the streets."

"That's not a problem but you must know that Prince Neno is in shackles in a dungeon at the bottom of a tower in the wall not far from here and our Queen is a prisoner in the palace. Though she is allowed to keep the palace guards, she cannot leave. Nevertheless, only once she was allowed to see her son."

Eloy and Pearl looked at each other.

"Yes, we already know that," said Pearl.

"Is there a way to send a message to the Queen?" Eloy wanted to know.

"Yes, one of her female attendants comes regularly out of the palace to visit her family who live not far from here. She collects water from the well in the square for her family."

"I would like to meet that woman," said Pearl.

"It can be arranged."

Pearl felt her blood boiling. "Eloy we'll have to do something to help the prince first."

"Yes, you're right but do we have enough warriors to do it?"

The man of the house interrupted them. "Excuse me, sir but if you intend to safe the prince we can help you."

"How?"

"With my family and the help of some friends we can create some trouble in the street near the square to distract the guards which will give you the chance to get inside."

Pearl was enthusiastic. "All right, we go in and rescue the prince but what will happen when we have to leave the tower with him?"

They all remained in silence for a moment and once again, the man of the house had the solution. "After the commotion, I will stay closer to the tower and when you are ready one of you will come out and signal to me. My friends will start the commotion again with the help of other city dwellers though in a different place."

"Isn't it dangerous?"

"Yes, of course it is but it is easy for us to stop anything and quickly disappear in the other streets. Usually when we run the soldiers don't chase."

They look at each other with complicity in their faces with Pearl feeling very enthusiastic.

"Eloy, that is so far the only plan we have and we should try. So far I think we better take things by stages."

"All right, first I want to go and mingle with the people, perhaps by going to the market first?"

"No, sir that cannot be possible because there is no market, the people in the city are starving and, in my home, all we have is flour. There is no food available and by now most of the people will be at home."

Once again, Pearl felt angry. "The more reason for us to do something to liberate the city."

"Yes, Pearl I know, shall we go then? First, we walk around to assess the situation," then he gave some instructions to the rest of the warriors. "Lera and a couple of men will come with us. The rest of you will stay here waiting for our return. Tell me good man which way are we supposed to go to find the tower with the prince?"

"First you go over the bridge close to the wall and then just follow the wall until you reach the second tower after the main gates and that's the one. Remember to walk very slowly, not to attract the soldiers' attention."

"Very well," said Eloy, "follow me."

*

Once outside and after the narrow bridge close to the wall they just walked slowly like everybody else though it was difficult because there were mostly soldiers and only a few city dwellers about with some of them carrying bundles of twigs. With the moon and the light of torches on the battlements was enough for them to see their surroundings.

They followed the wall doing their best not to attract the attention of the soldiers patrolling the streets and after passing the main gates, they soon arrived at the second tower's entrance guarded only by two soldiers with a shield and spear.

Pearl was feeling uncomfortable. "Somehow I feel unprotected not having my bow and arrows."

"Be patient Pearl."

*

They didn't stop and carried on towards the square. In that part of the city there was a pavement between the canal and the houses and soon they cross over another bridge and carried on to the square where the market was supposed to be. Most of the square was full of soldiers sitting around some fires. As the man said there was almost no city dwellers, only a few people just walking slowly in different directions and they did the same trying to go around the soldiers.

Suddenly they heard a commotion and noticed they were all moving aside to give way for something.

The enemy General came along surrounded by soldiers with torches making sure nobody could come close to him and walking towards the avenue leading to the palace.

Eloy with Pearl stood against a house wall together with other people and saw him pass.

A moment later, he was gone and they could walk again.

They had come to the bottom of the avenue at the side of the city square and they could see all the way until the end of it where the palace was. Cautiously they walked towards it and soon they realised it was surrounded by soldiers and there was not a sign of the city guards anywhere to be seen.

Pearl was curious. "Eloy, I wonder how the Queen's attendant can manage to leave the palace."

"Don't you worry soon we'll know."

*

Slowly but steadily they returned to the house using a back street.

"Did you see what you wanted to see?" asked the man of the house.

"Yes, we did," say Pearl, "and it is very sad to see people walking around mostly in silence."

"I was curious to see the palace surrounded by enemy soldiers but not a sign of the palace guards."

"That is because they are all well inside protecting the Queen.

"Very well," said Eloy, "now we plan our next move."

Pearl nodded. "We are ready."

"Good, now listen. I hope that commander Bo will manage to stay safe outside the city for him to protect our retreat. In the meantime, half of the warriors with commander Barum will move to cross the bridge near the square mingling with the people and move close to the tower sitting by the wall and be ready. Commander Marum will do the same with the other half but approaching from a different direction and sitting against the wall as commander Barum. Lera and Pearl will come with me."

Lera was curious. "All that sounds very good but how to disguise our bows and swords."

"We will not take the bows and arrows with us. Only swords."

The man of the house had the solution. "As you had noticed mingling with the people, some of them carry some bundles of twigs on their shoulders and you can use some of those bundles to hide your weapons. The soldiers are used to see people with those bundles and won't bother you. I have some of that wood in my house that you can use to make the bundles."

Their reaction to the man's explanation was a happy one and Immediately, they started making the bundles and, in a moment, the swords could not be noticed.

"Tell me," asked Eloy, "from where do you get the twigs considering you cannot go out of the city?"

"There's always a pile of twigs for everybody to use, close to the south gate."

*

The rest of the warriors came to the house from the other houses and Eloy looked at all of them overcrowding the man's house and gave the signal for Commander Barum to go first with some of the men down to the square and over a bridge to move towards the tower. "Make sure you don't walk in a group."

A moment later Eloy signalled for commander Marum to go leaving the house one by one.

"Now Lera are you ready?"

Lera nodded.

"I'm leaving now," said the man of the house, "I'll wait for you to be outside the tower for me to start the diversion."

Eloy waited for the man to leave. "Very well then, follow us." Lera and Pearl left the house one by one carrying the bundles following Eloy.

*

They went over the bridge and followed the wall.

They mingled very well with some soldiers walking without saying a word and soon they had passed the main gates and one of the towers. Reaching close to the tower where the prince was, they sat very close to its entrance and smiled to the guards while sitting against the wall with all the others doing the same though not together.

First, the soldiers guarding the entrance to the tower look at them but soon they just carried on chatting ignoring Eloy and companions.

Most of the houses were facing the city walls from across the street.

They waited until Eloy saw commanders Barum and Marum coming close to the other side of the tower and sitting against a house wall though not doing it as a group. Eloy dried his forehead with his handkerchief and close to him, one of his warriors with the bundle of wood did the same drying the sweat from his forehead that amused the soldiers guarding the entrance who mimic the drying of his forehead and laughed.

Eloy looked at his little force and as a signal for them to get ready, by nodded his head.

He stood up and so did the others but at that moment two soldiers with a commander came to the tower and they freeze.

That commander replaced the soldiers and left.

Eloy waited until the two soldiers settled down and once again, he nodded to the others. Barum and Marum moved to be by the wall at the side of the tower's entrance.

At that moment, some city dwellers started screaming, calling for the attention of the soldiers in the street near the square and suddenly they charged out of the square giving the impression they were moving towards the city south gates and the soldiers chased them. All that commotion distracted the two soldiers and attracted the attention of other soldiers and city dwellers passing by that went to see what the commotion was all about leaving the street in front of the tower with Eloy and warriors to do their job.

It was the signal for the warriors with commanders Barum and Marum to approach the tower.

Eloy approached the two soldiers and smiled at them. The soldiers smiled back and then Eloy rush them by pushing them inside the gate while Barum and Marum's warriors ran to help him. The soldiers on the wall had only eyes for the trouble.

Everything was completed very swiftly and soon all the warriors were inside the tower.

The two soldiers had been subdued though one tried to resist but Lera jumped on him forcing him to the ground.

Eloy was impressed with Lera's agility. "Wow, you are very agile." She just smiled and shrugged her shoulders.

"If you make any sound," said Eloy pointing his sword at them. "I'll cut your throat."

The two soldiers just nodded.

They were stripped of their uniform and two of the warriors put them on and grabbing the shield and spear, went outside to stand guard.

Eloy grabbed the keys.

The soldiers on the wall heard something and looked over but by then the street was empty. One of the soldiers on the battlements saw the two false guards coming out holding the shield and spear. "Everything all right?"

The warriors just smiled and nodded waiving their hands. Everything was going as planned.

"Barum you stay here with your men," ordered Eloy. "Marum you come with us and bring our prisoners."

With Pearl and Lera at his side and followed by Marum with his warriors pushing the two almost naked prisoners, he went deep down to the dungeons.

They encountered two soldiers guarding the corridor that tried to resist with their swords but had no chance and soon put their swords on the floor.

"Where is the prince?" asked Eloy with the tip of his sword at one of the soldier's throat and the soldier pointed with his finger to a cell close to them.

Using the keys Eloy opens the door.

"Who are you?" said a very surprised prince.

"Never mind my prince we are here to rescue you," said Eloy while taking the shackles of the prince legs and wrists. "Now come with us."

Pearl sniffed the air and looked at the prince pulling an ugly face. "Argh, I think you better stay behind me," she said grinning at him.

"Who are you?"

"I'm Pearl Your Majesty and right now what you need is a good bath."

"I'm sorry Pearl but in this dungeon, there are no facilities and why you call me Majesty? I'm not a King." Pearl just ignored him.

They gagged the four soldiers and tied their hands and legs.

*

They left with the prince still rubbing his wrists and went upstairs reaching the entrance.

Putting their weapons in the twig's bundles, they were ready to go.

"I might be recognised," said the prince and they all thought about it.

"Not for long," said Pearl and instructed two warriors to strip one of the dungeon's soldiers of his uniform.

Moments later, they returned not just with the clothes but the purses and swords as well. Enthusiastically the prince put the uniform on leaving his rich clothes on the floor and putting the belt with the sword on, he joined the others.

Eloy showed himself at the door. The man of the house saw him from a corner and the commotion near the square started again although at the other side of the square.

*

Once again, Lera and Pearl carried the bundles on their shoulders with the prince dressed as a soldier walking close behind them but not too close just following Eloy, Pearl and Lera walking towards the main gates with the warriors dressed as soldiers holding their weapons.

Barum and Marum with their warriors left after them one by one though going in opposite direction.

Eloy with Pearl and Lera looked like city dwellers followed by three soldiers and the commotion done by some city dwellers had stopped.

As soon as they could they started to break the group and once again they carried on separately not to attract any attention and though some guards on the battlements saw them they didn't say anything when they saw the soldiers with them.

Eloy felt very nervous when passing the main gates but the soldiers ignored them.

They went over the bridge close to the walls and immediately inside the house though they did it one by one. Prince Neno with the two false guards passed the house and after, the prince returned and quickly entered the house with the other two doing it individually. The darkness of the night helped them to walk without attracting the soldier's attention. After all, there was only the light of the crescent moon and the torches on the walls.

The soldiers on the battlements ignored their movements.

Moments later the man of the house with his wife entered the house looking exhausted.

*

Inside the house, the people were very happy to have their Prince Neno with them and did the best to make him comfortable for his embarrassment.

The first thing for you to do will be to have a bath," said the woman of the house, "after you'll wear clean clothes."

"Please, you don't have to be so nice to me."

"Yes, we do," said the woman of the house, "because you are our prince and on the other hand, you smell."

Neno felt embarrassed. "I'm sorry but in the dungeons, there are no facilities."

"Come with me," said the man of the house, "we might be very short of food but we have plenty of hot water and soap."

They all look at the prince holding back their laughter.

By then the warriors were provided with clean clothes by the old man and he started to put the uniforms in the cooker's fire.

Sometimes later, Neno came into the front room wearing some clean clothes and the woman of the house gave some clothes for the warriors to were. By then the uniforms had almost all burned inside the cooker.

Pearl approached him, sniffed the air and smiled. "Now you smell clean. Come and sit here," she said pointing to a chair.

The woman of the house came close to him holding a small basin and some cotton buds and a pot with cream. "Now you will sit still and let me treat your sore ankles."

The man of the house gave him a mug with tea. "Sorry but we don't have any milk."

The prince understood. "It's all right, sir, I like it as it is."

He sat close to the table taking his shoes off and the man of the house poured some hot water in the basin though not too hot.

Pearl was happy to help and she pulled his trousers up and saw the wounded ankles. "Oh dear, that must be painful."

"Well, not really."

The woman started to treat his wounds.

Neno was overwhelmed with their help, especially looking at Pearl. "Now it is a bit sore."

"Don't you worry," said the woman, "from now on it will be all right because the cream has some herbs that work as pain killers."

*

Suddenly they heard the sound of several horns.

"That's it," said Pearl, "the rescue of the prince has been discovered and that's why the guards are sounding the alarm."

"They might come here because they will start the search of all the houses," said the woman of the house and rushed to another room; soon returning with a straw hat for the prince. "Here, wear this hat. It will make you look like a peasant."

Immediately the man of the house gave him a lit pipe. "Here, pretend you are smoking."

"But I don't smoke."

"You don't have to. Just pretend by puffing."

The prince did so and took his feet out of the water pushing his trousers down to cover his wounded ankles and the woman of the house took the basin away while Pearl help him to put his shoes on. Soon there was plenty of tobacco smoke close to his head.

Then the man of the house noticed part of a uniform close to the cooker and immediately he put it inside the cooker to burn while the woman of the house put a pot with water on it. Most of them sat on the floor looking as natural as possible. After all, they didn't look different from anybody else in the city.

They heard some commotion outside the house and somebody pushed the door open.

Several soldiers entered. "Stay where you are!" said one of them and everybody stood still with the prince puffing some smoke.

For a moment, they all hold their breath but the soldiers didn't recognised the prince and after looking in all the rooms, left.

They all remained silent for a moment and the old man close the door.

"Strange but in a way, I think they could not recognise the prince because it seems to me they have never seen him," was Pearl's opinion.

Eloy addressed them. "So far so good and now we'll have to leave the city while is still night."

"Yes," said the man of the house, "but before you do so you two come with me and see the Queen's attendant."

*

The man left the house followed by Eloy with Pearl and commanders Marum and Barum right behind though at certain distance.

There were many soldiers going around looking at anybody outside the houses.

They reached another house and the man knocked the door.

A woman opened the door and let them in.

Inside they met a middle age man and a woman. At that moment, a young woman entered the room.

The old man spoke to them. "This is Eloy the rebel's commander and they have just freed the prince from the tower and soon they'll be ready to leave the city with him."

"You have really freed the prince?"

"Yes, we have."

"I am Amina and I am one of the Queen's personal attendants. I will go back to the palace to give the Queen the good news. What are your intentions with the prince? Will you try to rescue the Queen?"

"No," said Eloy, "unfortunately, we don't have enough warriors to rescue her but with the prince we will gather more people to help the resistance."

"The Queen will be very happy to hear the good news; thank you for coming to help us."

"It's all right Amina," said Pearl, "with him many more people will rally to us and we can organise those people to build up a bigger army."

"I'm leaving you now and the Queen will be very happy with all that good news."

Immediately and quietly, Amina left the house.

"From now on you can use our home as a safe house for meetings," said the man of the house.

Thank you for your help," said Eloy.

Eloy and friends left going back to the house closer to the walls.

*

As soon as they arrived, they had a meeting. Many of the warriors had come together although others remained in other houses.

"What we must do is to start somehow, something here in the city," said Pearl.

"I can do that," said commander Marum. "I can stay with some volunteers and start to organise the city dwellers."

Eloy was happy with the developments. "Very well commander you'll stay here and we'll go. When we attack the city, it will be somewhere to confuse them and you with your men and all the people you can put together will attack the guards guarding the main gates and open them. What you could try is to organise something to deal with the south gates. I will find somebody to attack those gates when the day comes."

"As you command," said Marum. "I need some volunteers," he said looking at the warriors and his surprise was total when all of them put their hands up.

"Very well," said Eloy, "from now you will work independently and I wish you good Luck."

Pearl was more solemn. "May the Holy Spirit guide you," and all of them bowed.

Quietly and doing it one by one, Marum left followed by the warriors leaving Eloy in the company of the prince, Pearl, Barum, Lera and the female archers.

"All right as soon as we can we'll go but we'll leave our weapons in your house for other people to use if you don't mind," said Pearl looking at the old man.

"Of course, you can; we'll keep them in the pile of wood for the fire."

"Please," say a giggling Pearl, "make sure you won't burn them."

"No, don't you worry. They will be safe but before you go I will go out and gather some city dwellers away from the canal close to the main gates and when you hear the commotion that will be the signal for you to leave."

Eloy was curious about something. Tell me good man is the water in the stream always so brown with floating debris?"

"Yes, it is because of the silt and sometimes when there's raining with a strong wind it becomes darker with many leaves and branches on it. We collect those floating pieces of wood for our cookers and there are some men that clean the canal from any extra silt keeping it deep enough for the boats."

"Is there any fish in it?"

"Yes, but only a few and they are too small."

*

Prince Neno was sitting on one side of the room and Pearl was looking at him and smiling. "I hope you feel better from your wounds."

"Yes, Pearl, you ladies are very good nurses."

"Now you are free you have nothing to worry about and I will protect you."

The Prince was surprised for a brief moment but then he smiled. "I know that Pearl but the point is that I can fight too and right now I wish I could have my sword and face those soldiers."

"It's all right. When we reach our people in the hills you'll have plenty of time to exercise and practice with a sword."

"Are there many people in the resistance?"

"Ah, yes and no. We don't have enough people to start a war but I hope more will join us. The people will be very happy to know you are free. From now on you are the royal symbol the people need."

"Pearl, I don't think I'm free because we are still inside the city and there's the danger of being captured."

"Okay," interrupted Eloy, "now we are ready to leave the city. Are you ready to get wet Your Majesty?"

Prince Neno has recovered from the excitement. "Yes, ready and willing but please don't call me majesty; I'm not a king and I want to be treated the same like anybody else."

Pearl grabbed him by the arm. "I'll be always close to you my prince," and they look at each other in a strange way without saying a word.

Prince Neno grabbed one of her hands and kissed it leaving Pearl in ecstasy. "Please do call me Neno from now on."

"As you wish, Neno," she said almost mumbling her words.

Once again, Eloy interrupted. "Get ready to leave."

His words broke the spell and immediately Pearl prepared herself to go.

"I'll go out first and you must wait for our commotion before you do anything," said the man of the house, "this time we'll do it close to the main gates."

*

In the meantime, Marum and his warriors were mingling with a few city dwellers in and around the city centre though separated and already talking to some of those people though individually.

*

General Agaram was resting in his room in the palace when a messenger arrived. "Yes, what is it?"

"Some rebels attack the wall by the main gates and somebody has rescued the Prince."

"What? Another attack? Somebody rescued the Prince?" He stood up in a rage. "I'm surrounded by idiots!" He looked at the messenger holding back his rage. "Tell my second-in-command to send some soldiers out of the city to search for those people right now!"

The messenger left running.

*

The man of the house with some city dwellers started throwing stones to the soldiers guarding the main gates and it works because those soldiers blow their horns that attracted the attention of those soldiers on the wall and any other soldier in the adjacent streets. Eloy and friends heard the street commotion and from the house door Eloy saw the guards on the battlements running away towards the main gates holding torches. "All right, the coast is clear."

"Let's go," said Pearl, "come Your Majesty, oops sorry I mean Neno, follow me." Saying that and without making any splashing noise, she walked to the wall and down the steps entering the water with her satchel on the head and the prince did the same behind her.

"All right," said Eloy in a whisper and followed them.

Barum with Lera left immediately after moving as fast as they could, considering the water was up to their necks. The ten fishermen with them followed as well.

The current helped them to move forward and some debris floating on it added to the camouflage.

Once they had passed the wall, they stayed under the road bridge for a brief moment to regain their energy.

They carried on and soon they reached a place with more bushes and small trees at the edge of the canal though away from the city walls. They left the water and started running as fast as they could under some protection of the bushes and small trees. Unfortunately, the crescent moon was high in the sky giving more light than the night before.

A couple of soldiers that had returned to their post on the wall saw them and raised the alarm while shooting their arrows; though the moon was shining on the land it was difficult for them to aim properly but by then Eloy and friends were already out of reach.

Commander Bo and the archers had been waiting for them.

"Where are your weapons? Where is Marum and the warriors?"

"We left them in the city," said Pearl, "commander Marum will organise the city resistance."

*

Amina had reached the palace and soon she was in the Queen's chambers, exhausted.

The Queen was sitting in her boudoir in front of a very beautiful ornamented mirror. It was a very beautiful and spacious room with yellow curtains in the windows facing east to catch the early sunshine. Many candelabras lit the room very well. "Did you find out anything?"

Amina recovered from her exhaustion. "The Prince has been freed."

The Queen stood up overexcited. "Please Amina tell me more."

One of the other attendants gave Amina a glass of water.

"A man called Eloy led a group of warriors and rescued him. It was very scary because the alarm was sound and they search all the houses. Though they entered the house where he was they didn't recognise him and now they are all away from the city but I don't know where they are taking him."

The Queen sat feeling very emotional. "It doesn't matter where they are taking him. At least my son is free. Did you learn anything else?"

"That man Eloy said they didn't have enough warriors to try and rescue you but with the prince they will rally more people."

There was a moment of silence and the Queen spoke. "Now we know there is some resistance and I hope the city dwellers will know about it.

"They will Your Majesty because they left commander Marum with his warriors to organise the resistance in the city."

"Good but we must not leave everything to others and we must find a way to do something here in the palace."

*

Soon Eloy and his little group had arrived at the cove looking for the footpath to go down to the beach.

Pearl looked back and felt scared. "We are being followed!" she cried and they all look back seen in the distance a group of enemy soldiers with torches running through the farm land.

"Hurry up," cried Eloy going down the narrow footpath and without saying a word they all followed him.

They reached the sandy beach and run to the boats.

Immediately the fishermen started pushing them in the water and they had no choice but to get their feet wet and by using the rope ladders, they climb aboard one boat.

The female archers did it by using two boats.

Where are the others!" asked Pearl's father.

"Commander Marum stayed in the city with the warriors!" answered Eloy.

"Come on!" cried Pearl's father, "we are leaving!" he cried and the other boats got ready to go.

"Use the oars and help us with the rowing!"

The prince and Eloy obeyed though in a clumsy way but it worked and soon they were moving steadily to the cove exit illuminated by the crescent moon while being followed by the other boats.

Prince Neno was very good with the oar and somehow Pearl was looking and admiring him. "You are very good rowing."

"I had some practice."

Pearl's father nodded. "He had some practice because he had visited our village and practice with fishing as well."

"How come I have never seen you?"

"Because he's done it early in the morning with other fishing boats when you are usually practicing with your bow."

Pearl was curious. "People get up early in the palace? Don't you have cosy beds to stay in until later?"

The Prince was surprised by her question. "What do you think we are lazy people?"

A few arrows falling close to the boats interrupted them.

"Arrows," cried Pearl.

It was all right because soon they were at a safe distance.

They could see some torches above the cliff but in a few moments they were in the open sea and still rowing like mad.

Because of the lack of clouds, the moon was shining beautifully showing them a calm sea.

The fishermen in all the boats put up the masts and sails and started their journey to the west. Though they knew very well how to use the stars to navigate, this time it was not necessary because thanks to the moon they could see the coast not far from them. All they needed was to keep well away from the rocks that in the night they all look black.

"Now you can relax," said Pearl's father holding the rudder and to his amusement, Eloy and the prince collapsed in the bottom of his boat.

Pearl came to sit close to the prince. "You'll like it in the hills."

"I know I will because I'll be close to free people." Then he looked at her. "Tell me about you."

"Oh, there's not much to tell. I live in a village by the seaside and help my father with the fishing and above all the collection of valuable pearls."

"Strange I have never seen you though I've been in your village and done some fishing from the rocks but tell me; is it true that sometimes you get black pearls?"

"Yes, we do and they are very rare, that's why they are so valuable."

"I don't understand why you live in the village when with the pearls you get you could live in the city and in luxury."

Pearl thought about it for a brief moment. "Well, that's not the point. By living in the village, we have a very healthy way of life. The fishing is good and from the farms nearby, we can get all the vegetables we need. My friend's father with other farmers, produce enough vegetables for us in the village and sell the rest in the market inside the city. Pity that now they cannot work the land."

"According to what you just said I realised that you and your family are very wealthy and, in a way, I envy your way."

"Why? You been a prince must have everything you want."

"No, Pearl people think that because I live in a palace with my mother and surrounded by servants I can have everything I want but in reality, that's not so. Plenty of protocol controls us and the Prime Minister organises everything we are supposed to do every day. I don't have the freedom you and the rest of the people have in the kingdom," and he said the last words with sadness.

Somehow, Pearl felt something and moved to sit closer to him. "As long as you stay with us you won't be alone and you will have the same freedom we have." Then she grabbed some smoked fish. "I hope you like fish because that's what we have more than anything else."

"Yes, Pearl I like fish."

She gave him some of it and they eat together. Somehow, being far away from the tragedy that has fallen on their country for Pearl those were happy moments.

Chapter Six

The day was still in semi-darkness and Eloy noticed they were not sailing in a straight line. "What's wrong? Are you changing directions?"

"We are not changing direction," said Pearl's father, "but we have no choice. Now we are going west and though we have the help of the current, the wind is blowing against us and so we have to use a different way and move in a zigzag for the sails to catch the wind from a different angle."

*

With no ceremony or respect of any kind, General Agaram pushed the Queen's chambers doors open approaching her boudoir in a rage, scaring the attendants that run to one side of the room.

"You think that because your son was taken away from the city you are free to do whatever you want?"

The Queen stood up adamant. "You know perfectly well there's nothing I can do without your permission."

For a moment, the General looked at her and then calmed down. "Very well but from now on some of my personal guards will stay outside your door so you won't try anything." Then he looked at her cheekily, "all these can stop right now if you accept me as your husband."

He waited for a brief moment but there was no reaction from the Queen.

His expression changed. "You two will stay outside these doors," he said pointing to two of his soldiers and left the Queen's chambers.

Her attendants came close to her.

"What are we going to do?" asked one of the young women.

"Calm down Nadia," said the Queen, "from now on we must use all our skills as women and find a way to pass those guards but it must be done in a very sophisticated way. Come on girls you think as well and we might find a solution. Now let's try to get some sleep for what's left of the night."

*

The boats were sailing going west with the sails catching the wind very well and the sea was calm. It was the time of the year without any storms.

Night was over and some hours later with the sun shining beautifully, they had reached the rocky islands and Pearl's father change direction. Eloy with Pearl were curious.

"Why are you changing direction?" he asked.

"Very simple; we'll go to the cavern first to get some food like smoked fish and muscles for you to take to the people in the hills."

"Good idea," said Eloy and sat close to them.

"Neno you'll soon meet some of the people," said Pearl.

Once again and to her surprise, the Prince grabbed one of her hands and kiss it.

"Why did you do that? My hands smell of fish."

Immediately the Prince released her hand. "Oh, I'm sorry it was just an impulse but my hands smell the same."

Pearl just look at him without saying a word though surprised.

*

It didn't take long for the boats to reach the cavern and they could see the light of some fires from inside that could only be seen from the sea.

Putting their sails down, they carried on rowing.

*

The fishermen and their families welcomed them with jubilation that turned into euphoria when they saw Prince Neno, with some of them starting to play tambourines and flutes giving a festive atmosphere.

They noticed several small stone constructions puffing smoke and Eloy realised those were places to smoke fish.

This time there were more people in the cavern and Eloy had to give instructions.

Standing on the bow of a boat, he called for attention and the music and singing stopped. "All the newcomers must choose a leader."

One of them came closer to Eloy. "I am Loni and I have led them here."

"Very well Loni now you must lead them to the hills where we are organising an army. All you need is to walk once again into the forest where you'll turn west and soon you'll reach the prairie. It's a beautiful day and you will not have any problems to see your way. It will be easier for you to see the hills."

"But how can I find the place?"

"Very simple my friend, by the time you reach the prairie you will be seen by the lookouts and they will send somebody to guide you."

"Aren't they afraid of been spotted by the invaders?"

"Not at all; it is an old fortress and the place is well defended.

"Very well."

"Before you go, will you ask some of the people to volunteer to come with us and help us to carry the food towards the village fortress? Ten will be enough."

"Of course."

Eloy and his warriors had something to eat while the fishermen families loaded their boats with seafood in baskets made of cane.

*

After having some rest, they were soon on board with volunteers who pushed the boats out of the sandy beach. The fishermen turned the boats to face the exit and started rowing.

"Thank you for all your help!" cried Prince Neno and with Pearl just waived their hands.

*

In no time, they were outside rowing happily while putting the masts and sails up. This time their navigation was easier because they had left the rocky islands behind and it was easier for the boats to use the wind; after all there was more open sea to manoeuvre. With the help of the current, their advance was fast.

"The people will be happy with all the smoked fish and muscles," said Pearl."

"And a few crabs as well," added Eloy with a crab in his hands that was moving his pincers. "Oh no, you won't get my fingers," and put it down inside the basket with other crabs.

"Here," said Pearl and gave the prince another smoked fish, "I know you like it."

"Of course, I like smoked fish. We get it in the palace and for me there is never enough. The only problem is the oil coming out of them," he added while licking some of it of his hands. "After eating smoked fish, the situation is that there is no woman in the world willing to give me a kiss."

Pearl's father started to laugh. "Only a fisherman's woman can do that."

Prince Neno immediately looked at Pearl who for a brief moment didn't know what to say and just giggled nervously showing some blush.

*

A few hours later they have reached the place with the sheltered cove. "There it is, we have arrived!" cried Eloy, "later on the boats can go out to do some more fishing."

Pearl's father agreed with him. "Yes, Eloy so they will."

*

A moment later, they hit the shingle and pulling the boats half way out of the water, downloaded the cargo of baskets with food.

"Now the problem will be on how to take all these baskets up to the hills," was Pearl's opinion but her father had the solution.

"You can use the extra oars we have and so two men can carry a basket between them and later on anybody coming to the seaside can bring them back."

"All right, you heard the man," said Eloy.

Moments later, they started their walk towards the hills. By then the sun started to warm the land.

Pearl's father decided to come with them.

"Somebody is taking your boat?"

"Yes, Eloy I thought better to go back to the hills and somehow help the resistance, after all, my wife is there and there are many things I can do better than to go back with the fleet."

"Good idea father that will make my mother happy but you call five boats a fleet."

"Yes, I know but together with the rest of the boats in the cavern we are a fleet and thinking of it, the fleet was in action for the first time."

Eloy thought about it and looked back at the boats leaving the cove. "Yes, you are very right."

*

It didn't take long for them to reach the top of the dune's barrier.

From where they were, Eloy and companions could see the boats moving to open sea and soon they saw the sails fully blown by the wind and they resumed their walk.

By then the sun was climbing beautifully already warming the air.

"I think that at the end of this new day, we'll be sleeping more hours," was Pearl's opinion.

"Yes, Pearl I'm sure we will," said a happy Eloy.

*

Prince Neno was working the same like the others and Pearl felt proud of him. "You are a prince and you shouldn't do heavy work."

The Prince was surprised. "Why not? I have always done heavy work in the palace and in other places as well. I practice with the sword every day and do some exercises with weights."

*

Not long after, they were all in a long column going up to the village fortress leaving the dunes behind following the path flanked by trees and bushes at either side.

They didn't have to walk far when some people joined them helping with the baskets transport.

Pearl was very surprised. "How did you know we were coming?"

"We didn't but we thought that you might need some help on your return so we came down the hills to wait for you."

*

Back in the palace, the Queen gathered her attendants. "We have two soldiers outside my chambers. I've being thinking but so far I don't have a solution for the problem yet."

They thought about it for a moment and one of the attendants had an idea. "Two of us can try to befriend the soldiers and maybe we can distract them from their post so Amina can leave and go out of the palace."

The Queen thought about it for a very brief moment. "Yes, that's a very good idea Nadia but you mustn't take too much risk. They must not feel suspicious."

"All right," said Amina, "you'll have to choose who will do it."

"I can do it," said Nadia and call another young woman and both stepped forward and cautiously they opened the door and smiled at the two guards who didn't react at the beginning. Then when the two women approached them coquettishly, they started smiling.

"Would you like to have something to eat from the Queen's kitchen?" asked Nadia but the guards didn't move.

"Don't you worry we'll bring something for you," said the other attendant and they returned to the Queen's Chambers closing the door.

What happened:" asked the Queen.

"It will take some time," said Nadia, "right now we'll try to give them something to eat. It seems to me they are hungry."

"Very well," said the Queen, "go to the kitchen and get them something."

Once again, the two young women left the Chambers. "We'll go now to get you something from the royal kitchen," said Nadia and the soldiers nodded. "Unless you don't mind to come with us."

The two soldiers looked at each other and shook their heads.

"All right," said Nadia, "you don't have too."

*

Eloy and his entourage had spent a good part of the morning on the sea and walking to the hills and now they were enjoying the sunshine and the warm air and soon they came close to the village fortress Pearl noticed something. "Look Eloy there are more animals in the corral."

Eloy noticed. "That means more people have arrived."

*

They entered the village fortress and the people were very happy with the extra food but above all, they were happy to see Prince Neno.

Some people started a spontaneous dancing with many trying to touch him, making him feel overwhelmed with happiness.

Pearl's mother was happy to see her husband. "I'm happy to see you have not been harmed."

"You know me; I'm a very good sailor."

Eloy's mother came to greed them and immediately with Pearl's mother they directed the warriors to where they could have something to eat and above all to get some sleep. By then the carpenters had made a very long communal table close to the cooking place.

The two mothers looked very happy chatting to everybody and Pearl noticed. "When helping people and dealing with cooking, our mothers are in their element."

Eloy smiled and nodded.

*

Commander Barum approached Eloy. "The people inform me that since we left many people from other villages have come to join the rebellion.

"Good," said Pearl, "more people we can turn into warriors and a few more are coming from the cavern. They should be here soon and their leader's name is Loni."

Eloy was happy though deep in thought. "I think that by now most of the villages must be empty." Then he talked to the prince. "Come with me my prince, from now on you will be with us wherever we go."

"As you wish but you must remember to call me just Neno."

"All right Neno but you must give me some time to get used to it."

*

Somebody gave Pearl a bow and a quiver with arrows and she checked how powerful the bow was. "All right this bow is more powerful than the one I left in the city. It looks to me like a powerful thirty pounders."

She put the bow on her shoulders and the quiver as well, then she went to a bucket with water and filling a small cup with it, she approached the prince. "Have some cold water."

"Thank you, eating fish makes me thirsty."

"Yes, I know it is like if the fish is asking for water."

The prince drank some and smiled at Pearl. "I should have met you before."

Pearl reacted with a little arrogance. "Yes, you should have but I'm here now," and touched her bow across her shoulders, "and this bow will protect you."

The prince drank more water. "Thank you. You are a good friend."

Pearl smile disappeared. "Friend?"

Prince Neno just continues. "Talking about protection I would like to have my own sword and protect you instead."

"Come with me you two," said Eloy interrupting them.

*

They started to walk around and Eloy saw that the wall around the plateau has been repaired and was getting higher turning the place into the fortress it was a long time ago and he noticed two workshops not far from the palace.

One was for carpentry where he saw the carpenter teaching some apprentices how to make bows and arrows while some young men were splitting some wood making tiles and the other was the blacksmith forge where several apprentices were making spears and arrow tips.

Eloy congratulated the carpenters for their work and then he went to talk to the blacksmith who was instructing his apprentices on how to use the forge and Eloy was curious. "From where did you get the metal to do your job?"

The blacksmith gave him some samples of arrow tips, which looked very well made. "We are using some of the people's cutlery and from now on they can only use their knives to eat with. All the spoons and forks were given to us but the carpenters are making wooden spoons."

Eloy was curious. "I think the only problem is to cut trees for your fire."

"No, we don't though the carpenters used a few cut trees we only use dead wood for our fire with some people going to the forest every day to collect and though it is a longer way for them, instead of going to the city, the charcoal makers are coming to us with their cargo."

"I'm happy to hear the good news my friend. Do carry on."

He approached commander Barum close to him. "Soon we'll have more armed warriors but tell me, have the warriors in the forest had any encounter with the enemy?"

"So far only your father with some warriors had gone to protect the people who might be in the forest and the others collecting the wood and the manure and I expect they are doing a good job hopefully they'll be back soon. Come you can see what's going on in the prairie."

They went on the ledge and from there they could see two thin columns of people, one going to the forest and the other coming from it.

Mingling with those people there was a wagon coming towards them. "Now that could be the charcoal makers wagon," was Barum's opinion.

The ledge was being made safe by a couple of men who were building a small wall on it in a semicircle.

"Look," said commander Barum pointing in certain direction and Eloy could see some people walking on the north side of the prairie from the direction of the cavern.

"Those are the people led by Loni and they will be here soon."

*

They went to one side of the village and had a meeting with the other commanders.

"We have many bows and arrows ready and the next step will be to have the warriors we have in here well-armed and after do the same with all the new comers. Now I think you better send somebody to bring my father and his fighting men back to safety" were Eloy's instructions.

Immediately the commanders Barum and Bo send one warrior each down to the forest.

"Make sure the people collecting the wood come with them. All the people going to the forest must be stopped!"

His mother came to him. "Eloy now you can get ready to have a good clean up and change your clothes."

Pearl was surprised as he was. "I wish to have the same. I'm beginning to smell."

Eloy's mother gave them a wide grin. "And so you will. Come with me."

Full of curiosity they followed her and they reached a place outside the wall on the west side of the village fortress. There they were surprised to see that the stonemasons with bricklayers had built not just the latrines down the hill but close to the west wall, there had repaired three big rooms already with a roof and plenty of water vapours coming out of the roof of two of them.

"What's all this?" asked Pearl.

Mother explained. "With so many people the problem with hygiene is big and so the boys repaired one room for the washing of clothes with boiling water and that's the one with no wooden floor and the other two are steam baths one for men and the other for women."

Eloy looked at Pearl. "What are we waiting for," they said in unison.

Neno approached them full of curiosity. "Eh, what's going on?"

"We are having a steam bath," said a happy Eloy.

"I'll love that. Though we have a very good bathroom in the palace we don't have any steam bath."

*

In the meantime, Eloy's father had commanded the people very well with only a few wounded.

They had managed to defeat several attempts from the enemy that send small groups into the forest.

Eloy's father had the advantage of having many trees to give them the protection needed and the results were always the same with the enemy retreating in disorder and losing some of their weapons.

One messenger arrived and reported to him.

Moments later, he gave the orders to retreat but to do it in silence, not giving the enemy the chance to know about it.

Retreating through the forest gave Eloy's father the chance to do some training though he was not a warrior but by instinct, he managed to form the people into two columns and though they didn't know how to march, they did it with some degree of discipline.

The rest of the people were already going up to the hills guided by the messengers send by the commanders with many of them carrying wood and many women were carrying sacks with dry animal dung.

*

Eloy, Pearl, Prince Neno and the three commanders stood on the ledge at the side of the plateau from where they could see the prairie and the columns coming close to the hills.

*

The column from the cavern led by Loni arrived and after a couple of hours, first the people carrying the wood and animal droppings arrived looking very exhausted.

The people who brought more tree trunks and dead wood arrived after.

*

Eloy's father's group of warriors came out of the forest walking behind the columns.

"Would you know it" said Pearl, "your father has managed to form them into a double line but I don't understand how because your father is a farmer and not a warrior."

Eloy was happy. "I know Pearl but sometimes necessity teaches people something and, in this case, it is discipline."

"I like that," said Barum, "and so all we have to do is to teach them how to use their weapons."

"Yes," said Pearl, "and so far, what we'll have more than anything else is bows and arrows."

Commander Barum agreed with her. "Not to worry because by the time we are ready, we'll have an army and some people had gone down to the streams to get some gold. With some of that gold we have bought all the weapons the merchants had."

*

A couple of hours later Eloy's father arrived with his made-up army group and was very surprised to see so many new comers. "From where have all these people come from?"

"Some of them come from the cavern though the others come from small villages and hamlets deep inside the forest," was Pearl's explanation.

Eloy continued. "From now on we must concentrate with the army organisation. In the meantime, the carpenters have managed to make many bows and arrows with the blacksmith making many arrows and spear tips."

Eloy's father was very happy and feeling very enthusiastic. "That is very good news and with my new army we have managed to defeat some enemies though small groups. Those enemies lost some of their weapons and now more people have a sword and a shield."

"Very good father but tell me how many warriors did you lose?"

"None, though a few have some scratches."

"Good and now you have become a new commander with plenty of experience. Because of it you must use your name to be recognised by the people turned warriors."

By then Loni had come closer to them.

Eloy's father felt confused for a moment. "So far my name has only been known by my family and a few friends."

Eloy called for everybody's attention. "Listen to me! From now on, my father is officially a commander and everybody must know his name.

"Go on," said commander Barum, "tell us his name."

"All right, I'm getting to it. His name is Choquero!"

Eloy's mother was close to them. "Funny but I have always called him Choqui."

Commander Choquero frowned at her. "Mavina don't tell everybody. I don't want the warriors to call me Choqui. They will stop respecting me."

"Oh, I beg your pardon commander Choquero," and putting her hands on her mouth held back her laughter. "Tell me now will I have a title been his wife?

"No, mother because you are not in charge of warriors and so far, you are already in charge of many women and you are doing all right."

At that moment, a woman approached her. "Sorry to interrupt but we need your advice with the cooking."

"There, you see what I mean?"

Eloy's mother sighed. "Oh, very well come with me woman. Why didn't you ask Sanila?"

"Because she's already very busy teaching some women about how to deal with the wounded."

Eloy and Pearl carried on with the meeting with him in charge.

"The first step will be to organise the army accordingly. We cannot count on commander Marum because as you know he is inside the city organising the revolt and so the structure will be as follow; Pearl and I are the commanders in charge, commanders Barum and Bo will command the male warriors and Lera will be the female archers' commander."

"Who will be in the front," asked commander Bo.

In the front of any military advance on the enemy it will be commander Choquero, Barum and Bo and with a small group of male and female warriors as bodyguards, me, Pearl and commander Lera with her archers will be right behind moving in different directions."

"Don't forget about me," said the prince.

"Not a chance," said a smiling Pearl.

"In the meantime, you father will carry on organising your own group of warriors using mainly the older people and who knows maybe you'll finish with more warriors than anybody else and be in the front line. Right now, you will have Loni who's leading the newcomers as your second in command."

Hearing his words Loni nodded enthusiastically.

"Son, I already have many warriors in my command and they have proven very efficient fighting in the forest and they are all of different ages."

"Very good for you father," he said realisation dawning.

Commander Barum was curious. "It looks all right but so far we don't have a great number of warriors. I have about fifty with Bo having the same amount and I can guess that very soon Lera too will have fifty.

Commander Choquero nodded. "He's right though I think I have more than all of them together."

Eloy put his right hand up and they listen. "You are right about the number of warriors we have but you must know that the number of warriors is immaterial. What we must use is tactics using our warriors in the best possible way so when we attack, the enemy will think we are more than them."

Pearl was curious. "Eloy, how can we manage that?"

"One of the tricks will be by staying behind the trees and the other is to make as much noise as possible. From the distance, it will sound as if we have many warriors inside the forest and because of so many trees the enemy will never know how many we are. So far our new army has all the groups needed and from now on what we need is more people to increase their numbers."

Pearl was happy with Eloy's opinion. "All right we have organisation but what do we do now?"

"Very simple from now on it will be for the commanders to have their warriors exercising every morning and to train them in the use of the weapons we have. Though today it is a different situation because most of them are sleeping."

"Eloy the only problem we have is the lack of space to do the training," said Barum.

"Not really because you can take your warriors to the lower grounds between here and the sea and you, commander Bo, can do the same."

"What about me?" asked Lera.

"You, commander Lera, will put some targets made of dry grass or straw at the edge of this plateau on the north side and start the training. It could be practical if you could make the targets to look like a standing person."

"Why?"

"Because by shooting human models, it will put in their minds the idea on how to shoot at people."

*

The meeting has finished and the commanders left.

"I want to go and have a meeting with the fishermen in the cavern; are you coming with me Pearl?"

"Of course, I am. We are supposed to be together."

"All right then let's take some food and go."

"And I'm going with you," said the prince very determined.

Pearl was surprised and then showed a bright expression. "Of course, you are."

Pearl's father approached them but he was the only one without a sword though he had the dagger. "You'll need me to talk to the fishermen."

"Very well father."

Commander Barum approached the prince with a sword. "Here is your sword. It's not specially made for a prince but I'm sure you know how to use it."

The Prince was overwhelmed and grabbed it. "It's not the sword that does the fighting but the person behind to use it properly," were his words.

Barum hit his chest with his right fist and bowed. "Well said my prince."

A moment later Eloy, Pearl and the prince with commander Barum and Pearl's father left going down the hill and to the north east of the prairie.

*

As soon as they entered the prairie, they came across some people coming from the south east carrying most of their belongings in sacks on their backs and with a small heard of goats.

"Where are you going friends?" asked commander Barum.

"We are looking for the resistance people," said an old man.

"We have managed to leave our village just before some enemies came to us," added a woman.

"You are going in the right direction," said Pearl, "just carry on towards those hills and soon you'll find the road."

"Thank you, friend," said the old man and signal for the group to follow him.

*

On that part on the north the prairie, coming closer to the hills, the terrain was becoming rougher with plenty of small trees and bushes in between some tall rocks.

Eloy signalled for them to stop and sat on the ground. "Come on have some rest and something to eat."

"I can guess these hills prevent the sand dunes to advance on the prairie," was the prince opinion.

Eloy agreed. "Yes, that's precisely what they do but at the same time by coming closer to the rocky hills we are better protected from any enemy that might come out of the forest."

Pearl was looking at the hills. "I've never thought there could be so many rocks at this end of the prairie," then she had a thought. "As a matter of fact, this is the first time I've been here," she said holding back her laughter.

Eloy looked in the same direction. "Same here but we don't have the time to explore."

"Hold on," said Pearl father, "look over there; it looks like the entrance to a path where that stream is running out."

"Yes," said Pearl, "now that is something I would like to explore."

Eloy look at them thinking and then he just shrugged his shoulders. "All right let's do it."

*

They noticed though the hills were steep at either side with plenty of vegetation in between, they were not too high and there was apparently a path in between though all covered with grass.

They carried on following that path at the side of a small stream.

The path widened and the source of the stream disappeared.

Though they could not see any surface water, they were surrounded by grass.

"Be careful," said Eloy, "I've got a strange feeling."

*

They carried on for a few moments until suddenly his feet started sinking and quickly, he tried to walk back but unfortunately his feet became stuck in mud covered with grass. "It's a bog!" he cried, "pull me out!"

Pearl's father came closer to him crawling on the grass with Barum pulling his legs and stretched his arm until he could grab Eloy's hand and gently started to pull, Neno, Pearl and Bo staying away for a while. When they saw that Eloy was closer to safety they moved closer and though their feet started to sink they grabbed him and by leaning on their sides started to crawl out of the trouble.

"Wow," said Pearl, "that was dangerous."

"Yeah," said her father trying to clean the mud from his clothes.

"Look at my clothes," said Pearl.

"This is not a nice mud because it has a strange smell," was Barum's opinion pulling an ugly face.

Eloy recovered from the ordeal. "From now on we must be careful because what we have is a kind of dangerous bog all covered by grass and if you observe you'll see that the grass growing on that mud is taller and of a deeper green than other grass."

Pearl look ahead. "If we stay close to the hill where the grass is shorter and drier it should be all right," she said walking ahead.

They all followed her in silence.

While walking Neno was trying to clean his clothes and Pearl was doing the same.

"How to get rid of the mud on our clothes?" she asked.

Eloy was more practical with the situation. "Don't do anything and let the mud to dry. Later on, it will turn to dust and start falling. It will be the same with the mud you have in your sandals."

"And feet," said Pearl's father looking at his feet.

"He's right," said Barum, "I've had some experience with mud close to our village."

They left the bog behind and reached a place with shorter grass on dry ground.

"Pearl's father was not a happy man. "We've been walking for some time with no signs of anything interesting apart of the dangerous bog."

He sat on a small rock flanked by smaller rocks at either side taking his sandals off and massaging his feet. Then he looked at his sandals. "You are right the mud is drying," he said hitting them against a rock, "though the smell is still on."

"Now that is a very good idea," said Eloy and sat on the ground facing them. "Don't try to clean all the mud of your sandals now, wait until the mud has completely dried out."

"I would like to have something to eat," said Pearl, "but there is no water to wash my hands."

"Don't you worry now," said Eloy, "there's an old saying that a clean pig doesn't get fat."

Pearl look at him shocked. "Are you calling me a pig?"

The others started laughing. Eloy opened his eyes wide and was quick to answer. "Oh no, I wouldn't dare; it's only an old saying."

They all had something to eat though not eating what their fingers were touching.

Suddenly Eloy stood up and started pacing and looking at the ground.

His expression brightened and Pearl noticed. "What? Do you see anything?"

"Yes, there is a kind of a trail going deeper in between the hills," he said and started to follow it.

Simply out of curiosity, they all followed him.

To their surprise, they reached a place with some steps chiselled out of the rocks going up to a small stony construction close to the top of the hill.

They did it carefully because there was no hand railing and it could have been very dangerous if they had fallen.

They were very surprised to see it was a small and strange stony construction built following the shape of the rocks and Eloy approached it and entered.

Once again, they followed him.

Inside they saw a spacious room with the dilapidated wooden frame of a bed and some scrolls in a couple of wooden shelves.

At the side of the bed there was a much-damaged table but above all, they could see something written on a piece of wood against the bottom of one of the walls.

"It seems to me," said Pearl, "this piece of wood was hanging on the wall a long time ago."

Eloy grabbed it and tried to read it. The writing was very simple.

"This place was one of the hiding places of the warrior King Bonamor and now you have reached this sacred place you must go south-west."

"I've got a strange feeling that this was written by somebody who visit this place after the country was liberated," was Pearl's opinion.

They looked bewildered but Pearl expression brightened.

"Eloy, now this confirms part of the story you told us."

"That's it?" asked Prince Neno.

"We found one of his hiding places but with no sign of the sword," said Barum.

Eloy approached the shelves and started reading one of the scrolls by unrolling it very carefully.

He carried on reading for a short moment and then he looked at them.

"This is very interesting."

"Interesting what?" asked Pearl.

He opened another scroll and after reading part of it, he looked at them.

"This too is very interesting."

The whole group asked in unison. "What?"

"I'm beginning to understand that Bonamor used this refuge to come here to write the story of the kingdom because all I can read is about how this country started and the people who build it."

They all started to murmur and Neno had an idea.

"If that is the case then we must come back at a later time and take all these scrolls, and put them in a safe place in the city library." Then he had a though. "If the library has not been burnt."

"Yes, Neno that's precisely what we will do and I hope for the library to be safe," was Eloy's opinion. "The animal hide is very dry and fragile. Some scribers will have to copy them on some new material."

Somehow, Pearl was confused. "All right, now we've got that clear our instructions are to go south-west but why?"

Eloy thought about it. "First we carry on with the original idea to go to the cavern and later on or another day we'll go down to Bonamor's tomb and find out."

It was a sensible idea and they all agreed with him. "All right shall we go?" asked commander Barum.

They all looked at Eloy but he turned away from them and outside the room, he started to climb more steps taking him further up.

It took him a few minutes to reach a place from where he could see the dunes and the sea on one side and well into the distance above the prairie.

A moment later he came down to join them. "That place up there is a perfect lookout. I could see miles away and now we better carry on to the cavern."

"I only hope we won't be stopped by enemies," was the prince's opinion.

"No, my prince," said Pearl coming close to him and grabbing his left arm. "No, Neno I don't think they will dare to come so far out of the forest and if they do we'll give them a good fight, eh?"

Eloy interrupted them. "Come on less talking and more walking, we'll use the narrow path on this part of the forest that will take us to the cavern entrance."

"That will take us to the cavern right on time for lunch," said Pearl.

174

"I wish I had some sleep," said Eloy, "I feel a bit tired."

"Not to worry Eloy in the cavern you can lay down on the sandy beach and have a little snooze."

*

By the time they reached the cavern, they noticed the entrance guarded by several men with spears and shields.

The cavern was well lit by the sun shining down through the gap at the top looking like light rays reflecting from the water in the lagoon and plenty of daylight coming from the sea through the main entrance.

Pearl went straight to the water washing her feet and hands with the rest of the group doing the same.

*

Soon the fishermen gathered close to Eloy, Barum, the prince and Pearl's father and Eloy explained the situation. "The main subject is to know how many more boats can be brought together in this cavern and how to do it. I can see that you have room for more boats and what we will need is a small fleet to carry many warriors," was Eloy explanation.

"I don't think the cavern will be big enough for more boats," was Pearl's opinion.

"That won't be a problem," said Pearl's father, "I can go to the fishing village in the east and hopefully a small fleet will gather in this cavern and we can use the cove with the shingle beach further west to keep more boats and don't you worry Eloy. We'll managed and probably find another place along the coast."

Eloy agreed with him. "Very well we'll leave you to it and as soon as that fleet is put together you will send a messenger to let us know."

"It will be done son but now you must have something to eat."

"Father I thought you'll never mention food," said a gleeful Pearl.

Some women approached offering them some fried fish on banana leaves.

"It is all right to use your mouth to talk but this is the time to use it to eat with," said Pearl.

Then a young woman offered some roasted muscles to the prince. "I thought that maybe you would like to eat some muscles instead of fish."

"Oh yes, please, thank you," said a happy prince.

Pearl father prepared his boat with some food and a couple of fishermen to help him.

"You are a good sailor but you must be careful Harmon," said one of the women.

Eloy was curious. "That's your father's name? I've known your father since I can remember but never heard anybody calling him by that name."

Pearl was giggling. "I know. Some people had called him many different names and one has been more common; they call him Pearly."

"Yes," said Eloy," that's the name I know," and Harmon who was listening just shrugged his shoulders.

Moments later, Harmon left the cavern in his boat into the open sea with the people looking at his departure in silence.

*

A man came to them with alarming news. "The enemy is in the forest."

Many people gathered around him. "I was doing my usual patrol at the edge of the forest when I heard them first and by hiding in thick bushes I saw a group of about ten soldiers holding bows ready with an arrow moving between the trees very cautiously and as soon as they passed I came to tell you."

Eloy agreed. "You've done well and I think you'd better go back with other men and keep an eye on anything that moves in there but above all be prepared to fight them if they come too close to the cavern entrance."

Immediately the warrior left running in the company of ten fishermen with spears.

"Eloy do you have any idea what to do with those soldiers in the forest?" asked Pearl.

"I think the warriors guarding the cavern will do the job and we better go back to the hills." Then he smelled his fish. "If you don't mind I would like to finish this delicious fish first," he said gleefully.

"And have some sleep," said Pearl while bringing him a blanket. "Go to those rocks over there where commander Barum is already sleeping and cover yourself with this blanket. I'll wake you up when we are ready to go."

"But what about you?"

"Don't you worry about me I'll have some sleep later on."

*

Time was passing slowly and Eloy with the prince were deep asleep while Pearl, after making sure she had her satchel with plenty of food, did the same by lying close to them.

*

They managed to sleep for about two hours and Pearl woke up waking Eloy. "Come on we can do some more sleeping later on."

She shook the prince to wake him up. "Come on Neno it's time to go."

Commander Barum didn't need any help to wake up and in seconds, he was ready. "Come on we can do more sleeping in the village fortress."

*

Moments later, they were leaving and soon they were following the narrow path meandering through the trees but they could not see any enemy soldiers.

By then most of the day had gone and by the time they reached the prairie the sun was beginning to go down in the west.

This time they did it by going straight towards the hills walking on the open prairie.

They carried on just strolling and chatting when an arrow struck the ground close to the prince. They turned and saw a group of ten enemy soldiers coming out of the forest with their bows ready.

"They are too many for us to make a stand," said the prince.

Without saying a word Pearl prepared her bow and shot an arrow but probably because of her excitement or the distance between them her arrow missed.

"Come!" cried Eloy and they followed him running as fast as they could.

A few more arrows came very close to them, nevertheless, they carried on.

Suddenly they saw a couple of arrows flying over them though in the opposite direction and to their surprise and relieve, a few of their warriors on patrol came to their help and after a few more arrows the enemy soldiers retreated.

They could stop running and welcome those warriors.

"I thought to give you a hand," said one of the archers.

"And you couldn't have come in a better time," said the Prince.

"You carry on," said the archer, "we'll stay here and keep an eye on them."

To their surprise, a group of ten men came out of the forest from the direction of the cavern, engaging the enemy in between the trees. Those were the men keeping an eye on the enemy.

Eloy took charge of the patrol. "Come with me!" he cried and they turned back joining those men in a skirmish, forcing the enemy further inside the forest.

This time Pearl was more accurate and managed to hit two enemies with her arrows while the other archers did very well. Then she saw Prince Neno with Eloy in between the trees engaging the surviving enemies using their swords.

Moments later those soldiers had disappeared inside the forest leaving their dead behind though some of the warriors from the cavern had been injured.

"Well, I must say that our warriors are getting better," said a gleeful Neno.

"And now we have more warriors with fighting experience with some extra weapons as well," added Eloy.

"All right," said a happy Pearl. "now we go back to the hills without having to run for it."

They all answered her with their laughter.

"Thank you, my friends," said Eloy addressing the warriors from the cavern. "You'll stay here and carry on inside the forest to keep an eye on the enemy. Your duty is to make sure they don't go too close to the cavern and above all take care of your wounded and don't you forget to take their weapons back to the cavern. Do you have enough food?"

They touched their satchels. "Yes, we have," said one of them and they went back to the forest in silence with their walking wounded while Eloy, Pearl, Barum and Neno with the rest of the group walked across the prairie.

*

Once in the village fortress they gathered the commanders around a big fire and Choquero joined them with Loni at his side.

Eloy gave his instructions. "Commander Barum, I know you need some sleeping but as you already know some enemies are in the forest and who knows how many more might be coming this way. You will go to the forest, join some of the men from the cavern that right now are keeping an eye on the enemy and lay in waiting for any soldiers trying to come out of it. If they do it, you will attack and get rid of them but don't forget to take their weapons. From now on your warriors will have some practical experience. If there is no encounter with enemies that will be the chance for you and your men to sit close to a tree and get some sleep."

Immediately Barum call some of his warriors and left trotting.

*

Another day was passing and many torches lit the village fortress with the help of the fires from the communal cooking place and the constant fire from the blacksmith forge.

Some workers were still on the roof of the palace adding more wooden tiles. By then many of the broken colour glasses in the windows had been replaced by wood until some glass could be found.

Some of the walls were already repaired and the other walls around the rooms were nearly finished.

"Now we will concentrate with the training," said Eloy.

"I know, I know," said Pearl. "Would you come with me your highness?" he said in a cheeky way looking at Neno who was startled.

"Yes, of course I would but you keep forgetting to call me Neno." he said and joined her while she was calling some of her warriors.

Many young women joined them but as it was expected, many just came to be close to the prince instead of practicing with their bows and for a moment Pearl had to be firm with them. "Come on girls! Let him be and show your skills instead!"

The place had a few torches so the young women could see the targets.

The prince didn't say a word; instead, he just smiled at them while the young women shoot their arrows showing their skills.

Neno was surprised with the human shape of the targets. "Why the human shape?"

Pearl was prompt to explain. "Because it put in the archer's minds the idea of shooting people," then she turned to Lera. "All right Lera, they had enough for today."

"Of course, all right girls enough for today, it's getting too late and you'll do some more practice tomorrow morning."

*

In the palace, things were getting a bid hectic and Amina with the other attendants were close to the Queen on the palace balcony.

From there they could only see a few lights in different parts of the city. Usually the light of torches.

"It is sad to see the city almost in darkness," said the Queen, "it used to be such a happy city with many lights in the night and we could hear music and singing. Look at it now, darkness and silence reins in it."

"What can we do Your Majesty," asked Nadia.

"There's almost no food left and by now most of what the people can eat is bread but even so the flour is almost gone," said Amina.

"I know but I have plenty of faith in the people organising themselves in the west. I only hope not too many people will die from starvation."

*

With his usual flamboyancy, General Agaram entered the palace surrounded by his bodyguards and went straight to the balcony.

"Leave us!" he shouted and the attendants left running.

Slowly he approached the Queen with arrogance. "Well? Have you made your mind or not?"

She carried on looking upon the city. "You know my answer perfectly well."

"I don't understand you. Your people will be soon starving and your slaves in the palace have not much food either."

"That's very cruel not to let the people to go out of the city to get food and on the other hand I have no slaves in the palace or anywhere in my country. My people are free or at least they were until your arrival."

The General gave a loud laugh. "Free? To do what? Nobody has come to rescue you and look at the city, all dark and gloomy." Then he saw the Queen with tears running down her cheeks. "Oh, I'm so sorry but I can put some light into it by burning a few houses," he said sarcastically.

For a moment, the Queen stood in silence and decided not to mention anything to do with the rebellion then she spoke with dignity. "A long time ago, as you know, we had a hero who was a nobleman coming from the farming community and leading the people he freed us from your evil ancestor and I'm sure this time there will be another hero and the people will follow him."

The General yawned. "All this is very boring but at the moment you change your mind and accept me as your husband, I will bring food to the city. The farmers will once again attend their farms, the fishermen will start fishing and we'll have a great celebration. Think about it," he said while grinning straight to her face. "Imagine the people singing and dancing in the streets." Then he smiled lifting his arms with some euphoria. "We can have plenty of fireworks illuminating the sky at night!"

"Carry on living in your fantasy world but your time will come."

The General looked at her first with surprise and then with rage. "My time will come you say but your time is here and now! And you will be my wife, like it or not!" saying those words full of anger he left.

The Queen attendants returned in silence.

"Have no fear Your Majesty," said Amina, "his arrogance will be stopped."

"I know my dear but the question is, when."

Amina shrugged her shoulders. "That I don't know Your Majesty."

Chapter Seven

Very early in the morning, Eloy, Pearl and prince Neno were having something to eat with coffee to push it down, sitting close to a fire and commanders Bo, Lera and Choquero with his permanent second in command Loni, joined them.

"How far is from here to the tomb of Bonamor?" asked Pearl.

Eloy looked at her with surprise. "Oh, I don't know but it should be." He looked in several directions and then pointed towards the south. "That way where the prairie is much wider and it should take at least one day or maybe two. I've never been there so I'm not sure."

"You just pointed to the south of the prairie."

"Yes, Pearl that's where the battle took place and the people build his tomb on the site of it."

They remained in silence for a few more moments and Pearl had an idea. "Considering we are not doing any serious fighting and the enemy is still in the city with only a small group of them inside the forest, why don't we go and visit his tomb?"

The commander's reaction was enthusiastic.

"I have never seen it," said Bo.

"Neither do I," added Lera.

"All I know is what some travelling storytellers told us," added Choquero.

"I would like to see it as well," said the prince, "considering that he is supposed to be my ancestor from my mother's side."

Pearl gave the prince a glance. "I'm sure you are as brave as he was."

For a brief moment, the prince was startled. "Well, I sincerely hope so, though I have never had the chance to find out; after all we have been at peace for two centuries."

"I saw you fighting earlier on and I think you're good."

The prince felts embarrassed. "Oh, I don't know about that, it was a very short fight."

"Yes, I know but for a moment you were fighting two of them at the same time."

Looking at the sky with only a couple of white clouds Eloy interrupted them. "If we are going to do it this is the best time. Come on let's go."

Then he gave some instructions to his father. "While we are gone you will be in charge and make sure the new army carries on training and practicing with their weapons but you must wait and above all keep an eye on the enemy just in case they decide to come out of the forest."

"Yes, son I can do that but how long will it take for you to be back?"

"I really don't know father. It could be a couple of days."

"Okay son. It shall be done."

They were leaving when Eloy and Pearl's mother came in the company of other women and gave them all some small bundles with food wrapped with banana leaves to put in their satchels.

"Here Pearl," said Sanila, "this will keep you going."

Eloy's mother approached giving Eloy some food. "This will keep you going son."

"Thank you, mother."

*

In the company of commanders Bo, Lera and the prince, they left the village fortress going down to the prairie and the only ones without a bow were Eloy and the prince. So far, Eloy has always relayed on his sword.

*

The prairie was peaceful and they couldn't see any animals, though they could see some little birds.

Barum was at the edge of the forest when he saw Eloy and friends going out of the hill road and immediately he signals for his men to follow him.

*

It took only an hour for him to reach Eloy and friends.

"I thought you were inside the forest."

"No, Eloy I send some of my warriors to explore some of the forest and I had the chance to get some sleep as you suggested. Those men didn't find the men you suggested for us to join with but where are you going?"

"We are going towards Bonamor's tomb," said Pearl.

"All right, I'm going with you," and instructed his men. "You'll go back to the village fortress and have something to eat and rest."

His warriors obeyed and left, and they carried on without any rush.

"I cannot see any birds of prey," said Lera.

Don't you worry about," said Barum, "when you hear the small birds stopping their chirping, it means one of them is not far from here."

They felt surrounded by peace and in the distance, they could see the high picks of the mountains crowned with snow. Barum was curious and wanted to know more. "Tell me, the battle where Bonamor died was it a big one?"

Eloy thought about that particular subject. "I'm not quite sure, I think it wasn't more than a few hundred warriors facing the same number of enemy soldiers. The situation was that during the battle Bonamor faced the enemy General in single combat defeating and killing him. Unfortunately, some enemy archers took advantage of the situation and shoot their arrows killing him."

"What about the magic sword he had. Could it not protect him?" asked Lera.

"In reality, I don't know but about the sword, I don't think there was any magic in it. The only magic was Bonamor's bravery and above all his leadership."

"We all know that," said Bo, "but people continued to say the sword was magical and whoever uses it will defeat any enemy."

"Well, in a way it is because by holding it and making sure the people saw it, which in itself was magic, it's better than many words haranguing the people."

"Eloy," said Pearl, "if we find it, will you take it?"

Eloy thought about it for a brief moment. "How can I use that sword? It is supposed to be used by a leader and above all a hero, which I am not."

Pearl looked at him and started giggling. The commanders and the prince started giggling too.

"What's funny?"

"What's funny is very simple," said Pearl, "from the beginning of our resistance you have led the people and now everybody looks to you as our natural leader."

"Why me? The natural leader is supposed to be the prince."

The prince interrupted him. "No, Eloy it is true that I am Prince Neno of Onuvar because my mother is the Queen but the people are following you and right now I am following you too," and bowed to Eloy with the commanders doing the same.

Eloy felt very embarrassed. "Oh, stop that nonsense and carry on walking," he said stepping forward leaving them to follow him though they were all smiling.

*

"Look over there," said Pearl and they look. A group of people were crossing the prairie and they were herding some sheep.

Eloy decided to stop and wait and it didn't take long for those people to reach them.

"Where are you going friends?" asked Bo.

To the west and hopefully find the resistance people we thing are somewhere in those tall hills," said a middle age woman walking with a shepherd's staff'

"It's all right," said Pearl, "you are going in the right direction," and pointed to where the road was. "Over there between those hills you'll find the road and I'm sure somebody will come down to help you."

"Thank you," said the woman and signalled for the others to follow her.

*

The undulating terrain prevented them seeing clearly what was ahead. Soon they reached a small stream with shallow waters and bushes at either side.

Not everything was grass and bushes; there were plenty of wild flowers as well.

Commander Lera looked at the surrounding land. "I thought a prairie was something flat and all covered with grass."

Commander Barum stood at her side. "Oh, I don't know about that but I don't think I would like to walk on a land all flat and monotonous."

"Well, at least we won't run out of water," said commander Bo while kneeling and drinking some.

Eloy look at the prairie in all directions and especially to the south of it. "Most probably there are many more streams further on though on higher grounds the terrain will be dryer."

They looked at him and without saying a word; they replenished their flat water bottles with fresh water putting them back inside the satchel.

Lera attracted their attention to something more attractive. "I'm happy to see that many bushes have ripe berries," and without any hesitation started collecting some and eating them, "and they are delicious."

The stream had many of those bushes at either side.

The rest of the group did the same and for several moments, they just gorged themselves with wild fruits.

*

They carried on walking for hours and several times they came across other small streams they had no choice but to cross making their feet wet because there were no bridges.

*

As Eloy had said, they encountered other streams coming from the hills in the west meandering in the undulating terrain towards the forest.

Bo started to laugh and Pearl was curious. "What are you laughing at?"

"I can answer that," said Barum, "after crossing a couple of streams we are the ones with the cleanest feet in the whole of Onuvar."

"And we have plenty of water to drink," said Bo splashing his feet in one of those streams.

"Make sure to drink the water from upstream or you'll be drinking the one you washed your feet in," added Bo.

"Argh," said Lera, "the water is turning into mud."

*

They reached a place where they felt strange feelings. Their surroundings make them feel tranquil and at peace.

Eloy put his right hand up and they stopped.

They looked into the distance and saw a mound in the middle of nowhere, all covered by grass. They could see what looked like the tip of some stones at one side. The forest on their left and the hills on their right looked far away. This was the widest part of the prairie.

"That is supposed to be the tomb?" asked commander Bo.

They stopped and just look at it without saying a word mesmerised with the size of the mound with no apparent entrance.

"What now?" asked the prince.

"Now," said Eloy, "we'll approach slowly and with respect we'll walk around until we find the entrance, if there is any."

They follow him looking at Bonamor's tomb that was coming closer and looking bigger.

"Wow," said commander Barum, "it's impressive."

Pearl looked at the prairie surrounding them. "You were right Eloy. The ground looks dryer and I don't see any streams. It looks so peaceful and there is no sign that there was ever a battle in here."

I don't understand," said Barum, "there are no graves either."

"Or a place showing a funeral pyre," said Lera.

"If there was a pyre, after so many years the ashes had been pushed underground mainly by the rain and on the other hand, if they were buried, I'm sure that the same rain had managed to flatten the graves as well.

*

Some grey clouds came from the west.

"Lovely clouds," said commander Lera, "they will give us some relief from the heat."

Barum look up. "They can also give us some rain."

*

They reached the mound and started to walk around.

Moments later, they saw the entrance on the west side of it.

It was not concealed and very impressive. What they saw were in fact two big vertical stones in front of either side of the entrance and one closer to the top, right across embedded in the vertical stones and when they came close to it, they could read some words carved on that horizontal stone.

"Before you enter make sure your mind is clear of bad thoughts. He who leads will be exalted with his followers.

Humility and honour shall be his real weapons. With him, the throne of Onuvar shall be safe. Once more a King will reign."

They read those writings and felt a bit confused. "I don't understand," said the prince, "the kingdom has a monarch with my mother the Queen and about having a King, it will be a matter of time for me to be the one but you must understand that I'm not in a hurry to see my mother dead to become a King; I love my mother."

Eloy shrugged his shoulders. "Let's not worry about those words now. After we liberate the country, we'll talk about it."

Pearl shook her head. "You say after we liberate the country but for that we need an army we don't have."

"But Pearl we do have an army, though a small one."

Pearl shrugged her shoulders. "Whatever."

*

Eloy led them through the entrance into what was a dark corridor though they could see everything under a dim light coming from the entrance with some light at the end of it.

The clouds had reached them obscuring the sunlight and started pouring. Commanders Bo with Barum started a fire with two pieces of flint stones, using some dry grass close to them and lighting several torches on the side of the corridor they carried on holding a couple of them.

At the end of the corridor, they came to a volt with a stone sarcophagus in the centre.

The place didn't look nice, all dark and through a hole in the roof above the sarcophagus, some rain was coming in.

They just stood looking at their surroundings.

The clouds passed and the sun shone through the hole in the roof right above the sarcophagus giving to it and the whole of the volt a magic touch illuminating the last of the raindrops.

They could see on it the sleeping body of the hero made in stone though partially covered with grass. He was not dressed differently than them though he shows to have had long hair, beard and moustache.

In front of it, there was a smaller stone container with some smaller writing.

"Remember humility."

"Why all this is covered with grass?" asked Lera.

Pearl look at it. I can only guess that grass seeds brought by the wind can enter through the hole in the roof and with some rain the grass just grows."

Eloy went down on one of his knees and his followers did the same.

"This is a sacred place and so it must remain."

"There is some writing at the side of the sarcophagus," pointed out Pearl and they stood up with Eloy approaching it.

"It's a kind of a riddle."

"What does it say?"

"Give me some time and I'll read it."

A moment later, he had cleared the dust and some grass on it and was ready.

"Search to the north, the west, the south and the southeast and open your heart."

"I don't get it," said the prince, "search for what?"

Pearl was feeling impatient. "Go on open the container and see what's inside. Maybe there are some instructions in it."

"I hope it is the sword," said commander Barum.

"No, it can't be because it is too small," was Bo's opinion.

Eloy opened it with some difficulty because after all, it was made of stone but to their surprise, there was nothing inside.

Eloy look at them and spoke solemnly. "There is only one way to find out and that is to follow the riddle. Come let's go outside."

They all followed him outside and stood waiting for him to speak.

The clouds had left and the sun was once again worming the air.

Pearl shrugged her shoulders. "All right, you said let's go but I don't think it means for us to go back to the north because we already found that place."

Eloy agreed with her. "Yes, you are right and in my opinion the west is our next place to search and from there we move south. So far all we have is the riddle in the tomb and that's what we are following and don't ask me why because I don't know. The only solution is to carry on and I'm sure the riddle will eventually be explained at the end of it."

At the end of it?" asked Barum looking at the others.

"Don't look at me," said Bo, "my knowledge is as good as yours."

Eloy had a thought. "It looks to me like if somebody is trying to show as all the places Bonamor had been and trying to teach us something at the same time."

He looked in all directions and pointed his right hand. "All right, that's the way north and we have already been there."

"That means we don't have to cross the prairie again," said commander Bo.

"You, silly man, we are still on the prairie and the tomb is almost in the centre of it and that means that where ever we go it will be like finishing the crossing," said a smiling Barum.

"All right, I know that."

They all followed Eloy but Pearl was curious. "Now we are going west and according to the instructions we still don't know what we are looking for."

"We are supposed to look for the sword," said Lera.

Barum nodded. "Yes, we are supposed to look for the sword but instead we are following a riddle. I only hope the riddle and the sword are connected."

"And I don't think we'll find the sword laying somewhere on the ground," was Bo's opinion.

"I agree with Bo and I think we are supposed to see something that will call for our attention," said the prince.

"Like what?" asked Barum.

"What about some stones?" said Bo.

"Or a cave?" was Lera's opinion.

Eloy shook his head. "Yes, I know but we won't know until we see it."

Pearl shook her head. "Still we don't know what we are supposed to look for; maybe it is some sort of container with the sword in it?"

"Ah," said Barum, "now that's a thought."

"Yes," said Lera, "I agree we won't find the sword lying on the grass just waiting to be picked up."

"Well?" said Eloy taking a deep breath, "are you ready to face the quest?"

They all looked at each other and nodded.

"Yes, we are and soon you'll get used to it," said Pearl.

He was surprised with her comment. "Use to what?"

"For you to be the leader."

For a brief moment, Eloy felt annoyed. "Oh, not that again."

She grinned at him. "Yes," and just carried on grinning with the others doing the same to each other holding their laughter.

"Something is puzzling me," said Lera, "so far all I've heard about Bonamor is that there was a battle and he was killed but I'm sure the fight against the invaders was much longer than just a battle."

They all look at Eloy making him uneasy.

"Yes, I know a few things about the story but you must understand that I'm not an historian and all I know is what I've heard from other people."

The prince thought about it. "Though Bonamor was my ancestor, I don't know much about him either."

"It's the same with us," said Pearl, "and now Eloy please do tell us whatever you know."

"The war was a long one and went on for over a year because the enemy was numerous and their commander was determined to capture Bonamor. To prevent been captured he used to change places and I wouldn't be surprised if he used the village fortress we are using now as one of his hiding places and that's all I know."

Then they looked at the prince who nodded. "Yes, that's what my mother has told me since I was a little boy."

"So far, yesterday we've been in one of his hideouts."

"That's right Pearl and I can only guess we'll find more hideouts from now on."

Without stopping, they all remained in silence for a few moments just eating something though without stopping.

Bo had a thought. "Maybe our quest is to find out about those places."

"You're right," said Barum, "those are precisely my feelings."

"I wonder what the people are doing in the city," said Pearl.

Eloy thought about it. "Difficult to say but we better leave those things to commander Marum; I'm sure he's very capable."

"And brave," added Pearl.

"All right," said Eloy, "the entrance to the tomb is facing west," and pointed his right arm in that direction. "and that's the way we go."

*

In the city, commander Marum had been busy and very careful not to attract any attention from the enemy soldiers and so did his men.

He was having a meeting in the safe house with some city leaders. Though they were important people, they wore simple clothes that will not attract any attention when mingling with the city dwellers.

"You are very important people not just in the city but in the whole of the country and so it will rest on your shoulders to organise the people into a revolt."

A man wearing black clothes, a black round hat and sporting a bushy beard spoke first. "I am the Prime Minister and now I have no choice but to be in hiding. I cannot use my good clothes and colourful hat anymore. Nevertheless, I have already been in touch with other dignitaries and they all assure me that many people are willing to subdue the enemy soldiers though so far, they don't know how to do it because unfortunately they have no weapons. Only the city guards have a spare weapon at home."

"I am the Foreign Minister and I have done something similar," said another man inconspicuously dressed though with no beard, moustache or a hat."

I am the Minister of the Interior," said a third man who was as well unattractively dressed with longer and dishevelled hair. "What we don't know is what the people outside the city are doing to help us?"

Commander Marum was happy to hear something positive. "There is something been organised at the other side of the forest in the hills on the west of the prairie but we must wait until I can get some more information."

The Prime Minister was curious. "How can you get that information considering nobody can enter the city?"

"Very simple Excellency I came in with the leader of the resistance and a few warriors, using the canal that runs out of the city and we were the ones who rescued the prince."

At that moment, Amina the Queen's attendant arrived and after giving her mother the jar of water, joined the meeting. "Is there any news? The Queen is getting very worried because the General is putting more pressure on her to accept his proposals of marriage. In the meantime, we are not starving because we still have plenty of flour to make bread."

The woman of the house approached her with some dehydrated fruit on a plate. "Thank you, mum".

Marum wanted to know more. "Did you have any problems coming to this house?"

"Yes, I did because I always go to the well in the square to provide my parents with some water and the soldiers always harass me mainly by whistling at me."

Marum was deep in thought for a moment. "We must start organising properly, you Prime Minister will tell your people to start putting together any weapons they can in a place close to the south wall gates and you Minister for the Interior will do the same in a house close to the north wall and close to the main city gates. You Foreign Minister will do the same close to the centre of the city. In the meantime, some of my warriors will start training your people in the use of swords and bows. One thing we must make sure is not to do anything close to the palace. We must not put the Queen in any danger by attracting the enemy's attentions towards the palace."

"But as I said, we have no weapons," said the Prime Minister.

"Yes, I know but they can use some of the bamboo growing in their gardens to make spears and the training in the use of bows will help them to be ready when the time comes."

The Minister for the Interior wanted to know more. "That will be very encouraging but what the people would like to know is if there is a leader."

"Yes, we have a leader. We came to the city with him."

They look at each other full of curiosity and the Prime Minister asked. "Well? Who is he? Is he a nobleman?"

"His name is Eloy and he is the son of a farmer; whose land is close to the city gates. He is the one who rescued the prince and I'm beginning to repeat myself."

"Now that in itself is very encouraging because the ancient leader Bonamor was a farmer too," said the Foreign Minister.

"How old is he?" asked Amina.

"He's old enough and you already met him. He's the one who came here to your home to talk to you."

Amina just open her mouth very surprised. "Yes, I remember him and he's very young and he had a young woman with him."

"That was Pearl and she is the leader of many female archers and right now she's giving a personal protection to the prince. Her father is a fisherman and pearls dealer and her mother is the priestess we have."

The three ministers stood up, "very well, we'll carry on with your instructions," said the Prime Minister and bowing they left.

"Now, how are you Amina with the use of weapons?"

Amina felt quite happy. "I'm all right with the bow, nevertheless, I would like to have some training with a sword and hopefully the other girls will have the same training."

"Very well, I will teach you the use of the sword and you must train the other women in the palace. Right now, and because you don't have a sword, we'll use pieces of wood with the same length. I'll give you a lesson now and every time you come to our meetings, you'll have some more training.

Amina's father provided them with two sticks and the training started. They did it for a few moments and commander Marum signal for them to stop. "Now go back to the palace and give the news to the Queen."

"All right but how can I get swords inside the Queen's chambers?"

"You do burn some wood in her chambers, don't you?"

"Yes."

"That's your answer. You must send the man who supplies you with cut wood in bundles to see me but above all you must make sure he is on our side."

"That's not a problem; his name is Mangro and though he's not a young man he has managed so far to go in and out of the palace without been stopped by the soldiers. In a way, he has managed to befriend some of them by smuggling some wine. At the same time, he is the only one allowed to leave the city using the south gates to get the dead wood from the forest." "How many attendants will need a sword?"

"We are six."

"Very well and with the Queen you are seven. I will send some of my men to find seven swords for Mangro." Commander Marum thought about something for a moment. "Tell me, is there anybody who can provide us with some sleeping drugs, like something we can use on the soldiers later on. Something we can put in the wine?"

Amina thought about it. "Yes, that's very possible and I know the right person for it. It is an old woman who sells herbs for medicinal purposes and I'm sure she could find something useful for us."

"Very well, that will be one of your missions but you must be very careful not to be captured."

"It's all right commander. All what the enemy soldiers see in me is a woman and as long as I keep smiling to them, they will leave me in peace."

"But what about if they decide to stop you?"

"Ah, in that case I have a secret weapon but I cannot talk about it now."

Though he was surprised, commander Marum nodded. "Very well, go and be careful."

Her mother approached her once again and this time with a small bundle. "Here, take this dry fruit."

"Thank you, Mum, but I cannot take the bundle. Some soldiers might take it from me.

Amina put the small pieces of dry fruit in some pockets and left.

*

Eloy and companions had walked for a couple of hours and the hills on the west of the prairie were still far away.

"I would suggest," said Barum, "when we reach the west, if we don't find anything, to turn south a little bid and then if we have not found anything yet we move further south where those mountains are and see what happens."

"Somehow it doesn't sound right because according to the instructions written in the tomb, we are supposed to find something in the west," was commander Bo's opinion.

Lera thought about it. "I think that when we reach the west of the prairie we'll have an answer. Personally, I'm sure we'll find something because our instructions are to go west."

"Good thinking," said Eloy and once again took the lead. "We must remember that place in the north of the prairie was very well protected."

"Oh dear," said Pearl, "it means we must be very careful because in the west there could be something to protect whatever is there. Remember the bog we encounter when visiting the place in the north."

"I'm beginning to get some pain in my legs," complained Bo distracting their conversation.

"Oh, stop whinging," said Lera, "you are supposed to be a strong warrior and leader of men."

"All right, I've got the message," he said for their amusement. "I'm not whinging and my legs are aching."

Once more, they walked for a long time and the sun was going down though they still had a couple of hours of day light left.

*

Back in the city, there were only a few people walking between houses and some soldiers were lighting some fires in the square while others started fires close to the walls and on the battlements.

Amongst the few people walking around was commander Marum who knocked at the door of the safe house and a moment later he was inside in the presence of the ministers.

"I can guess that by now many city dwellers are following your instructions and making mostly bamboo spears."

"Yes, commander Marum," said the Minister of the interior. "The people are doing a very good job and above all they feel enthusiastic with the news of some resistance."

"We started a system of communication," added the Minister for foreign affairs.

"Good and now you better carry on with the preparations."

The meeting was over and the Ministers left as usual one by one.

*

A moment later, he was moving slowly and trying to avoid attracting the attention of soldiers patrolling the streets.

He knocked at the door of the house closer to the bridge near the wall and entered.

*

On the west of the prairie, Eloy signalled for them to stop. "Once again this is the right time to stop and have something to eat," and the group collapsed on the grass in a manner of speaking.

Soon they were all enjoying something to eat though it was mainly bread pushed down with some water.

Commander Barum slapped his belly. "Look, I think I'm losing weight; all this walking has reduced the size of my belly."

"Same here," said commander Bo.

"In my case," said Lera. "If I lose more weight I'll be floating instead of walking."

Eloy shook his head. "You and your weight; think about how fit you'll be by the time we really go into action."

"Talking about fighting," said Barum, "what are your plans for the army."

"So far, not much; we all know that we won't have enough warriors to face the invaders face to face in a battle and so we have to think about how to do it."

"All right," said Bo, "I do understand that but what I don't get is how all this walking will help us."

Once again, Eloy had to explain. "So far we know that all this walking, as you say, it is to find Bonamor's sword and with that sword I'm sure more people will rally to us."

"I sincerely hope so because I don't want to spend a year or more fighting the invaders," said Lera, "we all know the people in the city are close to starving and we have no choice but to liberate them as soon as possible."

"We are not sure if that will be the case," said Pearl, "when or if we find the elusive sword, then we'll know if the people will follow it or if they will just follow Eloy."

"Even with the sword," said Bo, "and knowing about people, only a few will do something while the rest will stay cowering at home; not everybody is a fighter."

Eloy felt uneasy with his opinion. "Well my dear commander, we won't know until we find it and show it to the people, will we?"

"We won't know that," said Pearl crouching on the grass.

Eloy thought about how to answer that question. "We'll have to wait to see how many will fight and how many will stay at home."

Pearl looked at the prairie. "The rain water has evaporated and if you don't mind I'll try to sleep," and she lied down using her satchel as a pillow and covered herself with the cloak.

"Don't you think it is a bit too early for getting some sleep?" asked commander Bo.

Pearl sat up. "No, it isn't because if you think about it you'll realise that our country has a very warm weather and if we get some sleep now it means we'll wake up early and the best time to do any walk is early in the morning when the air is fresher," saying that she wrapped herself again with the cloak.

"She's right," said Eloy, "and we'd better try to sleep and we'll be rested before the sun is up," and using the satchel as a pillow, he lay down trying to get some sleep.

"Eloy," said Lera.

"Yes?"

"Strange but the message in the piece of wood mentioned Bonamor as the glorious Bonamor."

"Yes, you are right Lera," said the prince, "I had the same thought.""Try to sleep Lera and we'll talk about it tomorrow," said Eloy.

*

Amina has reached the palace going straight to report to the Queen who was in her chambers with her attendants.

"Amina, tell me, what news?"

"Good news Your Majesty as you already know many people are getting together in the west but that's not all. Commander Marum and his warriors are already working with the Prime Minister and the ministers for the exterior and interior affairs, organising the people to get ready for when the time comes."

"But what can we do?" asked Nadia.

"That is more good news I have. Every time I leave the palace, commander Marum will train me in the use of the sword and I am supposed to pass that knowledge to all of you."

The Queen was very curious. "But how? We don't have any swords."

"That's true Your Majesty but Mangro the old man that brings the wood for our fires will bring the seven swords commander Marum's warriors will start collecting from the city dwellers. Some of the city guards had spare swords at home."

The Queen thought for a moment and left her Chambers to go to the balcony with her attendants.

She looked upon the city and the attendants didn't say a word.

"It seems to me we should prepare to defend our freedom in here in the palace that will be turned into a fortress. The point is, is there a leader of the resistance?"

"Yes, Your Majesty there is a leader and he's the man that rescued the prince taking him out of the city. He's a very young man, his name is Eloy and he's the son of a farmer."

The Queen turned to look at her. "A common man?"

"Yes, Your Majesty and he's very handsome."

Her words make the attendants to look at each other smiling and giggling and the Queen did the same.

"It's all right because he is a son of Onuvar and if he's brave enough he must be treated as a prince. We must not forget that my heroic ancestor was a farmer too."

*

Back in the village fortress Choquero was giving his last orders for the day and was talking to several men and women that had just joined them as warriors and Loni was at his side. "It will take some time for all of us to be ready to start first our advance on the enemy in the forest and then to the city and considering I don't know how long it will take for our leader Eloy to return by tomorrow you will have your warriors selected and ready. So far, more people are coming to join us and it is your job to train them. Soon you'll see your forces getting bigger in number and so it will be your duty to train for when we'll be ready."

"Are we to be commanders later on?" asked one of those men.

"No, you won't because we already have enough commanders but you can be second in command."

His wife approached them. "It's all right with what you do but now it is dinnertime."

First Choquero look at his wife seriously and then he smiled. "You heard my wife and that means it is dinnertime for you too; I'll see you early in the morning."

They left and Choquero embraced his wife. "What are we having for dinner Mavina, fish again?"

"Of course, some people went to the seaside and returned earlier with more fish, crabs and muscles. Some of the merchants had plenty of vegetable oil for sale and now we can have more fried fish."

"Do you think that by eating so much fish I will learn to swim?"

*

Back in the prairie, most of them were asleep. Soon the night was upon them with the silence of the prairie only disturbed by some of them snoring.

Eloy, Lera and Commander Barum were the only ones not asleep.

"Eloy, I don't understand; all we are doing now is to walk following a strange riddle that is supposed to lead us to the place where the sword is supposed to be but we don't really know if we will find it or not."

"Yes, I know and there is only one way to find out and that is to carry on. The beauty of any quest is the mystery waiting at the end of it."

Lera was curious. "Why nobody else has looked for it before?"

Eloy smiled thinking of it. "I don't know commander, probably because it is so far from the city and any village. On the other hand, we haven't had any trouble with invaders for a long time and for many people it is not more than a legend."

Commander Barum thought about it. "If it is just a legend as you said why are we doing all this walking?"

"In my case it is curiosity, though the exercise is good for you and you must know that behind every legend there is a true story."

Barum thought about it. "Yes, you've got a very good point there." and drawing his sword he gave them a good spectacle in the use of it. "If I had the Glorious sword I could cut my enemies down."

They were all very amused with his exhibition.

"All right commander," said Bo sympathetically. "We know how skilful you are with the sword."

Chapter Eight

Pearl was right and after a good night sleep, they were ready to carry on.

The sun was beginning to shine from behind the eastern horizon and they could see their surroundings very well while enjoying the fresh breeze that was very invigorating.

They didn't start a fire to cook anything; instead, they had some bread with smoked fish, this time washed down with water.

"Somehow," said commander Bo, "I hope to run out of smoked fish as soon as possible."

Commander Barum reacted with surprise while munching some fish. "Why you say that?"

Holding back his laughter, commander Bo explained himself. "Very simple my dear friend, I'm getting fed up with the smell of it and whoever might be on this prairie, can smell our presence from any distance."

*

The sun was shining beautifully over the land and Eloy and his friends were coming closer to the hills and ready to search for anything that could attract their attention.

"I can guess by now being in the west we should start looking for another stone with some writing on it," said Pearl.

"Of course," said Lera, "what else?"

Eloy shook his head. "I think we should keep an open mind and look for anything; not just writing." Then he looked around. "The best place to look for something will be over there at the foot of those hills."

"What should we be looking for?" asked commander Barum.Eloy thought about that question. "Anything and not just a monolith with some writing. It could be something showing or pointing in a certain direction."

*

Pearl came closer to the prince and kneeled at his side. "Did you have a good rest?"

Neno stretched his arms and gave a long yawn. "No, Pearl I didn't. I can only guess that I will have to get used to it though I had some practice with sleeping on the ground when I was in the dungeons. I must say that it was a very smelly place to be, though it was a bit wormer than to sleep in the prairie."

Pearl looked at him fondly. "Oh, I'm sure you'll get used to it after all, you are a young and strong man."

Neno looked at her. "Just by looking at you I feel better."

Pearl was shocked and could not help blushing and stood up quickly. "You are just saying that."

Neno just smiled at her but Eloy interrupted them. "Well, Pearl you were right and the morning air is fresh."

Quickly and very determined, she put herself in front of them. "And I'm ready."

Eloy noticed her reaction and looked at Neno. "What's going on between you two?"

Immediately commander Barum, who had seen everything, approached him whispering. "They are young and very friendly."

Eloy realised about the situation and reacted accordingly changing the subject. "All right everybody, let's carry on."

"I've got an idea," said Pearl, "maybe all this quest was created by somebody two hundred years ago to make sure that anybody who reads the riddle in the tomb learns about part of Bonamor's life during his campaign against the enemy."

"Now that's a very good explanation," said Barum, "it teaches us that Bonamor was in different places during that war and we should learn from that."

Eloy agreed. "You have a very good point my friend but still we have not found the sword and so the quest continues."

"Yeah," said Bo, "it makes sense." Then he sniffed his hand. "Argh, my hands smell of fish," and they all ignored him.

*

Amina had left the palace to go to the well at the side of the square, carrying the clay jar on her head. This time there were more soldiers than usual and most of them had never seen her.

At one side of the well was a group of musicians playing some dull tunes in the hope the soldiers would throw some coins at them.

At the moment, when Amina came closer to the well, the old man carrying the bundle of wood tried to pass behind all of them and some soldiers stopped him. "What do you have there? Just wood?"

It was a very dangerous situation and several other soldiers approached him. Amina saw the problem and quickly reacted by putting the jar on the ground and grabbing a tambourine from one of the musicians started hitting it with a rhythm that distracted the soldiers and stopped them interrogating the old man. Hitting the tambourine several times on her hips and making some dancing steps, attracted the soldier's attention.

"Get out of here," said a soldier looking at the old man who didn't hesitated and left as fast as possible, though without running.

Her dancing started slowly at first, then she noticed that two soldiers looked at the old man leaving and immediately she hit the tambourine several times and called for their attention. "Hey you I'm dancing for you too!"

Her call worked because the two soldiers ignored the old man and go to look at her dancing instead.

She started to dance and the street entertainers joined in with their instruments. This time it was a happy tune.

The rest of the soldiers, with some city dwellers behind them, formed a circle though giving her plenty of room to dance and soon they were all clapping their hands following the rhythm.

All the soldiers in that part of the city were enthusiastically clapping their hands with her dancing rhythm that was faster and more exotic. She was after all a young and strong woman.

A moment later, she stopped completely exhausted and she was showered with coins and applauded by everybody. "Thank you, friends! I'll be back tomorrow!"

A couple of soldiers filled her jar with water while others collected some of the coins and put them in one of her pockets.

"Thank you, friends."

The musicians didn't waste any time collecting the rest of the coins. She left walking as fast as possible, taking the jar of water to her family house.

*

Moments later, in her family home she asked her parents for news. "Anything I can tell the Queen?"

"No," said her mother."

"Not now but maybe next time," added her father.

"All right. I was hoping for commander Marum to be here to give me more fencing lessons. Never mind perhaps next time. Now I'll have to go back to the palace to make sure the old man Mangro has arrived safe."

*

In the meantime, Mangro has entered the palace going straight to the Queen's chambers.

"I'm happy to see you have not been hurt," said the Queen.

Mangro opened his bundle of twigs and with a smile he gave her a sword.

*

Later on, Amina entered the Queen's Chamber and happily saw the Queen holding a sword while all of her attendants were overenthusiastic.

The old man was still there and Amina embraced him. "Thank you, old friend."

"It's all right and thanks for your help. For a moment, I thought they would have searched the bundle and find the sword."

"It's all right, anytime."

"With this trip, I've been here three times today and I'll try to bring another later on. Unfortunately, I can only bring one at a time."

"Tell me," asked the Queen talking to Amina, "do you think some of the other people in the palace would like to fight?"

Amina agreed. "Yes, they will but they don't have any weapons apart of their working tools."

"All right," said the Queen. "I think you better ask them but be very careful just in case some of them are on the side of the enemy."

"Oh no, Your Majesty they are very patriotic and your personal guards have a shield, a sword and a spear and they are all on our side."

The Queen addressed Mangro. "Very well my good man, now please be careful when you bring the other swords. We need four more."

Mangro bowed to the Queen. "Yes, Your Majesty it shall be done."

*

As soon as Mangro left, the Queen gathered her attendants. "So far we have only three swords and hopefully by tomorrow we'll have the others and Amina will pass the knowledge she has with the use of the sword to all of us."

"Shall we try now Your Majesty?"

The Queen was surprised. "Of course, and why not?"

One of the attendants gave Amina a sword and standing in front of them she started showing some of the movements and the Queen with her attendants tried to follow.

*

Commander Choquero had all his forces down on the north side of the village fortress and on flat grounds easier for them to use for the training required.

It was a place on the side of the corrals, on the path towards the seaside used to bring food for the village fortress.

He was instructing Loni his second in command to form their warriors in specific positions though there was a lot of confusion.

"No, no, no, archers, you must always be behind the warriors with a sword. You are giving them the aerial shield."

"What about us?" asked a woman, "we have a quiver full of arrows but don't have a bow."

"You must be patience, bows are being made and by the time your commanders Pearl and Lera return, you'll be ready to go anywhere you are needed."

At that moment, the carpenter with his assistants came down from the village fortress carrying as many bows as they could carry.

"There," he said, "now you have your bows."

"But they are not enough," insisted the same woman.

"I know they are not enough but you must be patience because we are not yet ready to face any enemy in battle."

He called his second in command. "Loni look at your warriors. They look more like sheep than warriors, talk and harangue them."

Then he looked at all of them. "Hopefully our leader will be back soon and I want for him to see how disciplined you are. Now try your best and form in straight lines."

"But why learn discipline when all we need is to learn how to use the bow properly?" asked one of the young women.

Choquero felt dismayed for a brief moment and tried to explain. "All armies move with discipline which helps during a battle and that's why small armies can defeat a bigger one. And that's all I know about the subject."

Mavina with other women of all ages arrived carrying trays with food for everybody and Choquero felt dismayed lifting his arms. "Oh, not now Mavina; what we need is more drilling instead of eating."

Mavina came close to him. "Oh, stop moaning and eat something."

"Very well then." He shook his head grabbing something and started eating. All the warriors sat on the grass to do the same.

*

The Queen was in the company of all of her attendants looking from her balcony upon the city and after a few moments, she signalled for her attendants to follow her.

They went to a spacious room behind her chambers with several trunks. "Now it is for us to learn more about the use of the sword and this will be the room for us to learn and practice. Those trunks with clothes will be ideal to hide the swords."

Amina had an idea. "One thing to do is for our guards to make sure no enemy soldiers will be in the palace corridors or near this room when we practice. They must not hear the sound of the clashing blades."

"Good thinking Amina but how to get rid of the soldiers outside the throne hall?"

"That won't be a problem," said Nadia, "because they are as you said, outside the throne hall and our guards are outside these thick doors and they will hardly hear the sound of clashing blades,"

"Good thinking Nadia now call the guards outside the door."

*

The two guards entered with Nadia and bowed.

"From now on every time we are here in this room, nobody will be allowed to enter apart of the old man that brings the wood in and if the General comes, you must warn us immediately."

The two guards bowed and left.

*

Harmon with his boat and a couple of fishermen had reached the last of the fishermen village in the east of the Kingdom of Onuvar.

After making sure there were no enemies in it, he finally beached his boat. Several men and women surrounded him.

"I'm happy to see there are no enemies in your village."

"But they have been and gone just before your arrival, taking all the fish and leaving us with nothing" said a man, "they said they will come back regularly to get fish for the army."

"There's nothing else for them to take from us, apart of fish," said a woman. "We were hiding in the hills but our men convinced them that women and children are needed for the fishing and they let us stay."

"All right then. I come from further west in the hills after the big prairie. Eloy, our leader, has managed to organise many people into a small army and right now, they are training in the use of weapons but what they will need is many boats to take them close to the city when the time comes. In our village, we don't have enough boats for that task and right now we are all in the cavern further west."

"I know the cavern you are talking about," said a man.

"Who is the leader?" asked another.

"He is the son of a farmer and together with my daughter Pearl they are leading the people. They managed to enter the city and had freed Prince Neno who is with them at the head of the resistance."

"We must help them," said a woman.

"Of course, we can help you," said the man with all the other fishermen approving enthusiastically.

"But if we do that they will punish us," was a woman's opinion.

"No, they won't. To prevent that you must do what we did and take all your people with you. In the west, you will be safe because you will join us in the big cavern and from there we will all sail further west to a cove where we will be sheltered from any rough sea and ready to do our job." Harmon felt happy and sad at the same time. "By doing so you will deny them the fish though the people in the city are beginning to starve, it is one of our weapons."

"All right then. I know the cavern and the cove you are talking," said the man.

"Good, what you should do is to leave with your families and catch some fish on your way to the west. I'll be going now and I hope to see you soon, I'll be waiting for you in the cavern."

A woman gave them some fresh muscles and some lemons. "This will keep you going for a while."

"Yes, thank you, we do like muscles don't we boys?" and his men nodded enthusiastically.

Several men and women help to push the boat back to the water while the village leader gave instructions. "Prepare to leave with just your essentials. Everybody out to sea! Bring all your boats close to the beach for the children to climb on board first while everybody else go back to the houses!"

While leaving, Choquero saw all those people running towards their homes while the fishermen started preparing their boats.

*

Eloy and friends had advanced well into the west and soon they had arrived at the foot of very rocky hills.

"Some of those rocks look like monoliths," was Bo's opinion.

"Why do we stop?" asked commander Lera.

"To rest and that's for sure," said Prince Neno and sat on the grass. "I'm beginning to feel that I'm developing flat feet."

"First," said Eloy, "we follow the prince idea and have something to eat," saying that he sat down and opened his satchel.

"All I see is many small rocks scattered around," said Pearl, "and we must be careful not to get a sprained ankle or worst, a broken leg."

Barum looks at the rocks and agrees. "I don't see those rocks as monoliths."

"Remember to keep an eye on any possible bog," warned Lera. "True," said Eloy and though still munching a piece of bread went to look in the company of Pearl. "I can see a narrow path between them."

"What are we waiting for," said Pearl also munching a piece of bread, "we have a quest to fulfil, come on."

Neno was the next to move coming closer to her.

"Do we have to? Can't we rest for a bit longer?" asked Barum.

"Oh, come on you brave and strong warrior," said Pearl and Barum frowned but didn't say a word.

Reluctantly the group stood up and followed them.

The path was narrow though easy to follow and the rocks were getting bigger.

They arrived to a place with short grass and Eloy noticed many small grey stones scattered on it.

"I don't see any message written on any of these rocks," said commander Bo.

Eloy started pacing and looking at anything that might give him an idea and suddenly he started to look at the small stones in detail.

For everybody's surprise, he run to a rock and climbed jumping on a taller one and from there he looked down and smiled.

"What do you see?" asked Pearl.

"From here I can see far away," he said putting his right hand on his forehead as a visor.

Pearl became impatience. "Stop fooling about and tell us."

"All right, I can see a message," he said looking down.

"What does it read," asked commander Bo.

"Give me a moment because most of the letters are made of small stones and somehow they have been moved."

Commander Bo grabbed a stone.

"Please!" cried Eloy, "don't touch them. Give me a chance."

Bo threw the stone back to where it was.

He carried on looking at the stones and started.

"By reaching this place you have proved to have stamina but the next part of your quest will be more demanding."

There was silence amongst them that the prince broke. "What we've done so far was to prove our stamina?"

Eloy had a thought. "I think all this is more than that. Somehow I'm beginning to think that our quest is more than just to find the sword."

"We know that," said commander Lera, "we have already learned something about Bonamor's life and something to do with his tactics and with so many tall rocks in this place it must have been one of his hideouts."

The prince shook his head. "I hope somebody finds the sword wherever it is so we can carry on organising the rebellion."

*

Eloy didn't have the chance to open his mouth because a group of five young women carrying bows and quivers arrived. They were from Lera's group.

"We were not sure where to find you," said one of them."

"Did you find the sword?" asked one of the women.

"Is it magical as people said?" asked another.

"Hold it!" cried Eloy, "no, we have not found the sword and we are still looking for it."

Pearl was happy to see them. "How did you manage to find us?"

The woman explained. "It wasn't difficult because we thought that if we went south towards the Tomb we will eventually find you and we were right."

"Though it was a long walk and we had to stop for the night, it wasn't really difficult because you didn't hide your footprints," said another, "and here we are."

"And the Tomb was impressive," added another.

They heard somebody calling. "Hoy! Where are you?"

A group of ten young men arrived and they too had their weapons with them. Those men were from Barum and Bo's group of warriors. They were only a handful but nevertheless looking very determined.

"I can guess that you boys followed the girls," said Eloy and they all nodded and giggled.

Eloy came down the rocks and was happy to see the group has swollen to a small fighting force.

"All right you lot now you have to come with us."

"Where too?" said one of Barum's men and the others started to murmur.

Eloy put his hands up and they silenced. "Now we must go to the south of Bonamor's Tomb."

"Why?" asked one of the women.

Pearl tried to explain. "Because this is a quest to find Bonamor's sword and yesterday we have already been in the north of the prairie where we found a small stony building that was once one of Bonamor's refuges and we read more instructions written at the side of his sarcophagus. Please from now on no more questions; so far you know as much as we do and hopefully soon we'll find out more."

Eloy decided it was the time to carry on. "Come on, follow us."

Pearl joined him. "Come on girls and boys."

*

Moments later, they were out on the prairie once again, this time going south.

"Peaceful prairie," said one of the young women, "difficult to believe that once a battle took place in this beautiful place."

Eloy looked at his surroundings. "That's true but battles are fought without thinking about the beauty of the land or the damage done to it."

*

They carried on in silence and looking at the distant mountains with snow in its picks.

"I only hope we won't have to climb up to the snow," said Bo, "we don't have more clothes."

"But if we have too we can make a snow man," was Lera's opinion.

They all gave her a look. "What? Haven't you ever played with snow?"

They all shook their head.

"Well, I have," she said with her chin up, "with my father we went to those mountains until we reached the snow. I was very little but still remember."

*

In the village fortress, Choquero had a meeting with the seconds in command. "I see some of the warriors had left without telling me."

"They have decided to go and find Eloy's party to see if they can help in anyway," said one of them.

"Well, there's nothing I can do about it now and I hope they can help him, the point is that I am in command and people should tell me if they want to do something. It's all to do with discipline." Then he gave some orders. "All right, there's no need to have a holiday. Organise your warriors properly and start drilling."

The seconds in command immediately obeyed and soon a column of warriors was marching down the north side of the hill with the archers, mainly women, doing it behind them.

*

In the city, commander Marum had another meeting with the three Ministers in the safe house they had used since his arrival. This time there were two young boys of about thirteen years of age.

"I have arranged for many of the city dwellers to gather whatever kind of weapons they can find, though so far what they have is bamboo spears though many of them have swords and they know where to gather when the signal for the uprising is given," explained the Prime Minister.

"I have done the same," said the Minister for the Interior.

"Same here," corroborated the Foreign Minister.

"I must say I'm happy with your news and now all we have to do is wait"

The minister for the exterior was curious. "I know we must be patient and wait but so far we are following your instructions without knowing what the resistance is doing outside the city. You said they are organising themselves in the hills west of the forest but we haven't heard from them."

"Calm down my friend. I will find a couple of messengers and I hope that soon we'll have some answers."

The two boys reacted with enthusiasm. "We can do it," said one of them.

"There," said Marum, "I have the messengers"

The ministers left and Marum spoke to the man of the house. "Now as soon as the messengers are ready you will instruct some of the city dwellers to make some commotion in the street to distract the soldiers in the battlements so the messengers can get away using the canal."

Marum called the two young boys into the room. "What are your names?"

"I'm Daba."

"And I'm Insa."

"Very well, I hope you are fast and above all you must be sure that you can do it."

"Do what?" asked Daba.

"To leave the city and go west well after the prairie to where the resistance people are. The point is, do you know the way?"

"No," said Insa.

"Yes, we can do it because we know how to go west without going through the forest and all we need is enough food and water," said the boy Dana.

Insa agreed with him. "Yes, you are right, we can do it."

"I'm curious and really want to know more on how you could do it without getting into the forest?"

"We've been west many times by following the coast," said Daba, "and now we are supposed to go further. Simple."

"This will be a great adventure," said Insa.

Marum was surprised. "Adventure?" and then he smiled. "Of course, it will be a great adventure though very dangerous and you'll have to be on the alert at all times. You can be captured and who knows, maybe tortured or maybe even killed. If that happens, then we'll be left without any communication and you must take into consideration that even outside the forest it will take you a great part of the day to do it."

The two boys look at each other this time very seriously. "We know," said Daba.

"And we'll be careful," corroborated Insa.

"What we need is some chopped wood to put on our heads as a camouflage," said the first boy.

"I'll help you with that," said the man of the house and with the boys approached the pile of wood at one side of the room and soon the boys had made a big hat with many twigs to cover their heads.

Marum look at them very seriously for a moment. "Very well, the message is that here in the city we are getting ready for the uprising but when the moment comes, we'll need to wait until the city is attacked because there are not enough volunteers for all the fighting. Do you understand?" The two boys nodded vigorously. "All right, off you go but you must wait until some people create a commotion in the street."

"Now go and create the havoc these boys need." He said to the man of the house that immediately left.

*

The two boys left the house and making sure the soldiers in the battlements were not looking they sat on some boxes at the side of the canal. They didn't have to wait long and soon they heard the noises of people squabbling and as soon as they saw the soldiers on the battlements running towards the main gates they stepped down to the canal with the twig hats making them look like floating debris. They had the help of some vegetation debris floating by and the brown colour of the water to cover them completely.

They moved further on to the road bridge and after they just followed the canal keeping themselves close to the bushes at the side of it.

A soldier saw the floating debris and raised the alarm. Many soldiers came to that part of the battements and look at the bundles of debris floating away from the city. By then the boys were too far to be seen.

The soldier's commander became irritated. "You, stupid man! You raised the alarm for some debris floating away from the city? I thought it was an army attacking us!" he said all that while slapping the soldier over his head and shoulders applauded by the rest of his laughing men.

*

The boys exited the canal on the left where there were some empty boats moored at either side.

"The water is very cold and full of silt."

"I know Insa but the air is warm and soon our clothes will dry."

"Yeah and the silt will dry so we'll be covered in dust."

*

Though they were at a safe distance from the city, they carried on for a while using the undulating land to prevent any soldier on the battlements to see them until they reached the coast.

"From now on," said the boy Daba, "there is only one way to go and that is that way," he said pointing west.

They moved towards the fishing village and in silence passed it walking close to the sea.

They followed the coastline using a path made by many years of people walking going east or west or maybe just admiring the sea.

For them it was beautiful to see waves braking against the rocks forming a white froth.

"I wish we were here in peace time so we could have done some fishing."

"Yes, Insa I know."

*

The two boys were doing all right walking close to the coast and it didn't take long for them to reach the north edge of the forest with plenty of trees reaching close to the coast.

"This is the best way to go west Daba."

"I know because inside the forest it could take longer by walking around the hills."

*

Their fears became real when they saw some enemy soldiers watching the sea and they stopped.

"I think we'd better stay here and wait until they go back to wherever they are supposed to be."

"That's right Insa but what about if they don't?"

"In that case we'll wait until nightfall and then we can bypass them without being seen."

*

Marum was in Amina's home teaching her some new tricks about how to use the sword, which for her parents it was very entertaining.

"I can see that you had some practice already but I will teach you a few tricks that probably the enemy soldiers don't know but don't you take it for granted."

"Thank you, commander and I'm sure the Queen will like them."

"I'm sure she will."

"Of course, she is very eager to learn and so far, the old man Mangro has brought some swords into the palace. She really wants to fight for the people with a sword in her hand and she is already thinking on how to turn the palace into a fortress when the uprising starts."

"I'm very surprised to hear that and I feel very proud of the Queen we have.

*

They carried on with the lessons and for commander Marum it was a bit too much because she was more agile than he was.

"All right, we'll stop now. I think you have learned something today."

"Thank you, commander," she said breathing heavily, "and now I think it will be the right time for you to come with me."

Marum was surprised for a moment. "To go where?"

Remember you ask me about getting some sleeping drugs?"

Marum opened his eyes wide and smiled. "Yes, I do remember."

"Well now, come with me to the old woman's home."

*

They left the house in silence and Marum followed her at certain distance, though they had to stop several times to let the enemy patrols pass by until they reached a house in one of the city suburbs.

Inside, the place was stuffed with many dry plants and herbs hanging from the ceiling and there was a small cauldron on an open fire in the centre of it.

The place was very smoky and because there was no chimney, the smoke was leaving through the tiles in the roof. Nevertheless, it was a very hot place where they could smell many different herbs, some pleasant and others not so pleasant.

A very old woman entered the room. "Sit down commander and tell me what you want."

Commander Marum and Amina sat on a small bench.

"What I need is something we can put in the wine to put people to sleep without killing anybody."

The woman thought about it for a brief moment and then she went to some shelves full of flasks of different sizes and colours, taking one made of red glass.

"This will do the job but you must not put more than three drops into each bottle and these will be enough," and she pour some of the liquid into a smaller bottle.

Commander Marum holds the little bottle in his hand for a moment. "Tell me, how much do you want for it?"

The woman smiled at him. "Nothing because I know you will use it for the benefit of the people. This is my way to help the resistance; now go and do your best."

Amina sniff the air close to the cauldron. "Is this something magical?"

The old woman looks at her and then at the cauldron. "I sincerely hope so because it is my meal."

Marum stood up and bowed to the old woman. "Thank you in the name of the people."

He gave the little bottle to Amina who put it in one of her pockets. "You know what to do with it and now go back to the palace."

In a moment, Amina had left the house holding the empty jar and soon after, commander Marum did the same in a different direction.

*

Amina reached the avenue between the square and the palace when some soldiers blocked her path and she managed to avoid them by smiling. "Sorry, I cannot stop."

"We heard you did some dancing in the city square."

"Is there any chance for you to dance for us?" asked another.

She quickly answered them smiling though without stopping. "Of course. I'll be back as soon as possible and as usual I will dance in the square."

"All right," said the soldier. "We'll be there."

*

Amina reached the palace and went straight to the Queen. "I was given this little bottle with a sleeping drug to put in the soldier's wine when the time comes."

"Very well," said the Queen. "Nadia give it to the servants dealing with the wine and make sure they will put it in the soldiers' bottles and not ours," she said gleefully, "but before you do that we better do some practicing with the swords."

*

Without wasting any time, the Queen with Amina and the other attendants went to the special room. By now, they had already four swords.

Amina was in command and ordered them to stand in a line in front of her, with the Queen in the centre of it.

"All right, now follow my movements," and she started to show how to attack and how to block.

Trying military precision, they all followed her movements and the attendants without a sword had to contempt themselves with a piece of wood, like dusters.

Nadia started giggling.

"What'd funny Nadia," the Queen asked.

"It could be very funny for me to fight an enemy soldier with a duster."

"Yes," said a laughing Amina, "with the dust in it you will make him sneeze.

*

In the meantime, those soldiers admiring the sea from the top of the cliff had prevented the two boys from carrying on and they had no choice but to wait until those soldiers decide to leave or wait for the night to give them cover to carry on with their mission.

"There must be a way for us to overtake them."

"Yes, Daba but for the time being we must wait."

"I'm happy to see that my clothes are already dry,"

"Mine too but we must get rid of the dust," said Insa while slapping his chest and arms though trying not to make any noise."

To their despair, the soldiers made camp and soon they had a fire burning.

"Well? There is your answer."

"Yes, I know."

They were preparing themselves to stay there for who knows how long when a group of more soldiers arrived.

"What do you think you are doing?" asked their commander, "you'll put that fire out right now and come with us! You are not here for a holiday by the sea!"

Reluctantly the soldiers put the fire out and left following their commander.

The two boys waited until all the soldiers were gone and slowly, cautiously at first, they left their hiding continuing their journey west.

*

Pearl's father had done a very good job with his visit to the fishing village. Those fishermen had left the cove and it was quite a spectacle to see out at sea many boats with their sails up packed with people and as Harmon had advised, they started to fish at sea.

The last resource of food for the enemy army has been cut off.

*

It was past midday and the sun was getting higher in the firmament and the temperature on the prairie was doing the same.

"We have run out of water," mentioned Pearl and Eloy looked back without stopping and saw some of the warriors drying their forehead with the back of their hands while others were shaking their water bottles, listening.

"Yes, Pearl, you are right but you must understand I don't know these lands and so I don't know if we will find a stream or not but don't tell them; just wait until they start complaining."

Pearl nodded and they just carried on.

"We are going to those snowy mountains," mentioned Bo.

"Yes," said Eloy sarcastically. "I've noticed."

Pearl whispered to him. "If we are coming closer to the mountains it means we will eventually find a stream."

"Yes, Pearl I know but still they have not complained."

Eloy stopped and so did the rest of the group.

"Why are we stopping?" commander Lera wanted to know with the rest of the group nodding and murmuring.

For a moment, Eloy didn't know what to say but had no choice. "In reality, I don't know which way to go. So far all we know is to go south and considering we have no directions south is south and that's it."

They all murmured once again and commander Lera spoke. "Aren't we supposed to look for more stones with something written on them?"

"Not necessarily," said commander Barum.

They all looked at Eloy who felt embarrassed. "What?"

Pearl stepped forward. "You are the leader and whatever you decide, we'll follow."

The rest of the warriors murmured and nodded.

Eloy just shrugged his shoulders. "All right, let's carry on and see what we will see."

*

They had walked for several hours, the hills before the mountains were getting closer and the land was changing. They were leaving the prairie and coming close to the hills before the mountains. It was already the afternoon.

Eloy noticed that there was no path. "If we keep an eye on the hills we might find a path between them."

"Look," said commander Lera, "over there just before the hills."

In the distance, they noticed a mound with some trees all around.

"Now that's a place to look," was commander Lera's opinion.

*

Without saying a word, Eloy led them towards it and they didn't complain about the walking.

They arrived and all what they saw was the mound.

"I don't know but it looks like a tomb," was the prince opinion.They walked all around but there were no signs on it.

"What do we do now," asked commander Bo.

"What we'll do right now," said Eloy, "is to rest and have something to eat.

They followed his instructions and Eloy had an idea. "Pearl come with me. We'll do some exploring."

"I really don't know what we are looking for."

"Neither do I but we must carry on looking."

"Perhaps if we climb the mound we will see better into the distance."

"All right let's do it."

They climbed to the top and for their surprise; there was a pond.

"I wonder if we can drink of this water."

"Smell it first. The smell will tell you."

So she did and pulled an ugly face. "Argh, stagnant water."

Eloy started to walk around and suddenly he noticed something unusual. "Come here, you've got to see this!"

Pearl joined him. "What am I supposed to look for?"

"Look at the shape of the pond."

She looked for a few moments and then she opened her eyes wide. "It has the shape of an arrow."

"That's right and that is our sign. The arrow is pointing straight between those hills further south east of the prairie."

They went to stand at the tip of the watery arrow and look into the distance.

All I see is hills with a gap in between and the mountains behind," said Pearl.

"Pearl, I'm sure we'll find something in between those hills, otherwise the arrow wouldn't point in that direction."

"To make a mound with a pond in the shape of an arrow to show us the way was clever."

He was looking towards the mountains and noticed many stormy clouds. "There is some rain in the mountains."

"It's all right with me," said Pearl, "as long as the rain stays in the mountains we won't get wet."

Eloy stopped. "I haven't been here or in those mountains but I remember people talking about torrents coming down between the hills though the sun was shining and all because of rain in the mountains and that is dangerous."

Though they saw everything covered with grass and bushes they noticed some more green vegetation in between those two hills with more bushes and some trees.

They returned to the group. "We know the way and I'm sure we'll find water over there. Follow us."

"More walking," said commander Barum sounding very unhappy.

Eloy heard him. "Yes, commander but the more walking we do the closer we are to find the sword. Remember that every step is a step closer to our goal."

His words put some encouraging into them and enthusiastically they overtook him with spontaneous running at first and laughing like children.

"We are getting closer! We are getting closer!" was crying Lera.

"Just look at them," said Pearl, "they are just grown up children."

Soon they slowed down and it took them a couple of hours to reach the place they had seen between the hills and soon they reached much abundant vegetation but there was no running water.

"Where is the water?" asked Lera.

Eloy was prompt to answer before their mood changed.

"Underground, start digging," he said pointing to a place with some sand.

Pearl was curious. "I don't see any stream."

"Don't have too. If you see bushes and trees it means, there is some underground water. Come on, they will be happy to know we are going in the right direction to find the sword."

They dug frantically and soon they reached the waterbed that was very muddy. Being country people they knew they had to wait for it to clear but Eloy knew they had no time to wait.

"Ready to carry on boys and girls? We cannot wait for the water to clear."

"But we need water," said Barum.

"Yes, I know but maybe we can find some further on. Come on."

"Just give me a moment," said Bo washing his hands. "Now that's better," he said sniffing his finger, "the smell of fish is gone."

They left following Eloy with their morale high.

*

In the meantime, the flotilla had arrived closer to the cavern and a fisherman as a lookout just outside the cavern saw them and run to tell the others.

Immediately some boats came out to join the flotilla.

Pearl's father standing at the bow of his boat gave some instructions. "When we reach the cove, you will keep the members of your family that can help with the fishing and send the rest with your children towards the village fortress where they will be safe and don't you forget to do plenty of fishing. The army will need plenty of food."

"We don't know the way," said a woman.

"That's not a problem because the people collecting shellfish from the rocks will eventually guide you when they go back to the hills."

*

The fishermen carried on with his instructions and sometimes later, they started to gather in the cove with Harmon fishing boats and this time looking like a proper fleet though made up of small fishing boats.

Harmon was ready to give more instructions.

"Some of you go out once more to do some fishing while the others will go inland to collect dry dead wood to smoke them."

"But how can we smoke them? We don't have a room where to do it," asked a fisherman.

"That's not a problem because some of you will start making some mortar in the nearby stream and we have plenty of stones by the seaside to make a room big enough for the smoking and make sure the walls are thick enough."

His instructions were followed and some boats left back to the sea and while other fishermen went inland for the wood; others started to make mortar with the water of the nearby stream that at the same time provided them with the drinking water.

Moments later a spacious room with thick walls started to take shape and thanks to the warm sun the mortar started to dry.

Not far from the seaside, there were some straight trees and some of the people went to get some for the roof.

*

With the camp well established it was just waiting for things to develop.

That was the moment for Harmon to leave. "I'm leaving now but I will see you later," he said and with the help of his men, they pushed the boats back into the water and a moment later, they were sailing towards the cavern.

*

In the city, things were getting worst and the people were really starving and the enemy soldiers had their food cut off as well because there was nobody coming into the city bringing anything. Their supply of fish had stopped.

The second in command approached General Agaram in his Palace room.

"Any news?"

"Yes, General we cannot get any fish from the fishermen."

"You must force them to do some fishing."

"I cannot do that, sir because there are no fishermen and the villages are empty; they have all gone to sea taking their families and we don't know where they might be."

The General stood up in a rage. "With all the power I have I cannot get any fish?" The General thought about it for a moment. "Though I have already sent some men to do some hunting in the forest, you will send a group of our soldiers to the forest and go hunting for any wild animal you can find and that will solve the problem." Then he had an idea. "You will send several small patrols into the forest to look for villages. They must have left some food in their homes before running away."

His second in command saluted in military fashion and left.

Moments later a group of soldiers on horseback left the city through the south gates and all of them had bows and plenty of arrows.

*

In the meantime, the Queen with the help of Amina were getting better in the use of the sword and Mangro the old man had managed to bring the rest of the swords into the palace.

The day was over and getting very dark.

By then the two enemy soldiers left outside the Queen's Chambers were more relaxed and the old man had managed very well to give them a bottle of wine every time he came to the chambers and as planned Nadia and another young woman had befriended them.

*

The system was working very well and every time Amina needed to leave the palace, Nadia and the other young woman lured the guards away to the kitchen to have something to eat.

*

Back in the village fortress Choquero had left his warriors to carry on training and was welcoming more people coming in and join them but his wife was not happy dealing with the feeding of all those people.

"We must do something my husband. We cannot feed all the people with just fish. They need bread and vegetables."

Choquero listened to her and carried on thinking about a solution while she carried on. "What about sending some warriors to the villages where the enemy has not entered and get what they have left behind? There must still be some potatoes in the ground and some vegetables and herbs as well."

Choquero expression brightened. "Very well I'll put several groups together to do that. In the meantime, find the owners of the animals we have in the corrals and buy a couple of cows and sheep, and goats."

"All right, I'll do it right now."

Immediately, he called for Loni his second in command. "Tomorrow with the first lights you will go and give protection to the groups of people going to the villages to collect any food left there."

*

In the meantime, the two boys carried on going deeper into the forest and suddenly when coming down a hill they heard the noise of many people not far from them and stopped to listen.

They carried on slowly and soon they realised they were enemy soldiers and they heard the sound of an animal screaming with pain. Those soldiers were there to hunt.

"Come," said Daba, "we must get away from here."

"Is there anything we can do to help that animal?"

"Don't be silly Insa, what can we do?"

*

At that moment, the fishermen's families arrived at the village fortress guided by the people carrying baskets with shellfish.

"Oh dear," said Mavina, "can you see the problem Choqui? More mouths to feed."

"It's all right Mavina we'll cope with it. You'll see." He embraced her. "Courage and faith in our cause is our main source of food Mavina but please do remember not to call me Choqui."

"As you wish commander," she said leaving and holding back her laughter.

*

Later on, and without knowing, the two boys passed close to the place with the entrance to the cavern and carried on towards the prairie. After all, they didn't know about the existence of the cavern.

*

They carried on until they reached the edge of the forest.

"There they are," said Insa pointing towards the hills and falling down on his back totally exhausted with Daba doing the same. "We'll rest for a while and have something to eat."

"It seems to me the prairie is a big place."

"Yes, Daba, nevertheless we don't have a choice and we'll have to cross it."

"Yes, I know and more reason for us to rest before we do it. we've being walking for most of the day."

They arrived on the north of the prairie and had come to the difficult terrain with rocks, bushes and trees on their right.

"Insa, I think those are the hills facing the sea."

"Yes, I think so too."

They changed direction and though still going towards the hills they did it walking on open prairie.

"You know what?"

"What Daba?"

"We'd better stay here for the night. My feet are aching and in this bay, we can be sheltered from any strong wind."

Insa look at his surroundings and agreed with his friend.

*

In the city, commander Marum was very busy visiting people in different homes while his men were training people in other homes in the use of the bow and swords.

*

In the palace, they were getting very short of food. There was no more meat and vegetables left but there was still plenty of fresh bread and quite a lot of wine in the wine cellar. Some of them were already surviving with bread and wine only.

*

Eloy and his entourage found it easy to walk to their destination because though they were leaving the prairie they didn't have obstacles blocking their path.

Finally, they have arrived at the foot of those hills.

"Here we are," said commander Barum, "and all we know is that we are walking between two hills and going who knows where."

"Yes," said Pearl, "but this time we are supposed to find the sword."

The sun is going down and we better find that sword soon," was Barum's opinion.

"If there is such thing as a sword," said commander Bo.

"Oh, come on," said Lera, "don't be so pessimistic. We all know he had the sword "Glorious" with him."

"Yes," said Barum, "but it wasn't in his tomb."

"Now that we don't know," said Pearl, "because we didn't open it."

"We know that," said Lera, "and I can guess that's why we are searching for it somewhere else."

"That's true," said Barum, "though I wouldn't like to look at a skeleton."

"Oh, I don't know. I wouldn't mind taking a look at my ancestor," was the prince's opinion. "After all bones are bones and they do no harm."

Suddenly they heard a rumbling sound and they could feel some vibration under their feet.

They stopped feeling nervous. "What's that noise?" asked Bo.

Eloy thought about it and started running to higher grounds.

"Quickly, run up the hill as high as you can!"

Pearls followed him and though some of the men and women hesitated for a moment, they too followed him.

The sound was coming close and seconds later, a torrential stream filled the land between the trees and they could see some tree branches and bushes floating on it.

"You were right Eloy," said Pearl. "So, what do we do now?"

"I can only give you my best opinion because I have never seen this and I can only guess it will eventually pass. This is the rain we saw earlier falling on the mountains."

"Well?" said Pearl looking at the others and giggling. "You wanted water and here it is!" her opinion was received by all of them with laughter.

He was right and a few moments later the torrent had passed and they could return though this time to a very wet ground but this time there was a stream of clear water.

"All right," said Eloy, "this is your chance to fill your bottles."

They were a happy bunch drinking and filling their bottles.

Prince Neno came close to Pearl. "When all this is over you should come to the palace and visit me."

Pearl felt a strange feeling. "I don't know but on the other hand I have never been in a palace."

"It's big and from the balconies you can not only see the city but well to the horizon all around."

She thought about it. "Now that could be something."

In the meantime, Eloy started to follow a very narrow path.

*

He carried on moving on the narrow path in between the hills and soon he reached a place at the side of the hill with fewer trees and stopped talking. It was a peaceful place only interrupted by some flying birds.

Eloy had advanced disappearing from their site and to his surprise, there was a small Monolith on higher grounds and he approached with great respect.

Some smaller rocks surrounded it and he could see there was some writing on one of them.

"Your quest is coming to the end and soon you will learn about what Glorious really means. From now on the last place for you to visit is on the east of this place. Prepare your mind and heart for it."

"Wow," said Pearl and Eloy turned to see that she with all the rest of the group had followed him in silence.

"Oh no, not another riddle," said commander Barum.

"What do you expect," said commander Bo. "So far, everything we have followed is a riddle and with quite a lot of walking."

"True," said Pearl, "and I have enjoyed every metre of it."

"I have learned something about our history," said Lera.

"And my feet are hurting," said Barum and they all look at him. "What? It's true they are hurting."

"I'm beginning to feel like a leader," said one of the young women.

Eloy look at all of them. "All of us are leaders from now on and because nobody else has come so far in search of something so important, the people will look at you for advice and children will ask for you to tell them about this adventure. Believe me my friends when I say that you are all very important in the quest to free our country from the invaders."

For a few moments, they all thought about his haranguing words.

Pearl broke that silence. "Come on put yourselves together; though we have learned something the quest is not finished yet."

They looked once again at Eloy making him feel more important than before and after a brief moment he just started to walk back to the prairie and they all followed him in silence with Neno left behind looking at the writings. "Strange but it tells us about the meaning of the word glorious, which is a bit strange."

Nobody heard him because they had all left and he quickly followed.

They reached the edge of the prairie and Eloy turned right going east.

The sun has started to go down in the west though they still had some daylight.

*

Later on, they could see the forest on their left touching the foot of the hills on their right.

It was easy for them to walk because there was another narrow path apparently made up by passing animals and it was getting darker.

*

Eloy and entourage had reached a place where the forest was almost touching the hills and they were walking under a canopy. Soon they saw a kind of a path with a hill on their left and a rocky cliff on their right.

Commander Lera pointed forward. "I think we should try this path. Maybe at the end of it we can find something."

"Like what?" asked Pearl.

"I don't know, some stone building or ruin. Perhaps another of Bonamor's hideouts?"

"So far, we haven't seen anything that might attract our attention," said Bo."

"What about Bonamor's tomb? What about the beauty of the hills and the beauty of the prairie?" asked commander Barum, "they really attract my attention."

"Same here," said Pearl admiring her surroundings, "though I was born and bred away from the city, the beauty of the land still amazes me."

They stopped and look at their surroundings and nodded.

Commander Barum had a thought. "According to what I've heard since I was a child. The sword was forged or created by the good magic of the earth and polished by the fairies and it was given to him by an old and wise woman living in a cave."

Eloy agreed. "Yes, we all know that part of the legend but what are you driving at?"

"Very simple; if the legend is true then we must be looking for a cave and in here we have a rocky face on our right to look for it."

They all look at each other and soon they were all nodding.

"Yes," said Pearl, "he's got a very good point."

Eloy reluctantly accepted their opinions. "All right then, let's go looking for a cave." Immediately he moved forward hoping they will not try to change the idea. "Remember one thing; we must keep an eye for any enemies that might come out of the forest. We know they are in it and it is possible for their commander to have send patrols to the south."

"Oh, come on," said Bo, "don't be so pessimistic; we can deal with any enemy patrol."

Commander Barum agreed with him. "He's right you know but only with a patrol."

Pearl walked faster taking the lead. "I think we are wasting too much time talking."

They stop talking and look at her; then they all followed.

The prince was prompt to follow her close behind.

But by instinct, they just carried on walking and soon found a path though difficult to see because of so much tall grass covering it with plenty of bushes and some trees at either side and still without any signs of a cave.

Commander Barum was not happy. "So far all we've done is walk."

"True," said commander Bo, "but in my case, I think it's been very good because I feel that I have lost some weight and I'm beginning to feel much lighter," he said and started doing some dancing for the group amusement. "And my feet are not aching anymore."

"Come on," said a giggling Pearl, "you are not the only one losing weight."

"Hey," said Lera, "maybe that's the intention with the quest, to keep us fit."

"I don't think so," said Bo.

"Neither do I," said Barum, "one thing is to lose weight and another is to fade away into thin air."

They all laugh.

"Now to fight the enemy like ghosts could be fun," was Lera's opinion.

"Come on, we're wasting time," said Pearl already ahead of them.

Eloy was deep in thought and suddenly he stopped.

Pearl looked back. "What is it?"

He stayed silent for a brief moment. "I think I can understand why all the walking going to so many different places. I know what it is."

Pearl cross her arms and look at him sympathetically. "It is a quest."

"Yes, Pearl, it is a quest but the point is what kind of quest."

The group stopped and gathered around him.

"The whole of it is to show us that when fighting an invader, we must change directions and attack in different places and that is precisely what we are supposed to do when we go into the offensive."

"Well now," said Lera, "it makes sense to me."

The other commanders and most of the group nodded.

"Yes, it makes sense to me too," said Barum.

"All right," said Pearl clapping her hands to call for their attention, "you had your little break and now we should carry on. Don't you think so?" She said the last words looking at Eloy who reacted quickly.

"Yes, Pearl is right. Let's go."

*

Eloy and friends had a part of the path with life size stone statues of warriors at either side, like silent guards holding a sword and a shield, surrounded with a very strange kind of silence. It was getting very dark and so the warriors started several torches.

Thick vegetation partially covered some of the statues and night was upon them with the moon starting to climb from the east.

They all finally slowed down and stopped.

"I don't know about you," said commander Lera, "I feel intimidated by these statues."

"I know what you mean," said Bo, "I feel that these rocks will come alive any moment now. It is like if they are under a spell."

"In my case the feeling is a bit different. It feels like walking on sacred ground," was Pearl's opinion and coming closer she touched the feet of one of the statues.

"Come," said Eloy, "I feel that in a way we are all safe from any enemies."

"Yeah," said Lera, "somehow I feel protected."

To continue they had to use their swords to chop their way forward.

*

They carried on slowly and soon they saw what it looked at first as a narrow crack in the rocks. Once again, they stopped and looked at Eloy.

"What are we doing now?" asked commander Lera.

Eloy simply shrugged his shoulders. "First we make up a few more torches and then we just go in hoping for the best. Personally, I don't feel any evil."

"Same here," said Pearl and with her usual personality she was the first to go in followed by the prince.

They did it slowly and very carefully though feeling somehow surrounded by peace.

It had taken them two days to reach this place.

It was not a cave but instead, it was an opening in the rocky heart of the hill; the further they went inside it turned into a cavern. Very wide in the bottom and at the top it was almost close. It looked like a magic place and they felt at peace.

"Somehow this reminds me of the cavern where the fishing boats are though here there isn't any water." was Pearl's opinion.

There were the remnants of a kind of a palace in the centre of it, all made of stones though partially collapsed.

Pearl was very curious.

"If this is the cavern where the sword was supposed to have been forged, where are the fairies or the wise old woman?"

"Yeah," said Barum, "and where is the forge and the anvil?"

"Barum," said Eloy, "according to the legend the sword was forged or created by the magic of the earth and not a person."

"Yes, I know that but what about the fairies who polished it; where are they? Fairies are not supposed to age."

"I don't know but I can give you an educated guess. It happened a long time ago and I don't think the old woman would have live so long. It happened more than two hundred years ago."

"And what about the fairies? As Pearl said they are supposed to be ageless," was Lera's opinion."

"Yes, that is what people believe but I don't think fairies really exist," was Eloy's opinion, "I've never seen one."

Pearl interrupted their conversation. "Why don't we look for anything that might tell us something about the sword instead of talking about it?"

"Yes, I agree with her," said commander Bo and immediately they all started to spread and explore this strange place.

Pearl had her own opinion about fairies. "I don't know about you but to me it is a little bit odd to talk about fairies because as Eloy said we have never seen one."

*

The ground was completely flat and it gave the idea of many people walking on it for hundreds of years.

At the bottom of the cavern, they found some more stone ruins that it looked to them as the remnants of an altar.

"Well? Here we are," said commander Bo, "and I don't see anything to tell us about the sword."

"What we need is a few moments of rest and the time to think about it," were Eloy instructions and they all sat on the ground to have something to eat.

Pearl sat close to the prince. "Quite an adventure."

Prince Neno looked around nodding. "Yes, though a very interesting one and in a way, I must be thankful to the invaders."

They all stopped doing whatever they were doing and looked at him, making him feel embarrassed. "What I mean is that without the invasion I would have been in the palace instead of been here with you in a so important quest."

"He's got a point," said Lera.

They all look at each other and nodded.

Eloy had a thought. "It seems to me that even from evil some good can come out."

*

They carried on wondering inside the cavern well-lit by many torches and a good fire just outside the ruins and Pearl was very close to him.

"I cannot see anything that might tell us about the sword."

"I know but I have the feeling that there is something in here that we have not noticed."

They carried on walking slowly.

"There," Pearl pointed her hand, "can you see that light behind the ruins, shining out of that opening in the rocks at the very end of the cavern?"

Eloy looked and nodded. "Yes, come on let's have a look."

They approached the place with that light and saw it was coming from between a crack in the rocks and though it was narrow, they managed very well to squeeze through.

"I can guess this place was not meant for fat people," was her opinion.

*

What they saw was well away from anything they had seen in their lives or imagination. It was a small cave and a bright light was emanating from cracks in the walls like pure magic.

They had to wait for a moment for their eyes to get used to it.

In front of them was a small throne made of stone and on it was the skeleton of a woman dressed with richly ornamented clothes and showing very long grey hair.

At its side was a pole with a flag on it. It was white and had a blue shield with a golden crown in the centre and a shining sun on top of it with golden rays pointing in all directions.

They didn't know what to say and just stood there impressed with their surroundings.

"It looks like the skeleton of a woman," Pearl managed to mumble.

Prince Neno nodded. "Looks like it."

In front of the throne was a small wooden box with the word "Glorious" carved on the lid.

"We found the sword," said Bo right behind them.

"You think the sword is in there?" asked a very nervous Pearl.

Eloy looked at it for a moment but he didn't move. "No, I don't think so it's too short for it."

"Go on try it. Maybe it is not a sword but a dagger instead?"

Eloy was feeling very apprehensive. "All this looks like very powerful magic and it could be dangerous."

They remained in silence for a moment and Pearl tried to gain some courage. "I don't feel any danger but peace instead and there's only one way to find out."

Eloy was getting excited. "I know."

At that moment, all the rest of the group came in keeping silent.

Prince Neno came close to Pearl and put his left arm on her shoulders. She opened her eyes wide and then smiled.

A short moment later Eloy put some courage together and approached the box but still looking at the skeleton very nervously. "I hope you don't mind."

"Why are you talking to a pile of bones?"

"I don't know. A kind of respect I think."

He kneeled in front of the box and slowly lifted its lid. "Do you see it?"

Without answering, he put his right hand inside and slowly brought out a scroll.

Pearl approached him with wide-open eyes. "A scroll?" then she looked inside the box. "Where is the sword?"

The people in the entourage started murmuring.

Eloy was trying to open the scroll but he had to be very careful because it was made of animal hide and it was very dry.

"Why are you doing it so slowly?"

"Because it's made of animal hide and been so old it is easy to break," he said and started to exhale and blow softly to put some moist in it.

It took some time and finally he managed to have enough of it unrolled and he felt happy. "At least it is written in our language."

He took a moment and started reading.

"You have reached your final destination and now it is the right time for you to know the truth. Glorious was the title given to the hero Bonamor and now you are the one to take the title of Glorious and lead your people to victory.

The flag will be your emblem from now on and where ever you go people will know where you are. It is a symbol of freedom."

Eloy stood up holding the scroll and looked at all of them.

"Somehow I don't think this was meant for me because it doesn't say if it's meant for a man or a woman."

Pearl looked around and shrugged her shoulders. "I don't see any woman with us to be the leader of the resistance."

All the female archers look at each other for a brief moment and they all shook their heads.

For a moment, they all stood there just looking at him and then Pearl went down on one knee in front of him.

Immediately the rest of the warriors with Prince Neno did the same and Eloy felt a lump in his throat.

"Why you kneel to me? The scroll doesn't tell I am the one for that title. It could be you Pearl."

Pearl had her eyes welling. "No, Eloy I already told you that I don't want to be the leader and you have already been recognised as such."

"She's right," said the prince, "and we have already recognised you as our glorious leader."

Pearl stood up and spoke to the warriors. "Now we know the truth about the legend and we have the leader we need. Now it is the time to go back to the hills and carry on with the preparations for war."

She went to the throne and picked up the flag putting the pole on her shoulders. Because the flag was covered with some dust she had a sneezing fit.

*

They started to leave and Eloy was the last. He turned to look at the skeleton on the throne and respectfully bowed to it. Then to his surprise, an apparition started to take human form at the side of the throne and he could distinguish an old black woman with long grey hair smiling at him and wearing the same clothes as the skeleton though with brighter colours and surrounded by little colourful fairies.

"Go and fulfil your destiny glorious warrior," she said with a voice that sounded more like a strong whisper.

Eloy could not articulate any words and the apparition faded away.

*

He joined the others and Pearl noticed something in his expression. "You saw something we didn't."

Eloy looked at her with a very serene expression. "Yes, the ghost of the old woman talked to me and she was surrounded by fairies; very impressive, very magical."

Pearl came close to him and gave him a kiss on the cheek. "You've been touched by the magic of the earth and that confirms you are our leader."

Commander Lera did the same by kissing him on the other cheek. "I'm very proud to be close to you."

Commander Bo shook his head. "Incredible but after all the walking searching for a sword we didn't know that we had the glorious always with us."

Pearl agreed. "That's true, nevertheless, all the walking has created a stronger bond with all of us."

"It is a very strong bond indeed," said Lera looking at Eloy with a bright expression.

Prince Neno touched his chest with his right hand and bowed to him with Barum and Bo. Soon all the rest of the group did the same.

*

By then the place had become very dark though they could see the entrance.

"I think we better go back to the village fortress," said Pearl.

"Pearl is right," said Eloy, "let's go."

By the time they came out of the cavern, a beautiful bigger crescent moon was shining over the land.

They just moved towards the exit and soon they were moving towards the prairie.

"Come on." said Eloy, "we have a long walk ahead and we don't need any torches from now on because the moon will be enough," was Eloy instruction and all the torches were put out.

"I can guess that now we'll go straight back to the village fortress," said commander Lera."

Commander Barum was happy to hear it. "Good because we are down to the last drop of water and almost no food left."

"Not to worry," said Eloy, "from now on our journey will be in a straight line and soon we'll be coming close to the streams in the prairie with fresh water."

"I think everybody will be very happy to know we have a glorious leader," was Lera's opinion.

Commander Bo was more preoccupied with the war than anything else. "By now we should have enough warriors to challenge the enemy in the forest."

"Yes, that's true but first we must make sure all the people in the kingdom of Onuvar get the good news about our leader," said Lera, "that will encourage them to join us in the hills."

"I guess that by now commander Marum has done some organising in the city," was commander Bo's opinion.

"Of course, he would have," said Lera. "Nevertheless, still we have a lot of work to do. We have an army to finish organising and we must not forget about our navy."

Eloy who was in the front heard her and stopped. "Our navy? All we have is some fishermen boats."

"Lera is right Eloy. They are fishing boats but nevertheless, I expect for them to transport part of our army to a place close to the city and that to me is a navy."

"Yes, Pearl to take us closer to the city." Then he realised all of them were staring at him and shrugged his shoulders. "All right, we have a navy."

*

Eloy and entourage had reached a place in the prairie where they could stop and have some rest and eat something. Mostly bread.

Lera was happy looking at her surroundings. "I like the prairie. I like to look at the stars."

"All right," said Eloy, "we'll stay here until the morning. Close to this stream we'll have some shelter from the wind."

There was no comment because they were all lying down and trying to get some sleep.

Chapter Nine

Early in the morning, Loni was leaving the village fortress leading a group of thirty warriors protecting some villagers and two four wheeled wagons pulled by mules. All of them were from villages in the south of the forest and they did it moving slowly.

*

Eloy and friends had somehow a comfortable night sleep and after having something to eat that was mainly dry and hard bread pushed down with plain water, they carried on though slowly.

*

North of the prairie, the two boys had already crossed part of it going towards the hills. Suddenly they encountered the group of warriors led by Loni protecting the wagons going to get food, coming out of the road from the village fortress.

"Are you lost?" asked commander Loni.

"No," said Insa, "we have a message for the people in the hills from commander Marum."

"But coming this way we saw some enemies hunting and they managed to kill an animal," said Daba.

"Thank you, boys and he addressed his warriors. "You heard the boys so we'll go further south before we enter the forest."

"Very good boys," said Loni, "you just carry on in the direction you are going and soon you'll find the road to go up. From there on you cannot go wrong.

*

The boys carried on for a while and stopped for a moment looking at the hills.

"Insa, that's a long way to go."

"I know but do we have a choice?"

"Come on Insa we are nearly there."

*

It took a few hours for the group of warriors and villagers to reach further south of the forest and entered following a path at the side of one of the many streams cutting a gorge in between the hills.

It didn't take long for them to find one of the villages and a few dogs welcome them by barking and wiggling their tales recognising the villagers.

*

This village was on some flat land between a stream and the foot of a hill and most of the vegetables were growing on terraces.

Soon after, and making sure there were no enemies, they divided themselves into several groups.

They started to collect everything they could carry. Most of it was flour in small barrels. Some of them went to the nearby terraces and started digging for potatoes, onions, carrots and parsnips, filling up as many sacks as they could carry on the wagons and a few more for the people to carry on their shoulders. Others went to collect as many lemons they could from many lemon trees including some fruit from other trees.

On one side of the village was a small plantation of coffee plants but they didn't have to collect any because for their surprise they found a few sacks with already roasted coffee.

The most important part of their collecting was to get a few horses feeding on the grass in some clearings close to the village.

A few warriors mounted some and gathered the other horses together in one place.

*

By then the two boys were halfway to the top of the hill. "I don't think I'll volunteer again. We've been walking since yesterday and I could not sleep properly and my feet are aching," said Insa."

"Yeah, the same here but we are the only connection with the city and so we must go on."

"Come on, we are nearly there. It's only a few more metres."

Daba looked at him. "A few more metres? It looks to me these metres are a bit longer than normal metres."

Insa looked at the hills. "You are right these will be the longest metres I have ever walked."

Forcing themselves forward they carried on though very slowly up the road and soon they were looking down the sharp slope at one side.

"I can guess this is one of the defences for the people up in the hills," was Daba's opinion.

Insa looked down and stepped back. "I agree entirely with you. I can see some graves in the bottom."

"In that case don't you fall down there or your grave will be joining the others."

*

They didn't have to go much further when some warriors aiming their arrows stopped them. "Who are you?" asked one of the archers.

"We have come with a message from commander Marum for the leader Eloy."

"Pass."

The boys carried on further up feeling very exhausted.

*

Some women saw them entering the village fortress and immediately run to help them and soon Choquero's wife came to them. "You poor boys."

Pearl's mother call from the communal table nearby. "Bring them here!"

They approached the table and sat while some women put a couple of wooden plates in front of them with some cooked fish.

By then there were several long tables close to the communal kitchen.

What are you doing here, did you come for refuge?" Sanila wanted to know.

"No, we come from the city and we have a message for Eloy the leader," said Insa.

Choquero heard them and approached. "Our leader isn't here but I am in command."

This time Daba spoke. "Commander Marum wants to know what's going on. He has organised some people in the city but there is nothing he can do until somebody attack the city first."

"Can you go back to the city with a message?"

Insa nodded. "Yes, we can but first we need some rest, my feet are aching."

"Of course, they need some rest," said Sanila, "part of the day is gone."

"Oh, I know that but when they are rested they will have to take the message." Then he looked at the boys smiling. "I hope you are fast."

"Oh, yes," said Daba giggling with Insa, "we had some practice."

"Of course, they are fast. They are young," said Mavina.

Choquero eyed the boys. "I can see you don't have any weapons."

"It's better for us not to have any. It's easier for us to run if we need to," was Insa's opinion.

"And we don't need any protection from the wild chickens in the forest," added Daba holding back his laughter.

*

After they had filled up one of the wagons, commander Loni send it back to the hills with half of the warriors carrying sacks on their shoulders while the riders guided the horses.

With the rest of the group, Loni carried on to another village south of the forest. This one is on flat land and cut right in the middle by a narrow river, made up by several streams coming from the prairie.

In this village, they found the same as in the previous one though this time they found many kitchen utensils and in a shed, they found steel bars.

"Now this will make the blacksmith very happy," was commander Loni's opinion.

As in the other village, most of what they found was flour in barrels and as before some of them went to dig for potatoes and other vegetables.

They also found several sacks with charcoal.

There were a few horses roaming close to the houses. They found many saddles in a shed and some warriors saddled some of the horses putting the rest of the saddles on the wagon. They found a few more horses that they easily rounded up.

Some of them went between the trees looking for eggs while others collected as many bananas as they could and finally they have put everything on the wagon and Loni signals for them to leave going back to the hills. This time his warriors too were carrying sacks with something on their shoulders.

The mounted men started herding the horses back to the hills and obviously, they were moving faster than everybody else was. This time they were using a different road meandering around the hills. By then the village dogs were with them and the sun was beginning to go down in the west.

*

Loni with some of his warriors were ready to leave the last village when a group of enemy archers arrived and started shooting their arrows.

For a moment, there was chaos but soon Loni and his few warriors recovered and started their retreat in a discipline way shooting their arrows using the trees as shields while the last wagon and warriors had reached the prairie.

Somehow, the enemy decided to retreat because they didn't know how many warriors they might face, giving Loni the opportunity to move faster.

*

Making sure nobody was following them, the warriors led by Loni came slowly out of the forest.

The crossing of the prairie was done as fast as possible and the horses had reached the hills first and the sentinels in the village fortress saw what was going on and Choquero asked for volunteers to go down to help.

Immediately some young women and men archers left running down the hill.

"I can guess that the warriors are overenthusiastic about getting into a fight," was Choquero's opinion and just sighed and nodded.

Soon those warriors had to move aside to let the horses pass.

*

In the meantime, Eloy and entourage were going in a straight line and as well coming closer to the hills.

"Once again it will take us most of the day to reach the village," was Bo's opinion.

"It's all right my friends," said Eloy, "this time we are not in a hurry and I hope our people are not in any sort of trouble."

*

The reinforcement with the female archers encountered the first wagon. "Where are the others?" asked one of them.

"The next wagon and some of the people are coming behind us but commander Loni is coming behind them to guard the rear," said one of the warriors. "But now with your help they might do a better fighting if they are attacked."

"Very well," said a female archer and while the male archers helped the first group to reach the village fortress. The female archers carried on trying to find Loni.

*

As the usual daily routine Amina went to the heart of the city and dance for the soldiers and a few city dwellers that had ventured out of their homes.

That sort of distraction was very helpful for the city dwellers preparing themselves for the day they will attack their enemy because every time she was dancing, most of the soldiers from the adjacent streets came to the square to see her dancing, giving the chance for some people to move using those streets without been noticed.

*

In the meantime, the crossing of the prairie was done without any dangers and soon the warriors with the second wagon had arrived at the village fortress.

Choquero was happy to see the horses. "If we can get some more we can have some cavalry."

*

In the prairie, the female archers found the other wagon and soon they found Loni's warriors already walking on the open, close to the south of the prairie. "What's going on?" asked the leading archer.

"The enemy is in the forest and they attack us but we managed and now we must do something to protect the animals in the forest," was Loni's explanation.

"All right but we must know where the animals are," asked the same archer.

Loni thought about it while looking at the forest. "I think the best place will be there right in front of us because we noticed that many of them had run north. We have seen others running south and, in my opinion, we must do it away from any path because probably the enemy is using them."

"Very well, what we must do is to find the enemy and when attacking them we must make a lot of noises for the animals still there to hear us and run towards safety in any direction."

"All right," said Loni, "let's do it. By the way what's your name?"

"My name is Alana."

All right Alana, from now on you'll stay close to me."

Alana opened her eyes with surprise and smiled.

Most of the day has gone and they were moving very carefully back to the forest led by him and advanced with their weapons ready back to where the enemy was supposed to be.

*

It took some time for them to go through that part of the forest and by then night was falling on them.

Finally, they found and engaged an enemy patrol that was not more than a small patrol and as planned, they did it with plenty of yelling.

They fought in the dark though the crescent moon was giving more light than the previous day.

Their attack worked very well because they not only scared the enemy but they saw a couple of gazelles running in a different direction.

Unfortunately, the enemy had managed to kill a couple of gazelles and they carry them hanging from thick bamboos.

"All right," said Loni, "we have them all on the run and now we'll go back to the hills."

*

Eloy's little fighting force decided to spend the night in another tranquil part of that magnificent prairie and choose a place where they found many ripe berries.

"Strange," said Barum, "but all this adventure has been to me like a holiday."

They all stayed silent for a moment, thinking about his words.

"In a way you are right," said Pearl, "because though we have done quite a lot of walking. It has been all done in peace."

Eloy was happy to hear their opinions. "You're right and I think this night I will sleep like a baby."

Lera started to laugh. "I only hope you won't wake us up in the middle of the night crying like a baby."

They all laugh while preparing themselves for the night.

*

Later on, Loni with his warriors and the female archers had arrived back to the village fortress and in the company of Alana reported to Choquero.

By then many torches and the fires in the communal kitchen lit the village. Some light was coming from the occupied houses as well.

"Thank you commander Loni. You have proved yourself as a good commander and now make sure your fighters get a good rest."

Loni and some of his warriors in the company of Alana passed on the side of the workshops.

"Thank you for the steel bars commander," said the blacksmith.

"It's all right and now you don't have to take the people's cutlery anymore," said a gleeful Loni.

The carpenter heard him. "It's all right. We are making some wooden spoons for the people."

It was getting late and everybody was preparing to sleep.

*

Commander Choquero approached the two boys. "I can guess that you are ready to go back to the city? If you do it in the night, you will have better chance not to be seen by any enemy patrol."

They nodded vigorously, showing plenty of energy.

"Very well then, listen to the message. The resistance is well and very much alive. Soon we'll be ready to march on the enemy and the attack must be coordinated with the rebellion in the city but for the time being all what commander Marum can do is to carry on organising until we send the final message to him, understood? You are the only contact we have with the city and so you must be very careful not to be captured." The two boys nodded smiling at each other.

Choquero's wife approaches them with a bundle. "Here, take this food."

As it was expected, they left running.

*

Later on, and well illuminated by the moon the two boys were walking at the edge of the forest and this time they did it closer to the rocky hills and it didn't take long for them to reach the place where the entrance to the cavern was and seen some guards outside they approached.

"Where are you going?" asked one of the guards.

"We are going to the city with a message from the people in the hills," said Insa.

"Come with me," said one of the guards. "The people in the cavern will be very happy to have some news about the people in the hills and from the city."

The two boys followed him and a moment later, they were surrounded by the fishermen and their families murmuring and asking questions.

Harmon put his arms up and they all listen. "Now boys, please tell us first about the resistance."

"There's not much to tell," said Daba.

"The people are getting organised by commander Choquero with several commanders and they have several groups of warriors practicing with their bows and swords," added Insa.

"We already know that but tell us, what about Eloy?" asked Harmon.

"Eloy the leader of the resistance has gone away in search of the magic sword "Glorious" and since his departure nobody has heard anything about him or the people with him."

All the people started once again to murmur very loudly and Harmon put his arms up to silence them. "Do carry on telling us more."

"Now we are supposed to go to the city and pass the news to commander Marum who is trying to organise the rebellion."

"So, there is something going on in the city," said Harmon.

Insa nodded vigorously. "Oh yes."

"The Ministers are organising some of the city dwellers and commander Marum warriors are mingling with the population teaching on how to use whatever weapon they have," added Daba.

"And most what they have is just bamboo spears," added Insa. "Though some of the city guards have spare swords and bows at home."

"Yes," said Daba, "and the Queen with some of her attendants are practicing with swords as well."

Those were the kinds of news those people were waiting for.

"Tell me," said Harmon, "how can you enter the city?"

"In the same way we exit. We use the canal that runs through the city," said Daba.

"And we put some twigs on our head looking like debris," added Insa.

"Thank you, boys," said Harmon, "now you'd better go but don't forget to stop and rest as many times as you can and get some sleep as well. I'll be going to the hills now taking some refugees with me and hopefully I'll see you later."

A woman gave them a small bundle of food. "Here, this is smoked fish and some smoked muscles but you must eat them soon. With the weather we have, you can only keep them for a short time."

The boys took the bundles and left guided by a guard.

*

From then on and because it was night, they had to be very careful not to trip or have an accident.

By then the almost full moon was lighting everything very well because only a few clouds were moving steadily going east though soon they had no choice but to find a place to spend the night.

Chapter Ten

By the time they woke up, the sun was already well above them.

"Boy, I needed that sleep," said Daba.

"Same here," said Insa while stretching his arms, "somehow that bed of dead leaves was very comfortable."

After having something to eat, they went further inside the forest looking for Bananas. Soon they found some in a clearing and spend some time eating to the point of bursting.

*

Harmon came out of the forest guiding some refugees and joined a small group of villagers on horseback going to the hills. "All right friends, I'm happy to see more people joining us and especially with horses. Very soon we'll have some cavalry but tell me, did you see any enemies in the forest?"

"Yes, we saw some of them in a gorge but we managed very well to avoid them because we were on top of a hill and they were too busy carrying a couple of dead animals."

*

In the village fortress, activity was plenty and some of the people had put the horses in a makeup corral outside the village fortress not far from the other animals, with many children coming to feed them.

*

By the time the boys passed the fishermen's village that was completely empty, the whole morning has gone and shortly after they reached the place by the canal.

From there they could see the city walls in the distance and stopped. "We must find the bundles of twigs to use as our camouflage," said Daba.

"True but we must put some short twigs with leaves to make a better camouflage." They look for the bundles and soon found them under a bush.

They were not in a hurry and so they sat to eat what they had.

*

In the palace, Amina was giving more instructions to the Queen and other attendants in the use of the sword though this time they were practicing with each other.

They stopped and Amina was ready to leave.

"Be careful Amina the city is becoming more dangerous."

"Not to worry my Queen, I'm always careful and many enemy soldiers already know me because of my dancing."

"Nevertheless, be careful."

She grabbed an empty jar from a table near the door and left the Queen's Chambers smiling at the two soldiers outside the doors. It was not necessary anymore for the Queen's attendants to distract them because by now they were used to see her.

"Going to the city Amina?" asked one of them.

"You know me this is the time to dance for the soldiers."

"Maybe one day you will dance for us," said one of them and Amina just waived her hands to them while leaving.

*

To go to the houses where she could meet commander Marum she had to go for water in the square well, where soldiers had acquired the habit to gather and wait for her.

This time there was no exception and as soon as they saw her, they started cheering and applauding. Somehow, the soldiers had kept that part of the square clean from manure most probably just for her dancing and obviously General Agaram let them be.

The musicians started first with their tambourines and then with flutes.

She left the jar at the side of the well and from that moment, she walked in a teasing way touching some of their faces and jumping away when some of them tried to grab her skirt.

Her dancing was exotic and sensual and the rhythm continues. That was the time for the resistance groups to move from one street to another without the enemy noticing anything. Some of them were carrying long bamboos and others longer bundles of twigs showing the tips of bows hiding inside.

*

Slowly, the boys approached and entered the canal with the bundles on their heads just above water, with the twigs on top. After negotiating the moored boats, they moved under the wall and entered the city doing it very slowly and though a couple of soldiers on the wall look at the bundles of twigs, they didn't notice they were moving against the current.

Suddenly one of the soldiers blinked his eyes and look at the canal outside the wall again but there were no bundles floating on it, only some vegetation debris. By then the boys had already left the canal and approach a house.

By the time the soldier went to the other side of the wall, the boys were already inside the safe house and getting warmer close to the fire in the hearth.

*

Moments later, commander Marum entered the safe house. "Any news from the resistance?"

"Yes, commander," said Daba.

Insa continued. "Commander Choquero is organising the people very well and by now they have more weapons taken from the enemy and some bought from merchants that joined them in the hills."

"And I saw two workshops," said Daba, "one making bows and arrows and the other making the tips for arrows and spears."

Insa interrupted. "Our leader Eloy has left the village and gone to the prairie where the tomb of Bonamor is, in search of the magic sword."

Marum felt enthusiastic. "All right, those are very good news and as soon as you are ready you will go back to them to let them know that we are almost ready. They must know that the Queen is all right and training in the use of the sword to be ready for when the time of the insurrection comes."

The people already know that because we told them," said Daba looking at Insa who smiled.

"We need some rest," said Insa.

"Of course; have some rest and as much food as you can get of course."

The boys started to enjoy some food though it was mostly bread pushed down with tea while the people in the house gave them clean clothes to change.

"Strange, we are changing clothes and maybe soon we'll be inside the canal once again."

"And all drenched," said Daba and they both laughed.

"Yes," said Amina's father grinning at them. "But by doing so you'll be the cleanest boys in the country."

"Oh, that's very encouraging: clean and very wet," was Insa's sarcastic opinion.

"And covered with dust when the water dries," was Daba's opinion.

*

In the meantime, Amina was coming to the end of her last dance and with many soldiers cheering and applauding her.

She finished the dancing and a couple of soldiers filled her jar with water and after collecting some of the coins she left walking coquettishly while throwing kisses making them whistle and howl.

A moment later, she arrived at her family home giving the jar of water and the money to her mother and sat to rest greeted by commander Marum.

"I'm happy to see you Amina but you look exhausted and I hope the enemy soldiers enjoyed your dancing."

She answered with a supercilious attitude. "Yes, commander I can guarantee that though I had to stop twice to regain my breath."

"Are you ready to practice with the sword?"

"Of course, I am," she said grabbing a stick and getting ready to start. She was after all a very strong and energetic young woman.

"We have good news from the resistance."

She gave a couple of strokes with the stick. "Come on, give me the news."

"The people are getting very well organised and our leader has gone to the prairie in search of the magic sword," said Marum attacking her very strongly with several strokes that she blocked very well.

"You are getting better," he said and attacked her again.

She blocked and attacked him. "Yes, I think so and I'm teaching the Queen everything I can though in the palace we are using real swords."

They stopped, feeling exhausted. "Let's sit down for a moment," said Marum and Amina's mother approached them with a couple of glasses with water.

"Tell me more about what the leader is doing."

"All I know is that he's gone to search for Bonamor's magic sword. It is supposed to be magical and with it, it is expected for more people to join him."

Amina thought about it. "What about if he doesn't find it."

Marum looked at her surprised and thought about it. "I don't know but thinking about that possibility, I think we'll have to carry on and do our best to expel the invader and free our country; magic sword or not."

"I understand commander and I will carry on training the Queen and the other girls."

The commander shrugged his shoulders and sighed. "Very well and I'll carry on organising the uprising in the city; let's hope for the best."

Amina left the house.

*

The two boys had left the city once again using their camouflage very carefully because they could be seen from the battlements.

This time they were lucky because the soldiers on the battlements gathering around a fire didn't bother to look.

It didn't take long for them to leave the canal. "Once again, we are wet," said Daba.

"I know but if we run towards the coast, we'll feel warm and our clothes will dry very quickly. After all the air is warm."

*

They managed to reach the coast and from there on, it was an almost straight walk to the west though they had to be careful with possible enemy patrols when going through the fishermen's village.

"This time we'll stop many times to recover." said Daba, "last time we did it too fast and my legs were aching.

"Good idea and we can do some sleeping at the edge of the forest."

"That means we won't enter the cavern where the fishermen are."

"It's okay with me although I don't want to eat more smoked fish."

They carried on at a steady pace though always listening for anything that might sound odd.

*

The boys carried on walking on the north of the forest stopping several times to rest and have something to eat; mostly bread.

The forest was very calm and soon they were following a small gorge without enemies or friendly warriors and they noticed some of the wild animals moving between the trees.

"Insa, now this is a good sign that the hunting has stopped."

"Yes, I agree with you."

"This time we are using a different way but we are still going west," was Insa's opinion.

"That's true but soon we must stop to rest once more."

They had reached a place where the charcoal maker had the smoky mounds and stopped for the night. After all, it was a warm place.

Chapter Eleven

With the first day light, in the village fortress, there was plenty of activity. After all there were many things to do and the would-be warriors were training with their weapons while others were feeding the animals.

Commander Choquero was doing his rounds in the company of Loni leading a couple of warriors and saw some people were still working in the rebuilding of the protective wall made of stones put together with mud.

"I'm happy to see the village is looking more like a fortress and hope Eloy will come back with the sword," said Loni.

"He's gone for nearly five days and I'm sure he's well protected," was Alana's opinion.

"I'm sure he is, after all some of the warriors left us without telling me and I'm sure they are with him."

Mavina came closer to her husband. "You've done very well Choqui and we have more people coming to join us."

Please Mavina don't call me Choqui."

*

After having some sleep, the boys restarted their walk.

They were fast walkers though it took some hours to cross the north of the forest. They had to stop to rest several times.

*

They reached the prairie and when they came out of it, Daba signalled for them to stop.

"What is it?"

"I can hear people."

They waited for a moment and they saw a group of villagers coming out of the trees riding horses.

Most of the group was made of younger women and children on foot and the two boys approached them. "Where are you going friends?"

An old woman walking with a staff was leading those people and signal for them to stop. "We are trying to find the resistance people to join them."

"All right friends, just follow us and we'll show you the way."

They took the lead and the old woman followed them with the rest of the people.

*

A sentinel came running towards Choquero. "Commander, some people are coming from the forest."

Immediately Choquero went to the ledge to look.

They could see those people moving and some of the warriors approached him, mainly female archers.

Immediately he instructed Loni. "You will go down to the prairie and give those people some protection; it could be our leader Eloy and they might attract the attention of any enemies that might be in the forest."

With a handful of male and female archers, Loni and Alana ran down to the prairie.

*

Eloy and entourage were walking without any difficulties when they saw those people going towards the hills and approach cautiously. Soon they heard some people talking and stopped.

Commander Barum run to the top of some higher terrain and looked.

"Who are you?" he asked the two boys ahead of those people.

The two boys approached him. "We are the messengers between the hills and the city and we are guiding these people to join the resistance."

Eloy and his group joined them and saw all those villagers led by the old woman. Above all, he was happy to see the horses. "Very well, now we'll do it together but there's still some more walking to be done."

The old woman stepped forward. "It's all right, though the children are tired I'm sure they will do all right. Some of them can ride on the horses behind the riders."

"We must hurry because if there are enemies in the forest they must have seen us."

"It's all right," said one of the boys, "we just came out if it and there are no signs of enemies and we saw some animals already returning."

*

They carried on and some of the warriors did something that impressed Eloy. They grabbed some of the smallest children and put them on their shoulders and some of the female warriors did something similar helping some mothers by taking their babies.

They didn't have much food left but they distribute what they have, like some small pieces of bread amongst the refugees.

*

Eloy's fears became real when some enemy archers came out of the forest and shoot some arrows wounding some of the people.

For a moment, there was panic but Pearl and Lera's archers turned back shooting their arrows forming a line of defence hitting some of the enemies.

Eloy reprimanded the two boys. "And you didn't see enemies in there?"

"Yes, that's right," said a very serious Daba but Insa had an idea.

"They probably come from the south or any other place."

"All right," said Eloy, "that's very probable."

They carried on as fast as they could to reach safety and were happy that their wounded were not badly hurt and though with some difficulty they managed to walk helped by some people.

Pearl and Lera's defence was very effective and the enemy retreated inside the forest.

At that moment, Loni with Alana and their archers coming down from the hills joined them and helped with the wounded.

It took some time before they reached the hills and shortly after they had reached the village fortress and safety. By then the sun was shining in all its splendour.

*

Commander Choquero was waiting at the village fortress entrance when he saw some refugees coming together with Eloy and entourage.

Immediately he called for his wife who approached them running. "Oh dear," she said looking at the women and children. Then she called for other women to join them. "Put some food on the tables for these people."

Immediately some women started to put on the long communal table some wooden plates with food and some fruit for the children."

Choquero gave some orders. "Take the horses to a corral outside on the north side!"

Pearl's mother came with other women to take care of the wounded. Some of those women had a white scarf around their necks.

In a few moments, the new arrivals were all sitting by the tables and standing around been fed by many women, with the commanders and seconds in command mingling with them.

Soon the newcomers had plenty of rest and above all enough food and thanks to the food brought in from the villages the new comers could eat salads and enjoy boiled potatoes as well.

Many people joining them with their happiness.

"I'm happy to see you back son. We saw some people coming across the prairie but didn't know which of the groups was you and that's why I send some of the archers to help but tell me where did you find these people? And above all where did you find that flag?"

"We found them in the prairie and the flag was in the cave where we found the scroll," explained Pearl keeping the flag straight up.

"From now on this will be our flag and symbol of freedom," said Eloy.

"In my opinion," said Prince Neno, "this could be our new national flag from now on and I'm sure my mother will like it as I do."

Eloy gave the pouch with the Pearls to his father. "We didn't have a chance to use them all father."

Harmon joined them. "Before I forget, here they are," said Choquero and gave Harmon the little pouch with the pearls.

"But I gave them to Eloy to buy some weapons."

"That's right and he gave them back to me."

"Eloy, why didn't you use them?"

"But I did and the other day, before we left, I used some of them to pay the merchants for some weapons. It wasn't necessary to use them all because we are giving them gold instead, gold that some people are getting from the streams down the hill. Those people saved some of the gold and donated it to the purchase of weapons and you know that from the encounters with the enemy we are getting some weapons directly from them." Then he giggled. "They have been very generous by losing them. Telling you the truth so far I don't understand how our boys managed to subdue some enemy soldiers because they are not yet fully trained fighters."

Choquero agreed with his son. "That's true but you must not forget that everybody is full of enthusiasm about fighting the invaders and that gives them some extra strength."

*

Choquero addressed the boys. "All right boys, this is the time for you to pass your message and I hope you have good news from the city."

"The message is very simple," said the boy Insa.

Daba carried on. "The Queen is training in the use of the sword with her attendants and she will be ready to defend herself in the palace. The palace guards are all preparing for any eventuality."

"These boys are the best messengers we could have and I'm happy to hear that the Queen is preparing herself to do some fighting," said Eloy, "but I would like to know what will she do; will she join commander Marum fighting in the streets or will she entrench herself in the palace with her guards?"

The two boys looked at each other. "Ups," said Daba, "that means for us to go back to the city just to ask that question?"

"That's another day walking," said Insa, "or night."

"I'm sorry boys," said Choquero, "but I thought you were enjoying been the messengers.

"But we are," said an enthusiastic Insa, "it's better than to be here most probably getting bored."

"And before you go I will give you more information for commander Marum. Now find some food and a place to rest."

The two boys left and the commanders stayed close to Eloy.

They all sat in a circle and a few curious people surround them.

"All right," said Choquero, "now we can talk about your adventure my son." Then he looked at him and Pearl. "All right, you have the flag but where is it?"

The commanders looked at Eloy and smiled. There was great expectation in the air.

"There isn't any sword," said Eloy and everybody become silent for a moment with their smiles wiped out of their faces.

Choquero just look at him and Eloy tried to explain. "We found the tomb and followed what it's written on a stone at the side of the sarcophagus."

"It was a riddle," said Barum.

"And we followed it in what it looked like a quest that took us five days to complete," added Lera.

More people joined them getting impatient and Choquero wanted to know more. "So, you went into a quest but what did you find?"

Once again, there was some silence between them and Eloy spoke. "It was a very strange quest because we had to go first to the south west and finally after been in the south we ended at the south east in a place between tall hills where we found a cavern."

"Yes, though we didn't have to go north," said Pearl, "because six days ago we already found what was in the north so this time we just picked it up from the west."

Somehow, her explanation was a little bit confused for all of them to understand.

"Yes, that's the way it happened," said Eloy very calmly.

"And there, at the end of our quest, everything was revealed," said Pearl solemnly.

They were all very calm but Choquero wasn't and he was becoming very excited. "Come on, tell us. What was revealed?"

"I will tell you but give me a moment," said Eloy and started. "We found a cavern and there was a small place in it with a throne made of stones and the skeleton of a woman sitting on it."

Pearl was desperate to talk. "In front of it there was a wooden box with the word Glorious sculpted on it, that Eloy opened," then she saw Eloy looking at her. "Sorry, do carry on."

Eloy coughed to clear his throat and continued. "Inside the box there was a scroll that explained the legend."

Commander Barum couldn't wait. "The scroll explained that there was no sword and the word Glorious was given to Bonamor and now Eloy has inherited the title. He is the glorious warrior to lead us into victory."

"What did you do with the scroll?" asked Harmon.

"He putted back in the box," said Barum.

"Why?" Choquero wanted to know.

Eloy shrugged his shoulders and smiled. "Because to me that place is a sacred shrine and if somebody wants to see it, it would be easy to go there. Well, there it is; that's the whole of the story."

Choquero smiled and sighed. "Well, I can guess that from now on we must get use to the reality of the legend and look at my son as the glorious leader the people have been waiting for, to lead us into war to liberate our country."

"Yes," said Pearl, "and I don't know about all of you but our glorious leader needs some rest and so do I."

Eloy shook his head feeling dismayed. "Please Pearl don't call me that."

She ignored his words and stood up with the commanders doing the same. "Come on."

*

In the city, the enemy General was doing his round walking on the battlements followed by his personal bodyguards.

"You must keep an eye on the city surroundings. I'm sure that some stupid people will try something stupid and if they do it we'll give them a bloody nose! We have conquered this country and now it is ours!"

The soldiers on that part of the walls cheered him.

He carried on inspecting the walls defences by walking all around the city and he could see in each tower was a catapult with a steal frame on a pedestal, used to burn wood in the night, strong enough to illuminate the battlement though by now those fires were off.

*

The Queen was on one of the balconies from where she could see the General on the wall behind the palace.

"There he goes wallowing in his power but his time will come and I strongly believe that very soon we will be ready."

Amina was close to her with the other attendants. "Yes, Your Majesty and I'm sure more people are joining the rebels in the hills; I'm sure that Eloy will eventually find the sword Glorious and use it to lead the people in rebellion."

"Yes, I hope he finds it and I hope the sword will be powerful enough."

*

Many people were very busy in the rebels' village that by now was beginning to look more like a village fortress with its wall getting taller; in some places, it was being built on taller rocks.

Eloy came out of the palace stretching his arms as much as he could and was very surprised to see his mother with Pearl's mother directing other women already preparing food in the communal kitchen.

Commander Bo approached him. "I think it will be a good idea to finally finish organising the warriors we have and send a few to the forest to search for enemies to get more experience."

"Yes, commander, it will be a good experience for them."

"Experience for whom?" asked commander Barum joining them.

"Commander Bo had the good idea to suggest sending some of the warriors to the forest to have some scuffle with the enemy to gain more experience."

"Yeah, Good idea," said Barum, "I'll choose some of my warriors with no experience."

"Take some of my archers," said Lera joining them.

"And let's not forget to put somebody already with some experience to give them some advice," was Bo's opinion.

"Now that's a very good idea," said Eloy feeling energetic. "All right, after you send some of your warriors I want to see the rest of our army and see if they are well trained or not."

"Commander Choquero has been very busy training them," was Loni's opinion.

*

Moments later, some warriors were leaving the village fortress led by Barum and Bo with Loni and Alana close to them.

Eloy with Lera and the prince were leaving as well though in different direction.

"Are you coming with us Harmon?" asked Eloy, "we are going to review the army in training."

"No, I'm a sailor, not a warrior."

Choquero came along. "If you want to see our warriors practicing you better come with me."

Harmon sighed. "Oh, very well."

Eloy and friends went down to the training grounds on the north side of the hill.

The warriors were all formed showing some organisation and Eloy was happy with it.

"All we need now is to have news from commander Marum to plan our attack."

They left the warriors to carry on with their training and went back inside de village.

The two boys approached them ready to go and commander Choquero gave his message.

"All right boys, now you will find out more about what commander Marum's warriors are doing in the city and what the Queen is planning and you will tell him about the reality of Glorious and that the army is ready with a small group inside the forest gaining experience by attacking any enemy they can find there with skirmishing. Got all that?"

The two boys nodded vigorously and left running for Eloy's amusement.

"At least they have plenty of energy."

"Come," said Eloy, "let's take a look at the warriors in the prairie."

Pearl joined them and with her, they went to the ledge from where they could see a great part of the prairie.

It didn't take long for them to see the warriors starting the crossing.

"Incredible," said Pearl, "only a few days ago we were all running away from the invader and now we have an army and, in a way, we are attacking."

Eloy agreed with her. "Yes, Pearl, you are right. We do have an army though a very small one."

"Yes," said the prince, "it is small but this is only the beginning."

*

Commanders Barum and Bo were crossing the prairie and forming their men into two columns, ready to enter the forest.

"I will enter the forest on the left," said Barum.

"Good idea and I will do it on the right," said Bo.

Barum gave a new order. "You Loni take some of the warriors and enter the centre and slowly move south eventually joining with Bo."

Immediately Loni with Alana formed a small group of men and women. "Come on men, follow me!" he cried and then he realised his wrong. "I mean warriors," he said smiling at Alana who was grinning at him.

*

Back in the hills Eloy with his friends were standing on the ledge getting a good and panoramic view of the prairie and thanks to the sun climbing to the sky they could see the three groups of warriors moving towards the forest.

"Many hopes go with them."

Pearl nodded and spoke solemnly. "I hope they won't get too many wounded," then she showed a cheeky face. "I hope they will get more weapons for our army."

Eloy smiled. "Yes, let's hope for the best."

"Somehow," said the prince, "I wish I was with them."

*

Soon Barum was inside the forest and gave some instructions. "Two of you will go ahead to scout while we stay here and rest. I need and hour or so to have some sleep."

*

The two boys were crossing the prairie a bit further north of the warriors.

"Look over there," said Daba, "we'll be all right because those warriors will attract any enemy that might be in this part of the forest."

Once again, they were following the path already known to them and later on, they had come close to the cavern entrance.

"Now, we get inside the cavern and hope for somebody to give us something to eat," was Insa's opinion.

"I only hope it won't be smoked fish."

"Why? Don't you like fish?"

"Yes, I do like fish but so far most of what we have eaten is fish. I would like to have something else."

*

They were recognised by some guards outside the entrance that greet them.

"Hello boys, going to the city?"

"Yes, we are but we hope to get some food first," said Insa.

"Of course, you can. Just go in," said one of the guards.

The two boys entered the cavern enthusiastically. "I like fish."

"So do I Daba but we've been eating fish everywhere we go."

"Oh, stop complaining; at least we have some food wherever we go, remember the people in the city have almost nothing."

Danna thought it was funny. "Lucky for them, they don't have to smell of fish."

"Oh, you and your strange sense of humour."

They reached the fishermen and at their surprise, it wasn't fish that they were offered but roast chicken with boiled potatoes instead.

"Oh yes, please give me roast chicken and potatoes anytime," said Insa while Danna just nodded with his mouth full.

"I'll give you some pieces of the chicken for you to take to the city," said a woman and gave them two small bundles wrapped with banana leaves.

*

Commander Barum's men were advancing cautiously on top of a small hill without any established paths, spreading his warriors in between the trees.

"Remember to use the trees as your shield," were his instructions.

As a leader is supposed to do, Barum led his warriors from the front with his sword ready and a couple of female archers behind him.

*

Commander Bo was doing the same and his men carried on advancing following a very narrow path at the side of a small stream at the bottom of a ravine, with their swords ready. The rest of the female archers advanced close behind them. "Happy to have some archers with us," said one of his warriors.

"Yes, I know but when we attack the enemy archers they will be shooting at us and when that happens you must remember the timing for the enemy archers to put another arrow in the bow and that will give you enough time to rush them."

Then he calls two of his warriors. "Go ahead of us as fast as you can but be careful."

Without a word, the scouts left running.

*

Commander Marum was having some meagre breakfast in the safe house. It was just dry bread and a big mug of tea. The bread was very dry and he had no choice but to dip it in the tea.

"I'm sorry for the poor breakfast commander, we don't have any sugar or milk for the tea," said the woman of the house.

"It's all right I like tea as it is. These will not be forever and soon we'll have our freedom back. When that happens, food will be brought in for everybody."

*

Moments later the three Ministers arrived and joined him at the table.

"Well, Ministers, are the people ready?"

The Prime Minister spoke first. "Yes, my group of people will be gathering close to the gates on the south of the city."

"And my people will do the same in this part of the city close to the main gates," said the Minister for the Interior.

With my people, I'll be in the centre of the city in the streets around the square," added the Foreign Minister.

"All right then, all we need now is to know what's going on with the resistance."

Amina's mother put a couple of wooden plates with pieces of bread on the middle of the table and gave a mug of tea to each of them.

"You are very kind," said the Prime Minister while the others nodded.

*

The two boys had walked for most of the day and had arrived at the sight of the city well into the afternoon.

"What are we doing now?" asked Insa.

Daba thought about it. "What we must do now is to find the twigs bundles we used to leave the city and with luck we can use them again but we must be careful not to make the pieces of roast chicken wet."

"All right, let's look for them."

The two boys started to crawl coming closer to the canal and a moment later; they found the bundles under a bush close to the water.

"Okay, this is it," said Daba and slowly entered the water and put the bundle with food on his head and the twigs on top with Insa doing the same close behind him.

As usual, the canal current was slow and they didn't have much difficulty to walk against it.

Suddenly they saw a guard looking over the battlement and they froze.

The guard on the battlement saw the bundles but ignored them.

Another guard came close to him. "Anything unusual?"

"No, just some debris and bundles of wood floating on the canal."

The two boys managed to enter the city and soon they had climbed out of the stream using the steps very close to the wall taking the bundles with them.

*

Suddenly the guard on the wall stopped and thought about the bundles. "Something's not right."

"What?" asked the other.

The canal water is running out of the city and the bundles were moving towards the city."

The two guards look at each other first and then ran to the edge of the wall to look at the canal outside the wall but there were no floating bundles, only some debris so they ran to the other side and looked at the canal but there were no bundles. All they could see were some people walking at the side of the canal close to the houses with some of them collecting debris floating in the stream.

"Are you sure you saw something floating there? You did this before and the commander wasn't happy with you."

The guard shrugged his shoulders. "No, I'm not," he said looking once again at the stream. "Maybe my eyes played a trick on me."

*

The place the boys used to come out of the water was so close to the wall that the only way for any soldier to see them was by leaning over and after nobody from the battlements could see them behind all the boxes piled up at the side of the canal. Once walking at the side of the houses they looked like any city dweller collecting some debris from the water. That's how the bundles in their hands look like; when the soldiers looked over the wall the two boys were already inside the second safe house safe house where commander Marum with the ministers were.

Amina's mother welcomed back the boys. "Come closer to the fire to dry your clothes; want something to eat?"

Insa shook his head. "Oh no, the people in the cavern stuffed us with roast chicken and potatoes." Then he put some pieces of roast chicken and a few potatoes wrapped by banana leaves on the table.

They all grabbed the fresh food and happily looked at the boys with the Prime Minister licking his lips. "Oh, I was dreaming with roast chicken."

"So did I," said commander Marum. "All right then, give as the news."

Daba spoke first. "We were there when our leader Eloy arrived back from his quest."

"Did he have the sword with him? You know the sword Glorious."

Insa shook his head. "Oh no, there was no sword."

Daba carried on. "We were told that Glorious was the title given to the hero Bonamor and not a sword at all."

They all remained in silence for a moment and Insa continued. "We were told that the title was inherited by Eloy and from now on he is the glorious leader of the resistance."

"Well," said commander Marum, "I'm shocked and I guess that from now on we must get used to treating our leader as glorious."

"That's not all," said Daba attracting their attention. "we now have a flag."

"And it is beautiful," said Insa enthusiastically, "it is white and has a blue shield with a golden crown in the centre and a shining sun on top of it with golden rays pointing in all directions."

"That's very interesting," said the Prime Minister, "because we have never had a national flag."

"We have some regional standards," said the Foreign Minister, "and a royal standard."

"What we had so far," said Marum, "is standards that represent different regions but this time we'll have something that will represent all the people of the kingdom because from your explanation the flag is royal and popular at the same time." Then he had a thought. "What about Prince Neno?"

"He's all right," said Insa.

"Last time we saw him he was with Eloy and Pearl and looking very happy," said Daba, "and before I forget, our glorious leader wants to know what the Queen will do when the rebellion starts."

"I understand she will stay in the palace and right now she is training in the use of the sword with her attendants," said commander Marum.

The Prime Minister was happy. "It will be a good idea to pass the news to the city dwellers that the prince is not just free but well. It will lift their moral; they'll have something new to talk about."

"Do you have more instructions for us?" asked the boy Insa.

"No," said Marum, "and now you can change your wet clothes and stay with us until later on for me to give you another message."

The woman of the house came to the room with some dry clothes for the boys. "Here, put these dry clothes on."

*

In the meantime, Barum was feeling very energetic and leading his warriors he was following a small path at the side of one of the many streams. "Maybe there are no enemies in here and perhaps they are all outside the forest, after all they were supposed to be forced out of it by Loni and some warriors earlier on," was his opinion and signalled with his right hand for his warriors to carry on.

*

It has taken the three groups the rest of the day and Loni's situation was different because by using some clean paths he had advanced faster than the others had and when he saw the enemy line of defence outside the forest, he decided to stay where he was and wait.

*

After visiting more houses in different streets, commander Marum had gone back to Amina's home and he didn't have to wait long for her to arrive carrying a jar of water.

"Welcome Amina. Did you have to dance before getting the water?"

"Yes. I did as usual," she said giving the money to her mother. "Any news?"

"Yes, the two boys' curriers have arrived with very good and surprising news. First, you must know the sword Glorious doesn't exist."

Amina was very surprised and disappointed. "You mean no sword?"

"That's right Amina there is no sword but the word Glorious does exist though in a different way."

Amina just listen with her eyes wide open and Marum continued. "Our leader Eloy found the cave where the sword was supposed to have been forged and he found an ancient scroll telling the truth. The great warrior Bonamor was the Glorious and now our leader bears the title."

"All right, I guess we must get used to the meaning of the word glorious but tell me, do you have any news about Prince Neno?"

"Yes, we do and he's well and happy."

For a moment, Amina stayed in silence just assimilating the news and looking at the two boys that were smiling at her. "Wow, it was quite a shock and I'm sure it will be the same for the Queen and everybody else. It will be for her very special to know her son is well."

Commander Marum was happy telling the news. "And there is something else. From now on we have a national flag that was given to our leader in the same cavern but we'll have to wait to see it until our city is freed from invaders."

Amina could not hide her enthusiasm. "I must go back to the palace with the good news."

"Very well my friend and we can practice fencing another time.

Amina just waived her hand and left in a hurry while commander Marum returned with the two boys to the house near the city walls.

There he spoke to the boys. "This time you will go back to our glorious leader and tell him we are almost ready. By coming and going, you are taking too much risk and considering all you have done I think this time you had better stay with the army.

The boys got ready to go.

"Very well," said the man of the house while leaving. "Wait until you hear the commotion close to the main gates."

By then it was getting very dark.

*

The boys didn't have to wait long and as soon as they heard the noises made up by some people squabbling not far from the city gates, they left and entered the water with the bundles of twigs on their heads and well camouflaged with some twigs and other vegetable debris floating with them. As usual, the water was not clear, which help to cover their bodies.

Moments later, they were away from the city and leaving the bundles under a bush they moved towards the coast.

"I only hope our glorious leader won't send us back to the city," said Insa.

"Yeah," said Daba, "commander Marum was right by saying we have taken too much risk."

*

Commander Bo had a different situation and his scouts were coming close to the edge of the forest at the south end of the enemy line of defence and as soon as they saw them immediately run back to report.

It took some time for them to reach commander Bo who was passed the centre of the forest. He listened to them and gave his orders. "We'll stay here in the forest well behind the trees for a while before we start our advance and there will be no chance for the enemy see us."

Then he called the two scouts. "You will go to commander Barum and tell him about what you've seen and you will go to commander Loni with the same message."

The two warriors left cautiously.

*

In the city, only some soldiers were walking in the streets holding torches and Amina reached the palace and went very fast through the corridors to the Queen's chambers.

The Queen saw her overexcited. "Give us the news Amina."

Amina sat on a stool in front of the Queen. "First, I must tell you the prince is all right and happy."

The Queen was overwhelmed with happiness. "Thank you, Amina, thank you so much. Now tell us the rest."

"When I heard about it I was shocked." The rest of the attendants joined them. "First you must know that there isn't any sword."

There was silence for a moment and the Queen asked. "If there isn't any sword the moral of the people cannot be improved."

Amina smiled. "Not quite because the word Glorious is being use in a different way; our leader Eloy with his companions found the cavern where the sword was supposed to have been forged and there it was revealed to him and his companions the truth about the legend." She paused for a moment regaining her breath. "Glorious was the title the hero Bonamor had and now our leader is the bearer of the title and that's not all. From now on we have a national flag."

The Queen thought about it and spoke solemnly. "As I learned a long time ago, things never stay the same and we must accept and live with the changes."

Amina showed a happy expression and they all look at her. "We have a glorious leader."

The Queen and her attendants started giggling.

*

The two boys had reached the north end of the forest from where they could see the enemy line of defence.

"We'll be all right if we carry on outside the forest," was Insa's opinion.

"Yes, Insa you are right."

*

A couple of hours later commander Barum reached the edge of the forest and saw the enemy line of defence he could hear clearly because they had several fires. "All right, form in two lines well behind the trees and get ready with your swords and don't let them see you."

*

One of the messengers sent by commander Bo took less time to reach commander Loni's camp and passed his message on.

"Very well, return to your commander and tell him we are ready."

At that moment, the other warrior sent by commander Bo arrived and passed on the message.

Immediately commander Barum gave his orders. "You will go back to commander Bo to tell him we have the same situation in here and we are ready to attack. When we do it, he should do the same on his side. What we'll do then is to fight for a few moments and then retreat inside the forest.

Hopefully the enemy commander will send his soldiers to give chase and then the real fighting will start inside the forest."

The warrior left running and Barum signalled for his men to remain where they were to rest for a while.

*

It didn't take long for the three groups to be ready at the edge of the forest.

They could see very well with the help of the moonlight and the light of the soldier's fires.

Bo was the first to give the battle cry and came out of the forest running against the enemy line.

Seconds later the other two groups came out of the forest doing the same.

For a few moments, the enemy soldiers didn't know what to do but their commander ordered his soldiers to advance and engage the warriors.

Bo's warriors were very inexperienced, nevertheless, they fought bravely though in a few moments the enemy started to push them back to the trees. Those soldiers were after all more experienced than the warriors were in the young liberation army and soon they had changed the swords for their bows. Bo's warriors in the three groups had good help from their archers and in no time, they were all behind the protection of the trees.

The same was happening with Barum and Loni's warriors. Without any hesitation, they ordered the retreat.

*

It was not a very successful attack, nevertheless, the enemy commander was surprised with it and being over confident he ordered his soldiers to chase the warriors.

Bo, Barum and Loni's warriors had quite some forest between them but the enemy didn't know how many they were and soon they were using the trees as shields managing very well to stop the enemy advance.

The battle carried on but not for long because the enemy commander decided for his men to leave the forest. In reality he didn't know how many warriors had attacked him.

Leaving some dead and wounded in between the trees he ordered for his men to once again form a line of defence facing the forest.

Barum gave the order for his men to stay where they were. "Now your job is to collect enemy weapons but we won't have the time to take care of their wounded. Nevertheless, we'll take our wounded back to the hills after we have buried our dead." He looked around and asked his second in command. "How many men we have lost?"

"I think we were very lucky because we only lost five though most of the rest are slightly wounded."

"Slightly wounded?"

"Yes, they are but they can all walk."

His warriors started immediately to follow his orders and it didn't take long for some of them to collect the enemy weapons with their purses and for others to start digging the individual burials at the foot of a small hill while the rest of them help the wounded to walk.

Commander Bo had done something similar though he had only lost two warriors and had less wounded than commander Barum had.

Loni was luckier with only a few wounded and happy to see that Alana was safe.

*

The enemy commander with the line of defence outside the forest was not a happy man and he called two of his men. "Go to the city and report to the General about our encounter with the rebels."

The two men left running and he started checking his casualties.

"We are supposed to bury our dead and taking care of our wounded and my men are afraid of getting into the forest. They think there are too many rebels still there," said one of his soldiers.

He went into a rage. "You stupid soldiers! By now the rebels are well away back in the hills and most probably getting ready to return! You will bury our dead and probably you will find more wounded in there!" he said pointing to the trees. "Go and do your job before the enemy decides to return!"

Reluctantly his men entered the forest though very slowly and sometime later they started to come out helping the wounded to walk.

We found the dead soldiers and they have all been stripped from their helmets, weapons and purses."

The commander went into a rage. "Argh! Those are not rebels but thieves!"

*

The boys had gone further west though still managing to do it on the north edge of it.

"I hope to find a clearing for us to spend the night," said Daba, "I don't want to do any walking like last time."

315

"I'm sure we'll find a place."

They didn't have to go much further when they arrived at the clearing used by the charcoal makers though they didn't see anybody."

"This is it Insa but we cannot sleep to close to the mounds, they are too hot."

*

Later and walking in darkness, the three commanders with Loni still in the centre came out of the forest and met facing the prairie where they stopped for a moment to have some rest.

"I think it's best for the warriors helping the wounded to carry on with the warriors carrying the weapons," said Barum.

Bo agreed with him. "Good idea and we can stay here to guard their rear, just in case the enemy commander decides to send some of his soldiers after us."

"I don't think he will be so stupid to do such thing."

Bo was firm. "Nevertheless, I'll do it."

"Of course, and so will I."

"Loni, you don't have to stay with us and it is better for you with your warriors to help the wounded."

"Very well and you can stay with them," he said talking to Alana."

He left helping one of the wounded and Alana stayed behind with the commanders.

Barum and Bo carried on moving together behind the wounded still formed in a line of defence though no enemy came out of the forest.

Chapter Twelve

A great part of the night had passed though the sun was not up yet and back in the hills, though many people were still asleep Eloy and Pearl with Choquero and the prince were standing on the ledge.

*

The boys couldn't sleep because of the noises coming out of the mound with the charcoal in it and at the same time the noises made by some animals walking by.

"Oh, come on Insa. I think it is better for us to carry on and maybe we can have some more sleep later."

*

From the ledge, Eloy and friends could see the three columns of warriors just outside the forest with many torches, moving back to the hills.

Prince Neno joined them. "I've got the feeling the beginning of the end is nigh now having warriors with more experienced."

"Yes, Neno," said Eloy, "I'm afraid you are right."

"Afraid? Why?"

"Because the closer we are to the end of the problem it means we'll be closer to the death of many."

The sun was beginning to shine though still behind the horizon.

Pearl interrupted them. "There is another group of warriors coming out of the forest."

Choquero observed the movements on the prairie. "I've got the feeling that those are the warriors forming a line of defence behind the wounded."

They looked for a moment and the prince noticed something. The columns in front are walking very slowly."

"I know what it is," said Pearl, "they have too many wounded."

Eloy reacted swiftly. "Commanders, send some people to help them."

Two of the seconds in command left followed by many people.

The sound of their voices woke many people and Eloy's mother approached. "Is there anything I can do?"

Pearl shook her head. "No, everything is under control."

Pearl's mother joined them. "I'm here, anything I can do?"

"Yes," said Pearl, "The warriors that went to the forest to fight the enemy are coming back and I can guess they have many wounded with them."

Pearl's mother sprang into action. "What we need is bandages and some medicinal creams."

"I'll help you with it," added Eloy's mother."

Both women left chatting enthusiastically.

"Well." said Eloy, "that's it, they know what to do."

"Oh yes, we all know my mother is dealing with the spiritual problems of the people and dealing with medicinal herbs. People trust her more than the doctors in the city and your mother is being always very good dealing with wounds. She has dealt with many wounded fishermen."

Eloy started laughing. "So, it is nursing with your mother and cooking with mine."

Pearl giggled. "That's right and I think they are both very good at it."

*

Sometimes later, the first wounded started to arrive helped by Loni, Pearl's mother and a small group of other women. They all went immediately into action attending to their wounds while Eloy's mother was preparing some herbal creams for the wounds.

Soon after more wounded arrived.

It was sad to see some people of different ages sobbing when they helped their wounded loved ones to walk while others were crying because their loved ones did not return.

*

The two boys came out of the forest and saw some people going towards the hills, slowly approached them.

*

Pearl's mother was going around stitching the cuts in arms and faces and at the same time showing some young women on how to do it while Eloy's mother was adding the herbal creams and the bandaging though they had the help of many other women.

Eloy and Pearl were very impressed with what they were seen.

"Pearl," said Eloy very calmly, "this is only the beginning and very soon we will witness more horrendous wounds when we go into the attack towards the city."

"In that case I wish for this war to be a short one. I don't want for anybody to suffer."

Everybody in the village was helping the wounded that were lying mainly at the entrance and Eloy with Pearl carried on talking to the people followed by the commanders.

"When are we going to the city?" asked a wounded lying on the ground. "My wounds are not serious and I can still use my sword. I had a very good experience there in the forest."

"So do I," said another.

"Come on Eloy, you know we can do it," said another wounded who was getting a bandage around his shoulders.

Eloy put his hands up. "I know you can do it but you must be patience, discipline is very important!"

Pearl talk to them loudly so they could all hear her. "The army is nearly ready and more people are joining us! Your duty is to pass your experience to others!"

*

Commander Barum and Bo arrived shortly after with more scenes of sadness by other families though commander Barum was very happy for all the experience gained by his warriors. "We don't have all the warriors we need but at least they are all in high moral and gaining experience."

*

One of the seconds in command approached commander Bo. "The enemy didn't follow us and that means they have gone back to their lines and that gives us the chance to go there to bury our friends."

"Of course, now go in there with some other warriors and start digging the graves."

*

Back in the city, the two soldiers found General Agaram.

He noticed them looking exhausted and as usual talk to them with arrogance. "What's the matter with you two?"

"We come from the line of defence by the forest," said one of them.

"Well? If you have a message, give it to me."

The second soldier continued. "We had an encounter with three groups of rebels that attacked us and then they fought us inside the forest."

"They fought very well and we lost several of our comrades."

The General started pacing and thinking. "Very well, go back and tell your commander to retreat back to the city."

The two soldiers saluted in military fashion and left.

The General call his second in command. "From now on you will be very vigilant and have more soldiers on the battlements."

The commander looked worried. "You think we'll be attacked?"

The General reacted violently. "Don't question me! Do as I say!"

The commander saluted and left running.

*

The rest of the day went on peacefully for friends and enemies.

In the village fortress, there was plenty of activities for everybody. The only ones not working were children that didn't waste any time playing all sorts of games.

Eloy with Pearl and Prince Neno just walked in all directions looking at the village activities.

They could see the daily routine for men and women going down to the streams to collect water. Many other people were feeding the animals while in a kind of abattoir some butchers were dealing with the body of a cow and Eloy could observed that some of them were slicing the meat very thin and after powdering with plenty of salt hanging those pieces on long strings to dry under the sun.

Some people were treating the cow skin by clearing all the grease out of it. And dusting it with salt.

In another place, they saw many women sitting in groups and doing plenty of knitting, mainly pullovers with some other women using several spinning wheels dealing with plenty of sheep's hair turning it into fine wool threats.

The bakers were very busy making mostly bread though some of them were making cakes under the watchful eyes of some children most probably waiting for the cakes to be ready out of the ovens.

Pearl was feeling happy. "I like to see a peaceful day in any village. Pity it won't last."

"I like to see the same everywhere I go," was the prince's opinion with Eloy just nodding.

*

In the city, everything was calm and relaxed for the enemy soldiers though there was a strange feeling with all of them because every time any one of them came to close to the city dwellers, those people were not smiling at them.

*

Once again, another day was coming to an end.

The two boys from the city approached Eloy. "Here we are commander and commander Marum told us to stay here close to you," said Daba.

"And we find out what the Queen will do," said Insa.

Daba continues. "She is training every day with a sword and her attendants are doing the same."

"And she will stay in the palace when the fighting starts," added Danna.

"Thank you for the news and happy to see you boys; from now on you will stay close to me where ever I go but tell me, how are things in the city."

Insa was quick to talk. "The people are starving and only some people have enough flour to make bread but so far the city dwellers are getting ready. We understand there are three main groups; one in the south close to the gates; the other north close to the main gates and the third is in the centre of the city."

"Yeah," said Daba, "they will be the ones to have a hard time because the main body of the enemy is in the centre where the square is."

"Thank you, boys and now we better have a good rest but above all, get something to eat from the communal kitchen."

Activities in the village fortress carried on though this time everybody was getting ready to go to bed apart of the sentinels mainly in the east wall with one on the ledge.

Chapter Thirteen

The new day started with plenty of work and Eloy could see many women and children leaving the village for the streams to get some water and as usual groups of people went to the forest to get dead wood though well protected by many male and female archers.

Many of the wounded were walking around while others started to exercise their arms.

At the same time and because there were no more repairs to the buildings, some men and women joined the training with the use of the bows and swords.

Eloy, Pearl, Choquero and the prince though they had almost no sleep, were walking around with something to eat in their hands with their entourage of commanders.

"More people have joined us but I need to know how many warriors you have," asked Eloy.

Lera was the first to answer. "When we started I had only a handful of archers but now I have counted hundred and we are all well provided by the carpenters making mainly arrows."

"My situation is a bid different," said Bo, "I have counted about hundred and fifty of which already some fifty have had fighting experiences and those are the ones that were wounded when fighting in the forest."

"Same here," said Barum.

Harmon just shrugged his shoulders. "Sorry to say this but I don't have any warriors in my command."

Not to worry," said Eloy, "because you can always stay close to us and above all close to your daughter and in that way action is guaranteed."

Pearl started to giggle. "Father, you never thought that you could be a warrior, couldn't you?"

"No, daughter and I'm still a bit apprehensive about it. I prefer to be a fisherman."

Eloy looked at his father. "What about you father?"

"In my case I have many warriors and it's been difficult to teach them to be warriors; they usually look at me like asking, 'All right, what can you teach us about fighting?' and I cannot tell them that my experience is the same as theirs."

"The point is; how many do you have?"

"I'm not sure but most probably about two hundred though most of them are older men or the too young; with many women of the same ages."

"I know father but nevertheless, they still follow you and don't you worry because so far you have learned a lot about the skills with the sword and so have your warriors."

Choquero nodded. "Yes, son you have a very good point there. I guess that war changes many things and me from been a farmer, I've turned to be a warrior. Still I prefer to be a farmer."

Eloy understood. "When this war is finished we'll all go back to our former way of life."

"So be it," said commander Barum, "but some things will be changed for ever."

Commander Bo was curious. "In my village, I was a woodcutter; what about you?"

They all look at Barum waiting for his answer and he felt a bit embarrassed. "I'm a cobbler."

"Well now," said Eloy, "maybe with the experience we are all getting with walking, you might create new shoe stiles. You know something more comfortable and not just the sandals we were."

Maybe a new kind of dancing shoes?" asked Lera and Pearl nodded vigorously.

Barum smiled at them. "As a matter of fact, I have a few ideas."

Pearl's mother interrupted them. "Come you lot, get something to eat."

Loni with Alana joined Choquero's warriors. "Happy to know you didn't suffer many wounded like the others," said Choquero.

"Yes, we were very lucky with only a few wounded." Then he looked at Alana, "Alana has been a great help with her skills in the use of the bow."

Alana just smiled.

*

By now, the village was looking its former glory as a fortress and right in the centre the palace was not a ruin anymore, with the wooden roof completely repaired. Nevertheless, the walls show the damage done by time.

*

The people searching for gold had been very successful and part of the gold has already paid for some things needed and that's why many of the colourful windows had been almost totally restored with some colourful glass brought in by some of the refugees; once again, it was treated as a palace though used as the command centre.

Eloy with his entourage was doing his usual round and saw that many families had prepare their shelter in a peculiar way like the people with wagons because they were using not just the inside of their wagons but under them as well, all covered with canvas like an oversized tent.

"Tell me something," said Pearl. "Why all the work to restore the walls, the palace and everything else in this place that we will eventually leave when returning to the city."

"I'm sure it is something to do with moral," was Prince Neno's opinion.

Eloy took a moment to answer. "The prince is right because by having the people doing something it prevented anybody to feel bored and do some mischief."

*

Later, inside the palace, Eloy and all the commanders were sitting around a table on some rudimentary stools made in a hurry by the carpenters.

There was a fire burning in the hearth.

Commander Barum was speaking. "Since the tragedy of the invasion and only in a few days, we have come a long way. Many people have run away from the enemy and now we have, though small, an army of about four hundred and fifty warriors and a small cavalry detachment of fifty."

"Commander Barum is right," said commander Bo, "and I think that with all the experience gain by several encounters with the enemy, our little army is ready and

I'm happy to say that almost all our wounded are walking, and their moral is high."

It was the turn for Lera to speak and she stood up. "It is true that we are ready but being a small army, we must use our intelligence to create tactics."

She sat down and for a brief moment they remained in silence and looking at Eloy waiting for him to say something.

"You are right, I think our army is ready and in need for us to think about the best tactics. We all know there is no shortness of bravery and in the last encounters our warriors have given us a good sample of it."

Pearl stood up. "The time has come for us to take the first steps and I would suggest for the army to remain with the organisation we have, which has proved to be effective."

Eloy stood up. "The first step will be to leave our little fortress and go down to the prairie where the army will camp in strategic places to go through the last passes of the organisation before we start the next step."

Some women with his and Pearl mother approached them with something to eat and after a few moments, he continued. "Commander Barum will move towards the north of the prairie and close to where the cavern with the fishermen is. Commander Bo will move to the south and make camp close to the hills where the ancient cavern is or he can use one of the villages in that part of the forest. Commander Choquero will make camp facing the centre. My place with Pearl and the prince with some warriors and archers will be anywhere."

Commander Lera was waiting for her assignment but Eloy didn't say anything.

"What about me and my archers?"

"Be patient Lera," said Pearl.

Eloy heard her. "Commander Lera and her archers will stay with me and later we'll join with commander Choquero. We will be a mobile force and the cavalry will stay with us as well."

"I would suggest doing something else before we do all that," said Pearl, "we must send scouts to the forest to make sure there are no enemies close to the prairie."

"I'll deal with that," said commander Choquero. "Loni will go in with some warriors and I was going to suggest that Loni is recognised as a commander. After all he had some experience leading some of the warriors and some experience in battle as well."

Eloy agreed with him. "Very well, from now on you are a commander."

Loni was happy with his promotion. "All right, that means I can name my second in command?"

"Of course," said a happy Eloy.

"Very well, I name as my second in command, Alana."

She was shocked for a moment. "Thank you, commander."

"Very well," said Eloy, "from now on Loni is a commander and Alana his second in command. Now we all know what to do and I think it is the right time to start but before you go we must make sure we have enough supplies and each group will take a wagon with all the preserved food they can carry."

His mother stepped forward. "We already thought about that particular subject and many women are already preparing some food. In the last few days, we have made plenty of dehydrated vegetables; all they need is boiling water. At the same time, we have plenty of dehydrated salted meat for the warriors to carry in their satchels"

Pearl's mother spoke. "In my case I have been preparing many young women with the skills of taking care of wounds and they will all take a small satchel with plenty of bandages and healing creams with them."

*

Eloy and the commanders were feeling very encouraged with all the positive organisations they had and very soon there was plenty of activities in the village fortress.

*

In the city, the commander has returned with his men to reinforce the walls defences when they heard the sound of horns and looking over the wall, they saw an army approaching the main gates. Most of it was infantry with a small cavalry squadron.

With them, they had a couple of wagons with plenty of supplies, mainly food.

*

General Agaram showed himself between the soldiers with his second in command. "Aha, now we are really powerful. Now I have all my army here with me."

"But sir, if all the army is here that means there is no army back home."

"Of course not, because I need them here you stupid!"

The second in command just kept quiet.

*

The army re-enforcements entered the city and immediately most of the infantry went up the walls, while the rest with the cavalry moved to the city square filling it up and some commanders started to distribute the food in the wagon but only to soldiers and the city dweller could only look and lick their lips.

*

Marum with many city dwellers had come out to look at the spectacle. "It looks to me about a thousand soldiers," was Amina's father opinion.

"Yes, I agree with you and with the soldiers already here they are about two and a half thousand."

"Will you have that many people ready for the uprising commander?" asked the man.

"Yes, I think we'll have that amount of city dwellers and we can defeat them as soon as our army enters the city. I'm very confident."

*

In the palace, the Queen and attendants noticed what was going on in the city and they gathered in the palace balcony from where they could see the enemy cavalry entering the city square.

"This could be terrible for any possible resistance in the city."

"That's the way it's looking right now Your Majesty," said Amina, "but we must wait and see."

"Yes, you are right Amina and as soon as you can, go and find out more."

"I'll do that right now Your Majesty," and left running.

*

The strict control on the Queen has being relaxed and once again, Amina managed to get out.

Using some side streets, she went straight to her family home but not without some difficulties because most of the people were on the streets either going home or watching the enemy army deploying in the streets around the square and she could see what was going on when passing close to it.

This time there was no chance for her to dance; even the musicians were nowhere to be seen.

The square was full of men and horses and she could see that even if they had asked her to dance there was absolutely no chance because of the horse manure.

This time the feeling of been occupied was very strong with the city dwellers and whatever happiness they have had by now it was all gone.

*

She entered her home and was happy to see that commander Marum was there chatting with her parents.

"How does it look out there?"

"Real chaos commander; it was difficult to walk with so many soldiers. It's beginning to look like a garrison city and the Queen is getting very worried but I noticed they are mostly in the centre, in and around the square."

Marum became very serious for a moment and then he smiled. You will tell the Queen not to worry. The enemy euphoria will soon be turned sour."

"I will tell her so; now do you think I need more training with the sword?"

"No, my dear there's nothing more I can teach you and from now on all we can do is make sure the people will be ready and waiting. My two messengers had gone to the hills and by now they should be with our army."

"Very well, Commander, I will go back to the palace now but you must know that though the enemies have received food they are not feeding the city dwellers that can only look at them eating. They are very cruel."

Commander Marum looked at her with a sad expression. "Yes, I know. I've seen it but don't you worry because their time will come."

*

Somebody knocks at the door and the man of the house opened it.

A man entered. "I'm sorry to disturb you but I know about you organising the people for a possible insurrection and I have been elected to be the city guard's commander. My name is Anton."

Marum was overwhelmed with the news. "Thank you, Anton and now all you need to do is to tell the rest of the guards to join the rebellion when we start though right now we don't know but when it starts all you have to do is to join the people that will fight the soldiers in the square."

"Very well, I will do so."

*

In the village fortress, there was plenty of activity and everybody could hear the carpenter's saws and the blacksmith's tools working very hard.

The blacksmith with several assistants was shaping hot pieces of metal into the shape of halberds.

Many women were preparing small baskets and bundles with food and loading three wagons while other women were giving the dehydrated meat to the warriors to put in their satchels.

Some boys and girls were feeding the mules while others were feeding the horses.

Close to the corral, there was a group of warriors saddling the horses while others were just cleaning their bows, shields and swords.

*

Eloy, Pearl and the prince still surrounded by the commanders could see the preparations.

Pearl's mother, at one end of the communal table, was showing some young women how to put a bandage around an arm and once again, Eloy saw those young women wearing a white scarf.

"You see that commanders?" she said, "next time you have some wounded you'll know whom to call for help."

Those words were very encouraging.

*

They carried on and commander Bo was curious. "What about the cavalry. They need somebody in command."

Eloy thought about it and looked at one of the riders. "What is your name?"

"I'm called Rony."

"Can you ride a horse?"

Rony shows a broad smile "Of course I can. I'm a country boy and I told some of them how to ride."

"Can you use a sword?"

"Yes, sir, I can. Until last year I was one of the city guards but I decided to return to farming instead."

"Very well Rony from now on you will command the cavalry and I hope you know how to ride a horse," he said looking at him and holding his laughter.

Roni was surprised. "Eh? Oh yeah right," he said understanding the joke and holding his laughter.

"Eloy," said commander Bo, "when do you want to give the order to leave?"

"We still have some day light and I think the best time to do it will be at dusk. By the time our army reach the place for camping, it will be night, which will be a very good camouflage."

Lera nodded. "So be it."

Eloy turned to Pearl. "I think you better make sure all your archers have the right amount of food in their satchel and a water bottle because we are going for a long walk."

"Right, Lera, come with me."

The two women left but Lera was curious. "What did he mean by a long walk?"

"So far we've done a lot of walking so once more doesn't make any difference to me."

"I don't mind walking but I prefer to know where I'm going."

"Come on Lera, where is your sense of adventure and by now, you are supposed to know we are going to the forest. Very soon we'll be facing the enemy in open war."

Lera nodded. "I knew I shouldn't ask." Then she had a thought. "We cannot have a proper battle inside the forest. There are no clearings big enough for that purpose."

"Yes, Lera you are right and the main fighting will be done by us from outside the city with the people inside starting their rebellion."

*

Eloy call the two boys. "I have known you for a short time but still I don't know your names."

"I'm Insa," said one of the boys. "I'm Daba," said the other.

"All right, now I know and you will stay with us."

Then he called his father. "Dad, this is the time for you to send the scouts into the forest."

"Very well, son, I'll send some of the warriors on horse," and called Rony. "Choose fifteen of your men and send them to the forest as scouts, five of them in the north, five in the centre and the other five in the south and you'll stay here with the rest of your force."

Moments later the fifteen riders left, all of them well armed with their bows, quivers, shields and swords.

*

In the city, there was still some spirit of freedom and a couple of young women saw their opportunity when some soldiers' open half of the gates in the south of the city and call for some people to come out with them and go to the trees and bushes nearby to get some dead wood for their fires.

Outside the city those people had to use a small bridge over the canal that in the forest was not channelled by walls because it was deep enough for boats.

One of the enemy commanders with some soldiers came out with them. "Get some wood and do not try to run away, my archers will kill anybody who tries."

The small group of people obeyed and soon they were coming back with wood on their shoulders piling it just inside the gates and out again to get some more.

The two women carried on and after a while, they noticed the soldiers left to guard them relaxed their attention and sat to eat something.

They left a bunch of wood close to them and one spoke. "We saw some more dead wood a bit further on. Do you want us to get it?"

The soldiers looked around and nodded. "Yes," said one of them, "but don't try to run away and hurry up."

"If you behave nicely to us, later on we will give you some food," said the other smiling.

The two women left but being very careful not to run and in a moment, they had grabbed some wood and returned.

By then dusk was upon them.

This time and without asking, they left once again though this time they went a bit further.

A soldier show himself in between some trees. "What are you doing there?"

One of the women waived her hand with a piece of wood. "We found more dead wood in here. We'll be back in a minute."

"All right, put it together and come back," he said disappearing behind the trees.

As soon as the soldier left, they just carried on following a narrow path.

"Malloa, I don't know which way to go."

"Not to worry, we just follow this path and hopefully we'll reach the heart of the forest but above all don't talk, they might still hear us."

In silence, the two young women carried on and the further they went, the more enthusiastic they felt.

*

Suddenly the soldier's commander came out of the city gates calling them. "All right, we have enough wood; bring them in!"

The soldiers guarding the people stood up. "All right you lot, come back here and don't forget the wood!"

Reluctantly those people started to move carrying the dead wood back to the city.

The two soldiers who were supposed to keep an eye on the two young women call them but there was no answer.

Immediately they run to where the two women were supposed to be but there was nobody.

They looked at the forest and shrugged their shoulders.

"I'm not going in there looking for them."

"Neither do I," said the other, "come let's go back to the city, I don't think the commander will notice those two missing women."

The rest of the soldiers called the people and herd them back like cattle carrying the wood bundles on their shoulders.

*

In the meantime, the two young women carried on and soon they were deep inside the forest.

"We can rest now Malloa."

"No, Mela not yet. First, we must make sure we are really safe.

They carried on and happy there were no other noises but the sound of their footsteps.

"Happy this time of the year the weather is usually dry," said Malloa.

"I wouldn't like to be in this situation with pouring rain."

"Personally, I wouldn't mind walking under the rain if I was going towards freedom."

"Perhaps that's why the enemy dictator did it this time of the year."

"Yes, Mela you've got a very good point."

*

The sun was beginning to go down in the west and in the village fortress, the warriors were getting ready with the commanders coming closer to Eloy once again waiting for his instructions.

Eloy with Pearl and all the commanders went to stand on the ledge looking upon the prairie and beyond. Pearl was holding the flagpole letting the flag flap freely with the breeze so everybody leaving the village could see it.

Then Eloy's mother joined them putting her hands up and closed her eyes. "Holy Spirit, hear my voice. Please guide our people in this our hour of need. Amen"

After that simple prayer, they remained in silence for a moment and Eloy broke it. "All right my friends, so far everything is going according to our plans. The scouts should be inside the forest by now and if there is anything wrong, they will report. Now Barum you will be the first to leave but make sure your men don't light any torches. Soon the moonlight will suffice.

Commander Barum saluted by touching his chest with his right hand and left, signalling for his warriors to follow him going down the hill followed by one of the supply wagons.

A group of ten women with the white scarf followed him and they all had a satchel with the first aid.

It was a magnificent spectacle to see the first part of their army walking to the prairie.

By then night has fallen and a beautiful full moon illuminated the whole of the land.

Then Eloy instructed commander Bo. "Now it's your turn Bo to move towards the south of the forest and I wish you good luck."

Bo saluted in military fashion by touching his chest and left with one supply wagon, followed by his men and ten women with the white scarf. Those women had two satchels, one with the first aid equipment and the second with their food.

"Now father you will go and please be careful but above all try to protect your warriors. You are leading a big group of fighters and you are supposed to be in the heart of the fighting."

"I know son and I will do my best but where are you going in the meantime."

"This time father the journey will be something to amalgamate with the past and the history of my country and I must do it before the fighting start."

"Very good son and good luck to you."

"Thank you, father," and turned to look at Harmon. "Now I have one of the most important missions in this war for you."

"All right," said an enthusiastic Harmon, "give it to me."

"You will join the boats and be the navy commander from now on. I will organise a group of warriors to be transported by you closer to the city. As soon as you have all the warriors on board, you'll go east and land the force in the cove you know. After, you'll stay with the boats just in case they are needed or if you want you can join them in battle."

"All right, I can do that; I'm more comfortable at sea than on land."

Moments later, Choquero left followed by his warriors, taking another supply wagon and some women with the white scarf.

Eloy, Pearl and Neno went back inside the village fortress and Lera formed her archers close to Eloy, Pearl and Neno.

The rest of the cavalry came closer to them and ready to go with Rony in the lead. "Rony instead of staying with me I think you better move forward and go down to join my father and his warriors."

Rony saluted by touching his chest and left at the head of the cavalry.

Then Eloy had a thought. "Commander Loni I think you have better go ahead and try to join with commander Bo. He will need you more than me."

Without a word, commander Loni with Alana left with their group taking the last supply wagon and the last women with the white scarf joined him.

*

Eloy look at them smiling. "Well my friends, we are leaving this fortress for the last time."

"Why do you say that?" asked Neno, "we can always come back here to have a holiday and who knows how many more people will do so just to have a break."

"Neno is right," said Pearl, "I can be one of those people."

"This can be a place for holiday makers from now on. It is well away from the heat of the land and the place has all the facilities for people to stay," added Neno.

Eloy lifted his arms feeling happy for them. "All right, so be it."

His mother and Pearl's mother approached them. "We'll stay with the wounded and the old," said Pearl's mother.

"We'll join you later on," added his mother.

Eloy and Pearl embrace their mothers and join their warriors starting their walk down the hill followed by Prince Neno, Lera with her archers and the two boys. Pearl was carrying the flag resting on her shoulder.

At the same time, the carpenter and the blacksmith put their tools on satchels and were ready to go behind them.

Mavina and Sanila with a group of young women went to stand on the ledge looking at them going down the hill. They had several torches around the ledge.

There Sanila and Mavina stood with their hands forward like in silent prayer.

Way down the road closer to the prairie Eloy looked back. "Look Pearl, over there on the ledge."

Pearl looked and for a moment, they both stood in silence looking at their mothers in prayer.

*

Behind them, the rest of the non-combatant people left the village fortress bringing the cattle and the rest of the animals including the dogs.

Soon most of the people left in the fortress were the old and the wounded with some difficulty to walk and they too were getting ready to leave.

Pearl had a though. "Eloy, I don't know why we are all leaving because if the attack fails we'll have no choice but to return and stay here, who knows for how long."

"I know and I had a similar thought but we must believe in our cause and hope for the best."

*

They were coming close to the bottom of the hills and Eloy with Pearl looked at the prince noticing he had a sad expression.

"What's wrong," asked Pearl.

For a moment, the prince didn't say a word and just swallowed several times feeling emotional. "It's just that when I saw you two saying goodbye to your mothers I realised that mine is far away in the city and when I left I didn't have a chance to say goodbye to her."

They stopped and approached him. "Don't be sad Neno. It's true that your mother is far away but here you are amongst friends," said Pearl and gave him a hug and a kiss.

Neno looked at her with a forced smile. "Of course, I know that; come let's go."

*

In the meantime, the two young women had gone deep inside the forest though by then walking in semi darkness because some of the moon light was filtering through the canopy and were beginning to feel exhausted. "Mela this time I will stop and rest."

"All right I'll do the same. You know, I think we have come deep into the south of the forest and there's supposed to be at least a couple of villages that maybe the enemy don't know about it."

*

They both sat in between some trees where there was a clearing. The moon was giving them some dim light coming through the tree branches.

"I don't know for how long we can carry on without any food and water."

"Stop thinking about it Malloa. I'm sure we'll find something or somebody."

A couple of gazelles came to the clearing and after looking at them for a couple of seconds, they run away.

"We could do with some meat but I don't think I have the energy to do any hunting," said Malloa.

Mela looked at her with surprise. "Malloa, how could we do any hunting with no weapons?"

Malloa open her mouth but could not say a word because some noises out of the trees and bushes interrupted her and they stood still with their hearts palpitating rapidly.

"This is it Malloa and I hope they are friendly."

A couple of scouts on horse came out of a path and stood there looking at them very surprised and for a moment the young women stood in silence holding hands.

"I never thought we could find people still in the forest," said one of them.

"Who are you?" asked the other.

"We are from the city and we managed to escape," said Mela.

"Well," said one of the scouts smiling at them. "You don't have to worry anymore," he said and took some bread and dehydrated beef from his satchel giving it to the young women who started devouring it.

"Do it slowly," said one of them laughing.

"Here," said the other, "have some water as well but tell me, what news do you have from the city."

Terrible news," said Malloa while chewing, "the enemy has been reinforced by a bigger army with cavalry."

"The two scouts were very surprised. "Come with us we'll put you in contact with our army."

"Mela was very surprised. "Army? I thought there was just a group of freedom fighters."

"Oh no, we have an army."

"We want to fight," said Mela.

"That's not a problem because many young women joined the archers," said the other scout.

"That's a thought," said Mela, "because I always wanted to try a bow."

*

Commander Barum was finishing the crossing of the prairie with his warriors formed into a well-disciplined formation coming closer to the north edge of the forest.

*

Commander Bo had entered the forest to the south and was moving his warriors' forwards though cautiously while commander Loni and Alana had reached a place not far north from Bo.

Bo reached one of the abandoned villages and it was better than to make camp further south because in the village they could take shelter in the abandoned houses.

*

Choquero with a greater number of warriors was doing it slowly in the centre of the prairie followed by commander Rony and his horses.

*

Commander Barum had reached the place on the north of the prairie and at the edge of the forest his warriors had started to make camp.

Immediately, he sends a couple of runners inside the forest as scouts.

*

Commander Choquero had reached the forest in the centre and behind all of them was Eloy with his small group of warriors moving across the prairie going southeast but without rushing.

The rest of the people were moving slowly not far behind them because of the animals with them though in the direction where commander Choquero was.

Pearl was in deep thought. "Eloy looking at the moving of the nonfighting people I think that everybody has the idea that we are going to win and nobody is thinking of been defeated and have to return to the village fortress."

"She's right," said Prince Neno, "I have the same feeling." Then he frowned, "I only hope for most of us to survive because in my case I intend to fight no matter what."

Pearl felt touched with his words and approaching him, she gave him a kiss in the cheek.

Somehow, the prince had a radiant expression smiling at her.

*

It didn't take long for Loni to arrive at the same village where Bo was and soon he approached him feeling quite happy. "Commander Bo, I hope you feel comfortable in my village."

Commander Bo was surprised. "Your village, well my friend, in that case you can show the warriors where they can make a fire and cook something. At the same time, you could tell them where to take shelter."

"Of course, I can and for what I can see, we have more supplies than the other groups."

"Yes, we have and as a group we have more warriors."

*

The scouts with the two young women reached another group of commander Bo's scouts on foot and Mela with Malloa were very surprised. Those scouts smiled at them and stayed there. "Commander Bo has made camp in one of the villages," said one of them.

"Come with us," said one of the riders.

*

They reached the village that by then had many lit torches all around and Bo was very surprised. "I can see you found somebody in the forest."

"Yes, commander and we don't know what to do with them; they come from the city."

"From the city? Come closer young women, do you have any news for us?"

"Yes," said Malloa, "an army has arrived with some cavalry and the people think the enemy is now stronger with more than two thousand men."

Bo thought about it. "I hope that Eloy will come up with a tactic to deal with cavalry." Then he looked at the two young women. "We cannot send them to the village fortress because by now everybody would be down by the prairie."

Some warriors felt amused with the idea. "But commander, we are supposed to go to war and not to babysit," said one of them while giggling.

Bo felt amused with their opinion and realised about the situation. "Yes, you are right but first they are not babies and second, we cannot leave them here on their own, they have not been trained as warriors, don't you think so?"

The warriors looked at each other shrugging their shoulders.

One of the scouts had an idea. "Why don't we take them with us and maybe somebody could give them some training? I volunteer."

Bo opened his eyes with surprise first and then he smiled. "No, we won't keep them with us but if they walk north towards the middle of the prairie they will eventually find the main group of people coming down to the prairie with our glorious leader." Then he called two of his men. "Now you take these young women to our glorious leader Eloy and good luck to you both,"

"Yes, sir."

"I'm sorry," said Mela, "we don't mean to create a problem to anybody."

"And I would like to be trained in the use of some weapons and help with the fighting," added Malloa.

"Yes, we can do that," said an enthusiastic Mela.

"I'm sure somebody will help you," said commander Bo.

"All we need is some food," said Malloa.

"That's not a problem because we have plenty of it," said one of the scouts.

A couple of warriors approached giving them a satchel each. "Here, take this, this will be enough. There's some food and a bottle with water."

"Thank you very much for your help," said Mela.

"And now," said commander Bo addressing the two warriors. "After you deliver these two young women you will pass the news to commander Choquero and then go north and pass the news from the city to commander Barum then you will return to us if you can. Now go."

The scouts left walking with the two young women heading to the prairie.

Moments later, they were out of the forest and as it was expected, the moon was giving enough light for them to see their way.

*

It took them several hours until they saw not far away many people encamped close to the forest. Those were the warriors led by Eloy's father and they approached. Choquero at the head of his warriors saw the two scouts with the young women. "Where are you going?"

One of the scouts explained. "We are taking these two women to the leader Eloy and their message is that the enemy had been reinforced by many more soldiers and cavalry."

"Very well, you'll find our leader not far behind us," said Choquero pointing to his rear.

*

They carried on until they found Eloy's group who signalled to stop waiting for the young women with the scouts to join them.

"Who are you?"

"I'm Malloa and this is my friend Mela. We were found in the forest by two scouts who help us and now we are supposed to join the people coming down to the prairie."

"Eloy," said Pearl, "why don't we take them with us? They are young and they can be of some help. On the other hand, there is nobody left in the fortress."

"Oh yes, please," said Mela.

Eloy was more interested with news. "Tell me, if you come from the city do you have any news?"

"Oh yes," said Malloa, "before we managed to run away, we saw more enemies coming to the city and this time with cavalry who are right now soiling the city square and the smell of manure is horrible."

Their opinion about manure made Lera's archers to murmur and giggle.

"And now the enemy is over two thousand men or more, like perhaps about twenty-five hundred," added Mela.

"I can only guess that the General has brought in the rest of his army and by now the city is well fortified," was Pearl's opinion.

They all looked at Eloy who was deep in thought and waited.

It didn't take long for him to give his opinion. "In a way, this can be taken as good news because by bringing all his army to our land, when we attack he will not get any reinforcements. On the other hand, it means if there is no army to control the people in his country, it could be very helpful for anybody trying for freedom. Who knows, maybe there might be a revolution."

"Shall we send messengers to the other commanders with the news?" Pearl wanted to know.

"Tell me," he asked. "Did you tell somebody else about it?"

"Oh yes, first we told the scouts and they were very surprised," said Malloa. "Later on, we joined commander Bo and told him as well."

"There, do you hear that Pearl? They already met commander Bo. Commander Barum with my father will soon know about it too and now we had better to carry on. Our fighting force will join with my father and I will carry on with just the female archers. I want to reach the south of the forest before the end of the night."

"Okay," said Lera, "you'd better join my archers. Do you know how to use a bow?"

The two young women shook their heads.

"It's all right, we'll teach you."

Eloy asked the two scouts to take a message. "Ahead of us you'll find commander Choquero with his warriors and after giving him the news you'll carry on north until you encounter commander Barum and you'll stay with him available as messengers."

"But we belong to commander Bo's group."

"It's all right my friend because later on all the groups will eventually be together."

"We already told commander Choquero about it," said a scout.

"In that case you just carry on further north and tell commander Barum."

The scouts left and Eloy carried on moving south and Pearl with Lera started to show Malloa and Mela how to hold a bow and to practice with the pulling of the string.

*

Commander Choquero was not far and closer to the forest. The two scouts reached him easily and passed the news given to them by the two young women.

"Thank you very much," said Choquero, "and I think you better carry on further north and pass the news about the enemy in the city to commander Barum."

The scouts overtook the army with commander Choquero and when they reached commander Barum they passed on the news. "Thank you scouts and you can go back to your command."

He called his second in command. "We'll carry on camping here for the night and you two," he said pointing to two of his warriors. "You will go inside the forest to keep an eye on any enemy movement. You might encounter the advanced scouts on horse in it. Don't you forget to take a blanket and don't you forget to take turns to sleep. We all must get as much rest as possible."

*

In the meantime, Eloy with his small entourage was walking slowly towards the south east of the prairie.

"Are we going to see Bonamor's tomb?"

"No, Pearl, this time we'll carry on towards the hills and to visit the cavern once more."

The two young women were learning how to use the bow and the archers were very amused with them. "Not to worry girls," said Lera. "Eventually you'll learn and who knows maybe you'll be better than the others."

"The only problem is that we don't have our own bows," said Mela.

"Well," said Lera, "not now but later on we'll find a couple for you."

*

Pearl walked closer to Eloy. "I'm beginning to have mixed feelings about this war."

"What is your puzzle?"

"I'm not really puzzled but uncertain more than anything else. We have a small but well organised army and we have the support of all the people in the country and still I'm not sure if we have a chance to win or not."

"I know my friend and I'm sure that many people have the same feelings, nevertheless, they don't say it; they just carry on with the strength hope is giving to all of us but you must be patience and wait."

Prince Neno agreed with him. "He's right Pearl and I know I will feel much better when we reach the city."

"Why would you feel better? Reaching the city means to be facing the enemy and obviously to get involved with heavy fighting. Who knows, maybe even killed."

"Yes, that's very possible but that means to fight for the people's freedom and who knows maybe be closer to the end of the trouble."

"It's all right for you to say that because you are a man but I'm a woman."

"And a beautiful one," the prince was quick to say which embarrassed her.

"Well, being a woman I prefer love instead of war but don't get me wrong; I want to fight as well and I have been ready for some time."

"So do I though now we have no choice but to continue with our quest."

"We are coming close to the forest where we should see commander Bo's warriors very soon," said Eloy, "maybe in one of the abandoned villages."

"Maybe they can spare a couple of bows," said Malloa.

"All right," said Lera. "I'll ask them."

*

They entered the forest and though it took them some time, they finally found the village used by Bo's warriors and joined his men in the centre of it.

His warriors had already built up a fire inside a public oven and were doing some cooking.

"What are you cooking?"

"Come closer Eloy and you'll see," said Bo, then he noticed the two women. "Those are the women I send to join the people coming from the hills."

"That's right and they are been trained in the use of the bow," said Pearl.

"And now we are all here by the forest and going to war," added a cheerful Eloy.

"Ah," said a gleeful Bo. "I'm happy for you young women and now you are here, you are very welcome to my camp. Or shall I say Loni's village."

Eloy was surprised. "Loni's village? Well, I'm happy to hear."

*

Some of his warriors had made some dough and were making a kind of very flat bread.

"You are making tortillas," said Pearl.

"Not quite," said Bo, "when they are finished you'll see but now have some rest."

They settled in the village sitting on the ground close to the waters and some warriors approached the female archers while Eloy with Pearl sat close to Bo.

"One thing is for sure," said Eloy, "and that is the friendship amongst our people. I have not seeing anybody squabbling or having a fight."

"Strange to say that," said Pearl. "Though people are usually friendly now we are at war that friendship has become more intimate."

Eloy felt philosophical. "Somehow it is something to do with the possibility of death been so close to all of us and it is logical for people to look for experience in human relation, like love."

"You are right," said Pearl. "Many of our young men and women will probably die tomorrow; many will never have the chance to have a family."

There was a moment of sadness in the air and nobody was talking. Suddenly, commander Bo's laughter broke the silence and they look at him with surprise and curiosity.

"Don't look at me like that," he said holding his laughter. "Don't you see?"

"No," they said in unison.

He looked at them with a wide grin. "Next year we'll see many new born babies and that's the happy side of the tragedy."

Once more, there was a moment of silence and suddenly with Pearl first, they all burst with laughter.

Bo looked around happy to see young women, especially Malloa who was not far from him. "Tell me," he said pointing at Malloa. "Is she good with some of our weapons? I can see that she doesn't have a bow or a sword."

Eloy and Pearl look.

"Oh, that's Malloa," said Pearl, "she doesn't have a weapon yet because so far she has join the archers but she still doesn't have a bow and as you noticed she doesn't have a sword either."

"Ah, maybe I can solve that problem."

"Any particular reason for your interest?" asked Eloy moving his eyebrows up and down while smiling.

Bo blinked his eyes but couldn't say anything because Loni approached them carrying a wooden tray with some of the flat breads that by now were covered with cooked tomatoes and sliced onions.

"Now the bread is cooked, try them," said Loni cutting them into smaller pieces with his knife. "This is the bread we eat in my village and it is quite popular with some city dwellers.

"Mmm, it's delicious," said Pearl, "but from where did you get the recipe."

"This is a very old recipe from far away countries where soldiers used to cook their own meals."

Bo stood up. "Excuse me I think I can provide that young woman with a weapon."

Pearl gave Eloy a complicity looks. "He mentioned a weapon."

Eloy look at her and then at Bo, smiling. "Yes, Pearl I've noticed."

Bo went close to the oven, grabbed a piece of flat bread with crashed tomatoes and the sliced onions on top and asked one of his warriors to get him a sword. Then he approached Malloa. "Would you like to have more of this lovely bread?"

Malloa was surprised for a brief moment. "Yes, I would thank you."

"And you can use this sword, can you?"

"For me? Oh yes, thank you very much but I have never used one and right now I've been instructed in the use of the bow."

"Don't you worry about the bow if you stay with us I can teach you how to fight with a sword and how to use a bow."

Eloy and Pearl saw what was going on and Eloy whispered to Pearl. "I think that commander Bo likes Malloa."

Pearl started giggling. "He's well after her."

"Yes, I can see that but now we must carry on. I want to reach the cavern so we can have some rest for the night."

"Okay girls!" said Pearl standing up. "We are moving!"

The archers prepared to go.

"Malloa will stay with us," said Bo. "She has decided to stay and learn how to use the sword and the bow."

"Are you sure Malloa?" asked Mela.

"Yes, I feel amongst friends in here."

"Very well then," said Lera. "Good luck to you."

Lera remember something. "Excuse me commander but is it possible to have a bow for Mela?" and she said that pointing to the young woman.

"Yes, of course," and he called for one of his warriors to bring a bow.

*

Once again, Eloy and Pearl took the lead with her carrying the flag and they left the village going towards the cavern and steadily going uphill.

"Are you happy carrying the flag?"

"Yes, Eloy I am."

*

The day was coming to the end and they carried on well into the night and they could admire their beautiful surroundings under a strong full moon light.

"Eloy, something is changing," said Pearl.

"What is changing?"

"So far, all the leaders, apart of my father and yours, don't have a female companion and now we've seen Bo trying to conquer Malloa and that could be the beginning of the change."

Eloy thought about it and then grinned at her. "And one of them is me, right?"

Pearl started giggling.

Prince Neno heard their conversation and came closer to her putting his left arm over her shoulders. "All the leaders?"

For a moment, Pearl was speechless and Eloy noticed her blushing.

"Well, Pearl? I don't think you are quite right."

"Er, well, can we change the subject?" she said while gently separating from the prince.

With a wide grin, the prince was moving his eyebrows up and down. "I think that right now commander Bo is doing very well getting acquainted with Malloa, don't you think so?"

Pearl felt under siege. "All right, I've got the message," she said trying to walk faster in front of them. "But still you don't have a partner with you," she said looking at Eloy and frowning.

Eloy thought about her words but decided not to answer.

Prince Neno whispered to him. "She's the right woman for a warrior you know."

Eloy whispered back. "Yes, I know and we must consider that you are not just a prince but a warrior as well."

The prince smiled while thinking and looking at Pearl. "You have a very good point there."

*

Though they were fast runners it took hours for the scouts sent by Choquero to reach the other side of the forest. They did it very cautiously without encountering any enemy and to their surprise when they came out of the forest; there were no enemies between them and the city walls.

Immediately they ran back to report.

*

Sometime has been spent by Eloy and his entourage moving towards the hills in the south and finally they came out of the trees facing the path towards the cavern.

They were enjoying the moonlight on open grounds and they could feel the tranquillity surrounding them.

Soon they had reached the avenue with the stone guards, which still make them feel apprehensive though full of respect. They were getting used to see those statues but for Mela it was all new and Lera noticed. "Don't you worry Mela you are amongst friends and these statues are here to protect."

"I can believe that because I can feel their presence."

Pearl looked at the statues. "I can guess that in a certain way they are doing their job."

"Yes," said the prince, "and they still impress me."

Eloy overtook them. "Come on, we are nearly there."

*

They reached the cavern entrance and after looking at it, they lit a couple of torches and entered.

Thanks to the torches light they could see their surroundings with some of the light reflecting from some rocks with different colours because of so much quartz and went straight to the side of the ruined alter entering the small room with the throne and the skeleton sitting on it.

The strange light was still emanating from the walls though they kept the torches burning.

Eloy sat on the ground and the entire group did the same.

"What now?" asked Pearl.

"Now we wait," said Eloy.

"There was a moment of silence. "Wait for what," whispered commander Lera.

"Maybe there will be an apparition? Maybe a ghost will appear and talk to us?" said Pearl looking apprehensive.

Eloy just shrugged his shoulders. "I really don't know but nevertheless, I have the strong feeling that something will happen."

"Oh?" said Lera nodding and looked around nervously.

Suddenly they all felt at peace and to their surprise some little fairies appeared in mid-air, like popping out of nowhere.

Commander Lera's jaw dropped and so did the others.

Nobody said a word and the ghost of the old woman materialised in front of the throne and she was wearing the same gown the skeleton had though the colours were more vivid.

"Glorious warrior," she said with a very strong whisper. "You have accomplished part of your task and the people are already looking at you as their rightful leader. You have many brave commanders and warriors at your command. Soon the war will end but its success will depend on everybody's cooperation and discipline though you must remember that goodness is on your side. May the Holy Spirit guide you in your quest; now go and fulfil your destiny. When that is done, once again, the kingdom will have a king."

The ghost faded away and the fairies did the same.

For a moment, they all stayed sitting and saying nothing.

"All right," said Pearl standing up, "we heard the old lady and you Lera can close your mouth."

*

Eloy looked at all of them with a serious expression.

"What do you want us to do now?" asked Pearl.

"What we'll do right now is to stay in the cavern for what's left of the night and I think that some of you should go outside and collect some dead wood to build up a fire."

Immediately everybody knew what to do and Neno with Pearl left the cavern to go for it followed by others while the rest of the archers started a fire with some scattered twigs in the centre of the hall facing the palace ruins.

They didn't have to go outside with torches because the moonlight was covering the whole of the land.

*

Outside the cavern, Neno and Pearl walk away from the others and Neno stopped collecting wood and looked at Pearl.

Instinctively, Pearl stopped collecting dead wood and for a moment, she did nothing.

"If it wasn't for the invaders and now with all what we've done preparing for war, I wouldn't have had the chance to meet you."

For a brief moment Pearl didn't know what to say but then she came closer to him with a radiant expression."

"Hey!" said somebody closer to them. It was Lera and some of the female archers with her. "Why you are not collecting wood?"

They were startled and immediately they grabbed some twigs and returned to the cavern while Lera and her archers carried on collecting more wood though looking at Neno and Pearl while holding their laughter.

*

Choquero heard the news from his scouts. "Very well, those are very good news and I think that the enemy General has called all his soldiers to be inside the city." Then he gave new orders calling for two warriors to approach. "Now you go to commander Bo with the news and you will go to commander Barum." Then he looked at the two exhausted scouts. Have a good rest and something to eat and then you'll go back there," he said pointing towards the forest, "to keep an eye on the enemy just in case the General sends some of them out of the city and do try to get some sleep."

*

After eating something, Eloy and friends make themselves comfortable lying around the fire.

Neno grabbed a piece of bread and went to sit close to Pearl who was close to Eloy.

Pearl had a thought. "I hope the other commanders will stay in the forest giving their warriors plenty of time to rest saving all their energy until tomorrow.

Eloy agreed with her. "Yes, I'm sure they will."

Lera came closer to them and sat close to Eloy. "In the morning, we'll have our bodies well rested and full of energy and if we go back to the village where commander Bo is, we can have some of that flat bread they make with tomatoes on top."

Lera was deep in thought. "Tomorrow will be the day Eloy."

He looked at her with a fade smile. "I don't understand why good things sometimes come to your life when there is no time for anything but fighting. I should have known you before but tell me, where do you live?"

"I live in one of the villages on the south east of the forest and far away from the sea though we have a small river and the land is fertile. The river is fed by many streams coming from the mountains way west of the prairie and the stream that feeds the city canal comes out of that river."

"So, you are a farmer the same like me."

"Oh yes, though our land is small, we have a big house that my father had built with the help of the family and some neighbours."

"Do you have a favourite vegetable? Mine is tomatoes."

"Mine too though they are not a vegetable but a fruit."

"Yes, you are right and I hope you don't mind to stay close to me from now on. I like to talk with somebody who knows about farming." She looked at him surprised and Eloy immediately changed that. "And I like your company."

Suddenly one of the young women started to sing one of the country's folklore songs and soon others joined in.

They didn't have any musical instruments but their beautiful voices didn't need any help.

Outside the cavern the land was at peace and in the sky because of the bright moon, only a few stars could be seen.

Chapter Fourteen

The whole night had passed with the morning well illuminated by a rising sun giving to all of them the energy the sun can give early in the morning.

"All right everybody," said Eloy, "we are leaving now.

Pearl and Neno left the cavern and strolled close to the statues guarding the path and once again he put his left arm on Pearl's shoulders but this time she didn't say a word.

"Beautiful day."

"And I feel happy to be here with you," she said almost in a whisper and turned to look at him.

It was one of those moments, when people don't speak and just look at each other; there expression was stronger than words.

Slowly their faces came together and they kissed.

"You forgot the flag," said Mela approaching them and gave the flag to Pearl.

Pearl with the flag took the lead in the company of Prince Neno with Eloy right behind them in the company of Mela and Lera. The rest of the arches fall behind.

*

A new dawn was upon the kingdom of Onuvar but still, in the city there was no happiness.

There were enemy patrols everywhere and very few city dwellers were brave enough to venture out of their homes. Nevertheless, commander Marum managed to have a meeting in Amina's home, with the ministers.

"Ministers, the time of the rebellion in the city is coming closer. I have not received any messenger from our friends outside the city but we have all noticed that the General had call everybody back to reinforce the walls and the rest of his army has arrived and that means he must suspect something's going on. Nevertheless, you must know that the city guards have managed to organise themselves and with their new commander will join in the rebellion."

"I'm happy to hear that but though our people are ready," said the Prime Minister, "it will be difficult for them to move to take position closer to the south gates as you have instructed us."

"In that case Minister, you must find another way to do it because we need those people close to the gates."

The Minister for the Interior had an idea. "I will instruct my people to start moving one by one to stay in the houses close to the main gates and wait there."

"Now that is a good idea and you could do something similar in the centre of the city," said commander Marum looking at the Foreign Minister.

"Yes, it will be done."

"And I'll do the same closer to the south gates," said the Prime Minister.

"Very well," said Eloy, "now go and do your duty."

*

General Agaram entered the palace with his usual arrogance and the Queen's guards had no choice but to move aside and let him pass.

Talking to his personal guards he was loud and the Queen's attendants heard him and immediately attended her to make sure she was properly dressed.

By the time the General pushed the chambers doors open and entered, she was ready standing straight and adamant.

"What brings you to my chambers this time General?"

For a moment, he just looked at her and then at her attendants. "Not much I can tell you, considering that by now your attendants must have informed you that the city is finally firmly in my grip and all my army is in control."

"That's what you think General."

He exploded in a rage. "Put it in your thick head! There is no resistance in the city and your pathetic rebellion is almost none!" Then he calmed down. "I'm going to ask you for the last time. Will you marry me?"

Still with her adamant attitude, she answered him loudly. "No!"

Her attitude was unexpected and her voice loud. Nevertheless, it startled the General who quickly recovered. "Very well, as you wish," he said and while leaving he shouted at her. "From now on nobody will leave these chambers!"

The attendants came closer to the Queen. "What are we going to do now Your Majesty?" asked Nadia.

"That I don't know but I wish I know where Amina is."

"We haven't seen her but I think she is still in the palace," added the same attendant.

Thank you, Nadia nevertheless, I need to see her."

*

In the meantime, Amina who had been outside the chambers in the corridor had heard everything and immediately grabbing a jar from a console table close to the chambers doors left the palace before the rest of the soldiers had their new orders.

*

She tried to go to her home but she had to go to the well in the square first.

She saw it was full of soldiers and horses leaving very little room for anything.

Many soldiers recognised her and started cheering. "Come on Amina! Dance for us!"

The street musicians had returned to the square and were playing to entertain them but with her presence, they started a different tune, which triggered the attention of soldiers in the adjacent street.

She had no choice but to dance though she could only do it at the edge of the square where there was no manure and grabbing a tambouring, she was ready.

"Come on!" she cried, "make room for my dancing!"

The horse soldiers moved their horses further away with some of them brushing some manure.

As usual, she started a slow dance and then her speed increased for the enthusiasm of the soldiers who by then were clapping their hands with the rhythm. The soldiers in the adjacent streets moved closer to the square.

That was the opportunity for the city dwellers to do something. None of the soldiers noticed some people moving cautiously using the adjacent streets though not in groups, towards the houses close to the south gates while others were doing it towards the north gates. Some of them were carrying long bamboos.

She noticed those people movements and her dance became more exotic for the soldiers' enthusiasm.

*

In the forest, there was some activity and the scouts send by Choquero had reached once again the edge of the forest and with no enemies out there they cautiously carried on using all the small bushes and small trees scattered in that area coming close to the city without being seen by the soldiers in the battlements.

The scouts send in by commander Barum joined them.

They stayed hiding behind their camouflage and from there they could hear the music from the square though it sounded far away.

"It sounds like they are having a good time," said one of them.

"We must go back and report," said another.

Slowly as they had approached, they left back to their commanders.

*

Amina carried on for a few more moment until she had no choice but to stop completely exhausted and many soldiers throw coins at her and as before some of them filled her jar with water.

With the help of some of the musicians, she put some of those coins in her pouch and bowing to the enemy, she left with the jar on her shoulder.

*

She had to negotiate her way between many more soldiers in the streets until she could reach her family home where she saw commander Marum.

"You look exhausted Amina."

"I am commander, I was dancing in the square," she said while giving her mother the jar with water and the money from her pouch. "I think my dancing has helped some people because I noticed that some crossed the streets way behind the soldiers watching my dancing."

Marum thought about it. "Very good Amina and when the time comes, that's precisely what you are supposed to do to distract as many enemies as you can."

"Yes, commander I know. Dancing is the secret weapon I mentioned before and so far, it's working because the soldiers didn't notice the city dwellers moving in the streets behind them carrying bamboos."

Commander Marum looked at her with a bright expression. "And a very good weapon according to what I've heard but tell me. What news from the palace?"

"Not much, apart of the usual. The General asked the Queen for the last time if she will marry him but once again, she said no and obviously, he exploded into a rage giving the orders that nobody will leave the palace. I managed to do it by reaching the gates before those soldiers knew about it."

"How will you go back inside?"

"I don't think that will be a problem but we must keep in mind that after I return to the palace I will have to stay there."

Commander Marum thought about it very seriously. "In that case it means you won't have the time to distract the soldiers in the square for us to start the rebellion."

Amina realised about the problem. "I'll have to think about that but so far I don't think so."

"Very well then, you will inform the Queen that we are very close to the uprising and to be prepared for it. Tell her the city guards are ready to join us with a new commander call Anton."

"Very well, Commander."

*

The scouts sent by commander Choquero had gone back to him and reported.

"There is music in the city but we don't know why."

"Not to worry now, I'm sure soon we'll know about it. Now we'll wait for Eloy's orders."

*

Eloy and entourage were coming closer to Bo's camp.

"Maybe we can have some more of that delicious flat bread they make," said Prince Neno.

"And some fresh coffee," added Pearl.

Barum's face brightened. "Hopefully some fried eggs, I can almost smell them."

"I can smell the fresh coffee and bread," said an enthusiastic Lera and her archers nodded enthusiastically.

The day was getting warmer and soon they reached the village where Bo and Malloa welcome them. This time she had a sword in a sheath hanging from a belt.

Some warriors approached them with bread, coffee and a frying pan with plenty of scrambled eggs.

Mela was happy to see Malloa. "Are you happy my friend?"

"Yes, I am and Bo is teaching me how to use a sword."

"So you are back and today is the day, Eloy," said an enthusiastic Bo.

They look at each other and the spontaneous happiness they had disappeared for a moment and they carried on eating and having some coffee without saying a word.

"Well my friends," said Eloy, "let's hope this day will be a short one."

"Come on," said Pearl, "we must go now; we must reach the core of our army with commander Choquero in charge."

Pearl approached Malloa. "Are you happy here?"

"Yes, I am and he's been teaching me how to use the sword. He's a good man and I want to be close to him in battle."

"All right, in that case I'll be seen you in the city later on. Hopefully inside."

"So be it."

"See you later glorious leader," said a happy Bo.

They all left Bo's camp still eating the delicious flat bread with plenty of tomatoes and onions on it.

*

The prairie was a big place and plenty of forest separated the three-army units but now they were all resting and just waiting.

It was easy to find Choquero's camp at the edge of the forest. They were so many and had several fires on for their cooking.

The cavalry was resting nearby with the horses feeding on fresh grass and not far behind the rest of the rebel population was still moving on the prairie herding the animals.

"Aren't you afraid for the enemy seen your fires?" asked Eloy.

"No, son because we are too far away from the city and my scouts would have report any enemy by now and so far, all they have told me is that there is music in the city."

The two young boys with Eloy stepped into their conversation. "We know what the music is about," said Insa.

"Yes, that's Amina dancing for the soldiers," said Daba.

Eloy had a thought. "I hope that commander Marum uses her dancing to distract the enemy before we attack."

"She's very good with her dancing," said Insa. "and she calls it her secret weapon."

"And we understand that her dancing has already been used by the city dwellers to move in the streets behind the soldiers when they are watching her," added Daba.

"She is a very brave young woman," said Eloy.

*

Pearl wanted to carry on. "I'm sorry to interrupt. All that information is very interesting but are we staying here with your father or carry on to commander Barum's camp?"

"In my case I must see all the commanders and so far, Barum is the last one. All right then, I'm ready and thank you boys."

"It's all right," said Daba.

"Any time," added Insa.

"Are you coming back here after seen Barum?" asked Choquero.

"No, I don't think so father because I have already started a plan of attack using our navy but you'll never know. I might come back."

"Whatever it is, I wish you good luck my son."

He left with Pearl and the prince, followed by Lera and her archers.

By then Mela had a little more experience with the bow and already had a quiver full of arrows on her back.

*

Though it took some time, they reached commander Barum's camp. Most of it was outside the forest.

"Welcome my glorious leader," he said lifting his arms as a salute.

"Thank you, commander and I can see all your warriors are well armed with swords and a few shields with a few female archers as well. I can see that some of them have a metal helmet."

"Yes, they have and a few more archers have joined us."

"Very well then, I have thought about a plan of attack and all we need now is to make sure the boats are ready to transport some of the army to a cove further east my village."

"All right Eloy I will send a scout to the cove and one to the cavern where they are supposed to be but with what message?"

"The message to the cove is very simple. To tell them to be prepared to receive more boats and wait for us and the message to the fishermen in the cavern is for them to join the boats in the cove." Immediately Barum sent two warriors.

"Now you can rest and have something to eat until they return."

"Thank you, commander," said Eloy.

"In commander Bo's camp, we had something very special," said Pearl while pushing the flagpole in the soft ground to stand up.

"Yes," said Lera, "it was a kind of flat bread with plenty of cooked tomatoes and onions on top."

"Oh yes," said Barum, "I've heard about that kind of bread but in my camp, we have managed to catch some wild chickens which as you know are very plentiful in the forest and right now some of my warriors turned cooks are roasting them in some mud ovens they have made."

"Yummy, yummy," said commander Lera and all her archers nodded enthusiastically.

"I don't think you can catch enough chickens to feed all your warriors," said Eloy, "there are not so many wild chickens."

"That's true and the rest of my warriors had to be content to eat bread and dehydrated vegetable soup." Saying so he burst with laughter.

*

Some archers came to sit close to Eloy, Pearl, the prince and Lera. One of them was Mela and somehow commander Barum noticed the young women and felt enthusiastic sitting with them and chatting.

"It's been a while since I had the chance to talk to young women because in the village fortress there was always quite a lot to do and no time to socialise with anybody. Young women were always very busy practicing with their bows."

Pearl started giggling. "Why don't you ask if some of them would like to join your warriors?"

Barum blinked his eyes and looked at the young archers that by now were giggling and looked at Mela. "What's your name?"

"I'm Mela."

"All right Mela, would you like to join me?"

Mela stopped giggling and looked at her commander. Barum noticed and asked. "What about you?"

Lera stopped giggling though still very happy. "No, I'm their commander and they are supposed to follow me to give our leader some protection with what's left of my command if some of them will join you, which I don't mind."

"Good but you haven't given an answer," he said looking at Mela.

"Erg, yeah, all right, I'll stay."

A small group of Lera's archer felt enthusiastic and wanted to join commander Barum.

"All right," said Lera, "You can stay as well."

"Good," said Barum, "now we have that settled we better have something to eat."

Some warriors approached them with a basket full of roasted chickens and in good old fashion they just grabbed them, ripped them with their hands and passed the pieces to each other. It was a feast.

"What do you want to do next," asked Pearl.

Eloy managed to swallow a piece of chicken. "As soon as we get the news from the boats, we'll go back to my father's camp."

*

Barum's camp was a happy one and after they finished roasting chickens, they used the ovens to bake bread, which they enjoyed with some cheese.

They had plenty of coffee to wash it down.

*

It took a few hours for the scouts to return. After all, they were not far from the cavern and the sea was just at the other side of the hills on the north of the prairie.

"That was very fast," said Eloy.

"We know this part of the country and all the short cuts in the hills near the sea," said one of them.

"Many boats are there in the cove ready in waiting," said the second scout.

"How many boats are there?"

"I could see about twenty-five," said the first scout.

"And more boats will join them soon," said the other.

Eloy thought about it. "Very well then and according to my calculations if each boat can take no more than seven, it means twenty-five can easily transport hundred and seventy-five warriors and with the other boats we can easily send two hundred warriors. Considering the number of warriors each army group has, you and Bo will provide twenty-five each and my father having more, will provide the other hundred and fifty," said Eloy standing up. "You commander Barum will now choose your warriors to go to the boats and wait for the rest of the warriors to join them."

"You heard our leader," said Barum, "now select twenty-five and send them to meet the boats," he ordered his second in command. Then he had a though. "Who will lead them?"

"That I have not decided yet but don't you worry my friend. I'll find somebody and now we'll have to go commander and I wish you and your men good luck."

"Thank you, Eloy and let's hope for the best."

Pearl put the flag on her shoulder. "I'm ready."

Eloy left with his entourage going back to Choquero's camp.

Pearl was feeling enthusiastic. "Your personal guards have been reduced in numbers and it was those archers' decision to stay with commander Barum. I could see the look in Mela's face. I think she fancies the commander."

"Pearl, you are beginning to sound like a matchmaker."

"What, me a matchmaker? Never."

*

In Choquero's camp, they had another meeting and Choquero was addressing them.

"This morning everybody was feeling very enthusiastic with the idea that today is the day for our attack but so far part of the day is gone and we are still here."

"Yes, father but we cannot rush anything. So far, all our army groups are in the right place and now we know that the boats, or the navy as some people call it," he said looking at a smiling Pearl, "are waiting for the warriors to board them."

"How many warriors I need to send to the boats."

"I have already calculated the total amount and your contribution will be exactly hundred and fifty."

"That will leave me with a reduced number of warriors but I must consider the female archers and some more warriors that just join me and my numbers will be all right and don't forget the cavalry with me. Very well, so be it" and he called one of his commanders, "Capana, choose hundred and fifty warriors and send them to join the boats with you commanding them."

There was some commotion with many of his warriors putting their arms up volunteering for the task.

"All right father, we'll stay here in your camp and this will be my headquarters." Then he had a thought. "I need to talk to the commander of your warriors to give him the instructions for the rest of the force going by sea."

"Very well, son, Capana! Come and join us!"

Capana approached holding a wooden shield with his sword in a sheath hanging from his belt. He was one of the warriors with a metal helmet.

*

Daba!" called Eloy and the boy came running. "You will go to commander Bo's camp and tell him to send twenty-five of his warriors to join the boats in the cove under the command of Capana."

Without any hesitation, Daba left running.

*

"Commander Capana," said Eloy, "from now on you will be the commander of the force going east by sea. When you reach the cove a bit further east of the city, you will advance and enter the city without letting the enemy see you."

"Yes, sir, I will do my best but how can I enter the city?"

"Very simple, Insa one of my messengers will go with you to show you the way. Once inside you will join forces with commander Marum and his warriors. The main objective was to take the main gates and open them for us."

"Very well commander."

Remember to pass my message to commander Marum to wait until he and you hear the sound of commander Barum attacking the main gates. That will distract the soldiers on the walls."

"Yes, sir, it will be done."

Then commander Choquero remembered something. "Before you go Commander, when the warriors are ready close to the city, I want you to send a couple of messengers to my camp, so I will know you are in position. By then my camp will be close to the other side of the forest." Capana saluted in military fashion.

"Wait commander," called Eloy, "Insa" he called and the boy came running. "You will go with commander Capana and show him the way to enter the city."

The boy joined commander Capana and a moment later, they were leaving towards the hills by the seaside.

*

Everything was moving accordingly and the whole of the army started to settle down to rest, though some of them carried on practicing with their swords and bows.

There was a sort of uneasy tranquillity with most of them and the singing by some women and men help others to relax.

*

It was a serious distance to commander Bo's camp but Daba did very well delivering the message.

"What?" said the commander, "I'll be left with only hundred and twenty-five warriors." Then he thought about it. "Oh, what the heck it has to be done." He called his warriors to gather closer to him. "Twenty-five of you will go to the seaside and join the boats in the cove under the command of Capana. Our glorious leader is planning something very important and I prefer if some of you will volunteer."

There was great enthusiasm amongst his warriors and in no time, the twenty-five warriors were leaving with Daba going with them.

*

With his headquarter well established in his father's camp, it was more relaxing for Eloy and Pearl to decide the rest of their movements.

Some warriors had improvised a small table using just dead wood and on top of it, there was an animal hide with a map and Eloy with Pearl, Prince Neno, Choquero and Lera were studying the situation.

Eloy put his right hand on the part of the map showing where the forest was. "We must advance our army inside the forest until the other side but we must make sure to stay well behind the trees until the moment of the attack. It must be a surprise and I will send instructions to commander Bo to do the same. He will be the one to attack first towards the south gates. When that happens, we will attack the west side of the city to create a distraction while Barum will wait for his time to attack the main gates. By then commander Capana will be ready to sneak inside the city to join commander Marum to attack and try to open the gates and when that happens hopefully the cavalry will be the first to go through."

They remained in silence for a moment and Choquero spoke. "That's it? That's the plan?"

"Of course, what else can we add to it?"

Choquero shrugged his shoulders. "I cannot think about anything else. Very well then, when do you want to start?"

"Now. We have what's left of the day and the whole of the night to reach our position."

Choquero gave the hand signal for his army to start moving and they all did it with discipline, though this time Eloy, his father with Pearl, the prince and Lera with her archers stayed behind just to check that everybody was going in the right direction, with the slower people entering the forest coming behind with the herds.

*

Later on, the twenty-five warriors from Bo's camp passed by with Daba.

This time Eloy let those warriors to carry on and he sent Daba with new instructions. "Daba, I'm sorry but so far you are the fastest messenger I have so I'm sending you back to commander Bo to tell him to advance towards the edge of the forest on the south-east side and be ready to attack the south gates when I send him the signal for it."

Somehow, Daba felt disappointed. "Very well but it will take me longer to reach him because I feel very tired."

"I understand Daba but so far you have been a great help and before you go get yourself some food."

"Yes, sir."

Eloy approached his father. "It will be wise to send a messenger to the people in the cavern for them to join commander Barum and for the fishermen still there to return to their villages though to stay at sea until it is safe for them to enter their villages.

Immediately Choquero send two warriors with the message.

*

Eloy gave the hand signal. "Now we follow the army. It will take us the rest of the day and part of the night to cross the forest."

As it was expected, Pearl was prompt to put the flag on her shoulder and was ready to go passing some of her confidence and enthusiasm to the rest of the group.

*

There was plenty of activity in the cove with all those fishing boats and the warriors getting aboard. The extra boats were already arriving.

It took some hours and the last warriors to arrive were from Bo's camp and quickly climbed aboard. All the boats had a kind of ladder made of manila ropes.

Harmon was giving instructions to everybody and soon they were ready.

The sea was calm and they started by rowing first until they were out at sea and there they put the masts and sails up catching the wind.

It was quite a spectacle to see all those sailing boats moving steadily east while all the warriors were cleaning and sharpening their swords.

Harmon was standing at the bow of his boat leading the flotilla like an Admiral.

In another boat, right behind him was commander Capana.

*

It was an exhausting trip towards commander Bo and it took Daba a good four hours to reach him and pass the message.

"Thank you, Daba. Now you come with us."

"No, commander I must go back to be close to our glorious leader."

"Very good Daba and thank you for your help."

*

Immediately Bo gave the orders for his men to put the fires out and they all left the village following a gorge with a road at the side of the stream leading them towards the city. Loni with Alana did the same and with their warriors fall behind commander Bo's warriors with the two supply wagons.

Daba was left alone and after having something to eat, he left going back to Eloy though this time walking slowly.

By then the day was coming to an end.

*

In the north, commander Barum was moving his warriors inside the forest and passing not far from the entrance to the cavern though they didn't stop but to his surprise some people came out of it joining him.

"You must be from the cavern."

Yes," said a man but we were instructed to join the people in the forest while our women will sail back to our villages."

"All right, you just fall behind us."

*

By then Mela was getting very friendly with Barum.

"If everything goes as planned we might be inside the city by tomorrow."

"Yes, Mela that's what we all want but we are not there yet and I think you better carry on practicing with the bow; I will need close to me a good archer to give me some protection," he said while smiling to her and she smiled back.

*

The three groups of the rebel army were moving slowly through the forest though in silence. By then the mood of enthusiasm has been replaced by apprehension with many of them and night was upon them.

"I think we better stop and wait until tomorrow morning," said Pearl.

"We'll need all the daylight we can get," was Choquero's opinion.

In a way, Eloy agreed with him. "Yes, father but we must try and make camp as close as possible to the edge of the forest.

"Very well, son and I remember a place which is only a couple of hours from the end of the forest."

*

The boy Daba arrived where Eloy's camp was supposed to be but they had already gone and though feeling disappointed he had no other choice but to follow their trail. He had the help of a full moon lighting his way.

It didn't take long for him to catch up with the people herding the animals that had stopped for the night but he decided not to stay with them and so he carried on.

*

Time was passing and several hours later, they had finally reached a place with fewer trees and Choquero gave the orders to stop and make camp in between the trees.

"Very good father," said Eloy, "now send messengers to commanders Bo and Barum to wait for the morning and not to make any fires, above all not to make any noises. The instructions for commander Bo are for him to use his initiative when to start moving towards the city south gates and hopefully with plenty of noise to attract the attention of the enemy on the walls. He is the one to start the attack and the instructions for commander Barum are similar, to start with the first daylights towards the main gates and start teasing the soldiers in the battlements but after a few moments he will retreat and disappear. He will repeat that system as many times as he can to create some confusion amongst the soldiers to give the chance for commanders Marum and Capana to attack the main gates and try to open them."

"You heard the instructions, now go," were Choquero's orders. The messenger warriors didn't waste any time and left running.

"Now what do we do Eloy?" asked Pearl while leaving the flag against a tree.

"Well, I don't know about you but I'm going to lie down somewhere close to a tree and try to have some sleep," and left disappearing behind some trees before Pearl had a chance to say anything.

*

Instead of looking for a place to have some sleep Eloy went to the top of a hill at the side of the camp from where he could see the city in the distance.

"I've never seen you on your own before," said a gentle voice from behind him. He turned and Lera was there smiling at him.

"Lera, I didn't hear you approaching. You are a good warrior if you can walk without been heard."

"Do you mind if I stay here and keep you company?"

Eloy was in a way surprised but quickly recovered. "No, I don't mind."

She came closer to him. "I'm a bit scared about tomorrow. Maybe some of my archers will be killed."

"I can see that you care more for your archers than for yourself."

Lera nodded. "Yes, I do. They are very good women and they really want to liberate the country. The point is that I don't want them to die before having a chance to have a family."

She started shivering and Eloy noticed putting his left arm on her shoulders. "Why are you shivering? It isn't cold."

"I know, in my case it is just nerves but don't you worry, I'll be all right in the morning."

"Come we must go back to camp where I'll get you a blanket."

*

They reached the camp coming close to Pearl, Neno and Choquero that were already asleep in a clearing and Lera sat against a tree.

A moment later, Eloy brought a blanket to cover her legs. "There, now you'll feel much better."

He sat at her side and she grabbed his hand. "You are a good man Eloy and the people have acknowledged you as their leader."

Eloy remained in silence for a moment and started to look at her.

Their talking woke up Pearl. "Yes, Eloy she's a very attractive woman."

Eloy looked at Pearl. "Eh?" then he looked at Lera and quickly stood up leaving.

Their talking woke the others up. "Where are you going?" asked Choquero.

"I'm going to see if everybody is all right."

Pearl and Lera looked at each other and started giggling.

"Come on girls," said Neno, "you embarrassed him."

"Leave my son in peace he's got many things in his mind," said Choquero while covering himself with a blanket holding back his laughter.

*

The boy Daba arrived coming close to Choquero and in a way collapsed close to a tree. "This time I hope to stay here, because I'm very tired."

"It's all right Daba, you have done very well and now is the time for you to have some sleep so go and get yourself a blanket."

"All right. I don't think I could have done any more walking."

"It's all right," said commander Choquero. We are going nowhere until the morning."

*

In the meantime, and with the help of a strong breeze, the rebel's navy arrived at the cove east of the city. Though there was plenty of moonshine, the dark of night was their camouflage. By then the moon had started to go down in the west.

"How will I know if it is safe for me to go back to my village later on?" asked Harmon.

"I don't know but I'm sure that our leader Eloy will send you the message," said Capana, "on the other hand, why don't you come with us and find out?"

"Yes, now that is a very good idea," then he gave his instructions to the fishermen, "you will stay here until I send words to you."

*

Leading his men, Capana followed the path to the top of the cliff and started their approach to the city.

They approached the canal cautiously and stopped doing their best to stay behind bushes and trees.

Capana called two of his men. "You will go to commander Choquero's camp and inform him of our arrival. Don't forget to tell him that we'll try to enter during the night but make sure to use any path close to the seaside to approach the forest. Before you reach Choquero you will come close to commander Barum and tell him we are ready to enter the city."

The two messengers left and he ordered his men to lie down and rest.

*

The moon was still giving some light for everybody to see their surroundings though by then it was going down in the west.

Eloy carried on walking through the camp and everybody was scattered in between the trees.

Some moonlight was still coming through the canopy giving the magic touch leaving many places in darkness.

This time he reached the edge of the forest from where he could see the city but there was no music coming out of it.

Lera approached him with the blanket over her shoulders. "Thank you for the blanket."

"It's all right but how do you feel now?"

"Much better, thank you. So, this time tomorrow we might be inside the city."

"Some people will but others won't."

"I know."

Eloy put his right arm around her shoulders and turned her to face him.

Lera rested her head on his chest. "I think that after this war is over people will have a normal life once again."

"Yes, Lera they will and I'll go back to work in the land with my father."

"Do you have plenty of land?"

"Yes, we do. Well, enough to feed our family and sell the surplus in the village and whatever is left we sell in the city market. What about you?"

"We are not really farmers though we farm the land close to the house but my father is a good carpenter and he makes plenty of furniture he sells to the villagers and some of it in the city. He uses the trees we have and he uses a system. For every tree he cuts, he plants two; the system has been used by the family for many generations and that's why there are so many trees close to the village."

"When all this trouble is over you'll go back to your village but tell me, where are your parents?"

My father was in the city with my mother when the invasion started and they didn't return home."

"In that case when we enter the city you can look for them."

"I hope they are alive."

"No, Lera you must think positively. All right, now it is time to try and have some sleep," he said and for the first time he gave her a kiss.

She left and he stayed there just looking at the city.

By then the moon had gone down in the west and the land was covered with darkness.

*

Slowly Eloy went to where Lera, Pearl, the prince and Choquero were. I think the warriors with Capana will have a good camouflage with no moon lighting the night." Saying that he lay down close to Lera and soon he was a sleep.

*

In the meantime, and using the darkness without moonlight Capana ask the boy Insa to enter the city with some of the warriors. "When you reach the first houses, you'll tell the people to send the message to many other houses to keep their doors open and above all with no lights inside the houses, in that way many more of my warriors will enter the city and go straight inside the houses, understood?" Insa nodded and left followed by ten warriors. Then Capana send a few more warriors into the water with the instructions of moving under the wooden bridge and as soon as the first warriors had entered the city for them to do the same.

By then there was almost no moon light.

*

On the walls, the enemy soldiers had gathered around the fires with only a couple of them looking over the wall though not all the time and Capana signalled for his remaining warriors to get some rest.

*

The messenger arrived at Bo's camp passing on the message.

"Very well and now you will stay with us. Get yourself a place where you can have some sleep."

"Yes, sir," and in no time the messenger was trying to sleep with his back against a tree.

*

In the meantime, Insa with the warriors had swum and walked in the canal towards the wall using some sticks on their heads.

The moon had gone behind the mountains in the west and because of the darkness any soldiers on the walls could not possibly see them.

Once inside the city and without making any sounds Insa left the stream followed by the ten warriors using the steps close to the wall and went to the first house and a moment later leaving the door open he carried on to the other houses.

The warriors under the wall obeyed their orders and soon one by one went to the houses and entered with the ones under the wooden bridge moving under the wall first and then up the steps.

It didn't take long for Capana with the rest of his warriors to enter the city under the cover of darkness and soon all his forces were in safe houses.

Chapter Fifteen

Many noisy birds woke all the warriors in the patriot's army and in a few moments, they were all walking around but without making any fires.

They had enough food in their satchels with many of them just chewing some of the salted meat pushing it down with water. After all, they all had a small water bottle in their satchels.

*

At that moment, the two messengers from commander Capana arrived to Choquero's camp and reported to Eloy. "When we left, our warriors were in position and ready to get inside the city."

"And he told us to stay with you," said the other messenger.

"We already passed the message to commander Barum," said the first messenger.

"Very good and now you'll stay close to me. I might need you later."

Prince Neno, Choquero, Lera and Pearl joined Eloy for instructions while many warriors were moving closer to them.

"This is the day Eloy," said Pearl.

"Yes, it is and the messengers from commander Capana had arrived and hopefully the commander will have some of his men or maybe all of them inside the city by now and ready to help commander Marum to attack and open the main gates when commander Barum attacks." Then he looked at Neno. "How do you feel Neno."

Neno stretched his arms. "Quite energetic my glorious leader."

Pearl gave him a hug. "That's my prince."

Lera started giggling. "Give him room to breathe woman."

Choquero was approaching them and saw what was going on. Though he was close to giggling he interrupted them. "All our forces are in place but we don't know about Capana. What we don't know is if he is in the right place."

"It's all right father, I just had two of his messengers telling me that by now he should have at least some of his warriors inside the city."

"All right, I'm happy to hear that things are moving."

"Commanders Bo and Barum must be moving to attack," said Pearl.

"Yes, I know but we must wait and be patience."

*

Commander Bo had started to move towards the city with Loni and Alana at his side and all his warriors were walking in certain kind of formation leaving behind the hills and gorges of the forest, this time using the flat land closer to the city. Malloa was close to him holding a small wooden shield. Her sword was hanging at her side.

Suddenly he embraced her. "I'm happy to go into battle with a beautiful woman at my side. Destiny has brought us together."

"Yes," said Malloa gently separating from him. "But now your warriors need you to lead them."

Bo shrugged his shoulders. "Ah, yes, duty calls."

Saying that he moved to be at the head of his warriors with Malloa at his side.

*

They advanced until they came out of the forest facing the south gates.

Those were some very nervous moments and after breathing deeply in he gave his battle cry. "Now, Attack!"

With the sound of many horns, his warriors started their attack by shooting a couple of arrows while yelling like mad, which make the enemy soldiers very nervous.

Some soldiers gave the alarm with the sound of many horns and mayhem invaded that part of the city with many enemy soldiers coming from other parts of the walls.

The enemy commander gave the order and the stones thrown by the catapults hit the grounds close to Bo's warriors.

General Agaram went straight to one of the palace balconies facing the city centre. A soldier came to the balcony. "The attack is against the south gates."

Without saying a word, he left and soon he was running followed by many of the soldiers in the palace, first to the city square and then straight up the wall close to the south gates. "Tell me is there any other attack somewhere else?"

"No, General," said his second in command, "so far this is the only one."

He looked at Bo's warriors for a moment and then he smiled. "This is not an army. Just save your arrows and carry on throwing stones instead."

*

Things were beginning to move and Eloy was still holding his warriors back waiting for news from commander Barum though he could hear the distant sounds of the attack in the south of the city. He could notice many soldiers had left going towards the south gates leaving only a few on the west wall.

Sometime later, a messenger arrived. "Commander Bo has started his attack towards the south city gates but the enemy is using catapults to throw stones at his men."

"Very well, tell him to continue with my best wishes. His distraction is beginning to work."

Immediately the messenger left running between the trees.

"Eloy, so far he is the only one doing something," said Pearl.

He couldn't answer because another messenger arrived.

"Commander Barum has started his move towards the city."

His message was the same. "Tell your commander to carry on with my best wishes."

*

The news reached the Queen's chambers and there was plenty of excitement amongst the attendants and all the palace guards and servants.

The guard's commander came to the chambers alone and the Queen signalled for him to approach. "Your

Majesty, most of the soldiers had left with General Agaram."

"This is it commander and now is the time to entrench ourselves in the palace and hold on until we get more news from the rebellion and hopefully some help."

"Yes, Your Majesty I will give the orders immediately."

"But who's doing anything about the enemy soldiers still in the palace?" She wanted to know.

Amina entered with a sword in her belt and the commander felt very encouraged.

"Well, Amina? What about the enemies in the palace?"

Amina answered her full of enthusiasm. "So far many servants have already given some wine to all of them but the bottles have been spike with a sleeping drug."

The Queen was feeling enthusiastic. "All right, let's hope it will work." Then she looked at Amina. "This time there will be no more dancing for the enemy soldiers."

"No, Your Majesty though commander Marum was hoping for me to use my dancing to distract as many enemies as possible but now there is an attack I don't see any soldiers going to the square to see me dancing," and he said the last words holding back her laughter.

At that moment, some of her attendants came close to the Queen and helped her to wear some light clothes and above all trousers with a belt. Immediately the attendants put the belt with the sheath around her waist.

The Queen felt very proud looking at them. "Well, girls? Are you ready?"

Amina and the rest of the attendants draw their swords and spoke in unison. "Yes, Your Majesty."

"All right girls, your first task is to make sure that only our guards are in the corridors."

Immediately Amina and Nadia ran to the chamber doors and exit but to their surprise the enemy soldiers were on the floor deep asleep.

Some guards came trotting with their commander. "The wine given to the enemy is working and the palace has been secured. The rest of the guards are on the walls all around it. Your Majesty the gates have been shut and secured with the cross bars and nobody can come in; the palace is ours."

"Very good commander, instruct your guards to put all the sleeping enemies in one room and lock the door but make sure to take their weapons away. You can give those weapons to the palace workers."

"Yes, Your Majesty."

"And don't you forget to strip them from their purses."

The Queen with her attendants went to the palace balcony to look upon the city. They could hear some clamour coming from the streets mainly from the south of the city.

*

Commander Barum came out of the forest and in full view of some soldiers left in the battlements.

With the sound of many horns, his archers approached the city walls shooting their arrows with the enemy shooting theirs.

Immediately the enemy General ordered some of the soldiers in the square to reinforce the ones on the battlements above both gates. By doing that the soldiers patrolling the adjacent streets moved closer to the square and that was the chance for the Foreign Minister to send

the message for his people to leave the houses inconspicuously and gather in the streets closer to the square.

*

As planned, Barum archers shoot one more arrow and
then he ordered the retreat back to the trees.

Some soldiers managed to shoot a couple of fireballs
but without any success because by then his warriors
were all inside the forest. All that the fireballs could do
was to burn dry grass and bushes.

*

The rumours of the attack reached the people under the
instructions of the other two Ministers and those people
started to get ready inside the houses.

Commander Marum and Capana received the news
inside the first safe house that by then it was completely packed with warriors.

"All right, it has started; go and take positions close
to the main gates and wait for the people under the command of the Minister of the Interior to start their attack
for you to join him." He left with his warriors going out
of the house one by one.

*

Moments later, Capana with his men had left the houses
one by one and using another bridge away from the walls
joined with commander Marum hiding in the streets
closer to the main gates. With these reinforcements,

Marum moved his warriors towards the main gates joined by the Minister of the Interior coming from another street leading his people. This time they did it as a strong fighting group.

Without making any sound, some of the warriors subdued the few soldiers guarding the gates while the three commanders led their men up the stone steps to the battlements engaging the soldiers. Somehow, they had a powerful force because most of the enemy soldiers were busy keeping an eye for commander Barum men.

*

Commander Bo was attacking the south walls using the tactic of attacking and retreating to the trees several times and so far, he didn't have any casualties.

Instead of using arrows, he instructed his warriors to throw stones using their slings instead. "You will save your arrows for later on!"

*

The second attack by commander Barum was more effective because there were almost no enemies facing him on the battlements and he could see many warriors on the wall pushing those soldiers away to the left and right.

*

The people close to the south gates received their instructions from the Prime Minister and came out of the houses near the gates and from nearby streets, attacking the enemy in the streets close to the gates. Most of those people had long bamboo spears but unfortunately, they didn't have shields.

The enemy on the walls reacted accordingly and many arrows hit many people though some of them managed to reach the gates and started to remove the heavy cross bar.

From the battlements above the south gates General Agaram ordered his cavalry to charge and so they did but then the Foreign Minister saw what was going on and ordered some of the people with long bamboo spears to face the cavalry formed into a wall with their spears ready.

The riders had no choice but to retreat to the square. They could not possibly attack a barrier of long bamboo's spears; they only had swords.

The city dwellers casualties were growing because of the arrows from the battlements. Nevertheless, they have managed to open the south gates and immediately they moved aside to let anybody outside the city to come in. Unfortunately, commander Bo was not close enough, which created a difficult situation.

*

General Agaram saw what happens and ordered his cavalry to charge once again, this time using the gap to come out of the gates. The people didn't have a chance to form a barrier.

By then Bo and his warriors were coming closer to the open gates.

The cavalry came out of the city charging against Bo's warriors but he ordered his warriors to let them pass and surrounded them.

With the help of many city dwellers with long bamboos coming out of the gates the enemy riders didn't have a chance. One by one, they were dismounted and their horses run away from the city followed by the riders running for their lives while his warriors throw as many stones as possible to prevent the soldiers on the wall to shoot their arrows.

*

At that moment, Choquero ordered his attack first against the west wall and after a couple of arrows; he ordered the retreat.

This time he led his people walking behind the trees to join Barum and his warriors with Eloy, the prince, with Pearl holding the flag and Lera with her archers coming right behind him.

*

Inside the city, commanders Marum and Capana could hear the commotion from commander Barum's horns that encourage them with their attack to the soldiers on the battlements and the city gates.

The warriors by the main gates were trying to remove the heavy cross bar.

The rest of Marum, Capana and the minister for the Interior's warriors flooded the battlements with such a force that those soldiers had no choice but to retreat although still on the walls.

The tactic was working because most of the soldiers were dealing with Bo's attack in the south.

The warriors trying to open the gates soon succeeded and the gates open with some cracking noises.

The warriors already on the battlements had gone in opposite directions forcing the soldiers still on it to go down and fight in the streets while others retreated on the walls going both ways.

*

In the meantime, Bo ordered his warriors to approach the gates and try to enter the city with his archers being very effective shooting their arrows to the soldiers on the battlements.

Malloa was close to his left side holding the wooden shield and she managed to stop several arrows protecting Bo's flank.

Alana was being very effective with her arrows and Loni wasn't bad at all with his sword.

*

In the meantime, Choquero has arrived and coming out of the forest joined with commander Barum.

Eloy with the archers led by Lera, Neno and Pearl joined him and together came closer to Barum.

Pearl was holding the pole with the new national flag on her shoulder.

One of the catapults on one of the towers manages to shoot a fireball injuring some of Choquero's warriors.

"Are you ready Neno," asked Pearl but the prince didn't say a word and just nodded. He, like many warriors, had a nod in his throat.

*

Marum, Capana and the Minister for the Interior with most of their warriors and city dwellers turned fighting people had already liberated the wall above the main gates and so there were no soldiers on that part of the walls.

At that moment and to everybody's surprise the city dwellers came out of their homes in all the streets, converging into the square first and then to the south and north gates holding their kitchen knives and garden tools. Somehow, the garden forks were very effective as weapons.

Many of those people went up the walls to attack the soldiers in the towers operating the catapults.

*

The uprising was general in the whole of the city. Harmon had been all the time close to Capana though doing no fighting because he didn't have a sword and though he had a dagger he managed several times to throw some stones.

*

It didn't take long for the main gates to be completely opened and Choquero ordered the cavalry to enter the city.

Some soldiers tried to stop the cavalry but Marum, Capana, the minister of the interior and Barum warriors finally defeated them letting the cavalry to pour through the gates.

They did it with Rony in command moving swiftly on the road alongside the walls to the right. They separated into smaller groups getting over the bridges to all the streets moving in the direction of the square. Some of them went riding through all the streets close to the centre. Any soldiers still in those streets had no choice but to retreat to the square.

*

Eloy saw the opportunity and cried his command. "Now people of Onuvar! Let's get in!" Choquero was at the head of those people and entered yelling like mad.

Close to the first warriors was Pearl though this time she was holding the pole straight up for everybody to see the flag.

*

As soon as they were inside the city, Choquero's warriors spread in all directions with some of them going up the walls to liberate them from any soldiers still there while others carry on through the streets towards the centre.The push was magnificent and a strong stream of warriors' flow through the open gates going right and left with Eloy.

Behind the warriors were the archers giving the aerial protection.

The boy Daba was behind Choquero and soon came together with Insa.

Their advance through the streets was easy because by then most of the enemy soldiers had gone to the square. By now, the size of the enemy army had shrunk considerably being completely outnumbered by the people of Onuvar.

Commander Barum been a big man, went straight up to the battlements to help Marum and Capana moving towards the south gates while sending some of the warriors towards the east to clear the walls from any remaining enemy soldiers still there.

The rebel army was attacking from all directions and though the enemy was more experienced, there was not much they could do.

It was very difficult for General Agaram to see how many warriors were attacking with so many city dwellers doing it from all directions.

It didn't take long for the enemy to be concentrating in the square and the walls close to the southern gates.

Commander Bo, leading his warriors, had managed to break through and was approaching the city square.

There was chaos with the enemy because of so many city dwellers attacking at the same time they could not form into battle line and those in the centre of the city had started to form behind their shields. It was only their infantry left.

By then the city guards had come out of their hidings and forming in the avenue between the palace and the square, started their advance led by their young commander Anton and they all had a sword and a shield. When coming closer to the enemy, the city dwellers saw them and moved aside letting them engage the enemy. Now, professional soldiers and professional city guards faced each other; it was spectacular.

On the battlements, small groups of enemy soldiers still there were running away chased by some city dwellers and desperately trying to reach down to the city square where their main force was battling the city guards and the city dwellers led by the Foreign Minister, the Prime Minister and Bo's warriors.

General Agaram had come down to the streets with his personal bodyguards and was trying to join his soldiers in the square. They were still a considerable force of about thousand soldiers though their will of fighting has been diminished.

*

In the meantime, the enemy soldiers left outside the palace were trying to break the main doors using a made-up ram head but the guards from the top of the walls were holding them back very well by throwing stones and arrows.

Suddenly the main doors were broken in and many soldiers entered wielding their swords.

Though they had to face the guards, they were surprised to see the Queen and her attendants with sword in hand, valiantly fighting them.

In front of the Queen was Amina using her sword very effectively with Nadia at her side.

The soldiers formed in a tight group and advanced against the Queen and attendants.

The Queen did the same and with her attendants, they proved to be tough women when it came to a fight. Amina was on her right and Nadia was on her left.

More of the palace guards led by their commander came to the Queen's aid and the enemy soldiers had no choice but to retreat.

At that moment, all the palace servants that by now had their own weapons together with the kitchen staff using their trade tools like the kitchen knives and cleavers came to the throne hall to do their fighting.

Some of them were the palace carpenters wielding their chisels, mallets and saws.

Moments later, they had surround and forced those soldiers to surrender and the rest of the enemy soldiers had left the palace and were running down to join their forces in the square.

*

The Queen with Amina and Nadia at her side and followed by the rest of her attendants and palace workers, left at the head of the Palace guards going down towards the city square.

It didn't take long for the Queen and her little force to reach the centre of the city joining the warriors and city dwellers.

There they saw the soldiers that had come from the palace with their hands up. They had surrendered, and armed angry people surrounded them.

*

The enemy General decided to leave the city. "Come!" he shouted to some of his soldiers. "We must reach the main gates and try to get out! I must form my army outside the city!"

Surrounded by his soldiers he tried to leave the square to cross the city to reach the main gates but though he tried to push the people aside, the rebel army and city dwellers had formed into a solid wall blocking his way through.

Commander Bo approached the square with his warriors from the south and Eloy, Pearl, Neno and Lera arrived in the company of Barum, Choquero, Marum and Capana with their small cavalry and with the minister for the interior's forces completely blocked the General with what was left of his powerful army. They never had the chance to cross the canal over the bridges.

All fighting had stopped and the city dwellers around the square were holding bamboo spears aimed at the enemy. The enemy soldiers were getting demoralised.

Many of the enemy soldiers in the streets around the square had surrendered throwing their weapons and putting their hands up.

The rest of the enemy soldiers around General Agaram were still holding their swords and shields though looking nervously in all directions.

The people stepped aside to make room for the Queen to approach and the General walked to the edge of the square still holding his sword and looking exhausted.

There was quite a lot of murmuring and the Queen lifted her arms for the people to stop talking and spoke. "Drop the sword General. Holding it makes you to look pathetic. Do it and save your life; we are not in the habit of killing prisoners."

The General looks at what was left of his army and dropped the sword.

Immediately the rest of his soldiers did the same.

The people and warriors shouted with happiness and once again, the Queen lifted her arms to silence them.

"You came with a powerful army to subjugate us and the people prove to you that we don't need an army because the spirit of freedom will be always powerful enough for a leader to lead us into victory. We are not barbarians and so now, you will leave this city and the kingdom of Onuvar with what's left of your army, never to return.

She signalled for the people on the side, where Eloy was, to make room for the enemy. "Let them pass!" and so they did, standing at either side of the street letting them go over a bridge and walk towards the north gates alongside the walls.

Escorted by the people shouting at them they reached the city gates and left. Many city dwellers had gone up to the battlements to see the enemy leaving though some people throw stones at them.

*

At that moment, the Queen saw the flag held by Pearl and approached her.

"Is this the flag?"

"Yes, Your Majesty and I hope you like it."

The Queen grabbed the tip of the flag. "Like it? I think it is beautiful and yes, I like it. May I?"

"Of course, Your Majesty," said Pearl giving it to her.

The Queen went to the top of the north wall above the main gates and lifted the flag as much as possible and cried. "This is our national flag from now on!"

The multitude cheered loudly and she gave it back to Pearl. "Guard well my dear."

*

They all watched the enemy retreat.

Daba and Insa were looking over the battlements.

414

It was quite a spectacle to see the Queen and the prince surrounded by Amina, Nadia, Eloy, Pearl, Lera, ministers, Anton and the commanders and the flag held by Pearl flapping slowly with the breeze.

*

The enemy led by General Agaram looked pathetic and had no choice but to walk.

"Look at them now," said the Queen, "they came with violence and arrogance and now they are leaving defeated and humiliated."

It was a sad spectacle to see the enemy leaving going back east to where they came from.

Many of those soldiers were limping while others were carried on stretchers.

At that moment, Harmon came up to the battlements to look at the retreating army.

*

The Queen turned to talk to the people down in the streets. "The gates will remain open for the people to go in and out as they please!"

The people rejoiced and started a spontaneous dance with plenty of singing.

Then she turned to her friends. "First we must organise the people to take care of all the wounded before we can have a day of festivities to celebrate our triumph."

Eloy addressed the people. "The first thing to do is to let the villagers to go back to their villages and to the forest. The city market will be active again. In the meantime, we will bring our supply wagons to distribute the food amongst the people."

"Very well," said the Queen, "I leave you to organise everything."

Immediately Eloy saw the youngsters Daba and Insa not far from him and signal for them to approach. "This time I have one last job for both of you if you feel to do it?" The two boys nodded.

"Very well, you must go inside the forest and tell the people with the herds to send some of those animals to the city and after you do that, you will tell the people taking care of the supply wagons to enter the city straight to the square and after you'll do whatever you want. You won't be in the army anymore."

Daba and Insa left running.

"Eloy."

"Yes, Pearl?"

Strange but after all that happened, it took only fifteen days to free our country."

Eloy thought about her words. "Yes, sadly though too many people died."

Harmon approached them "Wow that was quite a fight. I lost count of how many days it took as to defeat them."

"Fifteen days father."

"Wow," was the only sound make by her father.

*

The Queen left the battlements going down to the streets with Pearl at her side holding the flag.

It was sad for her and the people close to her to walk through the city streets with so many wounded and sad to see some carts pulled by people carrying the dead to the cemetery in the east of the city and followed by family and friends with many of those people crying.

She looked at those carts passing close to her and bowed. Her entourage did the same.

"It will take the rest of the day to take all the dead out of the city," said Eloy and he called Pearl's father. "Harmon send messengers to your people that by now they must have come inside the cove to return to their homes and the fishermen to go to sea and start doing some fishing. The people in the city are starving."

Harmon didn't waste any time and left running. "I'll do it myself!"

*

The cove was not far from the city and in no time, he had arrived at the top of the cliff and from there he lifted his arms for all the fishermen to see him and shouted. "The enemy has been defeated. The city has been liberated and the war is over!" The fishermen cheered with enthusiasm and he had to wait before talking again. "Now go to sea and start fishing. The people are starving!" Saying that he run down to the beach.

All the fishermen rejoiced once again screaming with happiness and without wasting any time, they boarded their boats and moved out to sea singing a fishermen's song. This time Harmon was following them though not as an admiral anymore but as a simple fisherman.

*

In the meantime, many people, mainly the villagers, were leaving the city. Many of them walked towards the south of the forest going back to their villages while others did it in different directions though walking west.

Some villagers took some of their animals back to the villages while others were herding the rest inside the city to be sold in the market.

The nurses that had come with the warriors were moving amongst the wounded helping the city doctors with Eloy and Pearl mothers helping them.

*

The whole of the city population was on the move.

For Eloy and Pearl was sad to see the damage done to the buildings and they could see many ruins blacken from the fire that destroyed them.

With his commanders Eloy went to the first safe house.

This time they could relax knowing there was no more dangers in the city.

"What are we doing now Eloy?" asked Choquero.

"Well, father, considering that food will come in from now on why don't we stay in the city until tomorrow but who ever want to go back to the villages can do it right now."

"Yes, "said Barum, "that's precisely what I want to do right now."

"Very good Commander and thank you for all your help. I'm sure we'll meet again."

Barum hold every bodies hand feeling emotional and so did all of them.

*

Queen Amanda was very emotional looking at all the damage and carried on visiting as many places as possible in the company of her three ministers.

"What we need is to build a hospital that from now on will deal with any person wounded or ill and it will be a place where people from all over the kingdom can bring their sick to be taken care by our doctors. I think the best place to have a hospital is close to the seaside and probably it could be a good idea to build it close to where the canal ends."

The Prime Minister felt enthusiastic. "Of course, that will be the best place because any dangerously injured person can be brought in by boat close to the Hospital entrance."

"And don't you forget to organise some builders to go around helping people to rebuild their homes."

The Minister bowed. "As you wish Your Majesty."

*

Though those were sad moments, already some city dwellers had started to clean the debris from the destroyed houses and taking the wood to the bakery though some of the wooden debris was piled up at the side of the square for other people to take it to be used in their cookers.

From the bakery in the heart of the city, there was plenty of smoke coming out of the chimney, telling everybody that soon there will be fresh bread for everybody.

*

It was a spectacle to see some animals coming in through the main gates and straight to the abattoir.

*

Lera has gone looking for her parents amongst the population doing what they could to help the wounded and suddenly she saw her mother with other women taking care of people lying on the streets near the square and overwhelmed with emotion she run to her and they both embraced with tears in their eyes.

"Where is father?"

"He's all right dear and right now he's helping with the distribution of food."

After a few moments with her mother Lera left to join with Eloy.

*

Eloy saw her joining him and still crying.

"What happened. Are you all right?"

"Yes, I am. I found mother and she said father was all right."

Eloy embraced her and kissed her on her forehead. "I'm happy for you. Now come, we have some work to do."

Lera carried on always close to Eloy and though his mother was around, Prince Neno stayed with his friends and above all, with Pearl making sure she was close to him at all times.

Chapter Sixteen

Several days had passed and the city was looking cleaner and tidy. All the manure had gone from the square and adjacent streets, mostly to the people kitchen gardens.

*

Eloy was helping his father with the collection of potatoes and Pearl was with them when a royal retinue arrived. It was the Queen on a horse at the head of them and they stopped working.

Choquero with Eloy and Pearl bowed to her.

"Commander Choquero I'm happy to see that your life and that of your family are back to normal."

"Yes, Your Majesty and quite happy with it."

The Queen came closer to them. "Eloy, tonight you will stay in the palace to be ready for a very special ceremony tomorrow at midday."

For Eloy, it was difficult to accept the Queen's invitation. "I'm sorry Your Majesty but after helping my father my intention was to do what I have been doing for several days and that is to visit as many city dwellers to see how to help them to recover from all the damage they suffered during the occupation."

The Queen understood. "Of course, and you should do that but tomorrow morning you must come to the palace because I am planning a very important ceremony and you Eloy must be there." Then she looked at Choquero.

"You must come too and with your wife. That invitation is extended to you and your parents too, Pearl. Please do tell your parents to come tomorrow to the palace just before midday. It is very important for your mother to be present."

Eloy, Pearl and Choquero bowed to the Queen and spoke in unison. "As you wish Your Majesty."

At the end of the working day, Eloy and Pearl left this time on horseback galloping towards the city.

Chapter Seventeen

The next day the palace gates were wide open and the people could see well inside until the throne room where the Queen was sitting with her son at her side with the other attendants close to her.

In between the thrones was the flag.

The Prime Minister with the Ministers of the Interior and Exterior were close by and this time they wore rich clothes.

In front of the throne was Pearl, Eloy with Lera, Barum with Mela and Bo with Malloa. Nearby was commander Choquero with his wife Mavina and Harmon with his wife Sanila. This time they were all wearing their best clothes though Sanila had a special cloak all blue and full of shiny pieces of polished glass resembling the stars.

Close to the Queen was Amina though this time she was wearing a guard's uniform with a sword hanging from her belt and Nadia was at her side and as well wearing a guard's uniform.

Marum and Capana were on their own nearby and enjoying what was going on.

In the front line of people were commander Loni and his female companion Alana with the boys Daba and Insa at their side and this time they were properly dressed.

Prince Neno came down the steps and approaching Pearl grabbed one of her hands and spoke loudly enough for the people close to the throne could hear him. "Dear Pearl, I know I should have asked this some time ago but nevertheless, I'll ask you now. Will you consider joining me as my wife?"

For a moment, she had a lump in her throat and just mumbled her words. "Yes, I would."

The people close to them cheered loudly.

Gently, Neno offered his arm and she held it.

Some trumpeters at the side of the throne blow a loud tune.

They walk slowly up the steps reaching the front of the thrones and the Queen signal for them to kneel.

"The Queen stood up and raised both arms. "Welcome to our family, Pearl daughter of Onuvar."

They stood up and Prince Neno sat on his throne with Pearl standing at his side.

The Queen signal for the trumpeters to play another tune and then she called with her hand for Eloy and Lera to approach.

"You have proved to be a good leader of people and the lovely Lera did a good job as your bodyguard with her archers and now I will confer the title of General to you Eloy. You'll be the General of our army."

For a moment, Eloy was confused and whispered. "Your Majesty we don't have an army. All I had was volunteers."

The Queen smiled at him. "Yes, General and your first task will be to organise one; not a big one because we must be careful with the nation's budget."

"Come on," said Pearl, "you can do it."

"And I agree with my future wife," said a giggling Neno.

Eloy realised he could not refuse. "Yes, Your Majesty as you wish," he said bowing to her.

They stepped down and a page approached commanders Barum, Marum, Bo, Capana, Loni, Rony, Harmon, Sanila and Choquero with his wife Mavina, inviting them to approach the throne to stand at the side of Eloy and Lera.

The minister of the interior approached the Queen with a tray and some medals with a blue ribbon and the Queen addressed them. "They are not big enough though they are the highest honour your country can give you."

The Queen put the medals around their necks and they turned to face the people who cheered them very loudly with the trumpeters playing a loud tune.

The Queen noticed two medals still on the cushion. "What happens Minister?"

"The Minister thought about it and call a page pointing to the first line of people facing the throne. "Bring those two young boys."

A moment later the two very surprised boys were in front of the Queen. "With these medals, you are recognised as the youngest heroes in Onuvar by risking your lives taking messages to the army right under the soldiers' noses."

She put the medals around their necks and signals for the boys to turn and face the people while lifting her arms. The trumpeters played a different tune while all the people cheered the two boys that felt very embarrassed.

*

Suddenly there was some commotion by the entrance to the throne hall and they all saw a group of five people, three men and two women, dressed like dignitaries with colourful robes, approaching the throne.

The boys stepped down joining the people, the Queen signalled with her hand for the people to let those dignitaries' approach, and they came closer and bowed. "We have come from our country to give the good news that the dictator has been deposed by the people and send into exile and from now on all what we want is peace between our two countries."

They bowed again and waited.

The Queen stood up. "Thank you for the good news and yes, from now on there will be peace between our countries; please do join our festivities."

The dignitaries bowed again and moved aside.

Then the Queen stepped aside of the throne and put her arms up to silence the crowd.

"The time has come for further changes in the kingdom and I have decided to abdicate in favour of my son Prince Neno. Come son, take your rightful place and sit on the throne as our King.

Neno sat on the left throne in the company of Pearl though she stood at his side.

At that moment, Queen Amanda waved her hand to Pearl's mother who approached the thrones and the Queen stepped aside.

Sanila walked up the steps to be as close as possible to the new monarchs. She lifted her arms facing Neno and Pearl and everybody stood still.

"This will be a memorable day in the history of Onuvar. The people have defeated an invading army and freed our country and today we have a King and a Queen in the throne. With the blessing of the Holy Spirit and the people as witnesses, I declare you both married. May you live long and reign with wisdom."

*

The Queen took the crown of her head and solemnly put it on Neno's head then she walked a few steps back and bowed to him.

Another dignitary approached with another crown. "I was wearing this crown when my husband was the King and now it belongs to you and the Queen put it on Pearl's head that by then had kneeled at the side of the throne.

Then Pearl sat on the throne at the side of Prince Neno now the King and the crowd cheered with enthusiasm.

The trumpets sounded again and a spontaneous party started in the palace.

*

"The prophecy was right," said Bo speaking to Barum who looked at him not really understanding what he was saying.

"What prophesy?"

"That the kingdom will have a King."

Barum opened his eyes. "Yeah, you're right."

*

Soon the party spread to the whole of the city and people were seen with something to eat in their hands; famine was history.

Many people had started several barbeques in the square for people to eat and there were several cow pieces in spits moved slowly on the fire by some strong men.

Amongst the crowd close to one of the barbeques were Daba and Insa enjoying some meat.

Suddenly some people started walking amongst the people giving small flags to everybody and moments later those flags were moving like waves in the sea.

*

King Neno went with his Queen to the palace balcony for all the people in the avenue to see them and right behind them stood the Queen mother with Mavina and her husband Choquero right behind them with all their friends and family. Lera was close to Eloy and Sanila with Harmon.

*

Pearl asked Eloy. "Who will help your father to work his land now?"

"I don't know but I'm sure that my father will find somebody." He said and started to wave his hand.

"And who will help your father to get the pearls?"

"Oh, I'm sure he will find somebody to help him," said Pearl while waving her hand.

*

In the city, the euphoria of freedom was everywhere and right in the centre of the square was Amina dancing though this time she was doing it in the company of many other young women though she and Nadia were the only ones doing it with their swords in their hands.

Happiness had returned to the Kingdom of Onuvar.

HERZ FÜR AUTOREN A HEART

novum 📖 PUBLISHER FOR NEW AUTHORS

The author

Lino Omoboni is a professional actor and an
artist (oil on canvas). Every one of his writings are
adventurous and educative.

novum ⬛ PUBLISHER FOR NEW AUTHORS

The publisher

He who stops getting better stops being good.

This is the motto of novum publishing, and our focus is on finding new manuscripts, publishing them and offering long-term support to the authors.
Our publishing house was founded in 1997, and since then it has become THE expert for new authors and has won numerous awards.

Our editorial team will peruse each manuscript within a few weeks free of charge and without obligation.

You will find more information about novum publishing and our books on the internet:

www.novum-publishing.co.uk